D1484390

Sign up for our newsletter to hear about new releases, read interviews with authors, enter giveaways, and more.

www.ylva-publishing.com

Other Books by
Caren J. Werlinger

Turning for Home

cast
me
gently

Caren J. Werlinger

East Baton Rouge Parish Library
Baton Rouge, Louisiana

44285 57913

East Baton Rouge Parish Library
Baton Rouge, Louisiana

ACKNOWLEDGMENTS

So what possessed me to write a book set in Pittsburgh in 1980? I have no idea, except I lived there in the early '80s during a very turbulent and formative time in my own life. It seems impossible that that was thirty-five years ago.

If we were to believe the news and literature these days, it would seem that all LGBT people are out and that all families and employers welcome them with open arms and that all is well in our world (unless you live in a state in the US with a religious freedom law). It isn't like that for everyone. I was in the middle of writing this book when I received a message from a young woman who had just finished another of my novels. She confided to me that she is still questioning, and part of what keeps her questioning rather than seizing her identity is a painful confrontation she had with her mother, who guessed what many of our mothers guessed about us. There are still so many for whom family, religion, work—you fill in the blank—any number of obstacles keep them firmly in the closet or keep them from pursuing any relationship at all.

Books such as *Cast Me Gently* helped me find my way when I was young, and I hope this book and others like it will continue to guide others along their way.

I owe several people a debt of gratitude for helping to make this book what it is. To Lisa T., your level of attention to detail astonishes me. To Sandra Gerth, who wasn't supposed to edit this book at all but ended up going through it three times with me, thank you! To Gill McKnight, I appreciate your thoughtful comments (and the snorks). To Michelle Aguilar, thank you for such a thorough polishing of the manuscript. To Astrid Ohletz of Ylva Publishing, you may have created a monster as Ylva keeps growing, but it's a wonderful monster. And to my partner, Beth, I wouldn't be able to write at all if not for you.

The soundtrack for this book was almost exclusively a Sara(h) list of songs: lots and lots of Sara Bareilles, especially "1000 Times" and "Breathe Again," Sara Ramirez's "The Story," and Sarah McLachlan's "Answer," which gave me the title for this novel.

Thank you for reading. I never take that for granted.

DEDICATION

To Beth, you will always have my heart

CHAPTER 1

THE SKY HAD LIGHTENED, but the sun was not yet peeking over the surrounding roofs when Teresa unlocked the store's front door from the inside. The musical tinkle of the door's bell served as a prelude to the metallic screech of the security grate as she unlocked it also. It rattled upward on its rollers, revealing the storefront behind. She stepped out onto the sidewalk, the odor of fresh espresso wafting out with her. She knew the grate was necessary at night, but she much preferred the friendliness of the store's old-fashioned façade, with its gold and black hand-lettered signage:

Benedetto's Drug Store
Est. 1898
Fine Italian candies, Espresso, Leather Goods

Wielding a stiff broom, she began vigorously sweeping the threshold of the store and the sidewalk in front. Each pass of the broom raised a small cloud of dust and grit. In an hour or so, when the sun rose high enough to reach the storefronts, the grit would twinkle like glitter, tiny metallic motes covering everything. On either side of her, other shops' security grates slid aside and other shopkeepers began the daily ritual of sweeping away Pittsburgh's steel grit.

"*Buongiorno*, Teresa," called the old woman to the right of the drug store.

Her open door let the aroma of baking breads and pastries tumble out into the street. It made Teresa's mouth water.

"*Buongiorno*, Mrs. Schiavo."

On the drug store's other side, a little man, already wearing a scarred leather apron, hung an oversized leather boot on a bracket next to his door. "You'd never know the steel mills are closing, eh?" he said with a heavy Italian accent. "They forgot to take their dirt with them."

Teresa laughed as she pulled a rag from her pocket and began wiping down the front window and sill. "I think you're right, Mr. Campagnolo." She paused her cleaning to stare at her store's lettering. She used to daydream about what it must have been like for her great-grandparents, leaving Italy with nothing but a few dollars, their dreams, and each other. She didn't know if she could ever be brave enough to do that. She tilted her head, and her eye was caught by the reflection staring back at her—a stocky woman, doing exactly the same thing she had done nearly every morning of her life for the past ten years. With a sigh, she gave the sill one last swipe.

Up and down the waking street, people appeared. Some of them materialized from lumps of rags tucked in alcoves and recessed stoops as the homeless woke from wherever they had bedded down. Other people, better dressed and not clutching bags of their belongings, began making the rounds of the shops, asking for work.

"No work today," they mostly heard. And occasionally, "I got a job for you."

Mrs. Schiavo brought out a tray of three-day-old bread and was immediately mobbed by people.

Teresa watched, shaking her head in pity.

A scuffle broke out between two women clutching the same loaf of bread. Mrs. Schiavo hit them both with her tray, scolding them in rapid Italian. She snatched the loaf back, ripped it, and gave them each half. The homeless people tore the bread apart, stuffing it into their mouths before anyone could take it from them. Others tucked their loaves under their jackets to take home to hungry families. The little mob scattered, and Teresa's gaze was drawn to a man she had never noticed before. She couldn't have said later what it was about him that caught her attention, but she would always remember that first day she saw him—"It was the day I met Ellie"—and the two things were forever linked in her mind.

He was in the alcove of the Italian grocery shop across the street, sitting on an unzipped sleeping bag that was pulled up behind him, wrapped around both him and the dog next to him. To Teresa, all dogs were pretty much alike, and this brown dog was no different except its ears were up as it watched the people. The man wore a hood over what looked like an old army cap. He and the dog had observed the scuffle across the street but made no move to join the people crowding around Mrs. Schiavo. Most of his face was covered in beard, but his gaze met Teresa's, and they stared at each other for a long moment before Teresa turned away and went back inside the drug store, locking the door behind her.

She punched a button on the cash register, which opened with its musical *ping*, and counted the cash drawer, even though she'd been the one to close last night and had counted it before she'd left. "Always count your drawer last thing and first thing," her father had pounded into her head for years. She then spent the next half hour re-stocking the pharmacy shelves.

The back door opened, and her parents' voices drifted over as they came in.

"How was your drawer?" her father, Lou, asked as he headed into the office.

"On the penny."

Her mother slipped an apron over her head and went to look out the front window before starting to rearrange the candies in the glass case. "She fed them again, didn't she?" said Sylvia from inside the case.

"Yes." Teresa went to the door and hung the *open* sign as she flipped the lock. The man with the dog was gone. She peered up and down the street, but there was no sign of them.

"I've told her a million times she shouldn't do it," said Sylvia. "But does she listen? No."

"The bread's just going to go to waste," Teresa said.

"Then let it go to waste," Sylvia said. "Better not to encourage them lazy bums to hang around here."

"Ma, they're not bums. They're out of work. They have families."

"Same thing," Sylvia insisted. "They should go to school, get a real job. Those steel workers thought they were so high and mighty, with their union. Getting above themselves. Never thought they would start bringing in cheaper steel from overseas. Wouldn't negotiate. Look where it got them. And now, we're all paying the price."

"Jesus fed the masses with a few fish and loaves," Teresa said.

"Mrs. Schiavo isn't Jesus. And don't blaspheme." Sylvia quickly made the sign of the cross.

Teresa rolled her eyes and wandered the store's shelves, straightening the shampoo bottles into neat rows and making a mental note that she needed to restock deodorant.

From behind the candy counter, Sylvia's voice continued. "That Jimmy Carter was the worst thing to happen to us in ages." Teresa sighed and silently mouthed along as her mother said, "Now Ronald Reagan! When he's elected, he'll get us back on the right track."

From the office at the back of the store, Teresa's father called her name.

"Here, Pop," she said, poking her head around the door.

Her father's salt-and-pepper head was bent over the open ledger on the desk. Without looking up, he held out a heavy moneybag. "Here, take this to the bank," he said as he continued to make entries.

"Pop, I have to handle the pharmacy today. Why can't you take it? Or Gianni?"

"Because he's working alone at the Morningside store." He shook the bag. "C'mon. I got to get to the Oakland store today."

"Why?" Teresa took the moneybag and tucked it into a cloth sling that she draped across her chest. She pulled a baggy men's sweater off a hook on the wall and buttoned it over the sling.

"Your cousin needed today off," he said.

"On a Wednesday?" Sylvia asked as she bustled into the office. "What does Dom need to do on a Wednesday that he can't be at work?"

"I don't know. I didn't ask."

"Lou," Sylvia said, putting her hands on her ample hips. "You pay your sister's son good money to manage that store for you, and you don't ask why he needs a day off in the middle of the week?"

"What's to ask?" Lou replied. "The man asked for a day off; I gave him a day off."

Teresa sighed. She checked her reflection again, this time in the office mirror while her parents continued their argument. What she saw looking back at her was her father's nose and her mother's hips—*not a good combination,* she thought, *and now I look like I have a third boob.* She slung a purse over top of her sweater and headed for the door. Why couldn't it have been the other way around? *The nose and hips, not the third boob.* Lou had been a good-looking man when he was young—an athlete's build, thick black hair, a strong profile. He had a belly now, courtesy of Sylvia's cooking, but his hair was still thick; his Roman nose had become more prominent over the years—not such a bad feature on a man, but not particularly attractive on a woman. Sylvia had been a beauty, with delicate features and flawless skin. She was still pretty, though she, too, had put on weight as she'd grown older. Teresa's three siblings—her older brother, Robbie, her younger sister, Francesca, and Gianni, the baby—had all inherited Sylvia's fine facial features, "and then there's me," Teresa often lamented.

"You have brains and a big heart," Sylvia always replied when Teresa voiced her woes.

"And a big butt," Gianni usually added, ducking whenever Teresa threw something at him.

Today, though, Teresa was glad of her powerful hips and legs as she walked quickly through the cool September morning, up and down Pittsburgh's hilly streets, avoiding eye contact and feigning deafness as she passed people asking for a handout. Suddenly, she remembered the man with the dog. *What would prompt someone who had nothing to keep a dog?* Funny, how sharply he was etched in her mind. Most homeless people—the ones who drank or used drugs anyway—had flat, dull eyes and seemed blurred around the edges as if they were fading away, bit by bit. But this guy, the way his eyes had bored into hers... She shook her head.

As she walked through Bloomfield into Polish Hill, the storefronts and flags and snatches of conversation gradually changed from Italian, so that by the time she got near the bank, it was like being in a different country. She passed a church whose sign was all in Polish, but she didn't need to be able to read it. Each of these neighborhoods had its own Catholic church, just as they had their own restaurants and shops.

She slowed a bit in front of one diner where the smells of simmering kielbasa and pierogi tugged at her. Those men lucky enough to still have jobs had been by hours earlier, picking up their lunches for the day. Her stomach rumbled as she sniffed and looked through the window.

"That's all you need," she muttered to herself and kept walking.

Despite the autumn chill, she was sweating slightly by the time she got to the bank. She stepped inside and twisted her purse behind her back before unbuttoning the sweater to pull the moneybag out of the sling. Spying an empty teller window, she stepped forward. Teresa and her family had been coming to this bank for years, and they were on a first-name basis with all of the tellers and managers, so it was with some surprise that she found herself looking at an unfamiliar face.

"Good morning... Ellie," Teresa said, reading the nameplate next to the window.

The teller looked up and smiled. "Good morning." She took the moneybag and dumped out the contents. "Miss Benedetto?" she added as she glanced at the store name on the deposit slip.

"You're new here."

Ellie nodded. "I transferred here a couple of weeks ago from our Squirrel Hill branch."

"Morning, Teresa," called the bank manager, who emerged from one of the offices along the right side of the lobby.

"Hi, Bill," said Teresa while Ellie began counting the change.

"How are your parents?" he asked.

Teresa stepped aside to chat with him while Ellie continued counting. By the time she turned back to the teller window, Ellie had finished counting the deposit and had zipped the receipt into the empty moneybag.

"Thank you," said Teresa, tucking the bag back into the sling and buttoning her sweater over top. She shifted her purse back into position.

"I like your security measures," Ellie said, watching the procedure.

Teresa shrugged. "I like to walk, and it's safer this way. Especially these days. If someone grabs my purse, an empty bag is all they'll get."

"Have a nice day, Miss Benedetto."

"It's Teresa."

"Teresa," Ellie repeated. "I hope we'll see you again soon."

"You'll see one of the Benedettos soon," Teresa said with an apologetic smile.

She took her time on the walk back to the store.

Five old women were emerging from the church where Mass was now over, their heads covered in scarves, speaking to one another in Polish and cackling at their own jokes.

Teresa smiled in greeting and walked on.

Despite the filth and the unemployment and the poverty and all the problems Pittsburgh was facing, she loved this city. She loved that five blocks' walk in just about any direction could take her almost to a different country—the Poles here, the Irish in Upper Lawrenceville; Ukrainians and Serbs and Germans. They all had their own enclaves within the city, with their own churches, their own foods and languages. Of course, her parents never understood why she would want to be anywhere but the Italian sections of the city. They had worked hard to expand what her great-grandparents started with the original store. They saved for years to buy their large house in Bloomfield and had set up stores in strategic locations to take advantage of cultural loyalties.

"It's heritage," Sylvia often said. "Our people miss what they had in Italy."

"It's good business," Lou answered. "They'll pay a lot to have what they miss from Italy."

When Teresa got back to the store, there were a couple of customers browsing the aisles.

"What took you so long?" Sylvia asked. "Mr. DiBartolomeo dropped off two prescriptions. Since you weren't here to fill them, I told him you'd bring them to him."

If you wouldn't keep sending me on errands, I'd be here to fill the prescriptions. But Teresa didn't say it. It never did any good to argue. She did anyhow, sometimes, just to get her mother riled up, but she didn't have the energy for it today.

She went to the office where she stripped off her purse, sweater, and the sling with the moneybag and hung them on the wall. She took down her white pharmacist's jacket from another hook and donned it as she stepped behind the tall pharmacy counter to check the dropped-off prescriptions.

With a sigh, she began counting pills. It was boring, but there was some comfort in the routine nature of her work. Occasionally, she glanced up to the street beyond the store. She liked to watch people going by, wondering where they were going and what it would be like to go somewhere different.

"Where would you go? What would you do?" Sylvia used to ask indignantly when Teresa wondered aloud what it would be like to be going somewhere. "This is somewhere. Our store, our home. Be glad you have somewhere to belong."

Teresa never had a response to that. As much as she loved Pittsburgh, lately there had been a kind of restlessness stirring in her, as if the hills of the city were closing in on her. But when she tried to think of where else she'd like to be, she couldn't think of anyplace. Still, she felt as if she was stuck in between.

"In between what?" her friend Bernie had asked when Teresa voiced this feeling, but, "just in between" was all Teresa could say. She wasn't sure how to explain it, but aside from her own siblings and cousins and now their families, it felt as if all the young people were fleeing Pittsburgh. She knew it wasn't actually so. The city's handful of colleges and universities were full of young people. "You're not that young anymore," Teresa reminded herself whenever she got nostalgic for the social life she used to have when she was attending Pitt for undergrad and then pharmacy school.

Thirty-four in a couple of weeks, she was too old for the college crowd, too young for her parents' generation, too single to want to hang around with the married people in her family with their demanding children.

She poured the counted pills into a bottle and affixed a label. "You're not going anywhere. Just do your job."

CHAPTER 2

ELLIE RYAN TURNED TO Suzanne, the head teller. "I'm leaving for my lunch break," she said.

The bank closed from noon to one—half an hour for lunch and then half an hour to reconcile the drawers from the morning. She went back to the staff room to retrieve her backpack from her locker. A middle-aged man in an expensive-looking suit was pouring himself a cup of coffee.

"You're new here," he said with a smile.

"Yes," said Ellie, backing toward the outside door.

"What's your—?"

"Sorry," she said, cutting him off. "I have to run an errand on my lunch break."

She pushed through the door without waiting for a reply. It was always the same. The guys who took two-hour lunches over drinks with clients wanted to chat away the tellers' precious thirty minutes.

The day had warmed, so that by the time she found a small park near the bank, she no longer needed her sweater. She carefully folded it and placed it next to her on the bench before unzipping her backpack and pulling out a sandwich wrapped in wax paper.

As she ate, she scanned the people around her. There were a few old men seated at chess boards on one side of the park,

CAREN J. WERLINGER

two of them arguing about the folly of a move one of them had made. A trio of young women sat on another bench, each with a hand on a baby carriage, pushing them forward and back, rocking the babies Ellie guessed were lying in each. People walked through and around the park, most of them busily going somewhere. She finished her sandwich and folded the wax paper into a neat square to use again tomorrow. Reaching back into her bag, her fingers closed on an apple. She munched on it, her face tilted toward the sun, enjoying the warmth. She was startled by a rustling next to her and turned to see an elderly woman wearing what appeared to be at least two coats and an old-fashioned bomber hat preparing to sit next to her on the bench. Ellie snatched her sweater up just in time as the woman landed with a grunt, falling the last several inches as if her knees had given out.

"Hello," Ellie said as the woman took off the bomber hat, her flyaway gray hair forming a frizzy cloud around her head.

She didn't return Ellie's greeting, though she mumbled to herself as she unbuttoned her outer coat and pawed at the pockets of the next one underneath. A potent mix of smells—body odor, sweat and dirt—enveloped the woman, spreading over to Ellie so strongly that she had to resist the urge to clap a hand over her nose and mouth.

She was about to grab up her backpack and go to find another bench, but *"Everybody is somebody to someone."* How many times had her mom said that? She forced a smile onto her face and said, "It's a nice day."

The woman grunted again, but Ellie thought it might have been a different kind of grunt, for there was suddenly a new, even more unpleasant smell. The woman evidently had found what she was looking for. She produced from one of her many pockets a battered McDonald's apple pie box. She wiggled her grimy fingers into the box and pulled out the squashed remnants of a half-eaten

16

pie. Ellie saw several ants scurry out as well, crawling along the woman's fingers.

"Stop!" Ellie said.

The woman recoiled, clutching the pie to her as if afraid that Ellie might try to take it.

"Here," said Ellie quickly, plunging her hand into her backpack and holding out a plastic baggie of chocolate chip cookies. "I'll trade you."

The woman squinted at her and then at the cookies. Ellie jiggled the bag. Quick as a flash, the woman grabbed for the baggie, but Ellie was ready for her. She jerked the cookies out of reach and held out her other hand. "A trade," she said firmly.

Scowling, the woman looked from her pie to the cookies, and then reluctantly offered the gooey cardboard container as Ellie handed over the baggie.

Ellie tried not to grimace in disgust as she wrapped the pie box in her wax paper and put it in her backpack. "I'll save it for later," she said, shaking a couple of ants off her hand.

The woman had already crammed one whole cookie into her mouth.

Ellie unzipped another pocket of her backpack. The woman eyed her curiously, waiting to see what she was going to pull out this time.

"Have you seen this man?" Ellie asked, holding out a cracked and yellowed photograph.

The woman leaned closer and Ellie twitched, prepared for the woman to make a grab for the photo, but she only peered at it through her watery eyes and shook her head.

"Are you sure?" Ellie asked. "He probably looks different now. Older."

The woman stuffed the remaining cookies into one of her coat pockets and jammed the bomber hat back onto her head. Mumbling unintelligibly, she heaved to her feet and shuffled away, leaving a lingering odor and a few ants behind. Ellie carefully zipped the photograph back into its pocket and pulled the wax-paper-wrapped pie out of her backpack, dropping it into the nearest trash can. She checked the interior of her backpack for any stray ants before zipping it closed and heading back to the bank.

"You are so weird."

She could picture Daniel saying it, lying on his back under the tree in their yard, a piece of grass in his mouth.

Ellie lay down beside him. Copying him, she plucked a blade of grass and put it into her mouth. She could taste the greenness of it. "Am not," she said with the grass clamped firmly between her teeth.

He laughed, that new deep, grown-up laugh he had that she wasn't used to. "Yes. You are, Jellybean." He said it as if it were a pronouncement. "Believe me. I know weird when I see it."

She looked over at him. She could see patchy dark stubble on his chin and his jaw.

"What's so weird?"

He shook his head. "You. Trying to talk to that crazy Mrs. Mallory."

Ellie frowned. "She's not crazy. She's just lonely."

Daniel laughed. "Sure. That's why she tried to swat you with her broom."

"She didn't mean it," Ellie said. "She's just so used to all the kids making fun of her and doing stuff to her house. They shouldn't tease her like that."

He turned to look at her. Ellie reached over to hook her pinky with his. "Definitely weird," he said, but he didn't pull his hand away.

A car horn blared, and a pair of strong hands yanked Ellie back up onto the sidewalk as a delivery truck made a right-hand turn.

"Watch where you're going, miss," said the stranger who had pulled her back.

"Thanks," said Ellie shakily. Cursing her carelessness, she hurried across the intersection to get back to the bank before her half-hour was up.

Later that evening, Ellie sat on the bus, lurching along with it as it braked and then accelerated at each stop. She stood as the bus approached her destination.

"Big plans tonight, Ellie?" asked the bus driver, pulling the hinged handle to open the doors.

"Yup. Going to a movie premiere and then to an all-night party," Ellie said with a smile. "See you tomorrow, Larry."

She could still hear him laughing as the door closed and the bus roared away in a cloud of diesel smoke. She walked the last six blocks to her apartment. The warmth of the day had gone as the sun sank low in the sky, and Ellie buttoned her sweater all the way up. Soon, she would be doing this walk in the dark. She looked around her as she walked. Even in this neighborhood, there were a few homeless people staking out places for the night—a couple of them daring to perch on the benches inside the bus stop shelters, knowing the cops would probably chase them off. Others headed down alleys where large sheets of cardboard were folded and stacked to offer a semblance of shelter. She quickened her pace as she passed the ornate façade of Our Lady of Fatima, the church windows dark at this time of evening.

When she got to her building, she climbed the stairs to her third floor apartment and unlocked the two deadbolts securing it. Once inside, she flipped the bolts again and engaged a third lock for good measure. She was greeted at once by a plaintive meow.

"Hello, there," she crooned, bending over to pick up her cat, the white patches of her calico coat just visible in the gathering darkness.

Ellie carried her into the kitchen where she flipped on a light and set her backpack down. The walls of the kitchen were papered nearly floor to ceiling with travel posters—Fiji, New York, Australia, Germany, Edinburgh—posters from cities and countries all around the world. Cuddling the cat, she went to the refrigerator and retrieved a can of cat food. She set cat and can on the counter where the cat sat politely, waiting for Ellie to spoon some of the food into a small bowl.

"Here you go, KC." Ellie turned back to the refrigerator and stood there with the door open. With a sigh, she reached for a container of leftover stew and quickly warmed it in a pan. She glanced over and smiled as she saw that KC was still sitting there. "Are you waiting so we can eat together?" KC answered with a tiny meow.

A few minutes later, they were both seated at the small kitchen table, or rather Ellie was seated at the table; KC was sitting on the table as she ate daintily. Ellie looked out her window at the fading Pittsburgh rooftops, watching the sky as it went from indigo to a deepening purple.

When they were both done eating, Ellie washed up the dishes and went to her living room, where more posters papered the walls. There was a quiet knock on a closed door. She flipped the lock and opened the door onto a hallway where there was a shared bathroom for the two third-floor apartments. All she could see at first was an image of green fields demarcated by stone walls. Below the poster was a pair of hairy legs and feet in Birkenstocks.

"Ireland," said a voice from behind the poster. It was lowered to reveal a man smiling through his scruffy beard.

Ellie took the poster and stepped back to let him in. "Oh, thank you, Sullivan. I've been wanting Ireland. I love it." She pointed across the hall to his apartment door. "You okay leaving it open?"

He waved carelessly. "It's not like my fish can wander off." He took a seat on one end of her well-worn couch, the springs groaning as his heavy backside settled into the cushion. "Am I in time?"

"Just in time," said Ellie. She went to the television and clicked it on, turning the channel dial to CBS. She adjusted the metal antennas until the picture was clear of snow and sat down on the other end of the couch as the theme music for *Magnum, P.I.* began. KC curled up in her lap.

"Higgins cracks me up," Sullivan said as the Dobermans chased Magnum across the estate's grounds.

"Shhh."

They watched in silence until a commercial break.

"Someday, we'll get to Hawaii," Ellie said. "Someday, we'll travel all over the world."

"You and your cat," said Sullivan, grinning.

"Yes," Ellie said, laying an affectionate hand on KC's back. "She's a great little travel companion."

Sullivan snorted. "How would you know? You've never actually travelled anywhere. The farthest KC has ever been is the bus ride from Duquesne Heights to Squirrel Hill."

"What about you?" she shot back. "The closest you get is working part-time in a travel agency." Ellie heard a distinct rumble from the direction of Sullivan's portly belly. "Hungry?"

He looked over at her. "Got anything for a sandwich?"

"Jumbo," she said. "Help yourself."

"Tell me what I miss." He pushed to his feet and went into the kitchen, returning a few minutes later with a thick sandwich. As *Magnum* broke for the next commercial, he shoved the last bite of his sandwich into his mouth, saying, "You do know the rest of the world calls this bologna, right?"

Ellie laughed. "Well, no one in Pittsburgh would know what you're talking about if you ask for bologna, so you'd better get used to calling it jumbo while you're here."

His expression darkened. "That might be forever."

"What's the matter?"

He wiped the back of his hand across his mouth, a few crumbs falling from his beard onto his shirt, where Ellie noticed there were also coffee and mustard stains. "My research advisor. He's such a prick. He looked at my latest results and told me I had to start over. He said my results were off and I must have made an error. If he keeps doing this, I'll never finish my PhD."

"He's just jealous," Ellie said stoutly. "You're more brilliant than he is, and he's afraid of you."

Sullivan shook his shaggy head. "You can't know that." But he smiled anyway.

"Shhh. Show's back on."

They finished watching *Magnum* in silence.

Ellie sighed as the closing credits ran. "I wish I lived someplace place like that," she said wistfully.

"If you did, you'd just want to leave it to see other places," said Sullivan, getting to his feet. "Thanks for the sandwich."

"Thanks for the poster."

He grinned. "See you."

"Night."

Ellie went to the bathroom to brush her teeth as he went across the hall to his apartment. When she was done, she locked her door and got changed for bed. Clicking the bedside lamp off, she slid under the covers. KC curled up, pressed against her side.

"Good night, Dad. Good night, Mom. Good night, Daniel," she whispered before closing her eyes.

CHAPTER 3

"Teresa, will you hurry up?"

"Coming," Teresa called as she came down the stairs, tucking her blouse into her slacks.

"You are not wearing pants to church," Sylvia said, glaring at her daughter.

Teresa clenched her jaw as she searched through the coats and jackets on the hall tree in the foyer. Finding the jacket she sought, she said, "Yes, Ma, I am. It's nineteen-eighty, not nineteen-fifty. Get used to it. I'm not wearing a hankie on my head." She glanced at the lace already bobby-pinned in place on her mother's hair. "And I'm not wearing a dress. If you don't want to be seen with me in pants, fine. I won't go at all."

"Stop already," said Lou. "We're gonna be late if we don't get going. Y'uns can argue about this in the car."

Sylvia continued to grumble under her breath as Lou locked the door and they all got into his maroon Cadillac Sedan Deville. Teresa, from long practice, ignored the grumbling. *It's not going to work.* She longed to say it but kept her mouth shut.

Lou drove three blocks and stopped in front of a two-story brick house that had been Sylvia's home growing up. He gave a loud honk of the horn.

"Don't blare the horn like that," Sylvia said.

Teresa opened her door. "I'll go." She walked up the porch steps just as the front door opened.

"Hey, Nita," Teresa said with a smile. "Everyone coming today?"

"Not Elisa," said her aunt. "She has a headache."

Two other women came out and locked the door behind them.

"Here, Ana Maria," Teresa said, offering an arm. "Let me help you."

"You're a good girl," said Ana Maria, grunting a little as her arthritic knees creakily lowered her down the steps.

The three aunts, all with their lace in place on their heads, their features clearly marking them as Sylvia's sisters, crammed themselves into the back seat while Teresa slid into the front seat next to her mother.

As they neared St. Rafael, Sylvia turned to Teresa. "Did you get to confession yesterday?"

Teresa looked at her mother. "Ma, I worked until closing yesterday. I didn't get home until after eight. When was I supposed to go to confession?"

"Then you don't take Holy Communion today," Sylvia said. "It's a sin."

Let it go, said a voice in Teresa's head, but "Oh, well, we wouldn't want sinners to go to Communion now, would we?" Teresa heard herself say.

"What did you expect?" Aunt Anita said, laughing at her sister as Sylvia fumed. "My goddaughter has a brain and she knows how to use it."

"She has a mouth and she knows how to use that, too," Sylvia replied testily.

All Teresa's life, it had irritated her mother when Anita came to Teresa's defense. Teresa turned and looked out the window with a small smile on her face.

Lou took two parking places in the church lot. "What?" he said when he saw Teresa staring at his blatant straddling of the line. "I just had it washed and waxed. I don't want any idiot dinging my doors."

Teresa shook her head. "So much for Christian charity," she muttered as she turned toward the church, helping Aunt Ana Maria up the steps.

Several people waved as the Benedettos and the Martelli sisters settled in their pew, third from the front on the right, the same pew they sat in every week.

"Where's Gianni?" Anita whispered as people shifted and coughed, waiting for Mass to begin.

"He went out last night," Sylvia whispered back. "He'll go to a later Mass."

Teresa coughed to cover her laugh. *Like hell he will,* but she didn't say that, either. Her mother would never hear anything against Gianni. Sylvia blindly chose to believe that Gianni was waiting until he married his girlfriend, Angelina, before having sex, but Teresa knew better. If Gianni was out last night, he was screwing some girl in the back seat of his car. If Lou knew, and he probably did, he would chalk Gianni's behavior up to "just being a man." She sat there, her anger rising at the inequity of all the things Gianni was allowed to get away with. The organ sounded its opening note and everyone stood.

"They've been like that since he was little!" Teresa complained an hour later. "They think he's an angel."

"Of course that's what your mother wants to think! And your father? Who knows? Like father like son? I don't even want to think about it."

Teresa sat at the table of her oldest friend, Bernie D'Armelio. She knew she was in for a talking to when she got home after stealing away from church while her parents and the aunts went to Communion. She was sure some variation of "it's a sin" would be awaiting her, but she didn't care.

"We've known each other since we were two," Bernie said. She took a deep drag from her cigarette and exhaled. "You always complain about how the boys get to do any goddamned thing they want and the girls have to behave. It's never going to change. We're fucking Italians, for Christ's sake. It's just the way it is." She tapped the ash off the end of her cigarette.

"I know, but it still makes me angry," Teresa said, reaching for another doughnut and dunking it in her coffee. "And poor Angelina. She thinks Gianni is waiting for their wedding night."

Bernie choked on her coffee. "Him? Those goddamned pants he wears are so tight, you can see him get a hard-on every time he looks at a girl. And she's stupid enough to think he's waiting?"

Teresa screwed her eyes shut. "Bernie, don't. Jesus. You just about made me sick."

Bernie laughed. "And you. Still a virgin. If you would ever let a penis get near you—"

"I don't want a penis near me, with or without a man attached to it," Teresa said flatly. "I've never met a man who wasn't a prick. Why would I want that?"

Bernie shrugged and took another drag from her cigarette. "You've got a point there. You know what Tom did last night? He cancelled on me. Said he had to be home with his wife. Goddamned bastard."

Teresa looked at her friend and saw tears shining in her eyes. "Why do you—?"

"Don't," Bernie cut her off. "I know it's stupid. I know I should stop. But I love him. Have you ever loved anyone so much you would have done anything—*anything*—to be with them? Even when you know it's wrong? God, just to feel him touching me, kissing me. No one has ever made me feel like that."

"You sound like a drug addict," Teresa said, secretly glad that she had never felt anything so... *destructive*, she decided was the right word. Not that she would ever say that to Bernie. No matter what, their friendship had always lasted, *and it always will*, Teresa thought now as Bernie ground out her cigarette.

Bernie sniffed and reached for another cigarette. "You want to stay for dinner? You know my mom would love to see you."

Teresa sighed. "I can't. I'm in enough trouble as it is. We're having the aunts over for dinner today. I gotta get home and help or there'll be hell to pay."

"When are you going to move out and get a place of your own?" Bernie asked.

Teresa laughed. "Who are you to be asking that? You still live here with your mom."

"Yeah," said Bernie. "But I don't work with my folks. And my mother doesn't care where I go or when I come home. Your situation is just weird. Too close."

"Well," Teresa said with a sigh. "I don't even know if I could afford to move out. I haven't had a raise in ten years. How do you ask your father for a raise? Then he'd ask why I need more money."

"You are fucked," said Bernie.

"Bernice Jean, stop with the language."

"Sorry. I forget. But you could get a job somewhere else. Some other pharmacy."

Teresa's eyes got big. "Oh, that would go over well. 'We paid for your education. We poured our blood, sweat and tears into this business. Why? To give you and your brothers something for when we're gone.' Yeah. I can just hear it now."

Bernie took another pull from her cigarette and tapped the ashes into the overflowing ashtray in front of her. "Well, Robbie got away."

"Way away," said Teresa. "So far away my parents won't even speak to him."

"That's because of the divorce," said Bernie.

"Yeah, but things were already strained even before the divorce," Teresa said. "I thought my dad was going to have a stroke when he dropped out of pharmacy school."

"But he's doing great in real estate," said Bernie. "Probably making more money than your dad."

"Maybe," Teresa said. "But that doesn't matter to Pop. All that matters to him is that his oldest son didn't follow in his footsteps."

"Maybe his daughter shouldn't, either," Bernie said, grinding out her cigarette and reaching for another.

———————

"How's my goddaughter doing? We didn't get a chance to talk in the car."

The house was noisy, filled as it was most Sundays with talk and laughter and the wonderful aroma of food. Some weekends, everyone gathered at the aunts' house, where the four unmarried sisters still lived in their parents' home, but today the aunts were here along with Lou's sister, Betty, and her husband, Dom Senior.

Teresa caught the not-so-subtle scold. She turned and smiled. "I'm good, Nita. How are you?" She turned back to the loaves of bread that she was preparing with melted butter and garlic.

"Oh, my feet hurt, my legs hurt, my back hurts," said Anita, sitting down at the kitchen table. The chair creaked ominously under her weight. "I'm just waiting for God to take me."

Teresa opened the oven and put the baking sheet with the bread inside. "Well, that's not going to be for a long time." She went to the sink to wash the brush and cup she'd been using for the butter. "How's Ana Maria doing since her heart attack? She seems weak."

"She's not so good," Anita said with a dismissive wave of her hand. "She's not so sure it was a heart attack. She thinks maybe it's cancer and those good-for-nothing doctors are too lazy to do more tests. She feels so tired all the time."

"Well, you do feel tired after a heart attack," Teresa said. "Even a mild one, like hers. Part of the heart is damaged and it doesn't pump blood as efficiently anymore."

"See? You know more than those doctors," Anita declared. "You should have gone to medical school. Then we'd have a doctor we can trust."

Teresa laughed. "You wouldn't listen to me as a doctor any more than you listen to me now." She dried her hands on a towel and turned to face her aunt. "How about you? Are you keeping an eye on your blood sugar? Watching what you eat?"

Anita waved her hand again, shooing away like an annoying fly a discussion she didn't want to have.

"See what I mean? Aunt Nita," said Teresa, taking a seat at the table. "Diabetes is serious stuff. You have to take care of yourself. I want you around as long as Nonna was."

Anita snorted. "Heaven forbid! I don't know if I could stand being here until I'm ninety-six." She looked shrewdly at Teresa. "And what about you? Haven't you met any young men? No one you're interested in? You're thirty-four now. You're not getting any younger."

Teresa was saved having to answer by the sudden and noisy entrance of her mother with Aunt Betty and two more aunts, Luisa and Elisa, whose headache was better now that there was food in the offing. Together, they were clustered around Teresa's sister Francesca, five months pregnant with her third child. The older women were fussing about Francesca's sudden craving for calamari and arguing whether that meant she was having a boy or a girl. Sylvia and the aunts took over in the kitchen, making Francesca sit at the table with Anita.

"Where's Chris?" Teresa asked.

"He got called in to the hospital this morning. I keep telling him he should have been a dermatologist, not an anesthesiologist," Francesca said with a wave of her hand that reminded Teresa of Anita.

Teresa quickly stepped back out of the way as Elisa brought a bowl of pepperoncini to the table. "If the baby kicks when you eat something hot, it's a boy," she said, pushing the bowl at Francesca.

"If it kicks when she eats something hot," argued Betty, "it means she's getting indigestion."

Is that going to be me? Teresa sometimes worried, watching her aunts mill around, all overweight, all with mounting health problems, all dependent on one another. *Except I'd be alone,* she realized. Francesca and Chris had a house close to the hospital so he could get there quickly when he was on call. No way Robbie or Gianni would stay here with her once Sylvia and Lou were gone. No, the only future she could see for herself was one with her staying on here, looking after her parents until they passed and then... what? She couldn't see any further, but no matter what she saw, it didn't look like this, loud and happy.

Her thoughts were interrupted by her mother pushing a steaming bowl of marinara sauce into her hands. "Go check on the table, will you?"

Teresa carried the bowl out to the dining room where the table was stretched to its max, and still they needed a card table set with four more places. In the living room, the men were gathered around the television, watching the Steelers game. There was a roar as Franco Harris charged through the Browns' defensive line to score a touchdown. Gianni had finally appeared, having slept in until almost eleven, "and not making it to Mass," Teresa had pointed out to her mother whose only reply had been to scold Teresa again for leaving Mass early. She could hear the kids running upstairs.

Ana Maria was already sitting at the table.

"Can I get you anything?" Teresa asked.

"A glass of wine would be good," said Ana Maria.

Teresa frowned. "Are you allowed to have alcohol?"

Ana Maria's temper flared. "If I can't have a little wine on a Sunday, then God take me now!" She slapped the table to emphasize her point.

"Okay, okay," said Teresa, going to the sideboard where three bottles stood ready to be poured with dinner. She uncorked a bottle of Chianti and poured a small amount in a glass. "Here you go. It's a good blood thinner."

Ana Maria chuckled. "So it's good for my heart?"

Teresa nodded. "Good for your heart."

Ana Maria reached out and squeezed Teresa's hand. "You're a good girl. I don't know what we'd do without you. I keep saying—" But whatever it was that she kept saying went unsaid as Sylvia called everyone to the table.

The men came slowly, stopping to watch "just one more play" as Sylvia and the aunts filled plates for them and for Francesca's two children, Daniela and Rickie.

"Sit with us, Aunt Teresa," they said, pulling her to one of the chairs at the card table.

The men were finally seated as Sylvia and her sisters fussed to make sure everyone had what they needed.

"Ma, sit down," said Teresa. She reached across the table and cut Rickie's ravioli for him. He already had a face full of sauce. Teresa swiped her napkin across his face before he could squirm away.

The women had barely sat down when Gianni shoveled the last of his ravioli and gnocchi into his mouth and stood. He untied the napkin from around his neck and wiped his mouth.

"Where are you going?" Sylvia demanded.

"I got a date," he said. He took a comb from his back pocket and ran it through his hair.

"Oh, John Travolta's got a date," Teresa said.

"Shut up," Gianni shot back. "At least I know what a date is." He gave Sylvia a practiced smile. "Got to go to another dinner at Angelina's."

"Tell Angelina's family we said hello," said Sylvia, her tone changing immediately.

Teresa almost choked. "If he's going to Angelina's, then I'm Annette Funicello," she said, but her comment was lost as the Steelers scored again and Lou roared, nearly upsetting the entire table when he jumped up. Lou carried his plate out to the living room where he could eat and watch the game. Dom looked around to see if Lou was going to get yelled at, and then followed with his plate. The women resumed their conversation, and Teresa turned back to her niece and nephew, who were squirting ricotta through their teeth. With a sigh, she reached for her wine glass.

CHAPTER 4

A HARD OCTOBER FROST had hit overnight and the windows of Ellie's bus were steamed up. People hunkered down into heavy coats and scarves, some with hats pulled low—*like armor,* she thought as she looked around. *Maybe that's why we need holidays in winter, because everyone pulls in and puts up armor. We need a way to keep from turning into hermits.*

She stood as she neared her stop. "Have a nice day, Larry," she said as she hopped down the steps.

"You, too, Ellie."

She briskly walked the last couple of blocks to the bank. Her breath puffed out in frosty blasts. Out of habit, she scanned the faces of people she passed, hoping for some sign of something that looked familiar.

"Morning, Mr. White," she said as she entered the staff room and hung her coat in her locker.

"Morning, Ellie," said Bill who was pouring himself a cup of coffee and talking to the man who had tried to ambush her lunch break a couple of weeks previously. "Have you met Aaron Myers? He's one of our loan officers."

"We almost had the pleasure," said Mr. Myers with a wide smile. He took Ellie's hand and held it longer than necessary. Ellie pulled her hand away and turned back to her locker as the men left the staff room, leaving the countertop littered with plastic stirrers and empty sugar packets.

The back door opened and the head teller, Suzanne, came in.

"Hi," said Ellie as she grabbed a paper towel to wipe the counter clean.

"Why are you always so cheerful?" grumbled Suzanne, who was struggling to shrug out of her thick coat.

Why are you always so crabby? But instead of saying it, Ellie smiled and helped her off with her coat. "It makes the day go by faster," she said. "You should try it, Suzanne."

She left the staff room, not waiting to hear whatever it was Suzanne was starting to say, and went to the vault to get her drawer. She took it to her window and counted her money, marking her money sheet as she counted. It was exactly as it should be. The other tellers, Suzanne and another young woman named Linda, carried their drawers to their windows and likewise counted their money while Mr. White stood at the front doors, holding a pocket watch in his hand. A customer stood shivering outside, but Mr. White waited until precisely nine o'clock before turning the key to unlock the doors.

From above her, Ellie heard voices. She looked up to see Aaron Myers talking to another man, gazing down over the balcony to the bank lobby below. His eyes met Ellie's, and she quickly lowered her head, rearranging her paper clips and pens.

She smiled her way through the morning, greeting each customer who came to her window, remembering some of them by name. That always made them smile in return and it had become a kind of game to her, to see how many people's names she could remember. Sometimes, it was the only way to keep from screaming at the sameness of the days. Lunchtimes lately had been spent indoors as it was too cold to eat in the park. Day after day, Ellie had listened to Linda talk about her upcoming wedding—the engraved invitations that the printer had messed up, the guest list her mother kept adding people to, her latest fitting for her dress, the squabbles among her bridesmaids. Ellie nodded and smiled, her eyes glazing over, but listening to Suzanne was even worse as she complained daily about her husband who had been laid off from a steel mill, sitting around the house in his underwear all day, not doing anything, not looking for work, waiting for her to get home and make dinner after working at the bank all day.

Ellie felt a rumble from her stomach, and looked at her watch. Fifteen minutes left before the bank closed for the lunch hour.

"He did it again," Linda said, turning from the drive-through window.

"Who did what?" Suzanne asked.

"Lou Benedetto," said Linda with a frustrated sigh. "He always drives off without his deposit receipt."

Ellie looked up. "I'll take it to him."

Suzanne looked at her as if she were crazy. "We usually just mail it."

Ellie walked over to Linda. "I have to run an errand at lunchtime anyhow. It's no problem. I can walk it down there... if I can take a little longer than my half-hour?" she added as Bill White came by.

"Lou is a good customer," he said. "Sure, take it to him if you don't mind. Linda can count your drawer. It'll make us look good. Thank you, Ellie."

Ellie stifled a laugh at the rancorous look on Linda's face. She took the receipt and went to the back to get her coat from her locker. Tucking the receipt securely in her pocket, she remembered to grab her sandwich from her backpack.

She walked quickly, eating as she went, but the smells of food as she passed through the Polish neighborhood made her jumbo sandwich seem less than appetizing. *You have food*, she reminded herself sternly. *You don't need to spend money on more,* but she gazed longingly at the plump pierogi steaming on the plates of the customers inside Kowalski's Diner.

She smiled and said hello to the people she passed, until, coming to an intersection in Bloomfield, she didn't know which way to turn. "Excuse me." She hailed a passing woman laden with a stuffed shopping bag hanging from the crook of her elbow. "Can you tell me where Benedetto's Drug Store is?"

The woman pointed. "One block that way."

"Thank you," said Ellie.

She found the store and paused outside, looking at the display in the front window. There were small figurines of the Madonna, Jesus, and what she supposed were various saints posed around small replicas of Italian landmarks—the leaning tower of Pisa, the Coliseum, St. Peter's Basilica. She pushed the door open, and a small bell overhead announced her arrival.

If she had thought the smell of pierogi was tantalizing, the aromas now assailing her senses were even more appealing. She recognized the rich scent of chocolate, but there were others she couldn't identify.

"Can I help you?"

Ellie turned to the candy case where an attractive woman with a white streak running through her black hair was standing, a starched white apron covering her front.

"Yes, I—"

"Ellie?"

Ellie turned to see Teresa Benedetto stepping down from behind the pharmacy counter. "Miss Benedetto," she said, smiling. "How nice to see you again."

"Ma, this is Ellie...?"

"Ryan."

"Ellie Ryan from the bank. This is my mother, Sylvia Benedetto." Teresa spied the paper in her hand. "My father drove away without his receipt again, didn't he?"

Ellie nodded. "Yes. I thought I would bring it to you. I wanted to take a walk on my lunch break anyway."

"That's nice of you," said Sylvia. "It's chilly out there. How about a cappuccino to warm you up?"

Ellie flushed. "No. I couldn't."

Teresa quickly said, "We can't send you back out into the cold without something. It's on us."

Sylvia looked at her sharply for an instant, and then echoed, "Of course. As a thank-you."

Ellie smiled. "That would be nice. Thank you."

Teresa stepped behind the coffee counter while Ellie looked around at the framed photos of various places in Italy dotting the walls behind the counters and the Italian products lining the shelves.

"This leather smells so good," Ellie said, holding a purse to her nose.

She took her coat off and sat at the counter.

"This store is really cute," she said. "I feel like I've stepped into Italy."

"Have you ever been to Italy?" Sylvia asked.

Ellie's face lit up. "Not yet. But I want to go. Someday. Italy and France and England." She stopped abruptly, as if she'd said too much.

Teresa turned to listen while the espresso machine churned and hissed behind her. The bell over the door tinkled again, and another customer entered. Sylvia greeted the woman by name and went to speak with her as Teresa poured frothy milk over top of the drink and slid it across the counter. Ellie's eyes widened as she took a sip, the frothy foam leaving a white mustache on her upper lip.

"This is delicious!"

"You've never had a cappuccino?" Teresa asked.

Ellie shook her head, taking another sip.

"But you want to travel?"

"Oh, yes," said Ellie, her face lighting up again. "I want to go everywhere. See everything."

"What's stopping you?" Teresa asked, curious.

Ellie's cheeks burned red yet again. "Well, I've been saving money. Starting a travel fund. I have my passport. I'll go."

"Someday," echoed Teresa with a smile.

Ellie cocked her head. "You've been?"

"What? To Italy?"

Ellie nodded, taking another sip of her cappuccino.

"No," Teresa said. She wiped down the gleaming marble counter. "My folks went back about fifteen years ago to see family that's still there. Tuscany. But I've never been."

"You grew up here in Pittsburgh?"

"Yes. Born and raised. You?"

"Yes," Ellie said. "My dad was a steelworker."

"Does he still have work?"

Ellie looked down at her cup, her brow furrowed. "He got hurt in an accident at the mill. When I was ten. He lived a few months, but..."

"I'm sorry. That must have been hard on your mother. And you."

"It was," Ellie said.

"Do you live with your mom now?"

"No. She died before I graduated from high school. Cancer."

"I'm so sorry, Ellie." Teresa looked mortified, an expression Ellie had learned to expect when she answered questions about her family. "Do you have any other family?"

"I have a brother," Ellie said brightly, but a shadow fell over her features. "He was in Vietnam, and well... he had a hard time when he got back. I haven't seen him for a while."

An awkward silence filled the air between them, while elsewhere in the store, Sylvia continued chatting with the other customer.

"Your window display is interesting," Ellie said. "What's it for?"

"All Souls' and All Saints'," Teresa said.

"Not Halloween? Does this neighborhood do Halloween?"

"Yes. I guess we just always do the religious part of it," Teresa said.

Ellie got up and went to the window. Teresa followed. "You might get more people buying candy if you did a Halloween display," Ellie said. "I mean, you sell candy, right? I don't think saints have much of a connection to candy."

"Not much."

"It's late in the season. I don't even know if you could stock cheaper candy now, you know, the kind people would want to give away, not the good kind you have in the case. You could stay away from devils and witches, if that bothers some people," Ellie continued, peering into the window, looking at the space available. "Do a whole display of jack-o'-lanterns and black cats and, if you have any little figurines—not saints or Jesus, I mean—you could dress them up in costumes like little kids trick-or-treating and—" She stopped abruptly. "I'm sorry. I don't mean to tell you how to decorate your store."

"No," said Teresa. "It's a great idea. You should work retail."

"Oh, I do," Ellie said. "Before I got hired as a teller, I worked at Kaufman's. I still work there during the holidays, to—"

She stopped, blushing yet again.

"Don't be embarrassed," Teresa said, walking Ellie back to the counter. "I think it's wonderful you have enough ambition to work hard to make extra money. My great-grandparents came here from Italy with less than fifty dollars. It's only in the last ten or fifteen years that we've had the three stores, but it means I work about sixty hours a week here. When I was growing up, things were tight."

"I'd like to hear more about your great-grandparents sometime." Ellie drained her cup and set it back on the counter. "Thank you for the cappuccino." She slipped her coat back on and donned her gloves. "I should get back."

"Thanks for bringing the receipt to us," Teresa said, opening the door.

"See you soon," Ellie said as she stepped back out into the cold and hurried down the sidewalk.

She got back to the bank and took her place at her window just in time for the bank to re-open. There was a distinct chill in the air coming from both Linda and Suzanne. *Should have kept my coat on,* she thought with a smile.

CHAPTER 5

Teresa looked up as the front door opened and she heard Bernie's voice call, "Bennie? You home?"

The childhood nickname made Teresa smile. "In the kitchen."

"Well, look at you, all domestic," Bernie said, taking her coat off as she stomped into the kitchen, where Teresa was rolling dough through the pasta maker.

How does someone so little make so much noise? Teresa picked up a strip of cut dough and threw it at her.

Bernie caught it and popped it into her mouth. "For dinner tomorrow?"

"Yeah. I keep trying to talk Ma into buying our pasta, but she won't."

"So you get to make pasta by hand? I haven't done this since I was a kid." Bernie went to the coffee pot and poured herself a cup. "I went by the store, but you weren't there. What's up with the front window?"

"What?"

"All the Halloween stuff."

Teresa looked up. "Don't you like it?"

"No, it looks fine," Bernie said. She pulled out her pack of cigarettes before remembering where she was. "Just not what I expect at Benedetto's."

"Someone suggested it, and I thought we should give it a try."
Teresa hung the neat strips of cut dough on a pasta rack.

"Someone like who?"

"Her name is Ellie. She's a teller at our bank," Teresa said. She
rolled another ball of dough flat to feed into the machine.

"Why is a teller telling you how to decorate the store window?"
Bernie sat, reaching for one of the biscotti sitting on a platter
on the table and dunking it into her coffee. "And why are you
listening?"

"She also works at Kaufman's and thought it might bring in
more Halloween business."

"Has it?"

"Yeah, it has." Teresa caught the long strips as she cranked the
handle. "We got some cheaper candy for people to give out and it's
selling really well. They can buy it here instead of going to the big
stores."

"What'd your mom say?"

Teresa grinned. "I did it without asking her. She started to
make a fuss, but then the customers started buying. Said they
didn't know we carried that stuff, so that shut her up."

They were interrupted by Gianni's entrance into the kitchen.

"Hey, Bernie." He flashed a big smile. "I didn't know you were
here." He leaned close to her as he reached across her to take a
biscotti.

"God." She leaned back and waved a hand in front of her face.
"How much of that goddamned cologne are you wearing?"

He gave her what Teresa guessed was supposed to be a roguish
grin. Teresa made a gagging face, which Bernie saw over his
shoulder.

"You like it?" he asked suggestively. "What if I told you it's all
I wear to bed, like Marilyn Monroe?"

Bernie laughed out loud. "If I want Italian meat, I'll go to Salvatore's butcher shop. You got nothing that interests me, Benedetto."

"You haven't seen the way this meat's wrapped," he insisted, scooting a chair closer to her.

"Weren't you supposed to be at the store at noon?" Teresa asked.

Gianni waved a hand. "Pop will cover till I get there." He turned back to Bernie. "You're just playing hard to get."

Bernie deliberately raised her coffee cup and took a sip before saying, "I'm not playing anything. I turned you down when you were five and tried to play doctor. I didn't want to play with you then, and I don't want to play with you now. Go away, Gianni."

Teresa laughed. "Get out of here."

"I'm going." He scowled. "Y'uns don't know a good thing when you see it."

Bernie pretended to look around. "Where? I don't see anything."

Teresa laughed again as Gianni stormed out. "That'll put him in a pissy mood for the rest of the day."

"Good," Bernie said. "He's really full of himself."

"Enough about him," said Teresa. "What brings you over here?"

Bernie shrugged. "Just wondered if you wanted to go out tonight? Dinner? Listen to some music somewhere?"

Teresa looked at her. "Where's Tom?"

Bernie shrugged again. "Who gives a fuck? Somewhere with his bitch of a wife. I want to go out and forget his sorry ass. Come on. It's Saturday. We haven't been out in ages."

And whose fault is that? Teresa wanted to ask, but didn't. "Okay."

"Can you make a day of it?" Bernie asked. "We could go downtown, go shopping and then go eat."

"I don't need to go shopping."

Bernie gave her a withering look. "What's that got to do with it? We live at home, for Christ's sake. We got nothing else to spend our money on. Let's go shopping, goddammit."

Teresa laughed. "All right. Shopping." She set the pasta rack on the counter to let the pasta dry. "Let me wash up and change. Just be a few minutes."

A short while later, Teresa sat in the passenger seat of Bernie's 1978 Toyota Corolla, her window down partway to bring fresh air into the car as Bernie puffed away on a cigarette.

"My dad would have a heart attack if he saw me riding in this rice burner," Teresa said.

Bernie smirked. "I know. My dad gave me shit about it when I bought it, but it gets three times the gas mileage as his old Thunderbird did." She glanced over. "Why doesn't your dad complain about your Volkswagen?"

"Oh, he does," Teresa said. "But a European car is better to him than a Japanese car. He'd rather I was driving a Fiat, but Gianni's is always in the shop and the parts cost an arm and a leg, so Pop can't say too much."

Bernie drove downtown to Kaufman's. "We haven't been here in ages. Is your teller friend working today?"

"I don't know," Teresa said. "She mentioned the holidays, but I don't know when she starts."

Bernie found a parking space that was just barely big enough for the Corolla to wiggle into after multiple adjustments. "No way Dad could have done that in his Thunderbird."

"Or my dad with his Cadillac." Teresa fumbled in her purse for quarters to feed the meter. "How long?"

"Max it out," Bernie said. "From here, we can go to Gimbels."

Teresa shook her head. "I should have known this could get expensive."

Bernie laughed and took her by the arm, steering her toward Kaufman's main entrance and directly through to the Misses department. "Clothes. We need clothes."

Three hours later, an exhausted Teresa sat on a chair near the mirror in the dressing room, her lap piled high with Bernie's intended purchases, while Bernie was in a dressing room, trying on yet another outfit.

"When are you going to wear all these?" Teresa asked, sifting through the clothes stacked almost up to her chin.

"Oh, you know," came Bernie's voice from the dressing room. "Work and such."

Teresa laughed, holding up a sequined blouse. "Work. Yeah. I can see you wearing this to work."

The dressing room door cracked open and one of Bernie's eyes peered out at her. "Well, that one maybe for New Year's."

Teresa gave her a look. "You're counting on New Year's?"

Bernie closed the dressing room door without answering, and Teresa let it drop. It was always like this. Had been for years. Tom would have some obligation with his wife or kids, Bernie would get furious and cry and swear she was going to break it off for real this time, but... she never did. All he had to do was call or send her flowers and she was right back where she had been—always available on his terms, whenever he could sneak away. It broke Teresa's heart to watch it, but she'd learned long ago that Bernie couldn't or wouldn't help herself get out of this mess.

"I've got to get something to eat," Teresa said when Bernie emerged at last from the dressing room. "Buy whatever you're going to buy and let's get to a restaurant."

Five shopping bags and a lot of money later, Bernie and Teresa left Kaufman's.

"Let's drop these off at the car," Teresa said, carrying three of the bags as she dodged people on the sidewalk.

"Didn't you buy anything?"

Teresa made a face. "Couldn't find anything that didn't make my butt look even bigger."

"You're crazy. There were tons of things that would have looked good on you," Bernie said.

"Yeah, like all the blouses and blazers with shoulder pads. Who thought that was a good look? I'm big enough without wanting to look like a football player. It's not as much fun shopping for clothes when you're five-foot-ten and wear size sixteen as it is when you take a six in petites. You make me sick."

Bernie laughed. "You're just grumpy because you're hungry. Where do you want to eat?"

"Miss Benedetto?"

Teresa and Bernie both turned.

"Ellie," said Teresa. "We were wondering if we might see you down here. This is my friend, Bernie D'Armelio."

"Nice to meet you, Miss D'Armelio." Ellie shook Bernie's hand.

"Are you working here today?" Teresa asked, nodding back toward the store.

"No," said Ellie. "I had to meet the holiday hiring coordinator to work out my hours." She pointed to the shopping bags. "Looks like you hit the jackpot."

Teresa shook her head. "All Bernie's, not mine."

"Here, Bennie." Bernie took the bags from Teresa's hands. "I'll take these to the car. Be right back."

"Bennie?"

Teresa smiled. "Childhood nickname. Bernie and Bennie. We were inseparable. Carrying all her bags has me starving. We were just going to grab a bite to eat," she said. "Can you join us?"

Bernie came back, a lit cigarette in hand.

"Yes," said the first woman, checking her watch. She caught Louise's eye. "The usual, Louise."

"Already put it in, girls," Louise said as she bustled by, her arms loaded with plates for another table.

"So, we'll see you in a few weeks?" asked the second woman of Ellie.

"In a few weeks."

"Sorry, gotta eat and dash," said the first woman as another waitress laid their drinks out for them at the counter.

"I know," Ellie said. "Go."

She slid back into the booth. "Sorry about that. Lots of the store workers come here on break or sometimes to get together after the store closes."

"You seem like the popular girl," Bernie said, stubbing out her cigarette. She pulled out another and was about to light it when Louise appeared.

"Here you go, ladies."

"Looks wonderful, Louise," said Ellie. "Thank you."

"Notice the pickle on your plate."

Ellie laughed, blushing a deep red. "I noticed."

Teresa looked curiously at the dill pickle on Ellie's plate, same as on hers and Bernie's. She was about to ask, when Bernie moaned next to her, chewing with her eyes closed.

"God, that's good."

Teresa took a bite of her burger and sighed in agreement.

"Bennie, you gotta taste this shake." Bernie slid the tall fluted glass to her.

Teresa stuck a second straw into the thick, chocolaty shake and took a sip. "This is my new favorite place to eat," she said. "Ellie, this place is the best-kept secret in Pittsburgh."

Ellie nodded as she took a bite of her sandwich, a thread of warm cheese pulling loose and dangling down her chin. She quickly plucked it away and wiped her mouth. "I know. Louise saved my life."

Teresa opened her mouth to ask what she meant, but Bernie said, "If you don't stop talking and eat, I am not saving half this shake for you."

Teresa turned her attention to her food. Ellie asked Bernie what she did.

"I teach," said Bernie. "At Holy Rosary in Homewood."

"You teach in Homewood?"

Bernie nodded as she popped a couple of fries into her mouth. "It's a hell of a rough neighborhood."

"Because it's black?" Ellie asked. Teresa was surprised to hear a note of challenge in her voice.

Bernie must have heard it, too. "No. Because it's poor. Most of our kids are being raised by their grandmothers because their teenage mothers are still screwing around somewhere or they're strung out on drugs. And fathers are scarcer than white people in that neighborhood."

"Bernie!" Teresa scolded.

"What?" Bernie refused to look abashed. "It's true. The only white people there are a few of us teachers and the nuns."

"So they need more white people to come in and save them?" There was no doubt now about the challenge in Ellie's tone.

Bernie smirked. "They need someone to step up. Don't get all righteous. I don't give a fuck what color they are. The mothers and fathers sure as hell aren't doing it. Listen to the news. After screwing the girls, the only thing the men do is get themselves shot. Every night there are two or three murders in Homewood or the Hill District. No one with any sense wants to go into that war zone. It's just the way it is. Our unemployment rate is double what it is for the rest of the city, so we've got too many bored people hanging out doing nothing productive with their time. If it weren't for our kids' grandmothers giving them some stability, I don't know what they'd do. Those grandmothers are the only thing that makes it possible for us to teach those kids anything. We have just as many black teachers as white ones, and they say the exact same thing."

A tense silence followed.

Louise came over as they finished off their sandwiches. "Dessert, ladies?"

"No, I couldn't—" Teresa started.

"We're splurging tonight," Bernie cut in. She looked at Ellie. "You said the pies here are good?"

"The best." Ellie passed them the dessert menu, and Teresa recognized that a truce had been called.

"I'll have coconut crème," said Bernie, giving Teresa an imperious look.

Teresa gave in with a sigh. "Chocolate."

"Cherry?" Louise said to Ellie.

Ellie nodded, smiling.

Louise was back in a moment, carrying three plates filled with large pieces of pie and a large paper bag for Ellie.

"What's with the bag?" Bernie asked.

"Some extra grilled cheese sandwiches," Ellie said.

"Who for?"

Ellie shrugged. "Friends."

CHAPTER 6

Teresa lay in the dark, listening to the night sounds of the house. She could hear her father's snores coming from down the hall. Gianni wasn't home yet. She might or might not hear him, depending on if he came home at all. Above her bed was a crucifix. Every room in the house had a crucifix on some wall. Her room was still furnished very much as it had been when she was a girl—the same twin bed and matching dresser and chest of drawers, the same mirror on the wall.

"Why don't you at least buy a double bed?" Bernie used to ask.

"Why?" said Teresa. "To remind myself that I'm sleeping here alone?" Except she never said that part aloud to anyone, not even Bernie. She had bought new bedding and curtains several years ago, and had freshened the pale yellow paint on the walls, but there was nothing else—"nothing of me," she could have said—no photos, no posters, no anything on the walls. If she died or moved out, someone else could move into this room without having to change a single thing other than the clothing in the drawers and closet.

Restlessly, she rolled onto her side, her mind racing around like a squirrel, just as it had the past few nights—ever since the evening with Bernie and Ellie, and she knew it wasn't Bernie that was keeping her up.

"She's full of herself," Bernie had muttered as they left Ellie outside the diner that evening. "She seems young. How old is she anyway?"

Teresa thought. "I don't know. She never said, and I didn't ask." Bernie was right. Something about Ellie did make her seem young—*and innocent*, said a voice in Teresa's head. *Like she needs someone to take care of her*—which was ridiculous. Ellie had been alone since high school. She obviously knew how to take care of herself and had friends like Louise and the girls from Kaufman's, and yet... What had she meant when she said Louise saved her life, and who were all the extra sandwiches for? Teresa's mind had been drawn back, over and over, to these questions. She had mentioned her curiosity to Bernie—but only the one time—as Bernie's immediate retort had been, "I wouldn't trust anyone who tries to be so mysterious."

"She's not," replied Teresa. The comment had stung in a way that intuitively let her know that this was not something she could talk to Bernie about. Trying or not, Ellie *was* a mystery to Teresa, one that intrigued her. She kept picturing Ellie's bright eyes—*what color are they?* she wondered. She couldn't remember for sure; in her mind, they were light, maybe blue or gray, because to Teresa, they seemed open and childlike—*There you go, thinking of her as a child again.*

She punched her pillow into a different shape as she rolled over again onto her other side. She reached for the rosary on her nightstand, forcing herself to concentrate as she said the prayers in Latin until, at last, she drifted into a restless sleep.

It seemed she had barely fallen asleep when the alarm clock woke her with its clang. Even a shower couldn't completely erase the drowsiness from her brain. She was alone in the kitchen as she made coffee and scrambled some eggs. Sitting at the table, poking at her eggs with a corner of her toast, she realized she was thinking of Ellie again. She finished her breakfast and placed her dishes in the dishwasher before taking her coat from the hook by the back door and letting herself into the early morning cold. Her Bug, parked outside the garage housing her parents' cars, started up with its *putt-putt-putt*, and she backed out into the dark. The streets were nearly deserted as she drove, turning down the alley that ran behind the stores. She pulled into one of the parking spaces behind their store, and her headlights caught movement. There, shielding his eyes from the glare, was the homeless man with the dog, camped out near the trash cans. Teresa sat for a moment, wondering if it was safe to get out of her car. She reached for the key and turned the engine off.

The man was getting stiffly to his feet as she got out of the VW.

"I didn't mean to startle you," Teresa said.

He was folding and rolling up his sleeping bag. His dog bowed down, stretching and yawning before coming over to Teresa, its tail wagging. She reached down to give it a pat on the head.

"We'll get out of your way," the man said in a raspy voice.

"You're not—"

"Come on, Lucy," he said, not waiting for her to finish. The dog trotted over to him, and, with the rolled-up sleeping bag now tied to a green canvas backpack, the pair of them headed down the alley, the man limping a bit.

Teresa watched them disappear into the darkness and went to unlock the security grate covering the store's back door. Re-locking the door behind her, she deposited her purse in the office and went to unlock the front grate and sweep the sidewalk as she did every morning.

As she swept, she looked up and down the street, but there was no sign of the man with the dog. Next door, Mrs. Schiavo came out carrying a bag filled with loaves of bread, and she was quickly surrounded by hungry people. Another scuffle broke out, and tiny Mrs. Schiavo was knocked to the ground.

Teresa pushed through. "Get away!" she said as she shouldered her way to where Mrs. Schiavo lay in a heap. "Let me help you." Other hands reached out to assist, and there were murmurs of apology. Teresa picked up the bag with the remaining loaves, but there were more people than bread. She tore the loaves in half, handing them out. "Take it or leave it," she said to one man who was balefully eyeing the half-loaf she offered. He snatched it from her and grumbled under his breath as he stumped away.

"Are you all right?" she asked Mrs. Schiavo, who was trembling. "Come on. Let's get you back inside." She steered Mrs. Schiavo into the bakery and made her sit down at a table while she poured a cup of coffee. "Here, drink this."

Teresa sat with her. She saw that one of Mrs. Schiavo's hands was scraped and bleeding. "Wait here." She went back to the drug store and got some antiseptic ointment and gauze. She locked the door behind her and returned to the bakery. Dampening a paper towel, she bathed the scrape to gently clean away the blood before smearing the scrape with ointment and wrapping Mrs. Schiavo's hand in gauze.

"I guess they were hungry today, huh?"

Mrs. Schiavo laughed shakily. "*Grazie*, Teresa. *Grazie*."

"It's nothing, Mrs. Schiavo," Teresa said gently. "But I think it would be a good idea for me to come over and help you in the mornings from now on."

"You're what?" Sylvia asked angrily a while later when she got to the store and heard what had happened.

"She needs help in the mornings," Teresa said, bracing herself.

"If she wouldn't feed them bums, she wouldn't need help! I've told her again and again..."

Teresa turned away and went behind the pharmacy counter. From long experience, she knew better than to interrupt her mother in the middle of a tirade. Once Sylvia got started, she needed to finish, "like a storm blowing itself out," Lou had said to a young Teresa many times when she would try arguing with her mother. "You can't win, so just let her have her say."

Over the years, Teresa had come to appreciate the wisdom of her father's advice and understood that it was probably the only thing that kept their marriage bearable. "It's not like divorce is an option for them," Bernie used to point out. "They gotta find some way of making it work."

Sylvia was still muttering loudly enough for Teresa to hear when Lou got to the store. Teresa went into the office where he was counting up the deposit from the day before.

"I can take that to the bank today," she said casually. "I need to do a couple things while I'm out anyhow."

He glanced up briefly as he punched numbers into the adding machine, its paper scroll of weeks' worth of numbers curling off the desk into a tangled heap on the floor. "Thanks."

Teresa briefly considered telling him about the man with the dog but decided against it. She knew her parents would call the police and insist they patrol the alley to chase the man and dog off. *They're not hurting anything*, she reasoned. *They just want a place to sleep.*

Her father called her when the deposit was ready.

"Just leave it. I'll take it later this morning," she said from where she was re-stocking the toothpaste.

"Fine," he said.

Lou left mid-morning to spend a few hours at the Oakland store. Teresa waited a while and then said to her mother, "I'm going to the bank, and I have a couple of errands I need to run.

Gianni's over at Morningside today, but if any prescriptions get dropped off, I'll take care of them when I get back."

Sylvia maintained an icy silence. Teresa sighed and went to the office to get the moneybag along with her purse and car keys.

Backing out into the alley, she saw no sign of the guy with the dog. There were a few people rifling through the dumpsters and empty boxes behind the stores, but not like the numbers there were at night. *Where do they all go during the day?*

It was nearing eleven by the time she got to the bank. Upon entering the lobby, she saw that Ellie had another customer at her window. She went to the lobby counter where she pretended to be filling out a deposit slip, stalling, waiting for the customer to leave.

"Hi, Teresa," called Linda when Teresa turned toward the tellers.

"Hi, Linda," Teresa said, going to Ellie's window as if she hadn't noticed that Linda's was free.

"Miss Benedetto," said Ellie with a smile. "How nice to see you again."

"Teresa," Teresa reminded her. "And it's nice to see you again, too."

"We haven't seen you here recently." Ellie shook the change out of the moneybag and began sorting the coins.

"No, my father's been bringing the deposits lately," said Teresa, feeling self-conscious now that she was there.

"And driving away without his receipt."

Teresa smiled. "Yes. I, uh—"

"Teresa!"

She turned to see Bill White coming out of his office. "Bill. How are you?"

"Good, good," he said, cleaning his eyeglasses on his tie. "Better now that the election is over. The financial market should improve with Reagan coming into office."

"I guess," Teresa mumbled.

"All set for Thanksgiving?"

"Um, I suppose so," Teresa said. "My mom and aunts usually take charge of that. I just go where I'm told."

He laughed heartily. "Give your mother my regards."

"I will." She turned back to the teller window where she was dismayed to see that Ellie had already finished counting the deposit. She watched Ellie write up and stamp the deposit slip and, in some desperation, blurted, "What time do you get lunch?"

Ellie looked up. "I take my lunch break at twelve."

"Would you..." Teresa almost gasped for air. She kept her voice low, but she could tell Linda was listening. "Would you like to have lunch? With me?"

Teresa wanted to crawl under the carpet as a slow smile spread across Ellie's face. "That would be nice."

"Great." Teresa grabbed the moneybag and gestured toward the front of the building. "I'll take care of a few things and meet you back here at twelve."

"Miss Benedetto? Teresa," Ellie said, correcting herself. "Your receipt."

Teresa could feel a hot flush creep into her face. "Getting as bad as my father," she mumbled.

She rushed out of the bank, grateful for the cold November air as she took deep breaths. "What in the world possessed you to do that?" she asked herself. She knew, without wanting to think about it too much, that having lunch with Ellie was exactly what she had hoped for. She felt an unfamiliar tingle in her stomach and suddenly wondered if she was coming down with something. What if she couldn't eat? There wasn't time enough now to do any other errands, so she wandered up and down the street, gazing into store windows until it was time to meet Ellie.

By the time she got back to the bank, Ellie was there, waiting for her. Again, Teresa felt that odd tingle in her stomach. "Where would you like to eat?"

"There's a little place two blocks down that serves really good food," Ellie said, snugging a scarf more tightly around her neck.

She guided them along the sidewalk to Falkowski's Family Restaurant. The interior was nicely decorated, with tablecloths and cloth napkins dressing it up.

They got the last empty table, situated in the front window so that they had a view of passersby hurrying past. Other diners came in behind them and waited to be seated.

"This is very nice." Teresa looked around as they opened their menus.

"Everything's made here," Ellie said.

Their server came by in a moment to take their orders. "Be right back with your drinks." She gathered up the menus and hurried off.

"So, what really brought you down here today?" Ellie asked, her head tilted to one side.

Teresa took in the way the sunlight glinted off Ellie's light brown hair as it fell in feathery layers around her face. *Her eyes are blue.*

"Teresa?"

Teresa realized she'd been staring. Thankfully, their server arrived with cups of fresh coffee. Teresa busied herself stirring some cream into hers as she said, "I really enjoyed bumping into you downtown the other evening."

"I don't know if I made a very good impression on your friend," Ellie said ruefully.

"Oh." Teresa chuckled. "You have to excuse her. Bernie can be kind of abrasive, but she's got a good heart. No matter how tough she talks, she loves those kids. She's had three batteries stolen from her car, right there in the school parking lot, and I think at least one radio. She could teach anywhere, but she sticks it out at Holy Rosary."

"I like her better, knowing that."

"You held your own," Teresa said with some admiration. "Believe me, that's not easy to do with her. She's like a terrier, a big dog in a little dog's body."

Ellie laughed. "She seems like someone who will always let you know where you stand with her," she said. "I like that."

Teresa snorted. "Yeah. That's for sure. With Bernie, what you see is what you get." She took a sip of her coffee. "What did you mean when you said Louise saved your life?"

"Ah." Ellie sat back. She seemed surprised at such an abrupt change of topic and, for a moment, Teresa wondered if she would answer. "I told you my mom died when I was in high school, so that meant foster care for a couple of years. My brother, Daniel, was still in Vietnam during that time. I was almost eighteen when he was discharged, and I thought..." She paused to take a sip of her coffee, and Teresa noted a slight tremor in her hands. "I thought he'd come get me and we'd make a home together somewhere, but... Daniel wasn't the same." Her eyes shone with tears and she turned to look out the window as their soup and sandwiches were brought to the table.

Teresa focused on her soup as she waited to see if Ellie would continue.

Ellie took a bite of her sandwich. "Anyway, I was legally allowed to be on my own once I turned eighteen. I got an apartment, the cheapest one I could find while I worked three part-time jobs—that was when I started at Kaufman's—but still, there were times when all I had left was three dollars to get me through to my next paycheck. Usually, I brought peanut butter and jelly sandwiches to work, but sometimes I would go to Louise's with the others and just order a cup of soup or something."

"Nothing else?" Louise had asked that first time, eyeing Ellie closely. "No, thank you," Ellie replied, keeping her eyes down. But then, "Miss, I think you made a mistake—" Ellie said when she tried to pay her tab and Louise gave her the whole two dollars back in change. "No," Louise cut in. "It's right. I double-checked it."

"Somehow, she always knew," Ellie said, smiling now. "When I had been paid, she gave me correct change. But when I was down to nothing, she never took my money." She blinked and looked up at Teresa. "So you see, she literally saved my life."

Teresa stared at her, almost wishing she hadn't asked. She ate her lunch, feeling guilty. She had never known a time of hunger, other than in between meals. There may have been lean times when her parents struggled with the store, and meals had been heavy on homemade pasta with no meat, and maybe Christmas and birthday presents were smaller, but they had never gone without.

Ellie seemed to read her mood. "It's okay," she said lightly. "I got through that period. Got a job as a teller, and a steady paycheck. Everything's good."

Teresa glanced up at her. "So, who were the extra sandwiches really for?"

"I told you. Friends." Ellie smiled. "When I can, I buy extra—Louise cuts me a break on the price—and I give them out to some of the street people around there. Doing for them what Louise did for me."

"Isn't that dangerous?" Teresa asked. "What if they robbed you or something?"

Ellie laughed again as she regarded Teresa. "They're homeless, not criminals. They don't want to hurt anyone. They're just hungry and cold."

But Teresa pictured the mob in the mornings knocking Mrs. Schiavo down over a few loaves of bread and she didn't believe for one second they wouldn't do the same to Ellie. Her mind was filled with images of Ellie—young, alone, hungry.

"Would you like to see a picture of Daniel?"

"Yes."

Ellie reached into her backpack and pulled out the photo. Teresa took it. It was grainy and yellowed, showing a smiling young man in army fatigues.

"He was in basic training," Ellie said. "One of his buddies took it. It's not the best, but it's the most recent picture I have."

Teresa handed it back. "He's nice looking."

"So, what are you going to do for your store for Thanksgiving?" Ellie asked as she zipped the photo back into her backpack.

Teresa caught the deliberate change of subject. "I don't know. Hadn't really thought about it."

"Would you like some help?"

"Yes," Teresa said, and her heart quickened in a way that was becoming familiar and had nothing whatsoever to do with the store. "I'd love some help. Otherwise, my mother will be pulling out all the Italian saint statues again."

"And dressing them up as pilgrims and Indians?" Ellie giggled at the thought.

Teresa laughed. "Something like that."

"Are you available this Saturday? I could come over mid-morning," Ellie said.

Teresa's expression brightened. "Saturday."

In a better mood, she finished her lunch and walked Ellie back to the bank where her VW was parked.

"Shit, how long can your mother stay mad?" Bernie used to whisper when Sylvia was in one of her snits.

"Forever," Teresa would reply with a roll of her eyes. "Or until the next time she wants to tell me I'm wrong."

When she got back to the store, Sylvia was still cool. "Sometimes, silence is golden," Teresa said to herself, ignoring her mother. She checked the prescriptions that had been dropped off while she was out. She filled them, and went out to deliver a couple of them to their older customers who couldn't get around easily. A light rain had begun to fall, making the chill day seem even colder.

At five, Sylvia left to go home and make dinner. Teresa closed up the pharmacy and busied herself watching the front of the store, restocking shelves, watching the clock. Sylvia came back long enough to drop off a plate of risotto and chicken for Teresa's dinner.

"I don't know why I bother," Sylvia grumbled. "I should let Mrs. Schiavo feed you."

Teresa hid a smile. "Thanks, Ma." Her stomach rumbled with hunger as Sylvia left to go back home. A couple of customers came in, so Teresa left the covered plate in the office while she waited on them. When the customers had gone, Teresa retrieved the plate and sat on the stool behind the cash register. Sighing in anticipation at the steamy aroma of the risotto, she raised a forkful to her mouth and suddenly remembered Ellie's tale.

"I wonder," she mumbled. She went to the back of the store, pushed the door open, and peered out. The cold rain was still falling, making it hard to see in the gathering darkness, but she thought she made out the gleam of two pair of eyes watching her.

She grabbed an umbrella from the office and went outside. There, sitting against a rusty chain-link fence separating their parking area from Mrs. Schiavo's next door, was Dogman and Lucy. They had pulled the sleeping bag and an old plastic garbage bag up over their heads and were huddled together for warmth.

Timidly, she approached. "Here," she said, holding out both the umbrella and the plate.

Dogman's eyes met hers, and even in the dim light cast by the lamp on the back of the store, she could clearly see his stare. Silently, he accepted the plate and took the umbrella, clamping it between his knees so that it sheltered both him and Lucy.

Teresa hurried back inside out of the rain, pausing at the door to look back. Dogman had taken a forkful of risotto and was holding it out for Lucy.

"Oh, better not tell Ma about this."

CHAPTER 7

"But why do you have to go?" Ellie sobbed.

With a patient sigh, Daniel turned from packing his suitcase and sat down on the side of his bed. "Come here, Jellybean." Ellie sat beside him, and he wrapped an arm around her. "I got drafted. I don't have a choice."

"They'll send you to Vietnam," she said, crying against his shoulder.

"Maybe," he shrugged. "But maybe not. They need soldiers all over the place. Maybe I'll be assigned somewhere else." He pulled away and lifted her face to make her look at him. "You'll have to take care of Mom until I get back. Make sure she doesn't work too hard. You understand?"

Sniffling, Ellie nodded. Daniel kissed the top of her head. "Be good, Jellybean."

A raspy tongue and a squeaky meow woke Ellie in the dark as KC licked the salty tears from her cheek. She sat up against the headboard, pulling KC to her. She hadn't had one of those dreams in a long time. She reached for a tissue and blew her nose. Talking to Teresa had roused a lot of old, unwelcome memories the last few days.

She squeezed her eyes shut. "Not unwelcome," she whispered. She didn't want to forget, no matter how much it hurt to remember.

She didn't want to forget Daniel, looking all handsome and proud in his new army uniform; she didn't want to forget her mother, even when her hair was falling out, and she had become skeletal from her cancer and the awful treatment. She didn't remember much of her dad, but she did remember sitting snuggled up next to him on the couch on the weekends, reading together—he reading the newspaper and she reading a book. The smell of newsprint always reminded her of him. "Reading can take you anywhere you want to go in the world, Ellie," he used to say, and sometimes, he would get distracted by her book and end up reading along with her.

The house had had to be sold when her mom died, but there were so many bills that there was no money left over, the lawyer said. The only thing they hadn't been allowed to take was Ellie's small college fund. When social services couldn't reach Daniel— the army said he was deployed on a classified mission in some undisclosed location, but Ellie knew it was Vietnam—they had placed her with a foster family in Duquesne Heights. The Lockes were nice enough people, especially in the beginning, sympathetic to everything Ellie had been through— they even got her KC as a kitten—but they weren't family.

Daniel had come to see her one time, when he was home on leave. It was like a stranger had walked in the door. His face was stretched, making his eyes look sunken in his face. He refused to wear any part of his uniform.

"You don't know... It's not good to be in uniform here," he'd said. His eyes darted around like he expected someone to jump out at him at any moment. Together, they'd gone by their old house, gone to the cemetery to see their mother's grave, in a completely separate section of the cemetery from Dad's. "Well, no one expected two such young people to die," the man from the funeral home had said matter-of-factly. Daniel had left her with the

Lockes that night, dashing her fleeting hopes that he would come home and they could be together again. "You're not coming back?" Ellie had asked, her chin quivering. Avoiding her eyes, he shook his head. "Can't. Gotta get back." He gave her a rough hug and said, "You're in a good place here. Be good, Jellybean."

As soon as she turned eighteen, she had come back to Squirrel Hill. The house, of course, belonged to other people now, but she liked to visit it sometimes, liked to imagine that it remembered her. She managed to find a tiny apartment a few blocks away—not much more than a sleeping room actually, with a hot plate and a shared bathroom that doubled as the kitchen sink. It was smoky and dirty, but the landlord let her keep KC.

When the war in Vietnam ended, there was no word from Daniel, no sign that he had even come back to Pittsburgh—not until she visited her mother's grave on Christmas Day in 1976, and saw a colored ribbon draped over the top of the tombstone. As she drew nearer, she saw that the red and blue ribbon held a Bronze Star. She looked around, her heart thudding wildly. The cemetery was empty, but she knew. "He came back." When she moved to a new apartment, she had stayed in Squirrel Hill, figuring the best bet for Daniel to find her someday was to be in their neighborhood. She kept a photo of him with her at all times, stopping street people to ask if they knew him. She often saw other men with old army caps or jackets. Their eyes had the same haunted look Daniel's had had, and she knew they must have seen terrible things in Vietnam.

"Oh, Daniel," she whispered now, reaching to her side and sliding open the drawer of her bedside table. From inside, she lifted the heavy medal with its red and blue-striped ribbon. "Where are you?"

She slid back down under the covers with KC pressed to her chest and fell back into a restless sleep. She woke to a knocking sound and couldn't at first tell what the sound was. Her bedside clock read six-ten as she sat up. Rubbing her eyes, she went to the living room and unbolted the lock on the door.

Sullivan bounded into the room. "Ellie! I—"

"Sullivan, do you know what time it is?"

"What? No," he said, looking around.

"How much coffee have you had?" Ellie asked, dropping onto the couch. "Have you been to bed at all?"

"No, I was working. Ellie, I found this incredible research this guy in Australia is doing." Sullivan paced excitedly as Ellie's eyes followed him. "This could completely change my approach to my research. It could change everything!"

He looked at her with a caffeine-fueled gleam in his eyes. She sighed.

"Let me get dressed and then we'll go for a walk."

She could hear his agitated footsteps as she quickly pulled on some warm clothes and went to the kitchen to feed KC. "Be back soon," she whispered and gave the cat a quick kiss on the head.

She grabbed her backpack as they headed down the stairs. From experience, she knew she only had to listen as Sullivan talked about things she barely understood, having to do with half-lives of certain elements and weird biochemical reactions and whatnot. She'd learned it was better to do this while walking since he couldn't sit still anyhow when he was amped up like this.

The sun was not yet fully up, and the world was visible only in tones of gray. Leftover campaign posters flapped limply from where they were stapled to telephone poles. As they walked, Ellie's eyes darted here and there. She spied a telltale cardboard shelter in an alley between two buildings and veered away from Sullivan.

Crouching down outside, she coughed and said, "I'm not here to hassle you. I'm looking for someone. A man named Daniel. He's thirty-one. Have you seen him?"

There was a rustling from inside the cardboard, and she saw a scarf-muffled face peering out at her. She couldn't tell if it was a man or a woman.

"Have you seen someone named Daniel?"

"No," said a croaky voice. "Go away."

"Thank you," Ellie said, standing up. She leaned back down and tossed a dollar inside the entrance to the shelter before walking back out to the sidewalk where Sullivan was waiting for her.

"What are you doing?" he hissed.

"Just asking about my brother."

"You're crazy! Walking up to street people like that." He flung his arm back in the direction of the alley. "You're going to get mugged or beat up."

Ellie laughed. "No, I'm not. They're not going to hurt me."

"How do you know that?"

She shrugged. "I'm one of them. They just know."

He stared at her. "You are not one of them. You have a job and a home. Maybe you were almost one of them once upon a time, but not now." He grabbed her arm and made her stop. "Ellie. Listen to me. I don't care if Daniel is out there somewhere. You are not one of them. And you are going to get hurt if you keep walking up to them like that."

Ellie pulled her arm free and walked on. Sullivan had to hurry to catch up. "I'm not going to get hurt," she said. "And Daniel is out there somewhere. I know it."

Sullivan walked beside her for a few blocks, neither of them talking. "Want to get some breakfast?" he asked at last.

"I can't," she said. "I told Teresa Benedetto I'd help her with a Thanksgiving display at their store." She stopped. "I should get back."

"Ellie, I'm sorry. I—"

"I know, Sullivan," Ellie said quietly. "But I have to believe he's out there. I have to."

⁂

"Maybe I should do that."

Teresa looked back. Her rear end had knocked over half the trees in their model of Central Park.

When Ellie had arrived that morning, she had with her an artist's folio. "I thought—I hope you don't think I was being presumptuous—but I already planned..." She unzipped the folio and pulled out cardboard and construction paper models of Central Park, buildings, cartoon characters. "How about if we build a model of the Macy's Parade in your window?"

"Are you allowed to do Macy's when you work for Kaufman's?" Teresa asked.

Ellie laughed. "It's only against the rules if you work for Gimbels."

"This is amazing," Teresa said, looking over the detailed miniatures.

Ellie reached back into the folio and pulled out a bag of plastic toy soldiers. "Our band and our balloon-handlers."

Teresa shook her head. "You thought of everything," she said, but when it came time to set up the window, "I'm like a bull in a china shop," she confessed. Every time she shifted, she knocked something over.

Ellie lithely climbed into the front window and straightened all the knocked-over trees. Carefully, she strung up the fake balloons—Popeye, Superman, and Donald Duck, anchoring them to the toy soldiers who were now serving in the parade. As a finishing touch, she sprinkled the scene with soap flakes to look like snow.

People stopped to watch, pointing and smiling. Mrs. Schiavo and Mr. Campagnolo from the shoe repair shop came by as well.

Teresa went outside. "What do you think?" she asked Mrs. Schiavo.

"It looks wonderful, *molto bello*," she said. "Like watching the parade on the television."

Some of the passersby came into the store to browse, enticed by the aroma of coffee and chocolate. Sylvia was kept busy making cappuccinos and lattes, but earlier that morning, she hadn't been happy about Ellie's arrival.

"I don't think this is a good idea," she'd whispered angrily to Teresa. "She knows nothing about us. Why are you bringing her here?"

"Ma, she knows retail," Teresa said. "We sold four times as much at Halloween as we ever have before. Why are you arguing about this?"

At Ellie's suggestion back when they did the Halloween window, Teresa had talked her father into ordering Thanksgiving-themed tablecloths, napkins and candles.

"Your store isn't big enough to move expensive items like china," Ellie had said. "But you could do specialty items, like serving platters and extra touches that people will buy to make their tables look nice. And what doesn't sell this year will save for next year. This kind of merchandise doesn't go out of fashion. Do the same for Christmas and you're set. As soon as Thanksgiving is over, people start their Christmas shopping."

Ellie's advice was already bearing fruit, as customers began buying some of the things Lou had stocked.

The decorating of the window took most of the afternoon. "What do you think?" Ellie asked. She shivered in the cold as she stood out front with Teresa to survey their work.

"I think it looks great," Teresa said. "The best holiday window we've ever had. I can't thank you enough. I never would have been able to do this by myself."

Early dusk was falling as they went inside to clean up the leftover bits and pieces.

"I wish you'd let us pay you," Teresa said. "This was a big job. And all the materials you used—"

"Oh, no," Ellie said. "This was fun. I never get to do the real windows at Kaufman's, only the displays in my department."

"Well, the least we can do is feed you dinner," Teresa said. "One thing the Benedettos know how to do is cook and eat."

Ellie laughed. "That, I will say yes to." She glanced over to where Sylvia was cleaning the espresso machine. "Are you sure it's okay?"

Teresa waved a hand. "Ignore her. She has a natural distrust of anyone not Italian. She'll get over it. Come on." To her mother, she said, "Ma, I'm going to head home and get some dinner started. Ellie's coming home to eat."

She didn't stay to see her mother's reaction, and Ellie followed her out the back door to where the VW sat.

"What?" Ellie asked as Teresa looked around in the gathering darkness.

"Nothing."

There had been no sign of Dogman and Lucy for the past few nights, not since Teresa had found the empty plate and fork left at the back door that next morning with the umbrella neatly rolled up beside them.

Teresa drove them home, just a few blocks from the store, and parked on the curb out front.

"Oh, what a nice house," Ellie said, looking up at the brick foursquare with its broad front porch and red door.

Teresa looked up at it, feeling as if she were seeing it with new eyes, Ellie's eyes—"well, that's how I felt about everything in those days," she would remember later. "Like I was seeing the world through her eyes." It was a nice house, she realized, warm and inviting.

They entered the foyer, and she was aware of the smells of garlic and bread as Ellie sighed. "This is lovely."

She took Ellie's coat and hung it on the coat tree. She watched Ellie look around the living room, going over to the fireplace mantel where there were several framed photos.

"Is this your First Communion?" Ellie asked, taking down a photo of two little girls in frilly white dresses, wearing white lace on their heads, their hands in white gloves clasping the new rosaries they'd been given to commemorate the day.

Teresa made a face. "Yes. The last time I was the same size as Bernie."

Ellie laughed and put the photo back on the mantel. Teresa saw a brief frown flit over Ellie's features as she turned and saw the crucifix above the sofa.

"Come on back to the kitchen," Teresa said.

Ellie gasped again as Teresa flipped on the lights. "This is just what a kitchen should look like," she said.

Teresa looked around. "It's just a kitchen."

"No, it isn't." Ellie's eyes shone. "It's the heart of this home. There's love here."

Puzzled, Teresa looked around again. What she saw was a half-eaten loaf of bread covered by a towel on the wooden cutting board. She saw a counter lined with a coffee maker, a small espresso machine, a commercial-grade mixer, a toaster. She saw a marble slab on the table where it had been left to dry after being used to knead the dough from yesterday's batch of bread. She saw a couple of hanging baskets, one filled with onions and cloves of garlic, another with potatoes.

Ellie smiled at Teresa's blank expression. "You don't see it because you're here in it every day. But if you didn't have this, you would see it. And you would miss it."

Teresa didn't know what to say. She handed Ellie a knife. "Why don't you slice us some bread and I'll put some water on to boil. Spaghetti and meatballs okay?"

They busied themselves putting a meal together.

"What about your parents? How much should I cut?" Ellie asked as she laid slices of bread on a plate.

"Do the whole loaf. They'll have some when they get home," Teresa said. "Ma will be home soon. The store closes in half an hour. My dad is at our Morningside store today, with my brother. They'll be in when they get in. My mom will warm something up for them whenever. Heaven forbid any man lift a hand to feed himself in this house."

A short while later, Ellie said, "Oh, my gosh, this is so good," as she and Teresa began to eat. She looked at her heaping bowl of spaghetti, topped with three meatballs. "Do you eat like this every day?"

Teresa looked down and gestured to herself. "Don't I look like I eat like this every day?"

Ellie glanced at her. "You look—"

"Whoa."

They both jumped at Gianni's entrance into the kitchen.

"Who do we have here?" he asked, immediately running a hand over his hair as he strutted over to the table.

"Oh, God," Teresa moaned.

Ellie turned to Teresa. "Your brother?"

"How'd you guess?"

Gianni grabbed the chair next to Ellie and sat. "Well, you know who I am, beautiful. Who are you?"

Ellie laughed. "Does that actually work for you?"

Gianni pulled back a bit. Ellie immediately looked contrite at the hurt expression on his face.

"I'm sorry," she said. "I'm Ellie. I'm a friend of Teresa's. We were working on the store window today."

Gianni, always one to press an advantage, took Ellie's hand in both of his. "Apology accepted. The store window, huh? You should come to Morningside and do me."

Ellie whipped her hand away. "On second thought," she said icily, "I'm not sorry."

Teresa smirked. "Couldn't leave well enough alone, could you?"

"Shut up." Gianni shoved to his feet. "Where's Ma?"

"She should be home soon," Teresa said. "But if you want food, you can get it yourself. I'm not waiting on you."

"Who asked you?" he sneered. "I'm going to Angelina's tonight."

"Nice," Teresa said. "Hitting on another girl on your way to your girlfriend's."

Gianni gave her the finger as he turned on his heel and stomped out of the kitchen.

Ellie tilted her head in the direction of the stairs. "Is he always like that?"

"Always." Teresa shook her head. "The sun rises and sets on Giovanni Benedetto."

Ellie twirled her fork, wrapping the tendrils of spaghetti around it. "I thought you had another brother?"

"I do," Teresa said. "My older brother, Robbie. Roberto. But he got divorced a few years ago and now he never comes around."

Ellie paused her twirling. "Your parents won't see him because he got divorced?"

Teresa tore a slice of bread and used a piece to soak up some sauce from her plate. "The divorce was bad enough, but then he got remarried."

"They don't like her?"

Teresa snorted. "She's older than him, she's not Catholic, and she's not Italian. What do you think?" She reached for a slice of bread. "I really like Karen. But my parents have made it clear she's not welcome, and Robbie says he won't come without her. So he doesn't come home and nobody talks." She glanced over and started to reach out, but stopped herself. "You have some sauce, just here." She tapped her own chin.

Ellie lifted her napkin and wiped the sauce away. "Do you see him?"

"Yeah, I do." Teresa spread a thick slab of butter on her bread. "I like them both, but I don't get to see them as often as I'd like. Robbie is a real estate agent, so he works crazy hours. Karen works in an insurance office not too far from your bank. I meet her for lunch sometimes."

Ellie's face took on an expression Teresa was beginning to recognize. "What?"

Ellie shrugged. "I just think... If your parents knew how easily they could lose your brother —or anyone really—they wouldn't waste life not talking."

Teresa stared at Ellie who was busily trying to twirl her spaghetti around her fork again. She heard Gianni moving around upstairs. It was hard to imagine missing him. She had often wished her parents had stopped after Francesca.

The back door into the kitchen opened with a clatter as Sylvia came in. Teresa covered a smile as Ellie stood up and said, "Oh, Mrs. Benedetto, your home is wonderful. Thank you so much for having me over."

Sylvia, nonplussed, said, "You're welcome, Ellie. Thank you for all your help with the store."

Ellie offered to take her coat for her while Teresa filled a bowl. "Here, Ma, come and sit down. Eat while it's hot."

Sylvia had just sat down to her dinner when Lou came in. Teresa introduced him to Ellie.

"So you're the genius helping us out," Lou said as Teresa filled another bowl.

"It's my pleasure," Ellie said.

"Kaufman's better watch it. I just might hire you away," Lou said. He chuckled at his own joke as he tucked a napkin into his shirt collar.

Teresa filled a glass bowl with the leftover spaghetti, covered it with plastic wrap and then wrapped the whole thing in aluminum foil.

"I'm going to drive Ellie home," Teresa said as she tucked the bowl under her arm.

"You don't have to—"

"It's dark and cold," Teresa said, cutting off Ellie's protest. "I'm not letting you take the bus. Come on."

They huddled in the cold VW. "Here." Teresa reached into the back seat and offered Ellie a folded woolen throw that she kept in the car.

"You never know when you might break down and freeze to death," Sylvia often fretted, ignoring the fact that Teresa never went anywhere where help was more than several blocks' walk.

Ellie gratefully wrapped the throw over her legs as she gave Teresa directions to her apartment.

The car was just beginning to put out slightly warm air when Ellie said, "This is it." Teresa pulled up to the curb. "Would you like to come up?"

"Sure," said Teresa, more curious than she would have admitted. She got out of the car and retrieved the bowl of leftovers from the back seat, and then followed Ellie through a side door and up the stairs to the third floor.

KC came to greet them as Ellie unlocked the door.

"Hey there," Ellie crooned, picking her up. "Did you think I wasn't coming home? This is Teresa. This is KC."

"KC?"

"Kitty Cat." Ellie smiled ruefully. "I was not very creative with her name."

Teresa reached out a hesitant hand. KC gave her a sniff and a little meow.

"Y'uns don't have any pets?" Ellie asked.

"Are you kidding? My mother and her sisters had a fit when my sister got a cat, said it would smother the baby." Teresa stroked KC's soft fur. "In my family, dogs and cats are only for farms, not for houses."

"Too bad," Ellie said, snuggling KC against her cheek before setting her down. "They're wonderful company. Come on in."

Teresa stepped farther into the kitchen. "Wow." She pirouetted, taking in all the travel posters papering the walls as she set the foil-wrapped bowl on the kitchen counter.

"All the places I'm going to go someday," Ellie said.

Teresa followed Ellie into the small living room. "Well, for now, they make pretty wallpaper," she said.

There it was again, that shadow that flitted across Ellie's face sometimes, only there for an instant and then gone. Teresa felt she'd said something wrong, but wasn't sure what.

"Hey," she said as a thought occurred to her. "What are you doing for Thanksgiving? Our family is crazy, and we'll all be at my aunts' house and there'll be lasagna along with the turkey, but I'd love to have you."

"Oh, um," Ellie said. "I can't, but thank you. I already have plans."

"What plans?" Teresa nearly blurted, certain that Ellie was lying, but instead she just said, "Well, if you change your mind, you'd be welcome." She walked back out into the kitchen. "I'd better go. I'm sure you're tired. That's for you." She pointed to the bowl on the counter.

"Oh, I can't—"

"We owe you a week's worth of food," Teresa interrupted. "Thank you again for all your help with the window. I never could have done that without you."

"You're welcome again." Ellie threw her arms around Teresa and gave her a quick hug. "See you soon."

Teresa stumbled as she backed over the threshold. "See you."

CHAPTER 8

TERESA'S VW CHUGGED THROUGH the snow like a little tank, its rear engine giving the back wheels the traction they needed to churn up and down the hills to the store. The snow that had fallen overnight made everything look fresh and clean—"the only time Pittsburgh looks clean," she muttered through chattering teeth—but she knew it would quickly become a gray sludge as the city woke up and traffic got moving.

In the back seat was a folded winter coat. "You cannot wear that anymore," Sylvia had declared when Lou had taken it from the closet a couple of weeks ago. "What will people think?" she said, clucking as she inspected the shiny elbows where the wool was worn thin and the one shoulder seam that had pulled away. She insisted he start wearing the new one he'd received last Christmas, folding this one into the bag headed for the Salvation Army.

As Teresa had come downstairs that morning, she had noticed the snow from the window on the stair landing. Down in the foyer, balancing on one foot to pull a boot on, she had nearly tripped over the bag that had been sitting there for days, waiting for someone to take it to the Salvation Army. Remembering that coat, she'd pulled it out of the bag and brought it with her. When she turned into the alley, she wasn't surprised to see Dogman behind the store, shaking the snow off his sleeping bag so that he could roll it up and tie it to his backpack. Lucy came to her as she got out of the car. Teresa gave her a scratch behind the ears.

"Wait," she said as Dogman called to Lucy. He turned to her. "I..." Now that she was face to face with him, his face expressionless except for those eyes—*why is that the only part I can ever remember?*—she wasn't sure what to say. She held out the coat. "I thought maybe you could use this, now that it's really cold." When he just stood there, looking at her, not the coat, she added, "It was my dad's. It was in a bag for the Salvation Army. I just thought..." She held it to him again, and this time he took it. "And," she reached back into the car. "I have this for Lucy. To keep her warm at night." She offered the woolen throw that Ellie had used. Wordlessly, Dogman accepted this also, then turned and limped on down the alley with Lucy beside him.

Teresa watched them for a moment, then closed up the car and worked the key into the lock of the back security grate. She had to wrestle the frozen links before they slid open. Once inside, she rummaged through the storage closet, looking for the snow shovel. She quickly shoveled a clear space for her mother to park. She looked down the alley, but Dogman and Lucy were gone. She couldn't have said what it was that made her feel a connection to them. She'd never felt like this about any of the other homeless or out-of-work people she saw every day—and there were lots of them lately—but, *there's just something about the two of them,* and it had something to do with Ellie. She paused her shoveling, enjoying the secret thrill she felt every time she thought of Ellie. She always remembered that the first day she had seen Dogman was the day she met Ellie. For some reason the two things were connected in her mind. And now, it was all tied up with that hug.

Teresa leaned on her shovel and closed her eyes. *That hug.* "Don't be so stupid," she'd told herself over and over, but... other than hugs from Aunt Anita every now and again, that was the first hug she'd had from anyone since she was a child. Her parents weren't huggers, nor were her siblings. She'd never been kissed—not really kissed—never been held, never had a boyfriend, had never been... intimate with anyone.

She felt her face grow hot and knew it had nothing to do with the exertion of shoveling. Every night for the past two weeks, she'd fallen asleep smiling and remembering the feel of Ellie's arms around her. *How could something so simple be such a huge thing?* She'd avoided going back to the bank, certain she'd make an idiot of herself again, but that didn't keep her thoughts from turning to Ellie at the most unexpected—*and inconvenient*—times, like yesterday when she'd been in the middle of counting pills for a prescription, and had to start over because she found herself standing there, daydreaming, with no recollection of how many pills she'd counted.

Part of it was every horrible thing Ellie had been through. It broke Teresa's heart to think about it, and she wanted to hold Ellie and try to make it better, but "you can't make any of it better," she reminded herself again and again. "It happened—her parents, her brother, all of it," but there was still something so vulnerable about Ellie, something that made Teresa feel protective and... tender. It was such a new feeling that she didn't recognize it at first. "Teresa is tall, she can reach it" or "Teresa's strong, she can do it"—those were the kind of things she was used to being needed for. Her family relied on her, even if they also forgot about her, but with Ellie, she felt different. It was as if she were being molded into a new shape, a new Teresa – *just by knowing her.* Ellie had a way of turning her inside out, seeing the bits of her that no one else had ever seen.

But she knew better than to try and talk about this to anyone, not even Bernie. For years, she'd listened to Bernie talk about Tom, cry over him, scream at him—and then watched as she went back to him time and again, but "this is different." Teresa had a feeling no one else would understand, because she didn't understand it herself.

"Teresa!"

She jumped, dropping her shovel. Mrs. Schiavo was waving at her. Teresa picked the shovel up out of the snow and went around to shovel the back entrance of the bakery. When she was done there, she went out front and shoveled the front walk of both the bakery and the drugstore. By the time she was finished, a small crowd had gathered. Mrs. Schiavo brought out her old bread and let Teresa hand it to the people waiting. They were more orderly with her. "Because I'm big enough to hit back," Teresa joked. She scanned the street for any sign of Dogman and Lucy, but they were nowhere. When the bread had been given out, Mrs. Schiavo made Teresa come back inside, where she tried to give her a plate of cannoli.

"Mrs. Schiavo," said Teresa. "Do I look like I need cannoli?"

Mrs. Schiavo cackled and waved her hand at such an absurd idea as anyone having too much cannoli. She shoved the plate into Teresa's hand and Teresa went back around through the back door of the drug store, leaving the plate on her dad's desk. "Not that he needs it, either," she said, but she knew he'd eat it.

By the time Sylvia got to the store, snowplows had cleared paths down some of the streets and traffic was moving. She placed a mop behind the cash register.

"We'll have to clean up after snowy shoes all day today," she said. "I don't want anyone slipping and suing us."

"We could just close for today," Teresa said from behind the pharmacy counter.

"What? And lose a whole day's business?" Sylvia said.

The telephone rang, and Sylvia answered. Teresa could hear her end of the conversation and stopped what she was doing, listening with a scowl on her face.

"What?" she asked when her mother hung up.

"Gianni is stuck at Angelina's. Your father is going to the Morningside store until Gianni can get there. He wants you to do the deposit and take it to the bank."

"Stuck at Angelina's my ass," Teresa said under her breath. She finished the prescription she was working on and went to the office, still grumbling.

"What are you saying in there?" Sylvia asked.

Teresa didn't answer for a moment as she got on her hands and knees, dialing the combination on the safe bolted to the floor under the desk. She lifted last night's moneybag to the desk and brushed her knees off.

"I said, it's a good thing one of us makes it to work."

"Your brother always has a good reason if he doesn't make it in," Sylvia said.

"Yeah, right. I got out and shoveled this morning. Why can't he get his butt out and shovel and scrape and get to work?"

"He will," Sylvia said.

"Why do you always make excuses for him?"

"I'm not making excuses." Sylvia's voice sounded far away from inside the candy case.

"You are. If he worked for anyone else and didn't show up at work, he'd be fired. But you and Pop just let him get away with it. And for not showing up to work, he gets paid more than I do. I haven't had a raise since I got out of pharmacy school."

"He's a man," Sylvia said. "He has to save up to take care of a wife and family. You just have yourself and you live with us. What do you need more pay for, huh?"

"Maybe I'm not always going to live with you and Pop."

There was a very prickly silence that stretched on and on, and then Sylvia's heels clicked on the floor as she came to the office. "So you're thinking about moving out?"

Teresa shrugged. "Maybe."

Sylvia threw her hands in the air. "Maybe you should."

"Maybe I will," Teresa shot back as her mother stalked away. Breathing heavily, she had to count the change five times before she got an accurate number. She threw the coins into the bag and marked the deposit slip. She finished counting the bills and checks and stuffed everything into the bag. She crammed her feet back into her boots, pulled a hat on, wrapped her scarf back around her neck, and donned her coat over top of the sling containing the moneybag.

"I don't know when I'll be back," she said as she stomped through the store. She didn't look at her mother and didn't wait for a response.

Outside, the sidewalk was a checkerboard of untouched snow in front of some buildings interspersed with short lengths that had been shoveled. Traffic was moving sluggishly. She passed more than one car whose wheels were spinning, trying to maintain traction going up a hill. She was glad she'd decided to walk as her legs pumped along like pistons. She was soon breathing hard with the effort of walking through the snow, but the exertion felt good. It wasn't long before she was away from the commercial section and walking past houses, most of them still quiet, the sidewalks untouched, as the city's kids had been given a snow day and weren't outside yet.

As Teresa walked, she muttered to herself, continuing her argument with her mother, until she passed two kids coming down their porch steps with a sled. They looked at her as if she were crazy.

She chuckled. "Yes, I'm crazy."

She got to an intersection and paused. Instead of continuing straight toward the bank, she crossed the street and headed toward her sister-in-law's insurance office. The front windows looked dark as she approached, but when she stood in front of the building, she realized the glare of the snow outside masked the weak fluorescents burning inside. She pushed the door open.

Karen was at her desk, phone to her ear. She glanced up, looking harassed. When she saw Teresa standing there, she smiled and held up a finger as she took notes. "We'll get someone out there as soon as we can to assess the damage. You stay safe, Mrs. Brezicki."

Karen hung up the phone and took her reading glasses off, rubbing her temples. "I hate snow," she moaned. "But I love seeing you." She got up from the desk. Even on a day like this, she looked great, her slim figure shown to its advantage in a pantsuit, her blonde hair perfectly done—*oh, God, what will mine look like when I take this hat off?* Teresa suddenly wondered.

"Want some coffee?" Karen was saying. "You must be freezing. I can't believe you walked here."

Teresa stood on the mat inside the front door, stomping her snowy boots as she unwound her scarf from around her neck and flapped her coat. "Some coffee would be great in a minute, but your walk isn't cleared."

"I'm the only one to make it in so far," Karen said with a fake smile. "The phone has been ringing since I got here, and none of the men have dug their cars out."

Teresa glared at her. "Sounds familiar." She rewrapped her scarf and buttoned her coat. Reaching for the shovel leaning against the wall, she said, "Have that coffee ready for me. Be back in a jiff."

Several minutes later, she was back inside, stomping again as she took off her scarf and coat. "That should last you for a few hours unless it piles up out there."

"Thank you so much," Karen said, waving her over to a chair by the desk where a cup of steaming coffee was waiting.

Teresa held the cup in her two hands, letting the warmth soak in. "Oh, this feels good. Thanks."

Karen sat back down behind the desk. "So what brings you down here?"

"I had to go to the bank," Teresa said. "And I just had to get away from the store before I said something I would be sorry for."

"What's going on?"

Teresa didn't answer immediately. She sipped her coffee, but just as she opened her mouth, the telephone rang.

"Sorry," Karen said, picking up the phone. Teresa drank her coffee while Karen took down the details of yet another car damaged when someone else slid into it.

"That's the third one this morning. Now," Karen said a few minutes later as she hung up. "You were saying?"

Teresa shook her head. "I don't even know what it is. I get up early to open the store, take care of whatever needs doing. I stay to close most nights. I have no life. Gianni goes in whenever he feels like it, leaves early to go to Angelina's or out with his friends. He gets paid more than I do because he's a man." She stopped, feeling sudden tears sting her eyes. She never cried. She blinked down at her coffee cup as Karen watched her intently.

"It's good to know some things in this world are constant, isn't it?" Karen said.

Teresa hiccupped with laughter. "You're right. It isn't any different from what it's always been."

Karen sat back, still watching her. "Something's different. Must be. Why is it bothering you now?"

"I don't know," Teresa said. "Maybe because it's been going on for so long…" Her expression darkened. "I am in the exact same place I was ten years ago. And if my folks have their way, I'll still be in that same place ten or twenty years from now."

"There's nothing wrong with that, if it's where you want to be," Karen pointed out.

"I guess," Teresa said. "I never questioned it before, but now... I feel restless. Like my life is just passing me by. Everyone my age is married and having kids. I don't want that, but I watch my aunts, all single, all heavy and unhealthy. I don't want that to be me, either."

Karen smiled. "Well, Rob found a way to break away. Maybe you should talk to him. Why don't you come over for dinner one night? How about Saturday?"

Teresa's expression brightened. "That would be great."

"Bring someone if you like," Karen said.

Teresa felt her face get hot. She leaned over to retie the laces on her boots. "Maybe. I'll see you Saturday. Six o'clock?"

"Six is good," said Karen, walking her to the door. "Thanks for shoveling." The telephone jangled again. "Gotta go. See you Saturday."

Bundled up against the cold again, Teresa headed back out into the snow. Inside the bank, the lobby was deserted. All of the tellers looked up at her entrance. "Hi, Teresa," came a chorus.

"I can help you here," said Linda.

Teresa stepped to her window, avoiding looking at Ellie.

"Cold day for a walk."

"Better than trying to drive in this," Teresa said, struggling to extricate the moneybag from the sling under her coat. She got it out and plunked it down on the counter. While Linda counted the deposit, Teresa stole a look in Ellie's direction, but she was busy doing something and didn't look up.

"Here you go," Linda said, handing the moneybag back. "The deposit slip is inside."

"Thanks," Teresa said. "See you soon."

She went to the counter in the middle of the lobby where she stalled, taking her time getting the moneybag tucked back into the sling. Another customer came into the bank.

"Need some help?"

Teresa looked up to see Ellie standing there. She looked very pretty in a navy turtleneck. "Thanks, I think I've got it." The other customer had stepped up to Linda's window. Lowering her voice, Teresa said, "Are you doing anything Saturday evening?"

"No. Why?"

"Well, my sister-in-law asked me over to their house for dinner on Saturday, and I just wondered if you'd like to go. If you're not busy."

Ellie's face lit up. "No, I'm not busy. I'd love to meet your brother and sister-in-law."

Teresa finished buttoning up her coat. "Great. I'll pick you up at five-thirty?"

"Five-thirty. I look forward to it."

Teresa didn't remember much about the walk back to the drugstore. Her mind was occupied with the anticipation of spending Saturday evening with Ellie, and her heart was racing. She knew it had nothing to do with the exertion of walking.

"I wondered when you were going to get back."

Teresa did a double take as she entered the store. Bernie was sitting at the counter, drinking a latte.

"Hey. What are you doing here?"

Bernie twirled on her stool. "Snow day. Thought I'd come over here and hang out with you for a while." She glanced over to where Sylvia was vigorously polishing the glass of the candy display case, her back to them. She looked back at Teresa with a questioning expression.

Teresa jerked her head toward the back. Bernie slid down off her stool, carrying her latte back to the office where Teresa was peeling off layers.

"What in the hell is going on?" Bernie whispered. "Your mother's been pissy since I got here."

Teresa rolled her eyes. "I got mad because I got my butt down here early to shovel and open, and Gianni calls to say he's going to be late over at Morningside. Do they yell at him? No. Do they do anything? No."

Bernie held up her hands, sloshing her latte over the side of the cup. "So? That's how it always is. Why is your mother so angry?"

Teresa grabbed a tissue and wiped up the spilled coffee. She closed the office door and sat down to unlace her boots. "I might have said some things."

Bernie perched on the desk. "What things?"

"I'm sick and tired of Gianni getting paid more than me for not working." Teresa sighed. "I said I might not always live with them."

Bernie's mouth opened and closed. "Holy shit! Are you moving out?"

"No," said Teresa quickly. "I just... I want them to not take me for granted." She shook her head. "I shouldn't have said it."

"Don't go feeling all guilty, Bennie." Bernie took a sip of her latte. "You always do this. When you finally get fed up enough to say something, you feel guilty about it. They know this about you. They use it. To hell with them."

Teresa looked up at her.

"I didn't mean that," Bernie said. "But, Jesus, you need to stand up for yourself and not feel bad about it."

Teresa flung an arm toward the store. "That's easy to say. Until you have to live with the silent treatment."

"You gotta get tougher. Outlast her. She won't stay quiet forever. You're not that lucky. She's got more to say to you." Bernie hopped down off the desk. "How about we go out this weekend? Saturday?"

"I can't," said Teresa. "I'm going over to Robbie and Karen's."

"I haven't seen them in ages. I could go with you," Bernie suggested.

"Um, not this time. Sorry. Robbie needs to talk to me about something."

Teresa tried not to squirm under Bernie's gaze.

"Okay," said Bernie, watching her. "Maybe next weekend."

"Yeah. Next weekend would be good."

CHAPTER 9

When Teresa and Ellie arrived at Rob and Karen's house, Karen greeted them, taking their coats. She looked elegant—her blonde hair carefully styled, her slimness accentuated by tailored slacks and a cashmere sweater. "She always looks that way," Teresa whispered to Ellie while Karen hung the coats in the closet. "Not like the rest of our family, that's for sure," Teresa added, looking down at her own baggy sweater hanging down over her hips to hide as much of her figure as possible. Ellie, she noticed, looked almost as dressed-up as Karen, wearing nice slacks and a tucked-in blouse.

"I love this neighborhood," Ellie said.

"Thank you," Karen said. "We really like Shadyside."

When they entered the kitchen, Teresa had to stop and stare at her brother standing there in an apron, tasting from a pot simmering on the stove.

"Hey, Resa," he said.

"Oh, my gosh," Teresa said, reaching out to steady herself against the table.

"What?" he asked.

"You. In an apron. Cooking."

Karen laughed. "You can train them if you're patient and consistent."

"Thanks," said Rob with a droll smile. "You make me sound like a dog."

"Not a dog, hon, just a spoiled male with bad habits we needed to break," said Karen, winking at Teresa. "Rob, this is Teresa's friend, Ellie."

"Hi," he said, reaching out to shake her hand, while continuing to stir the contents of the pan with his other.

Teresa noted how much thinner his hair was getting. "He didn't get that from my side of the family," Lou always said, running his hand over his own thick hair. But Teresa thought now that it made her brother look more handsome, with flecks of gray starting to show at his temples.

"Can we help with anything?" Ellie asked.

"Oh, no," said Karen. "Just pour yourselves some wine and keep us company."

Teresa went to the counter where a few bottles of wine were sitting. "White or red?"

"White, please," Ellie said. "Whatever is cooking smells wonderful."

"Thanks," Rob said. "We're having roasted lamb with cannellini and spinach salad."

"Wow," said Teresa. "I'm impressed."

"I have managed to expand his culinary horizons beyond lasagna and gnocchi," Karen laughed.

"Better not let Ma hear you say that," Teresa said.

"Little danger of that is there?" Rob said, and even though his tone was light, there was a hard set to his jaw.

"When was the last time you heard from them?" Teresa asked, pouring Karen a glass of Merlot.

"My birthday last July. They sent a card. Ma signed it for both of them."

An awkward silence filled the kitchen.

"Your home is lovely," Ellie said.

"Let me show you around," Karen said, taking Ellie by the arm and leaving Teresa and Rob alone in the kitchen.

He turned to look at her. "Karen said you were having a bad day when she saw you."

Teresa shrugged. "I don't know why I let it get to me. It's the same old stuff. You know how it is. Gianni gets away with whatever he wants and they expect me to pick up the slack. The dutiful daughter."

He gave her a sympathetic glance. "I didn't know how true that was until I was away from them." He nodded toward the living room where they could hear Karen's voice. "She doesn't let me get away with any of that. Sometimes I don't even know I'm doing it, but she always calls me on it."

"Like what?"

"Anything. From leaving my socks on the bedroom floor to expecting her to get me a drink. All those things we watched Ma do for Pop. Karen's right. There's no reason I shouldn't pick up after myself, and I can pour a drink as well as she can. It shouldn't be her job because she's my wife." He opened the oven to check on the lamb. "It won't change for you unless you make it change."

"How? I can't make him pay me more."

Rob gave her a look.

"What?"

"You've got to be ready to walk," he said.

"You mean, leave the store?" Teresa stared at him.

"You might not have to leave, but you've got to be ready to. Leave the store and move out. I did it."

"Yeah, but..."

"Look, I know it's hard. Believe me. It's still hard sometimes." He took a big drink of his wine. "I miss you guys. I miss Ma and Pop, but if you keep caving in to them, they'll never see you as anything but their kid, someone they can tell what to do, and nothing will ever change."

Karen and Ellie came back into the kitchen.

"Until they accept Karen as my wife, as part of the family, they don't get me, either. It's that simple."

Karen came over and wrapped her arms around his neck. Rob gave her a kiss.

"And that's why I love him," she said, wiping her lipstick off his lips. "But he better not let the dinner burn."

"Shit," he said, jumping back and checking the pot of cannellini simmering on the stovetop. "I think everything is ready."

A few minutes later, they were seated at the table.

"So what do you do?" Rob asked Ellie.

"I work at a bank," she replied. "That's where I met Teresa."

"She also moonlights as the window designer at Benedetto's," Teresa said.

Rob looked from Teresa to Ellie and back. "And Ma was okay with that?"

Teresa grinned. "I didn't ask her."

Rob looked at her appraisingly. "Good for you."

"So you've met the Benedettos?" Karen asked.

"Yes," Ellie said.

"And what did you think?"

Ellie flushed.

"Don't put her on the spot," Teresa said. "Ma was civil, but barely. Ellie's just too nice to say anything."

Rob reached for Karen's hand. "That's more than she's been with us."

"How long have you been married?" Ellie asked.

"Seven years," Karen said, giving Rob's hand a squeeze.

Ellie's fork clattered to her plate. "Sorry. And they still don't talk to you? Did they come to the wedding?"

Rob shook his head as he reached for another slice of lamb. "In their eyes, I'm still married to my ex-wife. We couldn't be married in the Church. We had a civil ceremony. Teresa was the only one from the family who came. I wasn't going to invite them at all, but—"

"But I told him we needed to extend the invitation and let it be their decision," Karen cut in. "If we hadn't invited them, we would have been the bad guys. This way, they can't blame it on anyone else."

Ellie turned to Teresa. "I'm not surprised that you did the right thing."

Teresa felt a hot flush creep up her neck to her cheeks. She saw Karen's sharp gaze flit back and forth between her and Ellie. Teresa focused on her plate.

"Ellie," Karen said, "is your family all here in Pittsburgh?"

"It's just me and my brother now," Ellie said. She hesitated a moment. "He's busy and I don't get to see him very often."

"Well, we're glad you could come with Teresa tonight," Karen said, and Teresa shot her a look of gratitude.

When dinner was over, Teresa and Ellie insisted on helping with the dishes. Rob poured more wine, but Teresa stopped him.

"I'm driving," she insisted. "Make mine a Coke."

Karen invited everyone out to the living room. "So, Teresa, what are you going to do?"

Ellie glanced up. "About what?"

"My folks," Teresa said. "I'm not sure." She looked at Rob. "Any ideas?"

"Well, you could try just asking Pop for a raise." At the expression on Teresa's face, he added, "Or you could put in a few applications with other pharmacies and see what happens."

Teresa gave a weak laugh. "Oh, yeah. And when they ask for a reference from my one and only job and they call my father to see if I've been a good employee, that'll go over just fine."

Rob spread his hands. "I didn't say it would be easy."

———◆◇◆———

Ellie shivered in the passenger seat as Teresa drove through streets still slippery with compacted snow.

"Sorry," Teresa said. "I need to get another blanket for the car."

"What happened to the one you had?"

"I'm not sure. Guess I used it somewhere else and forgot to put it back."

"It's okay," Ellie said through chattering teeth. "Your brother and sister-in-law are not what I expected."

Teresa glanced over. "In what way?"

Ellie paused and Teresa had the feeling she was trying to choose words that wouldn't offend. "I can see how different he is from your younger brother."

Teresa laughed. "He was different anyhow, but Karen really has changed him for the better."

"No." Ellie sounded so serious that Teresa looked over at her again, noting how the street lamps lit up the smooth contours of her face. "Love changed him. He would do anything for her." She turned to face Teresa. "Have you ever loved anyone like that?"

Teresa returned her attention to the street as she shifted gears, feeling her face grow hot under Ellie's scrutiny. She shook her head. "No." She opened her mouth and closed it again. She wasn't sure she wanted to know, but "Have you?" she heard herself ask.

"Not yet," Ellie said. "But I will."

"How do you know that?"

Ellie sounded so certain. Teresa had never known any such thing for herself.

"I just do. I know that someday, I am going to love someone so much that I will wonder how I ever felt whole without them."

Teresa thought about this. "I've never pictured myself in love at all. With anyone."

"That's not right," Ellie said earnestly. "Not for you."

"What does that mean?" Teresa tried to laugh, but couldn't.

Ellie reached out and laid a hand on Teresa's arm. "You have so much to offer someone. You're kind and sensitive and caring." Ellie stopped abruptly, pulling her hand away. She sat very still as Teresa shifted gears again.

The interior of the VW crackled with a sudden tension. Even through the layers of her coat and sweater, Teresa could have sworn she felt the heat of Ellie's touch and she wished Ellie would put her hand back on her arm—*and never let go*. That fleeting thought jumped into her head, startling her with the surge of emotion that came with it. She longed to continue driving, just to keep Ellie in the car with her, but soon enough, she was pulling up outside Ellie's apartment building.

"This was a really nice evening," Ellie said, breaking the silence at last.

"I'm glad you could come," Teresa said. "I'm really glad they got to meet you." And Teresa realized she was glad about that. It made her happy that Rob and Karen had liked Ellie, not like Bernie or her mother, where she felt like Ellie was under attack.

"Well, I guess I should go up," Ellie said, and Teresa heard the regret in her voice.

Not yet! She wanted to say it, but it was late. Ellie was probably tired.

"Would you like to come up?"

Teresa's heart leapt at the invitation. "Yes. All right. If you don't think it's too late."

Ellie smiled. "Come on."

Teresa followed Ellie up the stairs. They could hear KC meowing as Ellie unlocked the kitchen door.

"Oh, did you think I was never coming home?" Ellie asked, picking her up. KC immediately began making a vibrating noise.

"Is she okay?" Teresa asked in alarm as she took her coat off and hung it over one of the kitchen chairs.

Ellie laughed. "Yes. That's the sound she makes when she's happy. You really don't know anything about cats, do you?"

"The only person I know who has a cat is my sister, and it always hides."

"Would you like to hold her?"

"Um, okay."

Ellie placed KC in Teresa's arms and took her own coat off. KC stretched up, sniffing Teresa's face curiously. Teresa chuckled. "Her whiskers tickle."

"Come and sit down," Ellie said, leading the way into the living room.

Teresa set the cat down and followed Ellie to the couch. Now that she was here, she didn't know what to say. *What were you thinking, coming up here?* She only knew she hadn't wanted the time with Ellie to end.

She felt KC wind around her ankles.

"There's this guy, a homeless man, who hangs out around our store," Teresa said, watching KC. "He has a dog named Lucy."

"Really?" Ellie looked at her. "How does he feed Lucy?"

Teresa thought. "I don't know. I mean, I've left food out for him before, and I think he fed her some of that, but—"

"No," Ellie said. "She really needs dog food to stay healthy. She probably means the world to him. If anything happened to her..."

Teresa pictured Dogman sheltering Lucy with him under the sleeping bag, feeding her before he fed himself, and she knew Ellie was right.

There was a sudden knock on the living room door, startling both of them. Ellie unlocked it and Sullivan bounded in.

"Hey, how was—"

He stopped abruptly when he saw Teresa sitting there.

"Oh, sorry," he said. "I didn't know you had anyone up here."

"Sullivan, this is Teresa Benedetto," Ellie said.

"Hi," Sullivan said, bending forward to shake Teresa's hand.

"Sullivan's my neighbor across the hall. He's working on his PhD at Pitt," Ellie said.

"In what?" Teresa asked.

"Biomedical engineering," Sullivan said.

"Whatever that is." Ellie sat back down as Sullivan took the armchair.

"No, it's fascinating," Teresa said. "Things like surgical hardware and artificial joints. Synthetic ligaments."

"Yes!" Sullivan said, leaning forward. "I have so many ideas about how joint replacements could be so much better than they are now. And we're just starting to explore how computers and robotics—"

"Oh, don't get him started," Ellie said. "Talking about this stuff is like drugs for him. He won't sleep for days. Teresa is a pharmacist."

"So you know what I'm talking about," Sullivan said.

"Only a little. Things I've read in journals." Teresa looked at her watch. "I really should go. It's late." She stood. "Nice to meet you, Sullivan."

"Likewise," he said.

Ellie walked her back out to the kitchen. "Thanks again for asking me to go with you tonight. I had a really nice time."

Teresa looked into her clear eyes and felt lost. She stood there, not wanting to leave, but unable to think of any reason to stay.

Ellie impulsively flung her arms around Teresa. This time, Teresa held her tightly in return, breathing her in for several seconds.

Suddenly, she let go and reached for the door. "I'll see you soon," she said and nearly ran down the stairs. By the time she got to the VW, tears were running down her cheeks.

She got into the car and turned the ignition. She started to reach for the gearshift and then put her hands over her face and cried.

Ellie looked up as KC meowed and placed a gentle paw on her knee. Wincing, she uncrossed her legs and looked around at the drawings scattered all over the living room floor. Her eyelids felt like sandpaper. She squinted, surprised to see sunlight coming in through the windows. She hadn't meant to stay up all night.

She leaned back against the couch and closed her eyes. After Teresa left, Sullivan had shown signs of wanting to settle down for a long visit. "I'm really tired," she'd said with a yawn, ushering him back to his own apartment as soon as she politely could. Only, once she was alone, sleep had been impossible. She was filled with a restless energy. Going to a dresser drawer, she'd dug out a drawing pad and an old cigar box filled with her charcoals, pencils and a kneaded eraser. She wasn't even sure what it was that she was going to draw, but the sketches took shape—hands, eyes, a bowed head with dark, wavy hair. Looking at the images now, she flushed as she realized they were all images of Teresa, or at least her impressions of Teresa. She picked up a sketch of hands and remembered watching Teresa's hands as they'd worked on the store window, fine fingers tying fishing line to the pretend-balloons. Such a contrast to the awkwardness of her large body. Last night, she'd been watching Teresa—the way she lowered her eyes when she was thinking about something, her dark lashes grazing her cheek, her strong profile with a prominent nose, something so sensuous about the curve of her lips, her hands as she twisted the stem of her wine glass. She was such a curious mixture of strong and... *what?*

Delicate wasn't the right word. Maybe sensitive suited her better. Ellie had looked up once to see Karen watching her watch Teresa and she had known in an instant that here was someone who saw everything, and that if she and Karen ever were to talk, it would do no good to hide or lie.

Ellie flipped to the back pages of her drawing pad, to images she hadn't looked at in years. They were only sketches—the line of a cheek and nose; an eye, smiling and coy; a head of short, pixie-ish hair and the graceful curve of a neck—but they were instantly recognizable. Ellie reached out and traced a finger along the curve of that neck. Katie was the Lockes' youngest daughter, just a couple of months older than Ellie. *"She'll be good company for you,"* the social worker had said when she placed Ellie with the Lockes. The two girls had bonded quickly. Katie was an athlete and knew everybody. The Lockes' sons were away at college, and so Ellie was given the boys' room, connected to Katie's by a Jack and Jill bathroom that became a secret passage, one that let Katie come to Ellie in the night. Nights spent with the girls' lying in the two twin beds, talking and giggling, had been like an endless slumber party. But that had all changed the summer between their junior and senior years of high school, the night Katie crawled into Ellie's bed—"You won't tell, will you?" Katie had whispered.

Ellie's heart had raced, and a part of her knew she'd been wanting this for a long time as she felt Katie's soft lips on her own, better than any boy's kisses, Katie's hands sliding under her pajama top to caress young breasts. She got to touch Katie's body as well, the wondrous feel of Katie's hard nipples pressing into her palms. They never strayed beyond teasing little tugs on the waistband of their underwear, but with Katie lying on top of her, their thighs pressing against each other's crotches, Ellie had experienced her first orgasm as she bucked against the pressure of Katie's leg.

But then, one day just before they were to start their senior year, Mrs. Locke said, "Come with me."

Mrs. Locke had looked unusually stern as Ellie followed her. They got in the car. Ellie remembered how her heart had pounded, thinking maybe she was being returned to social services, but all her clothes and things were still there at the house... They had driven to St. Ignatius, the Lockes' church. Ellie had been going to Mass with them there and thought old Father Patrick looked a little like a beardless Santa Claus, fat and kind of jolly-looking, only he, too, had worn a very serious expression when Ellie was ushered into his office that afternoon.

"I'll wait outside," Mrs. Locke said, backing out of the office and closing the door.

Nervously, Ellie had stood as Father Patrick came around from behind his desk and invited her to sit in one of the two chairs there as he took the other.

She had only seen him in the robes he wore to celebrate Mass. In his black shirt and collar, he looked different, more somber. Ellie remembered how her heart had continued pounding so fast that she could hardly breathe, wondering why she was there.

"Ellie," Father Patrick began. "I understand this is a delicate situation." He folded his hands together, and Ellie thought his fingers looked like fat sausages, with nails that were too long for a man. "Katie went to her mother and told her everything."

It took a moment for his words to sink in. *Katie told?* "We understand that you've been through a very traumatic time, losing your mother, and maybe you come from a different kind of family," Father Patrick continued, his voice taking on the tone it did when he was giving a homily. "But the Lockes are a good, Catholic family. Katie likes you, but not in that sinful way."

Ellie felt her face go red and hot, and she dared not look up at him. She stared at his fat fingers and said nothing.

Father Patrick cleared his throat. "I've spoken to Mr. and Mrs. Locke, and they have agreed to let you stay in their house, but with the stern warning that you must not go into Katie's room again, and you can never..." Here, even Father Patrick seemed not to know what to say. "You must not draw Katie into sin again. If you do, the Lockes will have no choice but to send you back to Social Services for a different foster placement."

The ride back to the house had been a silent one. When Ellie got to her room, she found that the door from her bedroom to the bathroom had been fitted with a lock, so that the only way into the bathroom was now through the hall. The Lockes were taking no chances that Ellie might slip into Katie's room again—"except I never went to her room!" Ellie wanted to scream. She couldn't even look at Katie. For days, she stayed in her room, leaving only to go to school, where she avoided Katie. At the house, she refused to come down for meals, surviving on a bowl of cereal scavenged during the night. How could she sit at the table while Katie pretended it had all been Ellie's fault? That was when the Lockes got her KC, thinking the kitten would be good company, and she was. She kept Ellie company through the long, lonely nights. She kept her company when the Lockes went to church on Sundays—Ellie refused to go back there. KC became her lifeline, her confidante. Ellie kept a calendar on the wall over her desk, counting down the last six and a half months until she turned eighteen and could leave their house for good.

"But it's only March," Mrs. Locke had said. "What are you going to do about school?"

"I'll manage," Ellie insisted, and since Social Services couldn't legally make her stay once she was eighteen, there had been nothing any of them could do.

Ellie packed her few things, put KC in a carrier, and left Duquesne Heights without a backward glance, and without ever having said another word to Katie. She had to dig into her paltry college fund, just enough to rent that first room back in Squirrel Hill, promising herself she would pay it back when she could. She got a part-time job, registered herself for school—anywhere was better than where Katie was. She soon had to get a second job and then a third to earn more money, and even then, she had to borrow from her college fund which was getting smaller and smaller. Her grades suffered, but she graduated, thanks to Louise.

"Oh, God," Ellie said now, pressing her hands against her eyes. It had been ages since she'd thought about Katie. KC crawled up into her lap. Ellie picked her up and squeezed her tight. "What would I have done without you?"

She gathered up all the scattered drawings and stuffed them into the drawing pad. She put all her pencils and charcoals into the cigar box, and tucked everything back in the drawer.

Her bed called to her. She glanced at the clock. There was nowhere she really had to be today. Next weekend, she would start her holiday hours at Kaufman's, but today, she could do whatever she wished. She lay down on top of the covers and pulled the quilt over her. As she lay there, she could feel an upwelling of emotion—none of it good—and she knew thinking about Katie had not been a good thing.

"It never is."

CHAPTER 10

ANITA WAS SHUFFLING AROUND the kitchen. She stopped when Teresa entered and set down two large pans of lasagna and took her coat off.

"You've lost weight."

She grabbed Teresa and made her face her, placing a hand on either side of Teresa's face as she inspected her anxiously.

"Are you sick? Do you have cancer?"

Teresa chuckled. "No, I don't have cancer." She had lost some weight, though. After her evening with Ellie—*Why do I keep wanting to call it a date?*—she had bought a bag of dog food, safely stashed under the front hood of her VW. Each evening, she had halved her dinner, placing a plate of food for Dogman and a bowl of dog food for Lucy on top of the trash cans behind the store. Every morning, the plate and bowl were empty, neatly stacked up. Her stomach had complained initially at only getting half of what it was used to, but she was getting accustomed to it now, and actually felt better eating less at night.

"You sure you're not sick?" Anita's sharp eyes probed Teresa's face.

"I'm fine," Teresa said with a smile. "Happy Thanksgiving, Nita."

Further conversation was impossible as Sylvia and the other aunts came into the kitchen, all talking loudly. Teresa gathered her mother's coat, along with her own, in her arms and carried them upstairs to drape them across Aunt Luisa's bed. Downstairs, she could hear the arrival of more people. They were expecting about twenty today. Gianni was supposed to bring Angelina, and then they would go to her family's house for a later dinner. Their cousin Dom Jr. and his family were coming along with Aunt Betty and Uncle Dom.

Teresa sat on the side of the bed, wondering what Ellie was doing right now. She felt nauseous and her face suddenly flushed hot, and she briefly wondered if she wasn't sick—except the same thing had happened every time she remembered how she had nearly run from Ellie at the end of their evening. She tried to imagine having Ellie here with her today, introducing her to everyone, and had to laugh at the absurdity of the idea. "There's no way." It was impossible for her to picture the crowd downstairs welcoming Ellie. Angelina would be welcomed as Gianni's girlfriend and someday fiancée, but she knew her mother would say, "Thanksgiving is family time. It's not the right time to bring a friend." Vaguely, Teresa knew that "friend" wasn't precisely the right word for Ellie. She heard her name being hollered and, with a sigh, went downstairs.

Francesca, bigger than ever, was doing a slow-motion fall backward into the sofa. Privately, Teresa thought it looked as if the sofa might swallow her, but she smiled and waved hello to her sister. She would have offered to get Francesca something, but Aunt Elisa beat her to it.

"What can I get you? Wine? No, you can't have wine. How about some nice tea?"

Francesca shot Teresa a "Help me" kind of look.

"What do you really want?" Teresa asked as Elisa bustled off to get the tea.

"I don't want tea," Francesca said desperately. "I already have to pee every ten minutes. I'm dying for a pepperoni roll. Are there any?"

Teresa laughed. "Are you kidding? When are there not pepperoni rolls in this house? Be right back." She went into the kitchen and found Anita just taking a fresh batch of pepperoni rolls out of the oven. Teresa reached over the kids who were waiting to grab them and took three. "For Francesca," she said at her aunt's reproving glance, but she had one in her mouth before she left the kitchen. "Hot," she warned her sister as she handed her the other two wrapped in a napkin.

"Thank you," said Francesca. She stuffed one of the rolls into her mouth like a starving woman, closing her eyes as she savored it.

Teresa thought briefly about warning her sister against eating too many of those. Francesca had gained more weight with each pregnancy, and wasn't getting it off in between, but *who are you to talk to anyone else about being heavy?*

She looked around. Most of the main floor furniture had been pushed to the outskirts of the rooms, making room for four extra tables that snaked through the dining room into the living room. The men had all disappeared into the basement where there was another television. She could hear their voices echoing from downstairs.

The television in the living room was tuned to the Macy's Thanksgiving parade, but it only made Teresa think of Ellie again. She went into the kitchen. "What do you want me to do?"

The next couple of hours were spent in a kind of organized chaos, getting all the food cooked, warmed up, spooned into serving bowls for each table, warmed up again, and placed on the tables and then trying to get the men and kids all seated while Sylvia and the aunts hovered, making sure everyone had some of everything on their plate. Teresa sat at a table with Dom Jr.'s three kids, cutting up their turkey and lasagna into smaller bites for them.

"Oh, thank you," said Gina, Dom's wife.

Teresa remembered that she was pregnant again, also, and getting big enough to show. "Sit down," she said. "I've got this."

Gina gave her a grateful look as she sank tiredly into a chair at the main table while Dom stuffed his face, oblivious to what the kids were doing.

Teresa showed the kids how to use their forks to make ditches in their lumps of bread stuffing so that when she spooned gravy on, the gravy could run sluggishly through the channels. "Then you scramble it all together and eat it," she said, taking a forkful.

She saw Ana Maria walking around the tables with a platter of turkey, asking everyone if they needed more.

"Have you sat down at all?" Teresa asked her, taking another piece of dark meat.

"Of course I have," said Ana Maria as she hurried over to the next table.

The kids were soon done eating and were only playing with their food, so Teresa told them they could leave the table. She sat there alone, looking at all the food left on their plates, and had a sudden thought.

She carried their dishes into the kitchen and found three foil pie plates. One, she filled with uneaten food scraped from the kids' plates. The other two, she filled with food from the platters, a little of everything. She covered each with aluminum foil and carried them out the back door to her car. Hurrying back inside, she helped clear the tables and began doing the dishes while her mother and the aunts cut the pies—pumpkin, pecan, apple—arguing as they tried to remember who wanted what. While they carried plates of pie out to the tables, Teresa quickly wrapped two pieces of apple pie in plastic wrap and took those out to her car as well.

"What were you doing?" Sylvia demanded as Teresa came back into the kitchen.

"Taking some garbage out to the cans," Teresa lied. She went back to the sink and scrubbed the roasting pan.

"Didn't you have any pie?" Francesca waddled into the kitchen, carrying some empty plates.

"I'll get some later," Teresa said, wringing out the dishrag and wiping down the stove.

There was a parade of women in and out of the kitchen, carrying more dishes and platters. Teresa filled the sink with fresh soapy water and continued washing until all the dishes were done. She tried to figure out how to get her coat from upstairs without anyone noticing. She knew the men were already heading back down to the basement to watch football, and she could hear the kids running around upstairs.

With the dishes done, she dried her hands and slipped out of the kitchen. Anita and Luisa were taking the tablecloths off the tables to shake the crumbs off and put them back on the tables for a second round of eating later in the afternoon.

"I'll do that," she said. "Just let me run upstairs for my coat."

She hurried up the stairs and was back in a moment. "Be right back." She gathered the tablecloths in her arms and carried them outside to shake. No one noticed as she brought them inside and then went back out the front door. She retrieved her car keys from her coat pocket and slipped around the back of the house to where her VW was parked.

You are really going to catch hell for this, said a voice in her head as she started the engine.

"I don't care," she answered.

Late afternoon dusk was falling as she drove down the alley and parked behind the store. There, Dogman and Lucy were arranging their sleeping bag, settling earlier than usual since everything was closed for the holiday. Lucy trotted over to Teresa and received a pat on the head.

"I thought you two might like something a little special, since it's Thanksgiving." Teresa opened the hood of her car and retrieved three of the wrapped parcels there. "This one is for Lucy," she said, handing him the foil pie plate with the kids' leftovers, "and these are for you."

Dogman looked at her. "Why are you doing this?" It was the first time he'd ever spoken to her. His voice was hoarse and raspy, as if it didn't get used very often. "I don't see you doing it for anyone else."

"I don't."

"Then why?"

She gazed into his stony eyes. Up close in daylight, she could see that he was younger than she had thought, though his face was lined and his hair and beard were streaked with gray.

"I'm not sure," she said. Lucy sat down beside him and looked up at her. Teresa smiled. "I think maybe it's because of her."

"Because of my dog?"

"Because you care enough to keep her warm and dry," Teresa said. "Because you feed her before you eat." She shrugged. "It just made me want to help out, if I can. I figure you've got to work a little harder to keep two fed and warm."

"I don't need help," he said.

"I know that," Teresa said quickly. "I know you don't. But we have extra. And it's one less thing for you to worry about."

With a curt nod, he accepted the foil packages, and he and Lucy turned back to their makeshift shelter. Teresa got into her car and started it up. Driving to Ellie's apartment, she could feel her heart thudding in her chest, but was it anticipation or apprehension? She sat at the curb, her hands gripping the wheel, trying to decide whether to go up.

"Don't be stupid," she whispered. "You're just bringing some dinner."

The apartment looked dark as she got out of the VW, and she suddenly wondered if Ellie really did have somewhere else to go for Thanksgiving. She'd been certain, when Ellie said she had plans, that she'd been making it up so Teresa wouldn't feel bad, but maybe not. She retrieved the plates of food from under the hood and climbed the stairs to Ellie's kitchen door. She knocked, but there was no answer. Tentatively, she knocked again. When there was still no response, she stood there, undecided about whether to leave the food at the doorstep. Finally, she set the plates down and dug in her coat for a slip of paper. The only thing there was a bank deposit slip. She found a pen in another pocket and scrawled a note telling Ellie what time the food had been left.

Reluctantly, she headed back down the stairs. She was nearly down on the second floor landing when she heard movement in the apartment above. She paused. *Ellie was there, but didn't want to see you.* She turned to continue descending the steps, her heart plummeting faster than her feet. A door opened above her.

"Teresa? Is that you?"

Ellie's voice carried down the stairwell. Teresa stepped out on the landing to where she could see Ellie standing outside her door, holding the two wrapped dishes.

"I thought I heard something," Ellie said. "I was over in Sullivan's apartment, feeding his fish. Come on up."

Teresa's heart lifted as she climbed her way back up to Ellie and followed her into the kitchen.

"What's all this?" Ellie hefted the pie tins.

"I didn't think you really had plans for Thanksgiving dinner, and we always have enough to feed an army, so..." Teresa's voice faltered as Ellie turned away suddenly. "Are you okay?"

Ellie nodded, standing with her back to Teresa. She set the dishes of food on the counter and busied herself with getting a couple of plates down from the cupboard. "I'm fine. This was really nice of you."

Teresa thought she heard a catch in Ellie's voice. KC came trotting in, meowing and winding around Teresa's ankles. Teresa bent down and picked her up.

"Can you stay and eat with me?" Ellie asked.

"I've already eaten," Teresa said. "This is all for you."

"Just a bite or two," Ellie said, turning to her. "Keep me company."

I'll keep you company forever. Teresa had to bite her lip to keep from saying it out loud.

Ellie heard her hesitation. "Of course, you have to get back to your family," she said. "I'm sorry—"

"No," Teresa said quickly. "They're in between round one and round two. I did my bit. I'm fine. I'll stay."

Ellie's face lit up, and so did something inside Teresa. Ellie poured them drinks while the oven warmed up. "Sorry, I don't have a microwave," she said.

"Don't apologize," Teresa said, taking her coat off and hanging it on one of the pegs by the door. "My mom won't have one in the house. My aunts, either. Convinced it'll give them cancer. Of course, they think that about everything."

Ellie slid the foil-wrapped pie tin into the hot oven and joined Teresa at the table.

"What have you been up to?" Teresa asked, taking a sip of her Coke.

Ellie's expression darkened. It was so fleeting, Teresa wondered if she'd imagined it. "Tell me about your Thanksgiving," Ellie said rather than answering Teresa's question. "What does your family do?"

Teresa studied her face for a moment, but the thing she thought she'd seen was gone. "Well, the women are all up early, starting the cooking while the men get to sleep in." Ellie laughed and Teresa thought it was the nicest sound she'd heard all day. She continued talking, describing the mountains of food and all the people milling around the aunts' house. Ellie smiled as she listened.

"That sounds really nice," Ellie said wistfully. The oven timer went off, and she pulled the hot pie tin out, setting it on top of the stove. "Oh, everything smells wonderful." She dished out a little of everything onto one plate.

"Just give me a little stuffing," Teresa said.

Ellie pinched off a bite of turkey breast for KC, mixing it into her dry food, and then came to join Teresa at the table again.

"Oh, this is so good," Ellie said at her first bite. "Your family knows how to cook."

Teresa lifted her hands. "Cooking and eating. The things we're best at." She realized she was staring at Ellie and forced herself to look down at her plate. "You don't have any other family?"

Ellie shook her head. "No one."

"What were Thanksgivings like when you were growing up?"

Ellie was quiet for several seconds, and Teresa kicked herself for asking.

"Nothing special, I guess," Ellie said, tearing a bit of a roll off and putting it in her mouth. "My mom always made the regular things—turkey, stuffing, pumpkin pie. She did have a really good recipe for a homemade cranberry sauce with orange and a little clove. It was delicious."

Teresa felt a sudden impulse to reach out and take Ellie's hand. She clamped her hand between her knees.

"Do they know where you are?" Ellie asked unexpectedly.

"No. I kind of snuck away without saying anything."

"Why?"

Teresa's eyes met Ellie's and *I was trapped*, she would realize when she thought back. She felt helpless, snared like a bird by Ellie's gaze. Her mouth opened, but no sound came out at first. Ellie waited, watching her. "I had to see you," Teresa heard herself say. "I... I wanted to see you."

Ellie's eyes hardened suddenly. "Because you feel sorry for me?"

Startled, Teresa said, "No!" She leaned toward Ellie. *Because every day I don't see you feels like a day of my life that I've wasted.* Only she didn't say that. Instead, she said, "Because you're my friend."

Ellie's eyes glistened with sudden tears, and she looked down at her plate.

"What's wrong?" Teresa asked.

Ellie didn't answer immediately. She ate a bit and Teresa did likewise as she waited. At last, Ellie said, "I'm sorry. It doesn't very often get to me."

"I think," Teresa said softly, "that it would get to me all the time. I don't know how you get by as well as you do."

Ellie smiled. She tucked her hair behind her ear and looked up, the tears gone, her usual bright expression on her face. "I get by because I have to."

"I might survive because I had to," Teresa mused, trying to imagine being all alone—but with the household full of people she'd left behind, she knew that would never happen, not like it had to Ellie. "But surviving is different from living, isn't it?" She looked at Ellie with new respect. "You do more than get by. And I think you're allowed to have moments when it gets to you."

Ellie looked at her gratefully and the air between them was suddenly tense again like it had been in the car on the way home from Robbie's, only this time it wasn't dark and Teresa had nowhere else to look except into Ellie's eyes. She didn't know how long they sat there, but the tension was broken by a little meow as KC stretched up on her hind feet, reaching to Ellie's thigh. Ellie blinked down at her and picked her up.

"I'm glad you're my friend," Ellie said, half-glancing at Teresa but not quite meeting her eyes again.

"Me too." With a pang of regret, Teresa saw the clock. "I have to be getting back."

"Will they be upset?"

Teresa laughed. "Probably. But they'll get over it. That's what we do. We yell and argue, and we get over it."

"That sounds nice. KC never argues back."

Teresa laughed again as she got up and took her coat down from the peg. Ellie was at the counter, writing something on a slip of paper.

"Here's my phone number," Ellie said, handing the slip to Teresa. "Could I have yours?"

Teresa quickly wrote down the numbers for both the house and the store. "I'm often alone in the evenings. Give me a call."

"I will."

Ellie fingered the piece of paper Teresa handed her. "Thank you." She waved toward the table. "For the feast, and... for being my friend."

I want to be so much more than that. The words nearly spilled from Teresa's mouth, but she couldn't let herself say them. "I am," she said simply. "I always will be."

She opened the kitchen door and started down the stairs. On the landing, she paused and looked back up at Ellie standing there.

Impulsively, Teresa rushed back up the stairs and threw her arms around her, giving her a quick hug. "I'll see you soon."

"Soon."

Teresa felt as if she floated down the stairs, buoyed by the rush of emotions Ellie stirred within her. Never had anyone moved her the way Ellie did. *The things I almost said.* She shivered at her own boldness.

Except you weren't bold enough to say them, were you? said a voice inside her head.

I will, she countered. *When the time is right.*

CHAPTER 11

THE DINER WAS PACKED, even for a Saturday evening. Ellie took a seat at the counter, watching Louise rush around, pouring coffee, taking orders, checking customers out at the cash register. She had other waitresses and three cooks back at the grill, but "I started this diner because I love talking to people," she always said. "Why would I want to give that up?"

"You be sure and tell your wife I said Merry Christmas," she said to one man as she handed him his change.

"I will, Louise," he said with a smile. "And Merry Christmas to you, if I don't see you before." He went back to his booth and left a bigger tip.

Ellie sighed. Her feet ached and her back was stiff from standing for the past five hours.

"What can I get you, Missy?" Louise beamed at her.

"Grilled cheese—"

"—and tomato soup," Louise finished for her with a shake of her head. "Be right up." She scribbled the order on her pad and clipped it to the carousel hanging between the counter and the kitchen.

Ellie twirled on her counter stool, listening to the noises—plates clattering, customers' conversations, the cooks' yells from the kitchen when orders were up. She spun around to the counter to find a Coke waiting for her, and next to the glass was a saucer with a dill pickle spear.

She laughed, picking the pickle up to take a bite.

The diner had been busy that day, like this, only it had been late summer—her first summer after graduating high school. It was lunchtime, and Ellie and everyone else had to eat quickly and get back to work. She'd worked four hours early that morning at another store, unloading a truck, before changing clothes to come and work her shift at Kaufman's. She ordered a burger, no fries, just water to drink—it was one of those in between times, when she only had three dollars to get her through to her next paycheck tomorrow afternoon. At least she had enough food for KC. She'd eaten nothing but peanut butter and jelly, twice a day, for weeks and had used the last of the peanut butter that morning. She knew if she had a burger, there would be no dinner that night and nothing but buttered toast in the morning. That burger and the pickle that came with it would have to get her through until she could get her check cashed tomorrow. Louise had already saved her a few times, giving her all of her money back when she made change, but "you can't expect her to keep doing that," Ellie told herself sternly. Her stomach growled as she waited for her order, but the diner was so noisy no one noticed. When the plate was slapped down in front of her, there was no pickle. She stared at her hamburger for a moment and then burst into tears. Louise stopped mid-stride on her way to the cash register.

"Come with me."

She practically picked Ellie up off her stool—"well, you didn't weigh any more than a bird," she would say to Ellie later—and took her back to the diner's office. "You sit here." Ellie sat, crying as if her heart was breaking. "I'll be right back," Louise said. She left, returning a couple of minutes later with Ellie's burger and another plate heaping with French fries—"and your pickle." Louise chuckled. "You eat and then we'll talk." She left Ellie alone, sniffling and hiccupping her way through her lunch.

Ellie emerged from the office about fifteen minutes later. "I have to get back to work," she said, her eyes red and still watery. She fumbled in her pocket for her money.

"What time do you get off?" Louise asked as she rang up another customer.

"I work until closing." Ellie held out her three dollars.

"You keep that until tonight," Louise said. "I expect you back here at nine o'clock. We'll settle up then."

"Yes, ma'am."

When Ellie got back later that night, Louise had a hot bowl of vegetable soup and a grilled cheese sandwich waiting for her. The diner still had customers, but she sat down at a booth with Ellie and made her eat. The soup was delicious. Ellie couldn't remember the last time she'd eaten her fill.

"Now," Louise said, sliding the empty dishes aside, "tell me what's going on."

For the first time ever, Ellie had talked. She told Louise everything—not the part about Katie—but everything else had come spilling out. She started crying again—"I cried for three days over a pickle," she would always recall with an embarrassed laugh.

"Well," said Louise when she'd heard Ellie's tale. "What are you going to do about it?"

Ellie blinked. "What do you mean?"

"I mean, what are you going to do about it?" repeated Louise. "You say you're working three jobs, and still not getting a steady forty hours a week. You have got to find something else."

"Doing what?" Ellie shook her head. "I thought I was going to go to college, but..."

Louise slid a business card across the table. "One of my customers is a bank manager. He mentioned that they're looking for tellers. You tell him Louise Baker gave you his name."

"Oh, no," Ellie protested. "I can't—"

She stopped abruptly at the stern look on Louise's face. "Ellie Ryan, you are a hard worker. You are intelligent. You can learn anything you set your mind to. I'm not saying you have to make a career out of this, but if you get hired, it'll be full-time with benefits. You call him."

Ellie's eyes filled again as she reached for the card. "Yes, ma'am."

She munched on her pickle now, watching Louise affectionately.

"Any extras today?" Louise asked as she laid Ellie's order in front of her.

In Ellie's pocket was her Kaufman's paycheck that she would cash tomorrow. "Fifteen."

Louise's eyebrows shot up. "Fifteen? Well, aren't you Miss Moneybags."

Ellie laughed and picked up her grilled cheese sandwich.

When she left the diner a short while later, she carried a paper sack filled with fifteen grilled cheese sandwiches wrapped in wax paper. A biting winter wind blew between the buildings, so cold it made her face hurt. She wandered the side streets and alleys, offering a sandwich to any street person she encountered, asking each if he or she knew a man named Daniel. She didn't expect to get a "yes", not after all this time, but she had to ask. Sometimes, it was hard not to give up hope. It felt as if Daniel had dropped off the face of the earth. When the sandwiches had all been given out, she trudged back out to Fifth Avenue to catch a bus.

She yawned as she sank onto one of the hard plastic seats. *This is only Thanksgiving weekend*, she reminded herself. *If you're this tired now, what are you going to be like by Christmas?*

Christmas. It gaped before her like a black hole. She had good memories of Christmas when she was a kid, but the last few before her mom died had been tough. Her mom had been sick more often than not, and there hadn't been any extra money for presents.

"I wish I could do more," her mother had said that last Christmas, handing Ellie a box containing a hand-knitted sweater.

"No, this is perfect," Ellie had insisted. "My favorite colors. Thank you so much."

Ellie's gift to her mom that year was also hand-made—a simply framed version of part of the 46th Psalm—*Be still and know that I am God*. "You made this?" her mother asked, admiring the calligraphy and the intricate Celtic knots scrolled around the border.

The bus lurched to a stop to let someone off. Ellie had to reach out to steady herself. A moment later, the bus roared off again while she stared out the window into the darkness.

Some years were just like this. Ellie knew that by now. Knew it would always be so. Lonelier. Sadder. Thanksgiving had felt the same—until Teresa showed up. Ellie smiled as she remembered the unexpected happiness she'd felt at finding Teresa on her doorstep— happiness that had nothing to do with the food she'd brought. *She thought of me. She left her family to come see me.*

But don't read too much into it, warned a more cynical part of her. *She only felt sorry for you.*

Maybe, Ellie admitted. *But she said she had to see me. That must mean something.*

It doesn't matter, insisted that cautious voice. *You said it yourself— she had to leave her family to come see you. Because you wouldn't have been welcome.*

Ellie knew that. Rob and Karen's situation told her that she would never be welcomed—as what? She gave a tiny shake of her head. She couldn't even let herself imagine what a life with someone could be like. In her dreams—the only time she couldn't control her imaginings—she was never with a man. Usually, the women of her dreams were nobody she actually knew, sometimes just faces of women she'd seen, but lately, Teresa had been in those dreams. To Ellie, Teresa was like a Roman statue—classically beautiful, larger than life. "You got the larger than life part right," she could hear Teresa scoff. But Ellie loved Teresa's largeness. She flushed as she thought it. That was a word she never let herself use for anyone outside her family. She used to think, long ago, that she loved Katie, but any ability to love had been squashed that day in Father Patrick's office. *Until now*, said a little voice, sniffing the air hopefully, no matter how many times Ellie cautioned herself.

"Oh no."

With a start, she realized she'd missed her stop. She got off at the next stop and backtracked.

She could hear KC's little meow before she even got the kitchen door unlocked. "Are you starving, little one?" she said, hugging the cat and carrying her to the counter, where she dished out some cat food. She hung her coat and scarf on a peg and went back to keep KC company while she ate. An unexpected knock on the living room door made her jump.

"Hey," she said when she opened the door to find Sullivan standing there. "I didn't think you were coming back until tomorrow."

Sullivan came in and sank into the couch. "I had all the family togetherness I could take. Told them I had to get back to check on my research."

"Well, this ruins my plans. I had my entire weekend laid out around feeding your fish."

He looked askance at her. "If that was going to be the highlight of your weekend, you are pathetic."

"More pathetic than the guy who keeps fish for pets? Besides, KC likes to watch them. It's cat television."

"You bring your cat over to traumatize my fish?"

Ellie laughed. "They like to tease her. They come over to the glass and make fish lips at her."

"How was your Thanksgiving?"

"I had a surprise visitor," Ellie said. "Teresa Benedetto came by. Brought some food."

"That was nice of her," Sullivan said. "I thought she might invite you over."

Ellie shrugged. "I think she might have, but her family is huge and kind of insular from what I've seen."

"What? Like Italians only?"

"Italians only. Family only."

"That's too bad." Sullivan slouched lower on the couch, stretching his legs out and crossing his ankles. "Have you ever thought about volunteering at a soup kitchen or something?"

Ellie recognized the signs of Sullivan's getting ready to settle in for a long visit. More than once, she'd gone to bed with him snoring on her couch. With a resigned sigh, she settled back into the corner of the couch, her legs curled under her.

"I would," she said. "But they're all run by churches."

"So?"

"So, I'm not going anywhere near any church," she said flatly.

Sullivan looked at her sympathetically, and she knew he was thinking what everyone thought. Let him. It didn't matter that people assumed she was angry with God over what had happened to her family—"in fact, it makes it easier," she could have said. "Because then I don't have to explain the real reason."

━━━◦✕◦━━━

Christmas carols played from tinny-sounding speakers and golden light spilled from the downtown store windows onto the sidewalks as a light snow fell.

"Just enough to make it feel like Christmas," said Teresa.

"I feel like I'm in a goddamned Bing Crosby movie," Bernie said, but she smiled as she watched a family of young children with their noses pressed to the Christmas display in the Gimbels window.

They stood with other shoppers, watching an antique electric train chug around a track that ran under a beautifully decorated Christmas tree, winding its way among wrapped boxes and antique toys, little puffs of smoke coming from the engine.

"Makes you wish you were a kid again, doesn't it?" Teresa asked.

"Want to go sit on Santa's lap?" Bernie asked.

"I'd break Santa's lap," Teresa said dryly. "And don't even say it," she added as Bernie opened her mouth with a wicked gleam in her eye. "I don't want to know what you'd do on Santa's lap."

Bernie laughed. "Come on. Let's knock some of these presents off our lists."

They went inside, stuffing their coats into a large shopping bag as they hunted for Christmas presents for their families.

Teresa bought new nightgowns and robes for the aunts.

"Didn't you get them the same thing last year?" Bernie asked.

"It's what they asked for," Teresa said. "I don't think they ever shop for themselves."

Bernie checked her list. "Let's head to the shoe department."

Two hours later, they staggered out of Gimbels, each carrying four bulging shopping bags.

"Well, that's half the list done," Teresa moaned. They carried their bags to her car, depositing them in the back seat. "I gotta eat before I do any more shopping."

"That diner is just around the corner," Bernie said. "Let's go there. I'm in the mood for a burger."

They made their way to Louise's and had to wait a few minutes for a booth to clear. Teresa picked up a menu as Bernie looked around.

"Isn't that your friend?"

Teresa looked in the direction Bernie indicated and her heart leapt as she saw Ellie sitting at the counter.

"Ask her to join us," Bernie suggested.

Teresa shook her head. "She's probably only got a few minutes on her break. We shouldn't bother her."

"What the hell are you talking about? She hasn't even got her food yet." Bernie got up from the booth and went to where Ellie was sitting. She tapped her on the shoulder and pointed to Teresa.

Teresa quickly looked down at her menu, feeling her face grow hot. Ellie followed Bernie back to their booth.

"Hi," Ellie said as Bernie slid into Teresa's side of the booth.

"You're on break?" Teresa asked.

"Yes," Ellie said.

A waitress came over to take their order while Louise was kept busy at the counter and cash register.

"So are you working down here every night?" Teresa asked after the waitress left.

"Just about," Ellie said, and Teresa noted that she did look tired. "I finish up at the bank at four, catch a bus downtown, and start work at Kaufman's by five. With the holiday hours, I'm working until ten and then home to do it all again tomorrow."

"God, I think I'd do without the money," Bernie said. "Sounds awful."

Ellie shook her head. "If you'd ever needed the hours and couldn't get them, you wouldn't say that. I swore a long time ago that I would never turn down work." She looked at Teresa. "Did you get your window decorated for Christmas?"

"Kind of." Teresa grinned apologetically. "My mother insisted on our usual Nativity scene. I figured I better take baby steps."

Their waitress brought their drinks. Bernie dumped two packets of sugar into her coffee and stirred in some creamer. She tilted her head as she looked at Ellie.

"How old are you anyway?"

"I'll be twenty-six in March." Ellie smiled. "Why? How old are y'uns?"

Teresa and Bernie gave each other a wry look. "Thirty-four," Teresa said.

"God, I feel old," Bernie muttered. "You're just a baby."

"Not a baby," Teresa said, meeting Ellie's eyes. "She had to grow up fast. Not like us, still living at home with our parents."

"Thanks, Bennie. Like I needed to be reminded of that."

Ellie smiled thoughtfully. "Be glad you still have parents to live with."

"Jesus, I'm sorry," Bernie said quickly. "I'm such an asshole sometimes."

"It's okay."

"No, she is an asshole sometimes," Teresa said. "Ouch!" She reached under the table to rub her shin.

Ellie laughed. "So, I'm guessing you're down here Christmas shopping."

"God, yes," Bernie said. "I always think I have it bad, buying for my family until I see Bennie having to buy for thirty people."

Just then, the waitress brought their food, so Bernie didn't see the shadow that crossed Ellie's face, but Teresa did. She kept an anxious eye on Ellie, but the moment had passed.

"Have things been busy at Kaufman's?" she asked before Bernie could say something else stupid.

"Crazy." Ellie squirted some ketchup on her fries. "But I'd rather be busy. Makes the time go by so much faster."

"Well, we're heading to Kaufman's next," Bernie said.

"Make sure you stop and look at the window displays," Ellie said. "They're really nice this year."

"What department do you work in?" Bernie asked.

"I float wherever they need me. Tonight, I'm in men's wear."

Bernie gave Teresa a nudge. "Don't you still need stuff for your dad and Gianni?"

"I'll be glad to help you pick something out," Ellie said. "Do you exchange gifts with Rob and Karen?"

Bernie looked from Ellie to Teresa. "She knows Rob and Karen?"

Teresa's face burned. "Yes. They... we had dinner with them one night," she said, concentrating on her corned beef hash.

Bernie turned back to her plate and the table was silent for a moment.

Ellie, seeming to sense that she'd said something wrong, changed the subject. "You said the last time we met that you teach. What grade?"

"Fourth," said Bernie through a mouthful of burger. "They're still cute at that age. They want to learn and they're too young for the gangs and sex. Just two years later, and all of that changes."

"They're into that stuff in sixth grade?" Ellie asked, shocked.

Bernie nodded. "Sadly, yes. Not all of them. But some."

"I'm sorry about the last time we met," Ellie said. "I practically accused you of being a racist."

"Yeah, you did," Bernie said, appraising her. "But I liked it. You called me on it. That's more than most people do. Shit, I don't have any answers, and this goddamned economy doesn't help. Unemployment's bad everywhere, but it's worse in the black neighborhoods."

Ellie glanced out the window. "Sometimes it's hard to celebrate things like Christmas when there are so many people who need so much."

"God, if you let things like that stop you from living, you'll never have a life," Bernie said.

"Shut up," Teresa said in a low voice.

"What? I'm not saying you shouldn't care, maybe do what you can, but you can't fix everything. If that's what you're waiting for..."

Teresa nearly kicked Bernie under the table, but Ellie's expression grew thoughtful.

"You're right," Ellie said. "I think sometimes I let myself get too wrapped up in all the misery I see." She glanced at her watch. "Mmm, I've got to finish up and get back." She quickly downed the rest of her hamburger and ate a few more fries. "Come on by men's wear," she said, sliding out of the booth. "I'll help you pick some things out."

She went to pay her check and waved back at them as she snugged her scarf around her neck. Teresa gave a small wave.

Bernie moved back around to the empty side of the booth. "What's up with you?"

"What are you talking about?" Teresa lowered her gaze to her plate, but she could feel Bernie's eyes boring into her.

"You're weird around her," Bernie said. "And why didn't you tell me y'uns had dinner with Rob and Karen?"

Teresa shrugged. "It's no big deal. I didn't see you for a while and it just didn't come up."

"It was the day I asked you about going over there with you, wasn't it?" Bernie asked doggedly.

"I don't remember," Teresa lied.

"Look at me."

Teresa forced herself to meet Bernie's eyes.

"What's up?"

"Nothing. I told you."

Teresa could see in Bernie's eyes that she wasn't about to let this go. "I'm done. How about you?" she said. "We've got more shopping to do."

She grabbed the check and went to the cash register before Bernie could pepper her with more questions. By the time she'd finished paying, Bernie had put her coat back on and gone outside to light a cigarette.

"I have not heard the end of this," Teresa muttered to herself as she went back to leave a tip on the table.

CHAPTER 12

TERESA SAT AGAINST HER headboard, her knees hugged to her chest, listening in the dark. It seemed as if it was taking forever for her parents to get to their room. On her nightstand was an open velvet box holding a necklace—a gift for Ellie. She'd spied it in the case at Gimbels while Bernie had been looking at earrings—"as if you need more earrings," Teresa had teased. She wandered disinterestedly along the jewelry case until she'd seen the necklace. It was a heart, one of those lop-sided, asymmetrical hearts hung on a fine gold chain.

You cannot give a woman a heart necklace, she told herself over and over as she followed Bernie to the petites' department, but while Bernie was in a dressing room—"why are you trying things on when we're here to Christmas shop for our families?" Teresa had asked with a shake of her head—she'd hurried back to the jewelry counter to buy the necklace.

"What are you looking so happy about?" Bernie had asked when she emerged from the dressing room.

"Nothing," Teresa said. "I'm just glad to be getting this shopping done."

She'd smiled to herself, her hand clasping the small velvet box safely tucked in her coat pocket as they continued shopping. She'd nearly passed out when Bernie spotted Ellie at the diner. It was getting harder and harder to be normal around Ellie, but somehow, she had to figure out how to be. Bernie was relentless—once she got suspicious that someone might have a secret, she wouldn't stop until she'd found out what it was. For most of her life, Teresa had watched Bernie weasel things out of other people, but Teresa had never had a secret to keep before—*and she knows you inside and out.*

For the hundredth time in the past two weeks, she took the velvet box in her hands, touching a finger to the delicate little heart. She knew it would look beautiful hanging around Ellie's slender neck, but she hadn't plucked up the courage to give it to her.

What if she won't accept it? What if she thinks you're queer or something?

Even in the dark, alone, Teresa blushed at the words.

"Feelings of a romantic nature for another girl are unnatural and ungodly," Sister Marguerite had lectured the girls in Teresa and Bernie's fourth grade class while the boys were sequestered in the gym, being lectured to by Father Paul. "Those feelings, if they must be expressed at all," Sister Marguerite continued, "should be directed toward one particular young man who may be the father of your children."

"I can't believe we're being lectured to about our periods and getting married by a nun," Bernie had whispered in Teresa's ear, but Teresa had stared at her desktop, tracing her finger over and over along the gouged letters carved there by previous students. She was certain, if she looked Sister Marguerite in the eye, that she would be able to tell that Teresa was ungodly.

"How could she know?" Teresa asked herself in a panic. Three rows up and two seats to the right sat Penelope Jones, the prettiest girl in the entire school—at least, Teresa thought so. She said a silent prayer of thanks that she'd never said anything to Bernie, and she knew now she could never do anything to let Penelope know she liked her. As it was, "I'll have to confess to having impure thoughts." Sister Marguerite was preparing the entire class for an upcoming visit from the bishop and Teresa was sure she couldn't meet the bishop if she liked Penelope Jones—in *that* way. Even after the bishop's visit was over, the prospect of facing confession every Saturday weighed on Teresa's conscience. She knew she could never confess to anything unnatural, so, "better not to do it," she reasoned.

Teresa pressed her hands to her eyes as she sat in bed now. *It's been twenty-five years and I'm still afraid of Sister Marguerite.* Only it wasn't Sister Marguerite, was it? *I'm afraid of me.* Afraid of the feelings Ellie was stirring within her, afraid of the way her heart raced any time Ellie crossed her mind, afraid of the physical urges she couldn't seem to control lately. Ungodly or not, she knew she was setting herself on a dangerous path, and the thought was at once terrifying and exhilarating.

She listened intently. The house was at last quiet. She stole out of bed and opened her bedroom door quietly. It wouldn't have been out of the ordinary for her mother to hear her go down the hall in the night, but if she didn't hear Teresa going back to bed, she'd get up to check. Silently, she crept down the stairs, arguing with herself the entire way.

It's late. She's in bed by now.

I know. But I need to speak with her.

If she wanted to talk to you, she'd have called.

She's been working every night. When could she call?

Feeling as if she were being driven by something she couldn't control, Teresa went into the kitchen and picked the telephone off the hook. Her finger was trembling as she dialed the number she'd had memorized since Ellie gave it to her, hoping her mother wouldn't hear the whirring of the dial as it rotated. Once the number was dialed, she took the receiver into the pantry and closed the door, being careful to thread the cord through the gap under the door. Trying to muffle sounds further, she cupped her hand around both her mouth and the mouthpiece. Her heart thundered in her ears as the phone rang once, twice, three times. Just as she was getting ready to hang up, she heard Ellie's sleepy voice.

"Hello?"

"Ellie, it's Teresa. I'm sorry to wake you."

"It's okay." Ellie sounded more awake. "Why are you whispering?"

"I don't want to wake anyone here," Teresa said. "I won't keep you long. I just wondered if you have any free evenings coming up? Or any gaps in your weekend schedule? I know you're busy with all the hours you're working now—"

"I have Wednesday night off," Ellie cut in. "I'm only working at the bank that day."

Teresa was supposed to work until closing on Wednesday. "Wednesday would be great," she said. "Can I come by your place about five?" She'd find a way somehow.

"Five. Do you want me to make some dinner here?"

"No," Teresa said. "We can go out or order something in. You don't need to cook your one night off."

"Okay. See you then."

"See you then."

As quietly as she could, Teresa hung up the phone and stole back upstairs to bed. Her heart was still pounding, but not from fear now. Unable to wipe the smile from her face, she rolled over and looked at the jewel box. "Please like it," she whispered.

"What is wrong with you?"

Ellie looked around at Suzanne. "What?"

"All afternoon you can't sit still," Suzanne said irritably. "You sit down and jump up. You're all over the place. It's driving me crazy."

"Me, too," called Linda from the drive-through window. "You're worse than a five-year-old."

"Sorry," Ellie said. "I guess I'm just restless."

She made a conscious effort to stay still at her window, but the afternoon dragged on. *It can't be just five minutes later,* she said to herself as she looked at the antique wall clock for the thousandth time. As the hands ticked toward four o'clock, she had her drawer counted and ready for the next day. At the first chime of the hour, she was already depositing her tray in the vault. From there, she hurried to the staff room, dragged her coat from her locker, and was out the door almost before the fourth chime had faded away.

On the bus, she gritted her teeth in exasperation as it seemed someone needed to get on or off at every single stop. She was on her feet, standing behind the driver as the bus approached her stop.

"Got a big date, Ellie?" asked the driver.

"Yup," Ellie said with a grin. "See you tomorrow, Larry."

She laughed to herself as she nearly skipped down the sidewalk. "I do have a date."

She hurried upstairs to her apartment and tidied up the kitchen from the morning's dishes. "You be on your best behavior," she said as she scooped some food for KC who replied with a small squeak. She left the cat eating while she glanced around the apartment, straightening up the living room and running a dust rag over the coffee table. She peeked into her bedroom just to make sure it was in order. "Shoot," she said, remembering to go check the bathroom. Sullivan was usually pretty neat, but every now and then, he left the toilet seat up or the sink was littered with hair from his beard. Everything looked fine. Secretly, she hoped Sullivan would be working late in his lab. She didn't want him interrupting this evening.

Her bedroom window gave her a view of the street. She and KC both perched on the windowsill, waiting. Ellie's heart leapt when she saw Teresa's VW pull up to the curb. After pausing to check her reflection one more time in the mirror, she went to the kitchen and opened the door as Teresa came up the stairs.

"Hi," Ellie said breathlessly.

"Hi." Teresa stood there holding a grocery bag.

Ellie noticed how flushed Teresa's cheeks were. "Come in. Cold, isn't it?"

"Makes it feel like Christmas," Teresa said. She set her bag on the counter with a heavy clunk.

"What did you bring?"

"Well, we can go out if you'd like, but I brought ravioli, a container of sauce, a loaf of bread, and..." Teresa reached into the bag. "A bottle of wine."

Ellie stared. "You brought the whole dinner."

"Unless you'd rather go somewhere."

"No. I'd rather stay here with you." Ellie lowered her gaze. "Let me take your coat." She paused as Teresa slid her coat from her shoulders. "Wow," Ellie said, taking in Teresa's white V-neck sweater—was that cashmere?—and gray slacks. She suddenly felt underdressed in her khakis and black sweater from the bank. "You dressed up. You look really nice."

Teresa snorted as she looked down at herself. "Huh. White. Figures. I don't think I own anything that doesn't have sauce stains on it. You are dressed much more sensibly."

"Don't worry," Ellie said with a smile. "We can fix that." She hung up Teresa's coat and reached over to another peg. "See?" She held up an apron. "Got you covered."

"Very funny," Teresa said, but her smile was frozen on her face a moment later as Ellie reached up over Teresa's head to hang the apron around her neck.

For a second—it felt much longer—Ellie's face was just inches from Teresa's. Ellie stood there looking up into Teresa's eyes. This close, she could see her own reflection in them, but there was so much more there....

Ellie caught herself and backed away. "How's that?"

"Better. Thanks." Teresa turned away, fumbling with the apron strings.

"Here. Let me." Ellie took the strings from her, her fingers brushing Teresa's as she did, and she had to stop herself leaning against Teresa's back as she tied the apron. She stepped away. "Okay. Tell me what to do."

"I'll need a big pot for the water and a smaller pan for the sauce. And do you have a baking sheet?"

As Teresa got started, she pointed to the bag. "I brought a corkscrew. For the wine. I wasn't sure you had one."

"I don't," Ellie said, reaching into the shopping bag. "I don't have wine glasses, either."

"I don't care if we drink it out of coffee cups."

Ellie opened her cupboard. "How about juice glasses?"

"As long as they're big juice glasses."

Ellie laughed. She uncorked the wine and poured two glasses. She set one down next to the stove where Teresa was stirring the sauce. She took a sip from her own glass. "Oh, this is good. Too much of this on an empty stomach and it'll go straight to my head."

Teresa turned to look at her. "Maybe I should have brought a second bottle."

Ellie laughed again, feeling giddy in a way that had nothing to do with the wine. Teresa chopped a clove of garlic and mixed it with some butter melting in another pan.

"Here," she said a few minutes later, handing the pan to Ellie. "Brush this on the slices of bread and we'll put it in the oven."

Standing next to Teresa as they prepared the meal, their shoulders touching occasionally, Ellie couldn't help a fleeting wish that they could always do this together. *Don't be stupid,* she told herself harshly. *It's just dinner,* but it felt like much more than just dinner.

KC sat in the middle of the kitchen supervising. When the food was ready, Ellie fed KC a bit more wet food and re-filled their glasses with wine as Teresa carried the plates to the table.

"So what are we celebrating?" Ellie asked.

Teresa raised her glass and looked into Ellie's eyes. "Friends?"

For a long moment, they sat there. Ellie could see the pulsing shadow of Teresa's heartbeat in her neck. She longed to reach out and touch that place, to feel the life coursing under her fingers. "Friends," she forced herself to say at last.

KC reached up on her hind legs and prodded Ellie's thigh with a soft paw. They chuckled as they looked down at her.

"No, you're not getting any people food," Ellie said firmly. "And we'd better eat while it's hot." She took a bite of ravioli. "Oh, this is so good. Did you make everything from scratch?"

Teresa grinned. "Are you kidding? In the Benedetto house, that's the only way."

They ate for a few minutes in silence. Ellie, more curious than she would admit, said, "When you called, you sounded like there was something specific you wanted to talk about."

"Well, not so much talk about," Teresa said vaguely. "I just wanted to see you. You've been on my mind. A lot. You seemed so sad at Thanksgiving, and we've both been so busy working extra hours. I've wanted to call, but it was always too late."

Ellie gave an embarrassed little laugh. "I know. I'm sorry I was in such a bad mood on Thanksgiving. Your visit meant so much to me. I'm surprised you even wanted to come back after I was such poor company."

"You're never poor company," Teresa said.

Another tense silence followed as they ate a bit more. Finally, Ellie said, "I've thought about calling you on my breaks, but I hate to call at the store in case you're busy with customers or your mom's there with you." She looked up with a smile. "It was so nice to run into you and Bernie at the diner that night."

Teresa laughed sarcastically. "Oh, yes. Bernie. She won't let it drop that you and I had dinner with Rob and Karen."

"Why didn't you tell her?"

"I'm not sure," Teresa said, frowning into her wine. "Sometimes she can get ideas and then she runs away with them."

"Ideas about what?"

Teresa didn't answer right away. She took another bite before saying, "Like, why I would want to introduce you to my brother and sister-in-law."

"Why did you?"

Teresa glanced up at her. "I wanted them to meet you."

"I really liked them."

"I think they liked you, too," Teresa said.

Ellie took another slice of bread. "I'm glad. Karen seems very perceptive. I don't think much gets by her."

"No, it doesn't," Teresa said. "And she pretty much says what she thinks. I like that about her, but it wouldn't go over so well with my family if they ever start spending time together."

"I thought your family yelled and got over it?" Ellie asked.

"They do, when it's them," Teresa said. "There's some kind of unwritten rule. They'll take an insult from a family member, and yell and argue, but if anyone outside says anything, they bunch together and heaven help that other person."

Ellie started giggling.

"What?" Teresa asked.

"I just had this image of one of those wildlife documentaries where the herd bunches up and stomps their feet to scare away the lions," Ellie said, laughing.

Teresa grinned, too. "That's kind of what they're like. Benedetto bison."

Ellie took a drink of her wine. "Do you think they could ever accept an outsider?" She raised her eyes to Teresa's. "Karen, I mean. Do you think they'll ever welcome her so she and Rob can be part of the family?"

Teresa shrugged. "I'm not sure. I keep hoping they will. I miss not having Rob around more. Sometimes, I think my mom is on the verge of asking them over, but my dad's not ready. For him, it's a bunch of things. Rob didn't want to go into the stores, so my father took that as a personal insult. Then there was the divorce and then him marrying Karen. He's his own man. I think my dad admires that and hates it all at the same time." She gave Ellie an apologetic look. "It's complicated."

"It sounds complicated."

They finished their dinner. "I'm sorry I didn't bring dessert," Teresa said, carrying her plate to the sink.

"I'm stuffed," Ellie said. "I do have some ice cream in the freezer if you want some." She ran some soapy water in the sink.

"No. I don't need ice cream." Teresa placed her plate in the sink and pushed up the sleeves of her sweater.

"Oh no. You cooked," Ellie said, stepping in. "You sit and relax."

"I'm not leaving you to do all these dishes. You wash. I'll dry."

"Deal." Ellie looked at her again. "You've lost weight."

She watched with some amusement as Teresa blushed, looking embarrassed and pleased at the same time.

"I have. A little."

"Are you on a diet?"

To her surprise, Teresa scoffed. "You could say that." She glanced at Ellie as she plucked a plate from the dish drainer and began drying it. "I've just been eating less in the evenings, that's all."

They were done with the dishes and pans in just a short time—a time that Ellie wished could have lasted longer. Teresa held up the wine bottle.

"Just enough for a half glass more."

Ellie smiled. "Can't let it go to waste."

"My thoughts exactly." Teresa poured, and then reached back to untie her apron. "I think I'm safe to take this off now." She took it back over to the wall pegs and fumbled with her coat. For a second, Ellie thought she was taking it down to leave, but she turned around. "Thanks for the apron," she said, tucking something into her pants pocket. "You saved me from myself. I'm usually such a klutz."

"No, you're not," Ellie said. She led the way out to the living room. "I think sometimes your family makes you feel that way, but—" She stopped abruptly. "Sorry."

"For what?" Teresa sat beside her on the couch.

"I don't want to say anything against your family, but..." She looked at Teresa. "I don't think they see how wonderful you are. You're kind and generous. I think you'd do anything for anyone." She stopped, embarrassed. She lowered her eyes. "You've been more than kind to me."

Teresa didn't say anything, but Ellie was afraid to look up. *She'll see. She'll know how you feel.*

Time seemed to stretch on and still Teresa said nothing. She reached out and set a small wrapped package in Ellie's lap.

"I know Christmas isn't for a couple of weeks yet," Teresa said softly. "But I wanted to give you this."

Ellie looked up in wonder. "For me?"

Teresa nodded. "Open it."

Ellie's fingers fumbled clumsily with the ribbon. She tore the wrapping paper away to reveal a velvet jewel box. Prying the top open, she gasped. Her own heart thudded wildly as she stared at the gold heart lying on the velvet. *Does she–?* She couldn't bring herself to finish the thought.

"Do you...do you like it?"

"Oh, it's beautiful, Teresa." She looked up. "But it's too expensive."

"Don't. Please." Teresa's voice was a plea. "Don't tell me you can't accept it." She sounded as if she was having a hard time breathing. "You don't have to wear it. You can leave it in a drawer and never tell me. But please accept it."

Ellie searched her eyes. "I love it. Yes, I'll accept it." She fought the impulse to fling her arms around Teresa's neck and kiss her. Instead, she held the box out. "Would you put it on me?"

She turned her back so that Teresa could slip the necklace over her head. She felt the trembling of Teresa's fingers as she fastened the clasp, and she shivered at the lingering touch of warm hands against her neck as Teresa lifted her hair free of the chain.

"Thank you." Ellie felt the necklace, her fingers tracing the shape of the heart against her chest. "Is it my heart? Or yours?"

Teresa shrugged. "Either. Both. Kind of crooked and bent."

"But whole."

Without giving herself time to think about it, Ellie reached out and wrapped her fingers around Teresa's hand. For an instant, nothing happened. Her heart, thudding so jubilantly just a few seconds earlier, plummeted to her stomach like a rock at the realization that she'd misread Teresa's feelings. Just as Ellie started to yank her hand back, Teresa's fingers tightened, holding her fast. For long minutes, they sat there, staring at their intertwined fingers. *Is this really happening?* Ellie reveled in the warmth of Teresa's touch, afraid to meet her eyes.

A loud knock on the living room door startled both of them, and they jumped apart as if they'd been shocked.

Reluctantly, Ellie got up and opened the door. "Hi, Sullivan."

"Hey, I smelled garlic—" He stopped short at the sight of Teresa sitting there. "Oh, hi."

"Hi," Teresa said with a smile.

Sullivan sniffed the air hopefully. "You guys had dinner?"

From behind him, Ellie grimaced apologetically. "Yes. Teresa brought dinner over. Would you like some?"

"Yeah." He headed toward the kitchen and then stopped. "Hey, I wasn't interrupting anything, was I?"

"No," the two women said simultaneously.

"As a matter of fact," Teresa said, looking at her watch, "I really have to be going."

"I'll walk you down." Ellie took Teresa's coat down off the wall and handed it to her. "Be right back," she said to Sullivan.

She walked with Teresa to the bottom landing. "I'm sorry," she whispered.

"It's okay," Teresa said.

Ellie looked at her in the dim light coming onto the landing from the outside lamp. "Thank you so much. For dinner, and for my present." She placed her hand over the necklace. Without warning, she flung her arms around Teresa's neck.

Teresa held her tightly. "You're welcome," she whispered back.

Ellie kissed her on the cheek and released her. "I'll see you soon."

Wordlessly, Teresa nodded and stepped outside.

CHAPTER 13

"I THINK THOSE ARE burning."

Teresa jumped at the sound of Bernie's voice. "Shit!"

Smoke was just starting to rise from the pizzelle iron. She opened the lid and used a fork to lift two darkened waffle-like cookies out of the hot iron.

Bernie sniffed. "Anise?"

"Yes," said Teresa in disgust. She threw the burnt pair away. "The kids all like vanilla or chocolate better, but the aunts and our old-timers prefer anise." She glanced over. "You here to help, Beej?"

"Sure," Bernie said, shrugging out of her coat. "Got nothing done at school today. The goddamned kids are so squirrelly thinking about Christmas, they can't concentrate on anything." She noted the stacks of pizzelle cooling along the kitchen counter. "How many are you making?"

"That was five dozen vanilla," Teresa said. "If you can put more of the anise batter in the iron, I'll start mixing some chocolate."

Bernie scooped some of the batter into the iron and closed the lid. "So what were you so preoccupied with that you let those burn?"

Teresa didn't answer right away as she cracked six eggs into a large bowl. "Nothing." She stirred in the sugar and turned on the mixer. "Just trying to juggle all this and things at the store."

Bernie poured herself a cup of coffee. "Refill?"

Teresa nodded and Bernie poured fresh coffee into her cup.

"You all set for Christmas?" Teresa asked.

"Yeah. Finally got everything bought and wrapped. Mom's upset. Denny called and said he won't make it home this year."

Teresa looked up. "Why?"

Bernie went to check the cooking pizzelle. "Said he can't afford to take time away from work."

"You're kidding? Not even for Christmas?"

"He's an asshole," said Bernie. "He knows how much it means to Mom, especially these last couple of years since Dad died, but his girlfriend's family is all there in Philly. I'll bet my goddamned paycheck she talked him into staying there with her. To hell with his family."

Bernie's younger brother had never been one of Teresa's favorite people, but to not come home for Christmas? "Well, Rob doesn't come home anymore, either," she said.

"Yeah, but he would," Bernie said. "That's your folks' fault, because they want him to come without Karen. Denny knows he can bring horse-face."

Teresa snorted as she slowly folded in some flour and baking powder along with some cocoa, watching as the mixer blended it all together. "What would you do, if you met someone—" She stopped abruptly. "I mean, say Tom got a divorce and you could be together, but your mom didn't want you to bring him home for holidays and things. What would you do?"

"Like that would ever happen." Bernie turned suddenly from where she was picking the pizzelle out of the iron and setting them to cool. "Why are you asking something like that?"

Teresa kept her back to Bernie as she poked at the batter with a spatula to be sure everything was blended. "No reason. Just thinking about Rob and Karen. If you were in their shoes, would

144

you go home alone? To keep the peace? Or would you do what Rob did?"

She could feel Bernie's eyes boring a hole in her back. She stayed hunched over the mixer.

"I don't know," Bernie said. "Like Denny now. He could split his time and come without her. But if it was me, I'd want Tom there." There was a long silence. "I'm not sure what I'd do."

Bernie spooned the last of the anise batter into the iron and took the bowl to the sink. She picked two vanilla pizzelle off the cooling rack and took them to the table. "Bennie, sit down."

Teresa turned off the mixer and sat. Bernie handed one of the cookies to Teresa and began snapping hers into smaller pieces along the geometric ridges cooked into a snowflake design. She chewed on one piece thoughtfully as she studied Teresa's face. "Something is up with you," she said. "You're different."

Teresa felt her cheeks grow hot. She dunked her pizzella into her coffee and took a bite. "I'm the same as I've always been."

"No. You're not."

Teresa refused to meet Bernie's eyes—*she can read you like a book*—and she knew she could never lie convincingly.

Doggedly, Bernie went on. "I don't know what it is. I don't know why you can't talk about it. But, Jesus, Bennie, I'm your oldest friend. If you can't tell me, who can you tell?"

"No one! That's the problem!" Teresa nearly blurted, but she knew better. Sister Marguerite's lesson had been drummed into her long and hard. "Unnatural" and "ungodly" kept running through Teresa's head any time she thought about Ellie. Only... it felt like the most natural and holy thing that had ever happened to her. *How can it be wrong to love someone?* Because she knew now that's what this was. For the first time in her life, Teresa was in love, and the strength of the emotion was enough to make her feel almost sick at times. She couldn't eat, couldn't sleep, couldn't concentrate on anything for long before thoughts of Ellie crept back into her mind. She felt as if she were running a fever. Every time she remembered the light in Ellie's eyes as she accepted Teresa's gift, the warmth of Ellie's hand in hers, how close she'd been as she slipped the apron over Teresa's head—*I could have kissed her*—Teresa felt lightheaded. Just this afternoon, her mother had come upon her, leaning weakly against the desk in the store office, one hand clutching her shirt as she tried to calm her heart rate. "You're working too hard," Sylvia had declared, and so Teresa was home now, making the Christmas pizzelle—*and being interrogated.*

Realizing Bernie was staring at her as these thoughts ran through her mind, Teresa pushed up from the table. "These are done," she said, taking the anise cookies out and spooning some of the chocolate batter into the iron. Bernie sat at the table, silent, watching.

"There's nothing to tell," Teresa insisted, but she knew Bernie didn't believe her. She handed Bernie a stack of plastic bags and Christmas ribbon. "Help me wrap these, six to a bag. I'm going to deliver them this evening."

The ringing of the doorbell brought the muffled sound of startled voices. A curtain at the living room window was pulled aside, and Teresa waved. A moment later, she heard bolts and chains sliding, and one of their elderly customers opened the door, shakily supported by a cane while his wife peeked around his shoulder.

"Hello, Mr. and Mrs. Taliaferro," said Teresa.

"Come in, come in," Mr. Taliaferro said, shuffling back.

Teresa stepped into the foyer and pushed the door shut against the cold. "I can't stay," she said as Mrs. Taliaferro waved her into the living room where their Christmas tree was brightly lit. She reached into a large shopping bag and pulled out a wrapped packet.

"I just wanted to bring you some homemade pizzelle. Made fresh today."

"Oh, Teresa, *grazie*," said Mrs. Taliaferro. She raised the bag to her nose and sniffed. "What a treat. Can't you stay and have one?"

"I ate too many while I was making them," Teresa said. The old couple chuckled. "And I have to deliver many more tonight. You call when you need a refill on your medicines, yes?"

"Yes, we will," said Mr. Taliaferro. "*Buon Natale*, Teresa."

"*Buon Natale*." Teresa let herself out the door, waving as she went down the porch steps into the night.

She walked for blocks, checking off the houses on her list. The cold night air was soothing on her face, and it felt good to move. She couldn't have sat still at home anyway. "It's a good thing she's working late," she muttered to herself as she walked. "You can't call and you can't go over." But she wanted to. More than anything, she wanted to hear Ellie's voice, wanted to see her again. She stopped and leaned against a tree. There it was again, that weakness that overcame her at the mere thought of Ellie. "You have got to get hold of yourself," she said, taking a deep breath and continuing on to the next house.

It took the better part of two hours to get all the pizzelle delivered—no matter how many times she protested that she had to get on to other houses, some of those old people were so lonely and starved for company that Teresa couldn't bring herself to leave right away. Making her way back home, she suddenly realized no one would have left dinner for Dogman and Lucy tonight. Why hadn't she thought of that sooner? If her mother had seen them settling for the night as she closed up, there would be trouble. Nearly running the last block home, Teresa bounded up the porch steps.

To her relief, both Sylvia and Lou were in the living room. She took the fact that her mother wasn't yelling about homeless bums as a good sign. "Got almost everything delivered," she said. "Just have a few more. I'll be back soon."

Without waiting for a response, she went to the kitchen and quickly filled an aluminum pie tin with lasagna. It was cold, but it would have to do for tonight. She didn't dare take the time to warm it. Hurrying out to her car, she drove to the store. There was no sign of Dogman as she parked, but it wasn't unusual for him to not be there when she closed up. She found Lucy's bowl behind the trash can where Dogman had been leaving it. Opening the hood of her VW, she filled the bowl with dog food and set it on top of the trash can along with the tin of lasagna and a packet of pizzelle. She was just getting into her car when the pair of them came down the alley, Dogman limping along with Lucy beside him.

"Hi," she said, bending to pet Lucy, who trotted over to say hello. She pointed to the trash can. "Brought some lasagna tonight. Sorry, it's cold."

Dogman nodded. "She likes you."

Teresa smiled. "She's sweet. I'm glad you have each other." She turned to go.

"Thank you."

Teresa spun around. "You're welcome."

She got in the car. Looking in her rearview mirror as she drove down the alley, she could see Dogman setting Lucy's bowl on the ground. At the end of the alley, she stopped the car and sat there. A left-hand turn would take her home. She turned right.

Ellie's apartment, as expected, was dark when she pulled up to the curb. Teresa let the engine idle. *Why are you here?* she asked herself, and she couldn't answer. It made no sense. Ellie wasn't here. The only thing she knew was that she couldn't stand not having some contact, some connection. She opened her glove box and found a scrap of paper and pen—*from the bank*, she realized with a droll smile. For long minutes, she sat with the pen poised.

At last, by the yellow illumination of the street lamp, she wrote a few lines. She turned the car off and went up the stairs to Ellie's kitchen door. There, she hesitated. This was stupid. She turned around and had descended a half dozen steps before she stopped herself. "Which will you regret more?" she whispered. Without giving herself time to reconsider, she ran back up the steps and slipped the paper underneath the door. Returning to the VW, her heart felt a bit lighter as she headed home.

Impatiently, Ellie waited for the lobby clock to chime noon. She pressed her fingers to her chest, feeling the small heart necklace through her sweater.

"I'm going out for lunch today," she announced to no one in particular at the first chime.

Without waiting for a response, she hurried to the staff locker room and retrieved her coat and scarf. She opened her backpack and found her wrapped sandwich. Slinging the backpack over her shoulders, she ate as she walked.

"Hello," she said cheerfully to the people she passed. "Nice day." Tucking one hand in her coat pocket, she felt a scrap of paper. She pulled it out and read it for about the hundredth time, though she knew it by heart now. *Just wanted to let you know I'm thinking of you. Sweet dreams, Teresa.*

Ellie had come dragging up the steps a couple of nights ago and opened the door to find KC batting a slip of paper around on the kitchen floor. She picked it up, thinking the cat had gotten something out of the trash. All weariness was forgotten as she read the note and pulled KC into a tight hug.

"She was here!" she said, laughing. "She's thinking of us."

Newly energized, Ellie had fed KC and sat at the kitchen table to resume work on Teresa's Christmas present. It was nearly two a.m. when she sat back to inspect her work. "I think it's done," she said, waking KC, who was sleeping on the other kitchen chair.

Ellie reached back to her backpack now, feeling the bulge of the wrapped parcel tucked inside. She walked quickly and got to the drug store within ten minutes. She held her breath as she pushed the door open. The bell signaled her entrance and Sylvia looked up from behind the coffee counter where she was serving a couple of customers.

"Hi, Mrs. Benedetto," Ellie said, looking around. Her heart fell when she saw no sign of Teresa.

"Hello, Ellie," said Sylvia. "How can I help you?"

"Ellie!"

Ellie turned to see Teresa coming out from behind the tall pharmacy counter. "Hi, Teresa."

"Come on back to the office." Teresa shut the door halfway, just enough to shut them off from her mother's view. "What brings you down here?"

Ellie set her backpack down and unzipped the main compartment. "I wanted to bring you your Christmas present," she said, holding out a wrapped parcel.

"You didn't have to do that," Teresa said, but she looked pleased.

"It's nothing to get excited about," Ellie said quickly. "It's handmade, not bought."

Teresa looked up. "That makes it extra special." She turned the package over in her hands. "Should I open it now?"

"No," said Ellie. "I'd be too embarrassed. Wait until you're home." She zipped up her backpack and slipped the straps over her shoulders. "I have to get back. I only get a half hour for lunch." She paused as Teresa reached past her for the door. "Thanks for the note the other night."

Teresa's face broke into a shy smile. "You're welcome."

"See you soon?"

Teresa nodded. "Soon."

She walked Ellie to the door.

"Bye, Mrs. Benedetto," Ellie called. "Merry Christmas, if I don't see you before then."

"Merry Christmas to you, too, Ellie," Sylvia said.

Ellie hurried down the sidewalk. At the corner, she turned to look back. Teresa was standing there. Ellie gave a small wave and turned the corner.

CHAPTER 14

Sylvia came through the back door of the store carrying a covered plate. "I brought chicken piccata," she called, setting the plate on the desk back in the office.

"Thanks, Ma." Teresa finished making a cappuccino for a customer who was waiting for his wife while she browsed the aisles of the store.

"I'll have some of that," the customer joked, jerking a thumb toward the office.

"You drink your coffee." Teresa smiled as she slid the hot mug toward him.

"You have such nice things this year," said the wife. She carried an armful of little gifts up to the register. "These will be perfect stocking stuffers."

"Or Befana gifts," Sylvia chimed in as Teresa began ringing the purchases up.

"I haven't done Befana since I was a kid," the man said. "We got our stockings in January, after Christmas. We should do that for the kids this year, hon."

"What's Befana?" the woman asked.

"Italian Santa Claus," Teresa said. "An old woman who leaves gifts on the Epiphany."

"My family's Polish. I remember we celebrated St. Nicholas on December sixth," the woman said wistfully. "We could start a new tradition."

"January sixth," Sylvia said. "You hang the stockings up the night of the fifth, and Befana, she'll come."

"We'll do that," the man said. He finished his cappuccino and accepted the shopping bag from Teresa.

"*Buon Natale.*"

"*Buon Natale,*" the couple echoed, heading out into the cold night.

"Go on home, Ma," Teresa said as she cleaned the espresso machine. "I'll be home late tonight."

"Why? Where you going?"

"I want to check in on Nita and the aunts," Teresa said. "See if they need any last minute shopping done. I'll see you later tonight."

"All right," Sylvia said, slipping her purse over her elbow. "Don't let your dinner get cold."

Teresa smiled. "I won't. Thanks, Ma."

Teresa locked the back door after her mother and went to the office where Dogman's plate was tucked in a file drawer. She scooped half her dinner onto his plate and re-used the aluminum foil to cover it. She ate quickly in between customers. Promptly at seven, she pulled down the front security grate and locked the front door. She turned off the lights and took the cash drawer back to the office to reconcile it. When she was done, she grabbed her coat, put Dogman and Lucy's food out for them, and locked up the back of the store.

Traffic was light as she drove to the aunts' house. She rang the doorbell and waited. Nobody moved fast in that house. She smiled as she heard voices from inside.

"Who is it?"

"It's Teresa."

"Are you sure? Let me see."

"Of course I'm sure. I know my own goddaughter, don't I?"

"But I want to see for myself."

At last, Anita opened the door.

"Teresa. What are you doing here?" she asked, pulling her niece inside and closing and locking the door as Luisa hurried back into the living room to catch whatever was on the television.

"I wanted to talk to you." She peeked into the living room and said hello to the other aunts. "No, I can't stay," she said in answer to their invitation to come in and join them.

"Come to the kitchen," Anita said.

Teresa followed her to the back of the house. Anita pulled out a chair for Teresa and sank heavily into another. Teresa draped her coat over the back of the chair and sat.

"Now, what is it?"

"I have a friend—the girl who helped me decorate our front window at the store. She's all alone. Her parents are dead." Teresa decided against trying to explain about Ellie's brother. "She was alone at Thanksgiving and has no one to spend Christmas with."

"Oh, that's terrible," Anita said, pressing a hand to her chest. "You bring her here with you on Christmas Day."

Teresa broke into a relieved smile. "I was hoping you'd say that."

"Well, what else is the poor girl going to do?" Anita huffed indignantly. "Of course, she should be here with us."

"I might need your help with Ma," said Teresa. "You know how she can be about family holidays."

Anita patted Teresa's arm. "You leave it to your godmother. I may be the youngest, but I'm the most stubborn." She leaned close. "And I cook the best. If Sylvia gives me any trouble, I know how to get around her."

Teresa threw her arms around her aunt. "Thank you, Nita. I knew I could count on you."

Anita laughed. She laid a loving hand on Teresa's cheek. "You can always count on me, Teresa."

Teresa stood and put her coat back on. "I'll let you get back to your television. Thanks again."

When she got home, she found both of her parents in the living room where they were watching the news on the television.

"I miss Andy Williams," Lou was saying from his armchair, his legs stretched out on the ottoman. "They don't make Christmas specials like that anymore."

"And Bing Crosby," said Sylvia. "Remember his specials? Maybe President Reagan can bring them back," she added hopefully. "I bet they knew each other in Hollywood."

"Ma, Reagan isn't even president yet," Teresa said. "He doesn't get sworn in for another month."

Sylvia gave a derisive snort. "Another month of that Carter. It can't go fast enough for me."

Teresa sighed and rolled her eyes. "Ma, why—"

Gianni came into the living room and said, "I'm going out."

"You just got home!" Sylvia glared at him.

"And now I'm going out."

"Why don't you ever bring Angelina over here?" Sylvia asked.

Because he's not going out with Angelina! Teresa wanted to say it but clamped her jaw tight and turned back to Walter Cronkite as he wrapped up the nightly news.

Gianni gave his mother an embarrassed smile—a look Teresa knew from long experience was completely fake—and said, "We like to be alone, Ma."

"Did your register come out even?" Lou asked.

"I'll do it tomorrow," Gianni said with a wave of his hand.

"How many times I gotta tell you, you do your register at closing every night," Lou said.

"What does it matter?" Gianni asked. "Tonight or tomorrow. It's all the same."

"It matters because it's part of the job," Lou said angrily. He turned to Teresa. "Did your register come out even?"

"On the penny," Teresa said, not looking at her brother. She could feel his baleful gaze directed at her.

"See? Your sister knows," Lou said. "When it doesn't come out even, you'll never remember the next day. Before you know it, you're short twenty, then fifty. You lose money and you don't know where it's going."

But Teresa knew. She knew every time Gianni overspent his paycheck, an extra twenty or two went from the cash register into his pocket.

"You keep this up, and I'm going to put you back behind the coffee counter," Lou said, but Teresa knew it was an empty threat. Gianni knew it, too.

If you were going to punish him, you needed to do it a long time ago. Teresa clapped a hand over her mouth to keep from saying it.

Gianni muttered something about the Morningside store being busier and not having time.

"*Basta!*" Lou said. "You shape up or we're gonna have a talk."

Gianni opened his mouth to retort.

"Quiet," Lou said. "It's time for Perry Como. Teresa, change the channel and adjust the antenna."

Gianni stormed out as Teresa got to her feet and played with the rabbit ears until her father said, "That's good. Right there."

"He's in the Holy Land," Sylvia said reverently, crossing herself as the show opened.

Teresa sat there watching Perry sing until the first commercial break. "I'm going upstairs to read."

Sylvia reached over and gave Lou a nudge. "Tell her."

Teresa looked at her parents. "Tell me what?"

Lou cleared his throat. "Your mother and I were talking, and we, uh, we think it's time you had a raise." Teresa's mouth fell open. "You've been working hard, and we want you to know we appreciate it. So, with the new year, you'll get a five thousand dollar raise."

Teresa didn't know what to say. "Wow. Thanks."

"Shhh!" Sylvia flapped her hands. "Perry's back on."

Teresa turned toward the stairs, feeling as if a miracle had just occurred. "Thank you, Perry Como," she whispered.

She went up to her room and closed the door. She turned on the bedside lamp and plumped her pillow against the headboard. From the bedside table she picked up a frame. *May the road rise up to meet you...* She'd read the blessing so many times, she knew it by heart. Lifting it near, she inspected the intricate Celtic knots Ellie had painstakingly drawn and colored in. Up close, she could see the little imperfections of the hand-inked letters. *She did this for me.* Never had anyone made something so special, put so much care and attention into a gift just for her. She ran a loving finger over the frame. It felt as if she were holding a bit of Ellie in her hands.

It was Christmas Eve, and the stores were all closing as six o'clock chimed. People hurried home, last minute packages tucked under their arms. Store employees waved to one another, wishing each another a Merry Christmas. Ellie got out of Kaufman's as quickly as she could and peeked through the glass door of the diner. It was nearly empty. She saw Louise refilling a customer's coffee at a far booth.

Ellie came in and hopped onto one of the counter stools as Louise put the coffee pot back on the burner. "I'm so glad I caught you before you closed." She slid a wrapped present across the spotless Formica. "Merry Christmas, Louise."

Louise smiled. "Haven't I told you a hundred times to save your money for all those trips you're going to take?" She reached under the counter and laid a heavy square package in front of Ellie. "Got one for you, too."

Ellie's face lit up. "For me? Really?" She stood on the foot rail and leaned over the counter so she could pull Louise into a hug.

"Don't you even want to see what it is?" Louise said, laughing as she hugged Ellie back.

"I'll love it, no matter what it is," Ellie said happily. She released Louise and sat back down.

"You want anything?"

"Just a Coke. You have the kitchen all cleaned up," Ellie said.

"I kept one grill hot, just for you," Louise said. "Be right back."

Ellie pushed off to make her stool spin. One, two revolutions and—she suddenly grabbed the counter to stop her motion. "Teresa!"

Sitting in that far booth, Teresa was watching her with a bemused smile. She slid out of the booth and carried her coffee cup to the counter. "Merry Christmas," she said as she perched on the adjacent stool.

Louise peeked out from the kitchen. "She's been waiting to see if you'd come in."

"You were waiting for me?"

Teresa nodded. "You're coming to my aunts' house with me for Christmas dinner tomorrow."

Ellie's expression sobered. "No. I can't—"

With a clatter, Louise set a grilled cheese sandwich down in front of Ellie. "Now, you listen here," she said sternly. "I've invited you home with me for as long as I've known you, and you always say no. I've let you be, but it's not right, Ellie Ryan." She glanced at Teresa. "You got a friend inviting you home with her for Christmas Day. There is no reason for you to spend the holiday alone."

Ellie looked doubtfully at Teresa. "What about your mother? Won't she—"

"I talked to my godmother, Aunt Anita," Teresa said. "I told her you had no family and she insisted you come. She'll help if my mother puts up a fuss."

"See?" Louise said. "It's all taken care of. Eat while that's hot." She put a piece of apple pie on a plate and set it in front of Teresa. "And you keep her company while she eats."

Teresa smiled. "Thank you."

Louise moved away to clean up.

"Are you sure?" Ellie asked in a low voice. "I don't want to impose."

"You're not imposing," Teresa said. "You'll have to put up with about thirty people, so it'll be crazy. But you're not imposing. And it'll make me happy. Nice necklace, by the way."

Ellie's hand flew to the heart hanging from the chain around her neck. She met Teresa's eyes and what she saw in them made her insides tingle. "Okay. I can't think of anyone I'd rather spend Christmas with."

They ate while the last couple of customers paid their checks, wishing Louise a Merry Christmas, and soon they were the only diners left.

"And you're not doing extras tonight," Louise said. "We already took care of it. We gave out soup and sandwiches to anyone who wanted some before the dinner rush."

Ellie's eyes teared up. "I love you, Louise. Thank you."

Louise looked at her fondly. "I love you, too, baby girl. You made me realize how blessed I've been. Got to help others when we can. You don't know how much you've done."

When they were done eating, Teresa insisted on driving Ellie home. Ellie gave Louise one more hug and accompanied Teresa to where the VW was parked. She stopped suddenly.

"Listen," she said. The stores were all closed. Hardly any people were out. A deep hush lay over the city. "Have you ever gone out and just walked on Christmas Eve or early on Christmas Day, listening to the quiet?"

"Are you kidding?" Teresa looked at her watch. "Right now, most of the family is gathered at the aunts' house for Christmas Eve dinner. They'll eat on and off all night until midnight Mass. Only after we get home from church will it be quiet in our house. And then tomorrow, it starts all over again. We'll open presents at our house, and then we'll go to church and back over to the aunts' house to start cooking and eating again and opening more presents. We won't be back home until tomorrow night. Maybe then—if no one got in an argument—will it be quiet again."

Ellie sighed. "It sounds wonderful."

Teresa laughed and unlocked the car. "We'll see how wonderful you think it is tomorrow."

Teresa drove through nearly deserted streets to Ellie's apartment building. They sat in the car, neither wanting to say good night. Ellie slipped her glove off and bravely reached over for Teresa's waiting hand and looked down, half-expecting to see a glow from the heat of their connection. Forgotten was the cold—the VW never could warm the interior up properly. Forgotten, too, was any worry that Teresa's family might be wondering where she was. For Ellie, the entire world was contained in that small space in that instant. Time ceased to exist as she reveled in the feel of Teresa's hand in hers. The warmth of that touch spread up her arm to her chest until she wasn't sure she could contain the joy that blossomed there.

"I never got to thank you for my Christmas present," Teresa murmured. "I love that blessing. It must have taken you hours to make."

"It did," Ellie said. "But I loved doing it. For you."

"Do you..." Teresa hesitated. "Have you made many of those for people?"

Ellie raised her eyes to Teresa's. "Only one other." Even in the dark, she could feel the intensity of Teresa's gaze. "I should let you get to your aunts'."

"I guess," Teresa said reluctantly.

Ellie leaned over to hug Teresa, and the contact of their cheeks felt electric. Ellie froze for a long moment. Almost against her will, she felt herself gently rubbing her cheek against Teresa's velvet skin. She would never know for sure who initiated it, but she could feel Teresa's cheek sliding along hers until the corners of their mouths were barely touching. The world seemed to hold its breath for that instant, and then she shifted just a bit more, and felt the incredible softness of Teresa's mouth against hers. Any fear she'd had that Teresa would pull away disappeared as Teresa's full lips returned the pressure, yielding, opening to welcome Ellie, to pull her in. Nothing, not even the distant memory of Katie's kisses, could have prepared her for the power of this touch. Ellie lost track of time and place. She only knew Teresa's strong arms were around her, and when at last Teresa's mouth left hers, it was to place feather-light kisses on her forehead, her eyelids, her cheeks. Ellie nestled into Teresa's neck and felt the pressure of her pulse. *She's real. This is real.* Ellie raised her face and placed a hand on Teresa's cheek, drawing her mouth down again. She had no idea how much time had passed when they finally drew apart.

"You have to go now," Ellie whispered. "Or I won't let you go."

Teresa nodded in the darkness. "I know. It will take all my strength to leave you."

Ellie reached for the door handle.

"I'll pick you up tomorrow at twelve-thirty."

Ellie looked back in a panic. "Are you sure? After we—"

"Twelve-thirty." Teresa placed a gentle hand on Ellie's cheek. "Good night."

CHAPTER 15

TERESA, FOR THE REST of her life, would think of that Christmas as the Christmas she grew up. *It was just a kiss,* she kept telling herself over the days that followed, but it was so much more. *It would be laughable if it hadn't changed my entire life.* It felt as if she had been stuck in a time warp. While everyone else had grown up bit by bit, dating, having sex, getting married, and having kids, Teresa had remained almost as innocent as she'd been at fifteen. With one kiss, she'd been awakened, like someone who had been placed under a sleeping spell in a fairy tale—but even she couldn't call herself Sleeping Beauty.

In a daze that evening, she'd left Ellie, only to realize that she'd nearly forgotten to leave food for Dogman and Lucy. She quickly detoured by her empty house to get some spaghetti and then swung by the store before going to the aunts' house, where she found that her family hadn't really missed her. Dinner—or at least the first round of eating—was done, and people were scattered around the house. Lou and Dom Sr. were snoring loudly from either end of the living room couch while the kids played in the basement. Teresa put a little food on a plate, but had no real appetite. She nearly called Bernie to see if she could go over, but she knew better. Anita had already grabbed Teresa and placed her lips against her forehead—"Are you running a temperature? You're all flushed."— and Teresa knew Bernie would immediately guess something monumental had happened.

She had never before appreciated the truth of being lovesick, but that's how she felt. She felt giddy, feverish, shaky. Every time she remembered the kiss—which was every few seconds—she felt an explosion of feelings she had never experienced before, and not just emotions but physical things. Her face burned just to think of the wetness she'd felt down there. She'd never had an orgasm. She smiled as she recalled how she had stared in horror when Bernie passed her a copy of *The Happy Hooker* when they were sixteen.

"I stole it from Denny's closet," Bernie said. "I think he stole it from Dad. What's he gonna do? Ask me if I have it?"

"I can't read this!" Teresa had gasped.

"Why not?" Bernie said. "If some boy is going to do this stuff to us someday, I want to know more about my body than he does. Why should we be ashamed? The hell with Sister Marguerite."

Teresa had nearly fainted when Bernie leaned close and whispered, "It'll teach you how to touch down there to make it happen."

Teresa knew that if she ever did such a thing, she'd have to confess it immediately, and the shame of having to say it out loud to a priest was enough to keep her from ever trying it. But she did read parts of the book, equally fascinated and terrified that her mother would find it no matter how carefully she tried to hide it. She found herself skipping the chapters involving men and looking for the ones describing what happened with other women and remembering Penelope Jones.

Throughout their college years, she'd listened in bemused ignorance as Bernie and other women talked about urges that she'd never felt. Until now. Now she knew what they meant because she wanted Ellie to touch her down there; wanted to touch Ellie, to know that part of her, wanted to kiss her everywhere, not just on the mouth.

Teresa shivered and felt a faint pulsing in her crotch just thinking about it. Startled, she realized she was sitting in her maiden aunts' dining room, thinking about... *this*. She looked around to see if anyone had noticed, but no one was paying her the slightest attention. Restlessly, she went outside to pace the sidewalk, waiting until it was time to go to Midnight Mass. All she wanted was to be alone in her room with her thoughts. Mass that night was a blur. As soon as they got home, she excused herself and went to bed.

She hardly slept that night and when she did, her dreams were wild, filled with Ellie doing things that made her wake, gasping. Lying in the dark, she tried to imagine Ellie's naked body next to her and immediately realized, *I'd have to be naked, too.* That realization sobered her. Just because Ellie kissed her didn't mean she wanted to go any further; but if they did, how would she know what to do? She knew what Bernie's answer would be. Hesitantly, Teresa slipped a hand down, under her underwear, through the tangle of dark curls to the swollen, wet place between her legs. In wonder, she let herself explore those forbidden folds for the first time. She clapped a hand over her mouth to stifle the gasp that escaped when her fingers found her clitoris. Clinically, she knew the terms, knew the anatomy, but *oh, my God*. She nearly moaned aloud as her fingers stroked. Never could she have imagined what this felt like. She let the sensations build and build into a tension that was almost painful until... she tipped over the edge of her first climax.

Breathing heavily in the dark, she felt the continued throbbing of her orgasm. She tried to imagine what it would be like to have Ellie do that to her. Even alone in the dark, she felt her face burn at the thought. She threw an arm over her face and laughed silently.

The next day, Teresa sat at a light, smiling as she remembered. A horn honked, startling her back into the present. She put the VW into first gear and sped through the intersection.

When she got to Ellie's apartment, she sat in the car. Suddenly, it seemed risky to take Ellie home for Christmas after what happened last night. Teresa knew she was a horrible liar—her mother had always been able to tell if she tried to fib, and she had a feeling anyone who looked at her would know she was in love, but she couldn't take the invitation back now. With a deep breath, she got out of the car and went to the stairwell where she nearly ran into Ellie who was running down the stairs carrying a shopping bag.

Teresa stood there, thinking that she'd never seen anything so beautiful. "Hi."

Ellie looked up at her, but instead of the happiness Teresa hoped she'd see, there was only worry and doubt. "We need to talk," Ellie said.

"Okay." Teresa pushed the landing door shut as the blood drained from her face, leaving her feeling cold and empty. *You idiot,* said a voice in her head. *She regrets the kiss. She doesn't love you.* Composing her features, she turned to Ellie.

Ellie's eyes raked Teresa's features as if searching for something. "Before we're with your family, I have to know." Her cheeks burned scarlet as she lowered her gaze, but then she was staring at Teresa's chest, which only made her blush a deeper red. Flustered, she stared instead at Teresa's knees. "I need to know how you're feeling. About last night."

Here it was. Ellie was going to force the issue. No pretending it didn't happen, no wondering where things stood. Teresa's heart was thumping as she considered how honest to be.

"I've never been happier than I was last night," Teresa heard herself say. For a moment, she wasn't sure if she'd only said it in her head and not out loud, because Ellie just stood there, silent and unmoving.

When at last she lifted her face to Teresa's, Ellie's eyes were shining with tears. "Really?"

Dumbly, Teresa nodded. She opened her mouth, but no sound would come out. She tried again. "How about you?"

Ellie bit her lip. "I've wanted to kiss you for ages."

Teresa stood, dumbfounded. "Why?"

Ellie smiled. "Because I think you're beautiful, silly."

Teresa couldn't think of anything to say. She stepped near and, keeping her eyes open, pressed her lips to Ellie's. Ellie's lips, warm and soft, returned the kiss, her free arm wrapped around Teresa's neck.

"I had to be sure it wasn't just a dream," she said to Ellie a moment later. She held Ellie tightly. *I love you.* It nearly burst from her mouth, but she bit it back just in time. She could hear Bernie saying, "You're ready to tell someone you love them after a kiss? Jesus Christ!"

They stepped apart and Ellie asked, "Are you sure about this? With your family?"

"Not really," Teresa admitted. "I think it'll be okay, but we've got to be careful."

Ellie nodded, her expression hardening just a bit. "We will be."

When they got to the aunts' house, Ellie pulled a wrapped present out of her bag and left the bag in the car. Anita was waiting for them. She took Ellie under her wing as soon as Teresa introduced her.

"Merry Christmas, Miss Martelli. I wasn't sure what to bring." Ellie held out the parcel. "So I brought you and your sisters a Johnny Mathis Christmas album. Let me know if you already have it and I'll exchange it for another."

"This is so thoughtful, Ellie," Anita said, giving her a hug. "And you call me Anita."

Teresa hung up Ellie's coat as Anita took her by the arm and herded her into the kitchen. She watched from the dining room as Anita introduced Ellie to the other aunts and put her to work rolling meatballs. She couldn't hear what they were saying, but Ellie was chatting animatedly with them while she worked.

"I didn't know you were bringing that hot little thing with you today," said Gianni, pointing with his chin toward the kitchen.

Teresa smiled. *She wants me, not you*, she so badly wanted to boast, but instead said, "That hot little thing handed you your ass the last time you tangled with her. But feel free to try again." Looking over his shoulder, she said more loudly, "Hi, Angelina."

Gianni jumped, and Teresa walked away chuckling.

Where normally she would have been in the kitchen helping prepare dinner, Teresa busied herself setting the tables and arranging chairs while she kept an eye on the kitchen. When Sylvia went into the kitchen and saw Ellie there, she turned and looked sharply at Teresa, but Anita must have been watching as well, because she bustled over and led Sylvia to the stove to check something. Later, Ellie was talking to Francesca when she must have felt the baby kick. Teresa watched her sister place Ellie's hand on her bulging abdomen, and she smiled as she watched Ellie and Francesca laugh together when Ellie felt it, too.

Louise was right. Ellie had a way of changing people. Teresa thought about Dogman and Lucy. *If it weren't for Ellie, would I have looked twice at them?* Ellie had no idea of the impact she had on people—*including me*, Teresa mused, no longer surprised at the way her stomach tingled as she thought about her.

Teresa made sure she was seated next to Ellie at dinner, but to her annoyance, Gianni positioned himself on Ellie's other side. She smiled as Ellie ignored his attempts at conversation and spoke instead to Francesca, across the table. She was startled to feel the pressure of Ellie's thigh against hers, and tried to look nonchalant as she returned the pressure. As usual, Sylvia and all of the aunts milled around, making sure everyone had everything they needed, so that, by the time they sat, the men had finished eating and moved back out to the living room to watch television, while the kids went down to the basement.

Ellie leaned toward Teresa and whispered, "Is it always like that?"

Teresa nodded, but as she looked around the table, she listened to the women laughing and talking without any men or children clamoring to be fed. *Maybe there's a certain wisdom to this,* she realized.

"You stay here and keep Francesca company," Teresa insisted to Ellie when it was time to clean up. "She needs to stay off her feet anyway."

Francesca rolled her eyes. "I don't think this baby is going to wait one more month."

Ellie leaned forward. "What names have you picked out?"

Teresa gathered plates, leaving Ellie at the table. She filled the sink with hot, soapy water and began washing dishes. She paused once to look back out to the dining room and saw Ellie looking over Francesca's shoulder, watching her. She turned back to the dishes, filled with a warmth that had nothing to do with the hot water.

"She's sweet," Francesca whispered to Teresa, and "You be sure and come back again," Anita said, giving Ellie a big hug as she thanked the aunts for having her over.

"I think they liked you," Teresa said happily as she started the car.

"I liked them, too. Thank you for inviting me," Ellie said. She reached over for Teresa's hand. "Could we stop by Rob and Karen's for a minute?"

"Sure," Teresa said. "But we have to make a stop first."

She drove down the alley and parked behind the store. "Here," she said, opening the VW's hood and handing Ellie a wrapped plate of food. "Set that on the trash can, will you?" She scooped dog food into Lucy's bowl and set it next to the plate.

"For Dogman and Lucy," Teresa explained when Ellie looked at her questioningly.

"Dogman?"

Teresa shrugged. "I don't know his name."

Ellie looked from the food to Teresa. "Is this the man you told me about weeks ago? You do this every night?"

Teresa nodded. "Lately. They usually sleep here."

"You are such a good person," Ellie said.

Teresa swallowed. "If I am, you made me that way," she managed to say.

Ellie shook her head. "You just are."

Teresa looked at Ellie in the gathering dusk and wished she could kiss her there. Ellie must have been thinking the same thing, because she stepped closer. A noise from the alley startled them, and they jumped apart.

"We should go," Teresa said. She drove them over to Rob and Karen's house, where the two of them were watching television. Rob answered the door and invited them in.

"We don't mean to barge in on you." Ellie offered the bag she'd brought with her. "I just wanted to give you this. I don't know anything about wine. I hope these are good."

"You didn't have to do that," Karen said as she took out one of the bottles to inspect it.

"I know," said Ellie. "But y'uns had us over. Just wanted to give you a little something."

"Oh, it's so nice and quiet here," Teresa said, closing her eyes.

"Yes, it is," Rob agreed, but there was a tightness to his voice as he said it.

Teresa watched him as he threw another log on the fire. "Do you want me to talk to Ma? She might be able to convince Pop it's time to let this go."

Rob snorted. "I don't want someone to talk him into it."

Karen's lips pursed. "Who is his father's son?"

Ellie laughed, but Teresa turned away frowning.

Lying in bed later, Teresa stared at the ceiling. She'd just spent the best Christmas of her life —no, the best day of her life—with the woman she loved. "Who would have thought I'd ever utter such a thing?" she could have laughed out loud, but if her parents could never get to the point of accepting Karen, there was no hope that they would ever accept Ellie.

As what, exactly?

Teresa couldn't answer that. She wasn't able to picture what a life with Ellie might look like; she only knew she no longer wanted to face the future without Ellie in it.

CHAPTER 16

FRIDAY MORNING, THE DAY after Christmas, the bus chattered to a halt at the stop where Ellie and three others were waiting.

"Hey, Ellie," said the driver. "Have a good Christmas?"

Ellie smiled as she climbed the steps of the bus and handed her card to be punched. "I had a very nice Christmas, Larry. How about you? Did you get your wife those fancy shoes she wanted?"

Larry chuckled as he closed the bus door and released the brake. "I took your advice and bought 'em. Don't know when she'll ever wear 'em, but she's got 'em."

"That's all that matters," Ellie said, sliding into the seat behind him. "Even if she never gets to wear them anywhere special, she'll always remember that you remembered."

Larry glanced at her in his overhead mirror. "Thanks to you. I thought it was crazy, but that woman's put up with me all these years."

Ellie laughed. The bus lurched to a halt at the next stop, letting a few more people on.

"You know, you could take her out dancing for New Year's," Ellie said thoughtfully.

He looked up at the mirror again. "You think?"

Ellie nodded. "Take her somewhere she can dress up, wear those new shoes. And you dress up, too. Like you used to when you were dating."

Larry guffawed. "I used to cut a fine figure. Not no more." He patted his bulging belly, barely constrained by his uniform buttons. "Too much o' her good cookin'." He stopped the bus to let some passengers off. "Dancin', huh?"

Larry was clearly still thinking about that when Ellie got to her stop.

"See you Monday, Fred Astaire," Ellie said as she hopped down the bus steps. She could still hear Larry laughing as the door shut and the bus pulled away with a belch of diesel smoke.

It was bitterly cold as Ellie walked the remaining blocks to the bank, each breath hanging in a cloud of vapor for a moment. She looked around as she walked, but she didn't see any street people. *I hope they're all in shelters,* but she knew that wasn't likely. There were just too many of them lately. Sometimes, it was hard not to get discouraged about the poverty and unemployment in this city. She was lucky to have a job and she knew it.

Suzanne was already in the staff locker room when Ellie came in. "Good Christmas, Suzanne?" Ellie asked, pushing her coat into her locker.

"Hmmph." Suzanne sat nearby, changing from boots to shoes. "Not much of a Christmas with his new job. Barely making half of what he made in the mill. We only had a few presents each for the kids."

Ellie unwound her scarf and hung it in the locker as well. It was going to be an eggshell day. Linda had taken the rest of the week off, so it was only the two of them working the windows today.

"Hello, ladies."

Ellie jumped. "Mr. Myers," she said.

He smiled. "I think it's time you called me Aaron, Ellie."

"I don't think so, Mr. Myers." She turned back to her locker, pretending to be searching for something in her backpack as she waited for him to go away, but he didn't. Suzanne pushed heavily to her feet and Ellie quickly closed her locker so that they could walk together past him.

"What was that about?" Suzanne asked with a scowl.

"No idea," Ellie said in a low voice.

"Stay away from him. He's done this before, with other young tellers." Suzanne glanced at Ellie and did a double take. "What's that?" she asked, reaching out to Ellie's chest where the heart necklace lay on her sweater.

Ellie's hand flew to it. It must have caught on her scarf and pulled free.

Suzanne's sharp gaze locked on Ellie. "And who is that from?"

"No one," Ellie said, but she could feel her face coloring. They went to the vault to retrieve their trays and take them to their windows.

"No one, my foot," Suzanne said, and Ellie knew she wouldn't let this go. "You don't get a heart from no one."

"It's just a friend," Ellie insisted, tucking the necklace back under her sweater. "So, what happened with your Christmas?" She knew from experience that the best way to distract Suzanne was to get her focused on her own troubles.

She half-listened as Suzanne went on about no one appreciating all the time she took to buy and wrap presents, and how her husband and kids only gave her token gifts of perfume and stockings—"Stockings!" As Ellie listened, she felt an odd tingle running up her spine. She turned and looked. From up on the second floor, Aaron Myers was standing at the balcony, watching her. She turned back to her drawer, refusing to look up again.

Every time the door opened, she looked up hopefully, but Teresa didn't come in. She knew that Mr. Benedetto brought the deposit more often than Teresa did, but she'd hoped Teresa would find an excuse to come by. At lunch, she considered walking to the drug store, but *you just spent all day with her yesterday,* she reminded herself, sitting in the staff room with Suzanne as they ate their lunch. Ellie picked at her sandwich as Suzanne continued her complaints about all the time she'd spent preparing Christmas dinner with no one offering to help her.

The afternoon dragged on, and finally, at closing time, she said good night to Suzanne and hopped a bus headed downtown. She was scheduled to work her last holiday hours at Kaufman's over the weekend, helping with the after-Christmas rush, "and then I'll be home more," she'd promised KC, who had sat looking forlorn and lonely just that morning as Ellie rushed out the door.

The evening passed quickly. The store was packed with people exchanging presents or trying to use gift certificates. "It's been like this all day," Ellie's manager said in a harassed tone. She was grateful when Ellie took over the floor in the men's department, rushing about, helping people find the size or color they needed. By the time the clock ticked nine o'clock, Ellie was exhausted.

She punched out, grabbed her things and hurried to the diner.

"I'm not here to eat," she said as Louise looked up. "I know you're trying to close up. I just wanted to thank you for my atlas. It's wonderful!"

Louise beamed at her. "So you can start planning those trips to all those places you're going to see. And thank you for my silk scarf. Silk! And that blue. It looks like it came from a peacock."

"It'll look beautiful on you," Ellie said with a fond smile.

Louise looked at her more closely. "You look wiped out."

Ellie nodded. "I am. I think I'm getting too old for fourteen-hour days. I don't know how you do it."

Louise waved a hand. "It's different when it's your own place and you're doing what you love." She leaned her elbows on the counter as Ellie hopped onto one of the stools. "So how was your Christmas with Teresa's family?"

Ellie's face lit up. "It was so nice. Her aunts, especially her godmother, they were great." She reached out for Louise's hand. "I've never had a Christmas like that."

"Teresa seems like a nice girl."

"She is," Ellie said. "She's become a good friend."

Louise squeezed her hand. "I'm so glad, Ellie." Her expression sobered. "For as long as I've known you, you've never had a friend." She waved a hand as Ellie opened her mouth to protest. "I don't mean the people from the store or the bank. You get along with everyone. I mean a real friend. Someone you can count on to be there, no matter what. Teresa seems like that kind of person."

To Ellie's embarrassment, her eyes stung with sudden tears. "I think she is," she said, blinking rapidly. "Between you and Teresa, I'm set."

Louise laughed. "You know you got me, baby girl. Forever." She went to ring up a customer.

"See you soon, Louise," Ellie called as she went back out into the night.

⤙ ⤚

The low winter sun pushed its way through the blinds of Ellie's bedroom window, burnishing the edges of the petals of a single white rose propped in a small vase on the bedside table. KC made tiny snoring noises as she lay curled up against Ellie's side while Ellie stared at the rose. It had been left outside her door at the top of the stairs sometime yesterday. She'd nearly tripped over it coming home. No note. None was needed. It was like having a bit of Teresa with her.

She rolled over and stretched, luxuriating in being able to sleep in, just a bit. She had to be at Kaufman's at noon, but there was something she had to do first.

She got up and scrambled some eggs, mixing a little egg into KC's dry food. When they were done eating, Ellie showered and got dressed for work.

"I'll be home later, little one," she said as she pulled on a coat, hat, boots, and mittens.

On the unheated landing, two wrapped bundles of flowers sat where she'd left them the day before. She gathered them up and headed outside, where the refreshingly cold air helped blow the cobwebs from her mind. She walked for about a half an hour, climbing over a few remaining snow piles pushed up by the plows at the intersections. Presently, she found herself at the cemetery, the grave markers standing like sentinels rising from the untouched snow still covering many of the gravesites. Ellie stood listening to the hush of the place.

After her father's death, Ellie's mother had insisted they go to the cemetery every Christmas, Easter, and on her father's birthday. Daniel hated to go—"He was stupid enough to get himself killed working for that damned mill," he used to mutter, but only so Ellie could hear. "I'm never working in those mills." But he trudged along, sullen and resentful, with Ellie clinging to his hand as their mother tenderly laid flowers and cleaned the gravesite of any leaves or fallen branches from nearby trees. After Daniel was in Vietnam and Ellie's mother got too sick to go, sometimes Ellie had to go alone. "Bring him flowers," her mom had begged. "I don't want him to think we've forgotten him." Ellie had looked into her mother's eyes, luminous in her wasted face, and wanted to ask, "If he's in heaven, the way everyone says, why are we still acting like he's there in the graveyard?" But she could never bring herself to say the words. Before long, it wasn't one grave she was going to visit, but two.

Following the tracks of the cars that had recently wound along the paths through the cemetery, Ellie made her way first to her father's burial site. A little bit of snow had clung to the granite, like frosting. She brushed it away, taking care not to disturb the snow over the grave. *Michael Ryan, Beloved Husband and Father.*

Ellie unwrapped one of the bouquets and laid the flowers against the headstone. "Here are your flowers, Dad. I'm a few days late, but I'm here."

The only sound was the occasional soft plop of a clump of snow falling from a tree and the chattering of a few squirrels. She stood there a while, and then said, "I'll be back to see you again soon."

From there, she walked to her mother's grave. "Can't they be buried together?" Ellie had begged when her mother's arrangements had had to be made, but the cemetery man insisted that there were no available gravesites near her father, and unless she could afford to buy two sites and have her father's remains moved, they would have to be in separate places. That stone, too, had some snow clinging to it. She brushed it clean and set the second bunch of flowers against it. *Ellen Ryan.* Nothing else. Just her dates of birth and death. There hadn't been enough money to have anything else carved on the stone. Ellie had been named for her. Everyone always thought Ellie was short for Eleanor, but "Ellie *is* my name," she had insisted over and over to teachers and principals who tried to convince her that no one was named just Ellie.

She opened her mouth to speak, but sudden tears choked off the words. It was always harder to visit her mom. Things had been hard after her dad died, but they had managed. It had been so much harder when Ellen got sick, and then Daniel got drafted. *Why?* Ellie covered her face and cried. She knew it made no sense to ask that, but sometimes... sometimes she just felt so alone. She wiped her cheeks with her mittens, but the cold air chapped the damp skin, leaving her cheeks red and raw.

"I've met someone," she whispered. "I don't know how you'd feel about it. I think you'd like her." Ellie closed her eyes. "I hope you'd like her."

Sniffling, she stood up and made her way back through the silent cemetery toward the nearest bus stop.

———

Teresa stomped the snow off her boots and knocked on the back door before turning the knob. "Anyone home?" she called as she entered.

"Teresa!" cried Bernie's mother, standing at the sink in her robe and slippers. She was even smaller than Bernie—"which makes me look like a giant when I come over here," Teresa used to lament as she continued to shoot up during junior high and high school to her current height.

"Hey, Mrs. D'Armelio," Teresa said. "I brought some of Mrs. Schiavo's doughnuts."

"My favorites," said Mrs. D'Armelio. "Thank you." She took one from the box Teresa held out.

"Is Bernie up yet?"

Mrs. D'Armelio cackled. "Are you kidding? On Christmas break? She doesn't get up until noon." She scuffed to the base of the stairs and called, "Bernie! Teresa's here. Come on down."

Teresa poured herself a cup of coffee and reached for a doughnut. "Good Christmas?"

Mrs. D'Armelio refilled her own coffee cup and joined Teresa at the table. "Could have been better. You know Denny didn't come home this year."

Teresa nodded. "Bernie told me. Did he call?"

Mrs. D'Armelio snorted. "For about five minutes. He doesn't come home since the summer, and he can't spare more than five minutes to talk to us?" She dunked her doughnut in her coffee and took a bite.

Teresa chewed thoughtfully on her own doughnut. "Do you mind he went away?"

"No," said Mrs. D'Armelio. "He had to. There's no future for him here in Pittsburgh. I could stand him living somewhere else, but he never comes home to visit. That's the hard part."

"Hey," said Bernie sleepily, coming into the kitchen in her nightshirt, her hair tousled and sticking up on one side.

"Put some clothes on!" Mrs. D'Armelio said, scandalized.

"What? It's only Bennie."

Teresa grinned. "After all the times we slept over at each other's house, I've seen her in her nightshirt more than I've seen her in clothes."

Mrs. D'Armelio gave an impatient cluck. Turning back to Teresa, she asked, "Your mother and father are good?"

"Both good. Ma's more impatient than Francesca for the new baby to be born."

"Your mother is lucky. What I wouldn't give for some grandchildren," Mrs. D'Armelio said pointedly.

Bernie rolled her eyes and lit a cigarette. "Not gonna happen, Mom. I teach the little bastards all day long. Why would I want to come home to them? With or without a husband."

Teresa laughed. This argument had been going on for the past fifteen years, and she knew it would continue until the day one of them died.

Mrs. D'Armelio got up and shuffled out of the kitchen. Teresa waited until they heard the vacuum cleaner roar to life in the living room.

"So, did you see Tom?"

Bernie exhaled and nodded. "We got together Christmas evening, after they got home from his in-laws."

Teresa knew "getting together" meant sex in Tom's car in some back alley somewhere—a thought she never wanted to contemplate in any detail, but now, after what she'd been feeling for Ellie, she had more sympathy for how powerful that drive could be.

"What about you?"

Teresa looked up to see Bernie watching her closely. "I invited Ellie to spend Christmas with us," she said casually.

For days, she'd been debating whether to say anything, but there was too big a chance Sylvia or someone else might say something, and if Bernie found out about Ellie from anyone else, she would hound Teresa to death over it. *Besides,* Teresa argued with herself, *maybe her reaction won't be bad. Maybe, you'll be able to tell her the truth...someday.*

"What the fuck?"

Okay, maybe not. Teresa shrugged. "She's all alone. I just thought she might like to spend the holiday with people. It's not like one more mattered at the aunts' house."

"You took her home for Christmas? And you act like that's not a fucking big deal? What, are you thinking about marrying her or something?" Bernie sat with her cigarette suspended an inch from her lips as she watched Teresa's face.

Teresa cursed herself as she felt the heat rise up her neck to her cheeks.

"Oh, my God!" Bernie hissed. She ground out her cigarette in the ashtray and leaned forward. "What the hell are you thinking?"

"What?" Teresa forced herself to meet Bernie's incredulous gaze.

"Are you...are you queer? Is that why you've never dated anyone?" Bernie whispered.

"No!" Teresa felt her face burn even hotter at the lie. "She's just lonely. Why can't I be nice to someone without you turning it into something nasty?"

Bernie sat back and lit another cigarette. "Because I know you, Bennie. You like this girl. I've seen it before, when we were young, but not like this. You want to screw her—or whatever two women do together."

Teresa's nostrils flared. "Like you should talk?" she whispered back. "You, the paragon of virtue? How many years have I listened to you moan and cry about how worthless you feel, screwing your married boyfriend in the back seat of his car whenever he feels like leaving his wife and kids to fuck you?"

Bernie's face went white with anger, but before she could respond, Teresa pushed to her feet and stormed from the house, tears stinging her eyes. Her heels slammed into the pavement with every step as she walked home. She'd been an idiot to think Bernie would understand. That anyone would understand. She laughed mirthlessly at her fantasy hopes that somehow, her family might accept Ellie.

"It's never going to happen," she muttered, wiping tears from her cheeks.

But if it didn't, what then?

Can you make a choice?

It won't come to that.

But if it does?

Teresa couldn't face that thought. How could she choose between Ellie and her family? It was like asking her to choose between her heart or her lungs. How could she live without either?

She walked blindly. She didn't want to go home and she sure as hell didn't want to be at the store on her only day off. She found herself standing in front of St. Rafael's. Climbing the steps, she pulled open the heavy oak door and entered the empty sanctuary. Without the overhead lights, the church's interior was lit only by the sunlight coming through the southern-facing stained glass windows and by a few candles. The nave was still decorated for

Christmas, with a wall of poinsettias creating a backdrop for the Nativity.

Teresa went to the alcove dedicated to Our Lady and, dropping a couple of quarters in the coin box, lit a votive candle. She knelt at the *prie-dieu* and tried to pray, but couldn't. "What do I ask for?" she whispered.

She listened, but there was only silence.

CHAPTER 17

ELLIE RUSHED HOME AND changed out of her bank clothes into jeans and her favorite sweater. "Come on, little one," she said to KC. "Let's get you fed before she gets here." She jumped at a rap on the door as she scooped some wet food into a bowl, but the knock came from the living room. Groaning, Ellie set the bowl down for KC and went to answer the door.

"Hey there," Sullivan said, bounding in as soon as the door opened. "I thought we could spend another worthless New Year's Eve together." He held up a grocery bag in one hand. "I bought munchies and beer." From behind his back, he produced a small box. "And look! I got a Betamax machine for Christmas. We can watch *Phantasm*!"

"Oh, Sullivan, I'm sorry," she said, "but I have plans."

He stared at her with a lop-sided grin on his face. "No, you don't. You and I never have plans for New Year's. We are our plans."

She grimaced apologetically. "Not this year. I really do have plans. I'm going out."

"Really?" He looked crestfallen. "Oh, well. Guess I'll watch *Phantasm* by myself." He looked at the grocery bag. "If I have a hangover tomorrow, it's all your fault."

"It would be your fault whether I was there or not," Ellie said, laughing. "I don't drink beer, remember?" She glanced at her watch. "Gotta go. See you later."

"Have a good time," he said as he slouched back across the hall to his apartment.

Ellie locked the door and hurried back to the kitchen. "Be good, little one," she said to KC, who was cleaning her whiskers. "Not sure when I'll be back."

She ran down the stairs, yanking her coat on as she went. She smiled when she saw the VW pulling up to the curb.

"Hi," she said breathlessly as she got into the passenger seat.

Teresa turned to her. "Hi."

For a long moment, they sat looking at each other before Ellie cleared her throat and shifted in her seat. "We probably should move."

"Okay," said Teresa. "But you never said where we're going."

"Driver, take us to Station Square."

Teresa glanced at her as she put the car in gear. "Station Square? Did you make dinner reservations?"

Ellie grinned mischievously. "You'll see."

"All right," Teresa said, pulling away from the curb. She wove her way toward their destination. "I'm really glad you called."

Ellie turned to her. "Tell me what you normally do on New Year's."

"The usual. Go down to the aunts' house. Eat. Wait until midnight when everyone goes outside to bang pans and make a lot of noise. Go home and sleep." She shook her head. "Same thing I've done every New Year of my life."

"It sounds wonderful. Sorry. You must get tired of hearing me say that every time you talk about your family."

Teresa shook her head. "No. Don't be sorry. It's made me appreciate my family more. I really do love them, although I may not have conveyed those sentiments to you." Ellie smiled, and Teresa said, "It's just like anything else, I guess. When they're close, always there, you just don't see. We did have a Christmas miracle I haven't told you about."

"What?"

"My dad gave me a raise. First one I've had since I started working for him after pharmacy school."

"Oh, Teresa," Ellie said, laying her hand on Teresa's arm. "That's wonderful. Isn't it?"

Teresa glanced over quickly. "What do you mean?"

"Well," Ellie began, suddenly feeling she was walking on shaky ground. She pulled her hand away. "When we had dinner with Rob and Karen, it sounded as if you were trying to find a way to break free of the store. Rob was giving you advice on how to look for another job. Has that changed?"

Teresa considered it. "I don't know. The main reason I got angry was because I felt like they took me for granted. I work my butt off, and my brother gets away with doing so much less."

"From what I've seen of your brother, that's never going to change," Ellie said flatly. "I think the thing you need to do is figure out how happy you can be, working your butt off, because I don't see you doing things any differently. Not while you're there. You could work for someone else and maybe do less, just work your hours and leave. But if you stay with your dad's store, you have to accept that some things won't change. You have to decide what you can live with and what you can't."

Teresa chewed her lip as she thought about what Ellie had said. "I guess you're right. Maybe they sensed how close I've been to walking out."

"So the raise will keep you there?"

"For a while." Teresa downshifted as she braked for a red light. "I don't feel like I can leave now."

"Then it worked," Ellie said.

"Do you think I shouldn't stay?" Teresa asked.

"No," Ellie said quickly. "Not at all. Like I said, I think you need to figure out what will make you happy. Maybe you like working seventy hours a week, and the challenge of making the store successful. There's nothing wrong with that."

"Except—" Teresa stopped abruptly as she put the car in gear again.

"What?"

"The reason I work seventy hours a week is because I have nothing else to do. Nowhere I'd rather be. At least, I didn't." She glanced in Ellie's direction. "But that's changed."

"It has?"

Teresa nodded. Ellie laid a hand on Teresa's thigh. When Teresa didn't react, she started to pull away, but Teresa caught her hand and pressed it to her thigh again.

"Did you leave dinner for Dogman and Lucy tonight?" Ellie asked.

Teresa smiled. "Yes. Before I came to pick you up." She turned left. "What do you usually do for New Year's Eve?"

Ellie sighed. "I've spent the last couple with Sullivan. He was really disappointed. He had a movie, one of those new Beta machines that plays them on your TV. I felt bad telling him I had plans."

"We could have invited him," Teresa said wryly.

"No." Ellie laughed. "I don't feel that bad. I want this time with you. Alone."

Teresa turned to her, her eyes shining. "Me, too."

A loud growl suddenly filled the car over the chug of the VW's engine.

"We are going to eat, right?" Teresa asked, rubbing her stomach.

Ellie sat back. "Yes, we are going to eat."

"And then?"

"You'll see," Ellie said.

Teresa found a parking space near Station Square and Ellie led the way.

"I haven't been down here in ages," Teresa said, looking around as they walked.

"Me, either," Ellie said.

They entered a well-lit restaurant. The hostess checked their coats and took them to their table.

"That's a beautiful sweater," Teresa noted as Ellie placed her napkin on her lap. She looked closely at the cable pattern knitted into the body of the sweater. "Is it Irish?"

"In a way," Ellie said. "My mom made it for me."

"Really? The green looks nice against your eyes."

Ellie felt a flush creep up her neck at the compliment. She picked up her menu. Their waiter came to take their drink order. He was back in a moment with their wine and took their dinner order. "We have live music tonight as well," he said, indicating a small stage set up in one corner of the dining room.

"Tell me more about your mother," Teresa prompted when he left.

Ellie twirled the stem of her wine glass in her fingers as she thought. "When I was little, I remember her and my dad dancing and kissing a lot." She smiled, her eyes focused on the past. "Then, they would grab Daniel and me and dance with us. I knew how to waltz before I could ride a bike. We used to laugh a lot." Her smile faded. "After Dad died, we had a little money every month from his steelworker's pension, but Mom had to go back to work as a schoolteacher. It let her be home with us more than any other job, but it didn't pay much." Ellie paused, remembering. "She was pretty. Small, with long auburn hair. I look more like my dad, I think."

Teresa was watching her closely. "You said you were ten when he died?"

Ellie nodded. She didn't usually like to think about the accident. "Something fell on him at the mill, crushed him, and broke lots of bones. He finally died in the hospital of pneumonia."

"I'm sorry," Teresa said. "We shouldn't be talking about this tonight."

"It's okay." Ellie met Teresa's eyes. "I want you to know. Everything." She took a sip of her wine. "Sometimes, I feel like I'm forgetting them or at least forgetting the good parts. When I think of them, I think of them as they were after the accident or after the cancer." She forced a smile onto her face. "I want to remember them the way they were before, when we were all together and happy."

An awkward silence followed her words.

"And I want to thank you again for Christmas," Ellie said at last, to fill the void and change the subject.

"I'm so glad you accepted my invitation."

Teresa's eyes were soft and large as they shone a bit, and her lips as she smiled curved in a way that made Ellie long to reach out and touch them. The light from the candle on their table lit her face, and Ellie's hands itched for a pencil. So preoccupied was she with these thoughts that it took her a moment to realize Teresa was speaking.

"Sorry, what was that?"

"I said, Bernie was asking about Christmas," Teresa repeated. "I told her you were with us."

Ellie heard the hard edge to her voice. "What happened?"

"We argued. When I told her about you, she said... things."

An old, familiar shiver of apprehension ran up Ellie's spine. She didn't want to ask, didn't want to know, but she heard herself ask, "What kind of things?"

She couldn't meet Teresa's eyes any longer.

"She—" Teresa stopped abruptly as their waiter appeared with their salads. She waited until he left. "It doesn't really matter. She said some things. I said some things. It was ugly."

Ellie suddenly had no appetite. "I shouldn't have come. Shouldn't have intruded."

"No, that's not what I'm saying." Teresa leaned forward. "That was the best Christmas of my life," she said firmly. "Being with you made it the best Christmas of my life."

Ellie raised her eyes. "For me, too." They were dancing all around it, like an enchanted chasm yawning between them, spanned by an invisible bridge that could only be crossed if they had enough faith, if they could be true and say what was in their hearts, *but we can't*, Ellie realized. *Neither of us can say it.*

They were startled by the amplified strum of a guitar as a female musician tested her microphone. She said good evening to the crowd and began singing a Melissa Manchester song. Ellie watched Teresa watching the singer and felt kind of relieved that they'd stopped talking to listen. She'd wanted this evening to be special, to maybe even... She turned her attention to her salad. She knew what she wanted. Sometimes, she thought Teresa wanted it, too, but taking that next step was so terrifying.

"Are you okay?" Teresa asked in a low voice halfway through their dinner, and Ellie realized she'd hardly said a word since their entrées were served.

"I'm fine," she said. "Just listening to the music."

"Are we staying here until midnight?"

Ellie smiled. "No. I have other plans for after dinner. I hope you don't mind."

Teresa looked at her in a way that warmed Ellie through and through. "I won't mind anything, as long as I'm with you," Teresa said.

Ellie chuckled. "We'll see if you still say that when you see what I have planned."

"Can you believe this view?"

They stood at the top of Mt. Washington, looking down at a spectacular view of the Point, where Pittsburgh's three rivers come together. Most of the downtown buildings had left their lights on for the countdown to the new year, and the rivers visible far below were dotted with boats strung with colored lights. A half moon added her illumination to the scene.

"I've lived in this city all my life, and I've never been up here," Teresa said, staring in wonder.

"I haven't been since I was a kid," said Ellie. "We used to come up here and picnic, all four of us, when I was little. Dad would put me on his shoulders so I could feel even higher."

A few other people had ridden up the Monongahela Incline with them. Teresa and Ellie wandered off to an isolated spot. They found a large rock and perched on it, shoulders touching.

"What did Bernie say?" Ellie asked. "When you argued. What was it about?"

She felt Teresa tense against her shoulder.

"It was about you, kind of," Teresa said. "She guessed how I feel about you."

There it was again—hanging there, begging to be said aloud, if only one of them could be brave enough to take that first step.

"And how is that?" Ellie could feel the turmoil as Teresa struggled to know what to say. "I have to ask, because..." Her heart was beating so that it was hard to breathe. *You have to. One of us has to say it.* She shifted on the rock and forced herself to look at Teresa, whose features were dimly lit by the moon. "...because I love you."

The words hung in the cold air for what felt like a long time.

"If you don't feel the same," she went on before Teresa could say anything, "I understand. If you don't ever want to see me again, I'll understand. Just tell me—"

"I love you, too."

"—and I'll leave you alone."

Teresa took Ellie's mittened hand. "I said, I love you, too."

"You do?"

Ellie's free hand flew to her mouth and she gave a kind of hiccup as she fought to hold back sudden tears. She got up and walked a few steps away before turning to look back at Teresa.

Teresa glanced around, but the others who had come up with them were over at the incline, waiting for the next car to take them back down. She followed Ellie and stood there, her hands stuffed into her coat pockets.

When Ellie could speak again, she said, "How long have you felt like this?"

"I don't know for sure. I think I knew at Thanksgiving. Maybe before that." She dug her heel into the frozen ground. "That's what Bernie guessed. I lied, though." Teresa shook her head. "She said it like it was something to be ashamed of, but it isn't. When I was young, one of the nuns gave us a lecture on relationships, and she went on and on about how unnatural it was to love another girl. I was sure she was talking directly to me. I've never let myself..." She looked down at the rivers below. "I've never felt this way about anyone. I thought I never would, but it feels like the most natural thing in the world. More natural than anything I've ever felt before."

They could hear the incline rattling up the hill, and a new group of people got off to take in the view.

"I've never told anyone this before," Ellie said in a low voice. "There was a girl, the daughter of my foster family. We became friends quickly, and then, she started coming into my room at night. At first, she lay in the other bed, and we'd talk and stuff, but then for some reason, she—" Ellie stopped. Even here, all these years later, it was hard to talk about. She could feel her face burn with shame.

"What did she do?"

"She started crawling into my bed and we—I was so innocent. I didn't know anything. She was the one who came to me, who—" She paused to wipe a tear from her cheek. "I'm not saying I didn't want it. I did. Nothing really happened. Just kisses and cuddling, but for years, I've felt like I was contaminated, dirty." She forced herself to look at Teresa. "I guess she felt guilty or something, because she went to her mother. Except she made it sound like I was the one who... The mother dragged me to their priest, who lectured me on being a sinner against God and nature, and corrupting Katie with my sin." Ellie took a deep breath. "It was hell, staying with them after that, but I had to. The day I turned eighteen, I moved out. I never spoke to her again."

"And you've never forgiven her," Teresa said softly.

Ellie shook her head. "I've tried not to even think about her." She paused, searching for words. "But I could never forget how I felt when I was with her. I never let myself feel that way toward anyone else, but I knew I could never marry a man. Not after that." She met Teresa's eyes. "And then I met you. It... it brought up lots of old memories. That's part of what's made things so tough these last weeks." She looked back out at the city below them. "The holidays are usually kind of hard, but this year, wanting so much to be with you, made it even lonelier."

Teresa looked around, but the other people were all gathered near the incline. "I don't want you to ever be alone again," she murmured. "You told me once that you were sure you'd fall in love someday." She hesitated. "You said you were sure you'd meet someone you loved so much you would wonder how you ever felt whole without them."

Ellie gave an embarrassed little laugh. "You remember all that?"

"I remember because I already felt like I wasn't whole without you. I just didn't know how to say it."

"I can't believe I'm hearing you say it now." Ellie shivered. "Silly me. I thought we could stay up here until midnight, but I don't think that's going to happen."

"Do you want to go back to the restaurant?" Teresa asked.

Ellie looked long into Teresa's eyes, searching, hoping they wanted the same thing. "No," she whispered.

Teresa swallowed and nodded. She held out her hand. "Let's go."

CHAPTER 18

TERESA NEVER COULD RECALL much about the ride back to Ellie's apartment. She did remember that they crept up the stairs quietly and didn't turn on any lights for fear of Sullivan inviting himself over. Ellie tossed KC a catnip toy to keep her occupied. It wouldn't occur to Teresa until much later to ask Ellie if she'd kept that toy handy, "just in case?" Ellie only smiled and never really answered.

After they'd hung their coats up, Ellie led the way to the living room and they sat on the couch. Teresa was glad they hadn't headed straight to the bedroom. She was already having a hard time breathing, and was afraid she might pass out if they moved too fast.

After the things they talked about on Mt. Washington, Ellie must have felt released from some of her constraints, because she moved close, her fingers exploring the contours of Teresa's face. Teresa sat quite still and let herself experience Ellie's touch. She closed her eyes as Ellie traced a featherlight fingertip over her eyebrows, down her nose, tracing the outline of her lips.

"That tickles," Teresa whispered, smiling.

"Does this tickle?" Ellie whispered back. The trail of Ellie's fingers along her lips left Teresa's skin tingling everywhere they touched. *Is it possible to die from softness?* she wondered in some vague part of her brain that was still sluggishly working. When at last,

Ellie's mouth reached Teresa's, she was ready to respond, her lips parting of their own accord, her tongue gently searching, hesitant at first. Ellie returned the pressure and Teresa's confidence grew. So engrossed was Teresa in the sensations of Ellie's mouth, the light puffs of Ellie's breath on her cheek, that she was startled to find her hand reaching up into Ellie's hair, letting the fine strands sift through her fingers. Ellie's hand ran down Teresa's side to her hip, coming back up to caress the curve of Teresa's breast. Without breaking their kiss, Ellie shifted, pushing Teresa back on the sofa so that Ellie could lie on top of her.

Teresa had never imagined anyone could fit with her so seamlessly. She let her hands explore the contours of Ellie's body—the curve of her waist and the soft swell of her hips—but when Ellie slipped one thigh between hers, Teresa nearly moaned out loud. She involuntarily lifted her pelvis to press against Ellie, and again, some part of her thought, *how does my body know what to do?*

Ellie pulled away and looked down at Teresa. "Come to the bedroom."

She got up and took Teresa by the hand. She led her into the bedroom, where the blinds were still open, allowing moonlight into the room.

"Shouldn't we close the blinds?" Teresa asked.

Ellie shook her head. "No one can see us. Let me see how beautiful you are." She gently tugged Teresa's sweater over her head and began unbuttoning her blouse. Teresa's hands flew up to cover Ellie's and stop her.

"If we're moving too fast, you can tell me." Ellie said. "I don't want to push you if you're not ready."

Ellie lifted her face.

As Teresa lowered her mouth to Ellie's, she forgot to be afraid and let Ellie undo the buttons, pushing the blouse off her shoulders so that Ellie's hands were now touching bare skin. Teresa couldn't suppress a moan as goose bumps erupted in the wake of Ellie's trailing fingers. Teresa reached for the hem of Ellie's sweater and eased it over her head. She stood gaping at the beauty of Ellie's slender body. Moonlight glinted off the heart hanging around her neck above a lacy bra covering small, firm breasts. Ellie stood still and let Teresa slide the straps down, running her hands over Ellie's collarbones and down over her chest, teasing the edge of the lace. She reached around behind and tried to undo the hooks, but she'd never done it from that angle and fumbled with it until she decided to simply slip the bra down around Ellie's waist. It was Ellie's turn to moan as Teresa placed her hands over Ellie's breasts, feeling the stiff nipples pressing against her palms. She rubbed gently against them, enjoying Ellie's evident pleasure. Ellie stepped closer and, with more dexterity than Teresa, unhooked Teresa's bra and let it slide to the floor, freeing her breasts. She placed her hands under the soft weight of them. The nipples didn't harden like Ellie's did, but that didn't stop Teresa from gasping when Ellie bent to take one in her mouth. Teresa had never felt anything as exquisite as Ellie's lips and tongue. She wasn't sure her legs would continue to hold her. Ellie's hands slid down over Teresa's hips, and her fingers came around front to undo the button and zipper of Teresa's slacks.

"Not here," Teresa said, looking around the room, which felt huge all of a sudden.

"Meet me under the covers?" Ellie went to the bed and folded back the sheet invitingly. Teresa nodded and waited for Ellie to go around the other side of the bed while she quickly pushed her pants down around her ankles and then grabbed the nightstand as she nearly fell over.

"You okay?" Ellie asked, already in bed.

"Shoes," Teresa said, blushing at her stupidity. She kicked her shoes off, and managed to get her slacks off without any further accidents. She quickly slid under the covers, the sheets cool against her flushed skin. She lay on her side and reached out for Ellie, running a tentative hand over her waist and discovering that she had taken her panties off as well.

"I don't know if I'm ready." Teresa rolled onto her back, trying not to hyperventilate.

"It's okay," murmured Ellie. She shifted closer, close enough that Teresa could feel Ellie's breast pressing against her arm. In spite of herself, she turned toward Ellie and met her waiting mouth. Ellie raised her body and gently lowered herself on top of Teresa. Teresa could feel a slight trembling in Ellie's arms and knew that she was ready to move away at the first sign that Teresa didn't want her there. Driven by a storm of desire so intense she thought it might scorch Ellie, Teresa wrapped her arms around her and pulled her close. Ellie slipped one thigh between Teresa's and Teresa could feel the soft curls of Ellie's crotch pressed against her. If Teresa had thought Ellie fit seamlessly with her when they were on the couch, it was nothing to the sensation of their naked bodies pressed together—*or nearly naked*, she thought, wondering what she'd been so afraid of. *No wonder people kill to feel this.*

Her kiss became more assertive as Ellie rocked her pelvis against Teresa's thigh. Teresa bent her knee to increase the pressure, and brought her hands to Ellie's nipples, gently pinching and kneading them as Ellie's rhythm against her increased. She could feel Ellie's wetness on her skin and moved in sync with her until Ellie suddenly gasped and arched her back. Teresa could feel the wet pulsing of Ellie's orgasm as she collapsed against her, breathing hard. She wrapped her arms around her, inhaling the scent of her hair and feeling the light sheen of sweat that covered her body.

"Sorry," Ellie whispered in Teresa's ear. "I didn't mean to get so carried away."

"It's all right," murmured Teresa. "I felt like I was carried away with you."

Ellie rolled partially off Teresa and propped up on one elbow. "Not quite," she said, trailing a finger over Teresa's lips. "We can make it much better for you." She bent to take first one, then the other of Teresa's nipples in her mouth while her hand stroked Teresa's stomach, sliding under the waistband of her underwear.

"Not tonight," Teresa whispered, laying a hand over top of Ellie's.

"Don't you want to?" Ellie asked, drawing away a little.

"Yes," Teresa said quickly. "I do, but this was perfect for tonight." How could she put into words her relief—relief that Ellie had found pleasure without Teresa's fumbling about in unfamiliar territory, without growing frustrated at Teresa's inability to bring her to a climax. This *had* been perfect, in Teresa's mind. And even though she ached with her own unresolved need, this was enough for tonight.

"Really." She pulled Ellie back down to rest her head on her shoulder.

"You're sure?" Ellie asked doubtfully.

"I'm sure."

<hr />

"Where were you until four o'clock in the morning?"

Teresa was too sleepy—*and too happy*—to be annoyed by her mother as she scuffed into the kitchen in her robe and slippers. She poured herself a cup of coffee.

"You were out until four?" Lou asked, lowering the paper.

"Happy New Year, Pop." Teresa sat at the table and closed her eyes as she inhaled her coffee.

"Everyone wondered where you were," Sylvia said. "I kept telling them you'd be there, but you weren't."

"But I wasn't."

Sylvia's eyes narrowed at Teresa's lack of fight. "Were you with a man?"

Teresa laughed. "No. I was not with a man." She looked at her mother. "Was Gianni there?"

"Well, no," said Sylvia.

Lou picked the paper back up and hid behind it.

"Did he come home at all last night?" Teresa asked. "Because his room is empty now."

"No, he didn't. He was probably with Angelina."

Teresa nodded, not bothering to argue that tired point. "I'm thirty-four years old. If I want to spend my New Year's Eve somewhere other than with my aunts and nieces and nephews banging pots and pans at midnight, I think I'm allowed."

"Well, you slept in so late, you'll have to hurry to be ready," Sylvia said.

"I'm not going to Mass today."

"It's a holy day," Sylvia said indignantly. "It's a sin not to go."

"And I'm not going to the aunts' house for dinner," Teresa added, bracing herself.

"What?"

Teresa took a sip of her coffee and said calmly, "I'm going to Rob's for dinner."

"Why?" Lou said, lowering the paper again.

"Because I want to spend the holiday with my brother," said Teresa. *And Ellie,* but she thought it best not to add that bit.

"Are you sure about this?" Ellie had asked worriedly when Teresa proposed the idea. It was the middle of the night and Teresa had crawled reluctantly out of bed to put her clothes back on when it occurred to her.

"I want to spend New Year's Day with you," she said. "I don't think it would be smart to have you back over to the aunts' this soon, but I'll call Rob. He and Karen are probably staying in. Say you'll come."

Ellie, wearing only goose bumps and her necklace as she crawled out of the warmth of the bed, wrapped her arms around Teresa's neck. Teresa nearly forgot what they were talking about as she kissed Ellie and ran her hands along Ellie's flank down to her butt and back up again.

"I'd go anywhere to be with you," Ellie whispered against Teresa's mouth.

Teresa groaned. "I have to go."

Too late, Teresa realized her eagle-eyed mother was scrutinizing her face as she allowed those unguarded thoughts to cross her mind. She quickly tried to compose her features into something that only looked tired—*which shouldn't be too hard, considering I've only had four hours of sleep,* she thought, trying not to smile.

"So you'd rather spend the day with that woman—" Sylvia began.

"Ma, her name is Karen. Rob loves her, and I like her," Teresa said. She looked at the newspaper hiding her father's face from view again, but she could see the paper crinkle as his fingers tightened. "If something happened to either of you or Rob, you and Pop would have to live with letting all this time go by and not speaking to him. How would you forgive yourselves if that happened? And you'd have nobody to blame but yourselves." She stood and pushed her chair back in. "I think y'uns should call Rob and invite him and Karen over for dinner next Sunday."

She left the frigid atmosphere of the kitchen and went upstairs to call Rob. "Please be awake," she whispered, using the phone in her parents' room. "Happy New Year," she said when Karen answered. "What are you two doing for dinner today?"

"Nothing much," Karen said. "I bought pork and sauerkraut. We'll have football on all day. Why?"

Teresa hesitated. "I just wondered if you'd mind two more. I'll bring extra food," she added quickly.

"We've got plenty," Karen said. "We'd love to see Ellie again. And you, too, of course."

Teresa could hear the amusement in Karen's voice at her clumsy attempt to wrangle an invitation for Ellie. "Great. We'll see you about noon?"

"Sounds good."

She called Ellie quickly. "Hey, it's all set. I'll pick you up about eleven-thirty. Okay?"

"Okay."

Teresa could hear KC's little meow in the background. "I can't wait to see you again."

"Me, either. Bye."

"Bye."

As Teresa went back to her room, she heard low voices downstairs as her parents talked, but what they were talking about, she had no idea.

A few hours later, after her mother had left for church in a huff —"You call your godmother and tell her why you're not with us today"—Teresa pulled up at the curb in front of Ellie's apartment. A thought suddenly occurred to her....

How am I going to look at her now that I've seen her naked? Now that we've...? Teresa's face burned, remembering that Ellie had seen her naked, too—well, close enough. "She's seen parts of you no one else ever has except your doctor." She chuckled as she reached for the door handle and got out of the car.

"Hey, Teresa."

She turned to find Sullivan on the sidewalk. "Hi, Sullivan."

"Here to see Ellie?"

Teresa nodded. "We're going to my brother's for dinner," she said and immediately felt guilty at his crestfallen expression. "I'll save some leftovers for you."

He smiled. "Have a good time. I can tell Ellie you're here."

"No need."

They both turned to see Ellie coming down the sidewalk. Teresa was mesmerized. How could she have grown more beautiful in just a few hours? She was radiant as she smiled at Teresa. Sullivan mumbled something about seeing them later, but Teresa wasn't sure if either of them replied.

They both got into the VW where they sat staring at each other.

"Hi," Teresa said at last.

"Hi," Ellie said with a musical laugh. She reached for Teresa's hand. "Are you okay?"

Teresa nodded. "Yes. You?"

"I'm wonderful."

Teresa couldn't remember now why she thought it might feel awkward to see Ellie after last night. She briefly considered calling Rob and Karen to say they wouldn't be coming over after all.

"We should go," Ellie said, as if reading Teresa's mind. "They're expecting us."

Reluctantly, Teresa turned the ignition.

"But we can come back here later," Ellie added with a wicked gleam in her eye that made Teresa blush again.

***

Lying in bed late that night, Teresa remembered with a pang of guilt that she'd forgotten to go by the store and leave food out for Dogman and Lucy. By the time they left Rob and Karen, Teresa had only had thoughts of being alone with Ellie. They hadn't gone back to bed, but they had spent a long time sitting on the couch, kissing and holding each other before Teresa reluctantly left for home as they both had to work tomorrow.

She wondered if she should run over to leave food now, but the bedside clock read nearly midnight, and she was tired.

"I'll leave extra tomorrow," she whispered, rolling on her side.

Tomorrow. Tomorrow, she and Ellie would head back to their normal lives, except nothing felt normal any more. It was hard to quiet the jumble of emotions tumbling around inside her. Karen and Rob had been great—it already felt like they and Ellie were old friends. At one point, Teresa had been standing at the stove, stirring a glaze for the pork roast, watching Ellie from across the room. Ellie and Karen were talking. It had only been a moment. Ellie glanced up and met Teresa's gaze with eyes so clear and full of love, and it struck Teresa—*no one has ever looked at me that way.* And no one ever would again. Even if, God knows how, Ellie was no longer in her life somewhere in a distant future, and Teresa met someone else, it would never again feel like this, *because I'll never be the same.* Ellie had changed her forever, and it somehow seemed appropriate that this sea change should have happened at the New Year.

Lying alone in the dark, the smile on Teresa's face slid away as she realized she had no one she could share this happiness with. She, who had never had a secret of her own to keep before, now had one so fragile and so precious that it felt as if her entire world balanced precariously on her ability to keep it safe.

CHAPTER 19

"Damn."

A couple of rats scurried away as the VW's headlights swept by the trash can where Dogman's dinner and Lucy's bowl of food sat. The rats had been in the food again. It was the fourth night in a row that the food had sat untouched.

Teresa got out of the car and grabbed a broom to shoo the rats away. She scraped the plate into the trash bag inside the can and poured Lucy's dog food back into the bag in her car.

"I don't owe them dinner every night," she grumbled to herself. "Just because I didn't bring them food one night, they're punishing me by not coming back?"

But her angry muttering didn't stop her from feeling guilty about not leaving them dinner on New Year's Day. She hadn't seen any sign of them for almost a week.

Still muttering, she unlocked the back security grate and let herself into the store. She went out front and began sweeping the store's entrance and sidewalk. Mrs. Schiavo came out a few minutes later and handed Teresa the loaves of old bread. The crowd that gathered was much more orderly these days. A couple of times, when scuffles had broken out, Teresa had simply turned around and taken the rest of the bread back inside. "No manners, no bread," she said over her shoulder, closing the bakery door and locking it. Mrs. Schiavo cackled and shook her head.

This morning, everyone waited calmly for their bread. A few people even said, "Thank you." Teresa was getting to know their faces. There was a young woman there most mornings, a baby on her hip. Teresa always saved her a whole loaf. There was an old man whose left hand had no fingers, only a thumb; he was grizzled and stooped and Teresa wondered what his story was. She began to wonder what all their stories were.

"No one dreams of ending up on the street," Ellie had said to her once when she talked about buying extra sandwiches from Louise. "It can happen to anyone. All it takes is one illness—lose your job, medical bills. You get behind on your rent or your mortgage and your life starts to fall apart around you like dominoes, then—one day, you find yourself out here."

"But isn't there help?" Teresa had asked. "Shelters? Employment services?"

Ellie had looked at her almost pityingly. "How do you fill out a job application with no address or telephone number? How do you dress for an interview when you haven't had a shower or clean clothes for weeks or months? Even if you get a job, how do you save for a security deposit for an apartment? Do you have any idea of the deposits you have to put down to get utilities? And some people just can't handle all that. For them, it's overwhelming. They'd prefer to be on the street."

Teresa handed out the last of the bread and took the empty tray back inside.

"It always smells so good in here," she said as Mrs. Schiavo set a doughnut and a cup of coffee down on a table for her.

"Sit down, Teresa," Mrs. Schiavo said, taking an adjacent chair.

Teresa sat.

Mrs. Schiavo peered up at her, her crinkled eyes scouring Teresa's face. "You're different lately."

Teresa felt her face get hot under Mrs. Schiavo's scrutiny. "What do you mean?"

Mrs. Schiavo shook her head. "I don't know exactly. But you're different. Is there a young man?"

"What? No," Teresa said with a laugh.

Mrs. Schiavo's eyes narrowed thoughtfully. "I thought maybe that was it."

"No," repeated Teresa, gulping her coffee so fast it scalded her throat, making her choke and cough. She took the rest of her doughnut with her. "Thanks."

She breathed a sigh as she went back over to the drugstore. *You're going to have to be more careful.* She wasn't sure exactly what it was that Mrs. Schiavo was picking up on, but she suspected there must be something different about her. She'd caught her mother staring at her from across the store the last couple of days. The weird part was, she felt no different and completely different—all at the same time.

"I'm the same as I've always been," she would have said if there had been anyone she could have talked to about this—reliable, hard-working, the dependable daughter—and yet, there was a side of her now that only seemed to have come to life since Ellie brought it to life. This side—and Teresa blushed even to think it—felt the thrill of being desired by someone. *She thinks I'm beautiful.* It made Teresa's heart leap every time she thought it. That knowledge seemed to stretch her, take her beyond herself and make her feel alive in ways she never had before.

She hadn't seen Ellie since she'd left her New Year's night, but it wasn't by her choice.

"I'd like to see you this weekend," she'd said to Ellie that night after they'd left Robbie and Karen.

"I'd like that, too," Ellie said, her arms around Teresa's neck as Teresa held her tightly. "But we shouldn't."

"Why not?"

Ellie lifted her face. "Your mother is already upset about you not spending the day with the family. We need to be careful."

Reluctantly, Teresa had agreed, but she didn't want to be careful. She felt reckless and defiant—things she had never been, not like Gianni or Bernie—but she knew nothing would get her mother's attention faster.

"Ellie's right," Teresa said aloud now as she turned the lights on and flipped the door sign to *open.* The telephone rang jarringly in the empty store.

"Benedetto's Drug Store, how may I help you?" Teresa said as she picked up.

Everything she had just been thinking about being careful was forgotten as Ellie's voice said, "It's been four whole days since I've seen you. You can help me by coming over tonight, if you're free."

Teresa laughed. "I close tonight, but I can be there by eight."

"I'll be waiting."

Ellie turned her head and listened to the soft sounds of Teresa's breathing. The winter sun made its way to the bed where the low slanting rays gilded the tiny hairs on Teresa's arm as it rested on the covers. Smiling, she nestled closer to Teresa's back and smelled her hair.

Never had she been happier than she'd been these last few weeks—*three weeks, two days and...about six hours, but who's counting?*

And it had taken three weeks and two days before Teresa could bring herself to let Ellie touch her, really touch her.

"Don't you want me to?" Ellie had whispered in the dark their third time together when Ellie slid her hand under the panties

Teresa still refused to take off, fingers moving through the curls there, cupping the warmth and beginning to work their way into the wetness. Each time, Teresa caught Ellie's hand to stop her. She could tell Teresa wanted it, too, could hear her moan a little from her desire, but Ellie never pushed, only saying, "You know I'll wait until you're ready."

She let Teresa explore her body, feeling a little guilty about the pleasure she was receiving, but she understood. Every now and then, Katie and Father Patrick would pop into her head and she could feel herself close in, like a flower folding its petals against the cold, so she understood why Teresa couldn't open up. Teresa was learning quickly where Ellie liked to be touched and how she liked to be kissed—featherlight kisses on her ears caused goose bumps to erupt everywhere, and when Teresa flicked her tongue over Ellie's rigid nipples, there was an explosion of sensation that was almost enough to push her over the edge before Teresa even touched her between her legs.

Last night, Teresa hadn't stopped Ellie as she tugged Teresa's underpants down and tossed them to the floor. She hadn't protested as Ellie hovered over her, gently lowering herself and allowing Teresa to feel their full nakedness, skin to skin, breast to breast, crotch to crotch. Ellie had taken her time, her hands exploring Teresa's curves while her mouth teased and tickled Teresa's breasts, kissed her ears and neck. At last, Teresa, biting her lip, had opened her legs, inviting Ellie's touch for the first time. Tenderly, patiently, Ellie had stroked, waiting for Teresa's body to tell her what she liked, moving with her as her excitement mounted and hung, suspended for an agonizingly long time before her orgasm shook her. Teresa's legs clamped on Ellie's hand, holding it there where Ellie could feel the continued pulsing against her fingers.

She laid her head on Teresa's shoulder. "Are you okay?" she whispered.

Teresa nodded, wiping tears away, still breathing raggedly. She wrapped her arms around Ellie and held her tightly. "It was just so much more than I thought it would be."

Ellie moved her hand, making Teresa gasp. "And that was only the beginning."

Afterward, they'd lain cuddled together, drifting off into a satisfied sleep. Ellie wasn't sure how much time had passed when she was startled awake by Teresa's jumping up.

"I've got to get home!" Teresa said, looking at Ellie's bedside clock.

"You could just stay," Ellie said sleepily. "Tomorrow, or I should say today, is Saturday.

Teresa looked down at Ellie as she held up the covers invitingly. A slow smile broke across her face. "Might do my mother good to think I'm up to no good."

Ellie sighed now watching the sunlight play on the contour of Teresa's ear. Propping up on her elbow, she nuzzled into Teresa's hair and whispered, "I'm glad you stayed, but I don't want you to be late to work."

Teresa stirred, rolling onto her back and stretching. She smiled when she saw Ellie. "Good morning."

Ellie bent her head and kissed her. "Good morning. Do you want to shower? I'll make some coffee."

"I didn't bring any other clothes," Teresa said. "I hadn't planned on staying here."

Ellie looked at her with a satisfied smile. "From now on, you'd better leave a few things here. Just put your pharmacist jacket on. No one will notice."

Teresa snorted. "Believe me, Sylvia Benedetto will notice."

Ellie got out of bed. "Here's my robe. You can wear this." She looked down uncertainly at the intense expression on Teresa's face. "What?"

"You are just so beautiful," Teresa said reverently. She slid out of bed also and came to Ellie, taking her into her arms. "I feel like I'm in a dream—one I've had my whole life but could never let myself actually live."

Ellie stood on tiptoe to give Teresa a kiss, a kiss that Teresa returned with a passion that made both their insides burn again.

"I really do have to shower and get to work," Teresa groaned.

Ellie chuckled as Teresa pulled on the robe and opened the door to a meowing KC.

A few minutes later, Teresa was back, dressed in her clothes from last evening, her thick, dark hair still damp. She found Ellie in the kitchen, waiting for the coffee to brew and stroking KC as she ate.

"Well, I don't know about my mother," Teresa said wryly. "But you're going to have some explaining to do to Sullivan."

Ellie's eyes widened. "I forgot about him."

⟶ ⟝⟞ ⟵

"Don't push me."

"I didn't push you, but there's no room."

Teresa was crammed into an elevator with all four of the aunts. She looked over their heads at the elevator inspection notice behind the little glass panel and wondered if their group exceeded the weight capacity.

The elevator chugged up to the third floor of Allegheny General, and spit the group out as the doors opened.

"Which way?"

"It says Maternity, this way," said Teresa, leading them to the right.

They passed the nursery and stopped, scanning the tiny cribs with their pink and blue bundles.

"There!"

"Where?"

"Third from the right." Teresa pointed. The aunts jostled one another, trying to see the newest member of the family. All Teresa could see was a tightly swaddled cocoon in a pink knit cap.

They stood for several minutes, the aunts craning their necks to get a better look.

"Let's go see how Francesca is doing," Anita said at last.

They found Francesca's room and burst in. Chris was there, wearing his white coat over scrubs. He gave Francesca a quick kiss.

"Don't let them tire her out," he said in a low voice to Teresa. "How are the kids?"

"They're fine. I left them watching television when Ma and Pop got home."

He glanced at his watch. "I've got to get back to the OR."

"We won't stay long," Teresa said.

The aunts were gathered around the bed, patting Francesca's hand, straightening and tucking in her sheets, plumping her pillow, all talking at the same time. Francesca looked up at Teresa.

"You okay?" Teresa mouthed since she would have had to shout to be heard.

Francesca nodded with a tired smile.

"What's her name?" Anita asked over the tumult and the others quieted.

"Annalisa Maria," said Francesca.

Four pair of eyes instantly teared up.

"You named her after Mama," said Luisa, dabbing at her eyes with an embroidered handkerchief.

Francesca nodded. The aunts gathered closer to the bed, wringing Francesca's hand and kissing her, but Anita shuffled over to Teresa. She took Teresa's hand in her own.

"I remember like it was yesterday, when it was you in the nursery we came to see," she said.

Teresa smiled. "I was the one in the extra large crib?"

Anita clucked her tongue. "You were a beautiful baby. Not all wrinkly and shriveled like some of them are." A shadow passed over her face.

"Do you need to sit and rest?" Teresa asked.

"Just for a minute." Anita lowered herself with a sigh into the armchair near the wall. She looked up at Teresa. "Do you ever wish it was you?"

Teresa blinked. "What, having a baby?"

Anita nodded.

"No! Not at all," Teresa said. She looked at her aunt. "What about you, Nita? Do you ever wish you'd gotten married, had a family?"

To Teresa's astonishment, Anita's eyes filled with sudden tears, but she brushed her hand quickly over her face. "Don't be ridiculous!" She heaved herself back to her feet and returned to Francesca's bedside.

Teresa frowned at the abrupt change in her aunt's demeanor. She let the aunts hover and fuss a few more minutes, but when her sister gave her a pleading look, she said, "I think we need to let Francesca rest now. We can come back tomorrow."

With more hugs and kisses from all of the aunts, it still took several minutes for Teresa to get everyone out of the room and headed back toward the elevator. She tried to catch Anita's eye again, but Anita charged to the front of the group as they left the hospital and got into the back seat of the Cadillac for the trip home.

CHAPTER 20

Teresa was kneeling on the floor, shelving a shipment of antibiotics when she heard the bell announce someone coming into the store. The low murmur of voices travelled back to her for a few minutes, and then Sylvia called in an unnaturally loud voice, "I'm going to run home and see about dinner." Teresa looked at her watch.

"Ma, it's only three o'clock," she said. She got to her feet and froze.

Bernie was seated at the coffee counter and Sylvia was already closing the back door.

Teresa turned back to the pharmacy, breaking down the box the antibiotics had come in as she stalled. If she had thought her mother's silence about her nights away from home meant that Sylvia had decided to let her live her own life, *boy, was I wrong.*

Teresa and Bernie had had their share of petty arguments growing up, and always, it had been Teresa who initiated making up.

"But not this time," Teresa had insisted to herself again and again since she'd stormed out of the D'Armelio house nearly two months ago. She and Bernie had never gone this long without talking—*hell, we'd hardly gone two days without talking.* Guilt had pricked at her, prompting her again and again to pick the phone up or go over, but Teresa had stubbornly refused. Bernie hadn't just insulted her. That, she could have dealt with, as she had done her whole life, but when Bernie had derided Teresa's relationship, she'd also insulted Ellie; at least that was how it felt to Teresa. *Funny, how much easier it was to stay angry when I was angry for Ellie.*

At last, she pushed the flattened box into the trash can and came out from behind the pharmacy counter, pulling the door shut behind her.

"School going okay?" she asked lamely as she stepped behind the coffee counter.

"Yeah," said Bernie, who was playing with a stack of sugar packets.

"Cappuccino?"

"Sure."

Teresa busied herself for several minutes, making two cappuccinos. In the mirror behind the espresso machine, she could feel Bernie's gaze locked on her as she moved about. She refused to look up, but when she could no longer avoid it, she turned to face Bernie, setting a steaming mug in front of her as she cradled the second in her hands.

"So, you and my mother are in cahoots now?" She met Bernie's eyes for the first time.

"She's worried about you."

Teresa took a sip of her cappuccino and didn't say anything. Bernie took a drink as well. The silence between them stretched on uncomfortably.

Don't say a word, said Teresa to herself.

Bernie seemed unaccustomed to this strangely stubborn Teresa. She squirmed on her stool and finally said, "I'm sorry. About the things I said."

Teresa nodded but still said nothing.

Bernie frowned. "Aren't you going to say anything?"

"Apology accepted," Teresa said coolly.

Bernie set her cup down and leaned her elbows on the counter. "C'mon, Bennie. I really am sorry. I shouldn't have... I just didn't know what to think, you know? I mean..." Her voice trailed off.

Teresa's eyes narrowed. "You didn't say anything to my mother did you?"

"Jesus, no!" Bernie's eyes got big. "What kind of friend do you think I am?" Apparently, the expression on Teresa's face said exactly what kind of friend she thought Bernie was, because Bernie burst out, "Holy shit, Bennie. Give me some credit. I mean, okay, the whole idea kind of shook me for a while, but I've had some time to think about it. You're my oldest friend. Nothing comes between that. Right?"

Teresa bit her lip. "Right."

Bernie sagged with relief, a puzzled look on her face. "So, are you two really...?"

Teresa frowned. "I am not going to talk about that."

Bernie blinked. "Okay."

Another long, uncomfortable silence crackled in the air between them as they negotiated the new boundaries of their friendship, carefully testing to see what was safe and what was not.

"How was your New Year?" Teresa asked at last, searching for some new topic of conversation.

"It was kind of quiet," Bernie said with a shrug. "Tom was at a company thing with his wife, and—"

Teresa heard the unspoken, "—and you and I weren't speaking," but she remembered where she'd been on New Year's Eve and felt the color rise in her cheeks.

Bernie's gaze searched her face curiously, and Teresa turned away suddenly, busying herself cleaning the espresso machine.

"You want to go shopping this weekend?" Bernie asked.

Teresa's heart sank. She really, really wanted to see Ellie this weekend, but she didn't want to hurt Bernie's feelings just as they were finally talking again.

Bernie seemed to sense Teresa's hesitation. "You could call Ellie and see if she wants to come with us."

"You would be okay with that?" Teresa asked, her back still to Bernie as she continued cleaning.

"Sure. As long as the little piss-ant doesn't jump on me again about being a racist," Bernie said.

Teresa grinned. "I think we can swing that." She turned back around.

"Okay. You call her," Bernie said. She looked at Teresa. "We're good?"

Teresa nodded. "We're good."

<hr />

"I'm going to get more coffee," Ellie said to Linda and Suzanne. "Can I get y'uns anything?"

Suzanne tipped her cup and saw that it was empty. "Sure, I'll take some. Cream—"

"—no sugar," Ellie finished for her. "I know." She took Suzanne's cup with her back to the staff room where a half pot of coffee sat in the coffee maker. She refilled their cups of coffee. With a shake of her head, she dampened a paper towel and wiped down the counter, which was littered with granules of sugar and creamer, along with empty sugar packets and plastic stirrers. "Do they do this at home?" she muttered aloud.

"Probably."

Ellie jumped and turned to find Aaron Myers standing there. He pushed the door shut behind him.

"How about making a fresh pot?" He pulled a chair out from the table and sat.

Silently, Ellie refilled the coffee basket with fresh coffee grounds and went to the sink for water, feeling Myers's eyes on her the whole time. She got a fresh pot brewing and reached for her cup and Suzanne's.

"It'll be ready in a few minutes," she said.

"Why don't you wait and have some fresh?" he said, crossing his legs so that his foot blocked her path to the door.

"I should get back to my window," Ellie said, but realized, with two cups in her hands and the door now closed, she couldn't open it without setting one cup down on the table. Forcing herself to smile, she said, "Could you open the door, please?"

For a moment, she wondered if he would, but at last he stood and reached for the doorknob, forcing Ellie to brush up against him as she squeezed through the narrow opening he left for her.

Linda looked up as Ellie came back out to the tellers' windows. She took a second look at Ellie's face. "You okay?"

"Fine," Ellie said with a dark glance in Aaron Myers's direction as he sauntered out of the staff room to go back upstairs to the loan offices. She noticed he didn't have a coffee cup in his hand.

It was late morning when Ellie heard, "Good morning, Teresa." She dropped a handful of change with a loud clatter as she looked up to see Teresa standing at Linda's window. She scrambled to scoop up the dropped coins and turned back to her customer, but she could feel the heat in her face. She stole a glance in Teresa's direction as her customer left, and Teresa pointed to her watch. Ellie gave a small nod and waited impatiently for the clock to crawl toward noon.

"Going out again?" Suzanne asked as Ellie locked her drawer at the first chime and headed for the staff room.

"Want some fresh air at lunch," she said, hurrying back to the lockers to grab her coat and backpack.

The March sunlight was weak but felt good on her face as she walked quickly to Falkowski's, where Teresa already had a table in a back corner.

"Hi," Ellie said breathlessly. She hung her coat on the back of her chair and sat.

"Hi."

The light in Teresa's eyes made Ellie's insides tingle.

"I already ordered so you have time to eat and get back," Teresa said.

"Thanks." Ellie's hand itched to hold Teresa's, but she busied herself spreading her napkin on her lap.

"I'm glad you could get away today," Teresa was saying. "You're sure it wasn't a problem?"

"Not a problem." Ellie opened her mouth to say something more just as the waitress brought their soup and sandwiches. She waited until the waitress left before leaning nearer and saying in a low voice, "I wasn't sure I could wait until tonight to see you." She chuckled at the color that rose in Teresa's cheeks, and picked up her sandwich.

They ate in silence for a few minutes, Ellie keeping an eye on her watch.

"I have a favor to ask you." Teresa glanced up from her lunch. "Two favors, actually."

Ellie sat up, Teresa's tone making her wary. "Yes?"

"Well, Bernie came by and we talked, kind of." Teresa paused, stirring her soup. "She'd like to go out, with us."

There was a loud clang as Ellie's spoon dropped into her bowl.

"What?" Ellie coughed a little as she choked. "With both of us? She said that?"

"Yes." Teresa smiled. "She knows I won't talk about, you know, us. But she wanted to go shopping and asked me to invite you. So will you? Go with us?"

Ellie met Teresa's gaze, but didn't answer immediately.

Teresa leaned closer and said in a low voice, "I know it's going to be hard, every time we take one of these steps, to do things with Bernie or my family, but it's a start."

Ellie took a drink of her water. "Okay. I like Bernie. I'll go. What's the other favor?"

Teresa stalled, chewing and swallowing before she said, "Annalisa's baptism is a week from Sunday. I'd like you to come. Francesca asked me to invite you especially. And Karen will need someone to sit with."

Ellie's head snapped up. "Really? They're coming?"

Teresa nodded, smiling. "I talked to Francesca and Chris. I told them I would only be godmother if they asked Robbie to be godfather."

"What did your parents say?"

"Well, I think Ma was relieved. Pop just grunted and walked away, but this allows everyone to get over themselves and come together without anyone having to apologize. It's not perfect, but I hope it works."

"I think it's brilliant," Ellie said. "If your father is anything like your brother, then the two of them would never have swallowed their pride. This way, they're doing it for Francesca and the baby." She frowned. "What about your priest? I thought the Church would only let practicing Catholics be godparents."

"Our priest has known Robbie for years," Teresa said. "I know he's bending the rules a bit, but he said as long as I was the godmother, he'd allow it. Karen won't be allowed to receive Communion, and they'll never recognize Rob and Karen's marriage, but this is the best I could do."

She looked questioningly at Ellie. "So, will you come? Please?"

Ellie met Teresa's eyes as she fought with herself. Teresa reached under the table to squeeze her knee.

"I know you said you'd never go back to church, but it won't be like it was before," Teresa said. "For me?"

Ellie took Teresa's hand under cover of the tablecloth. "For you."

"Most Sacred Heart of Jesus, we ask that You accept the soul of our dearly departed sister, Ellen Ryan, into the light of Your presence. We cannot know the depths of Your mercy, but we beg You to forgive her sins, and all the sins of all the souls in Purgatory. Lord, those who die still live in Your presence. We pray that one day, we will be united again to sing Your praise, forever and ever. Amen."

The social worker's arm settled around Ellie's shoulders, but Ellie shrugged it off and moved away. It was meant to be a comforting gesture. She knew that, but she didn't care. In the trunk of the social worker's car were two suitcases and a backpack—all of the things Ellie could take from the house. From the cemetery, she would be driven to her new foster family. Earlier that morning, she had toured her home for the last time, still filled with furniture that would be auctioned off in a few weeks to go toward the medical bills, followed by the sale of the house. She'd had to leave all of her mother's clothes, their books and dishes, most of Daniel's varsity letters and trophies, his guitar. She'd gone through the house, plucking things here and there—her mother's few pieces of jewelry, the family photo album, the calligraphy she'd made for her mother, a few of Daniel's favorite albums. Those things had gone into one suitcase, her clothes into the other.

She looked at the group gathered there as the prayers droned on over her mother's coffin. The priest, a man from the funeral home who had to be there, the social worker who had never met her mother, and her. That was it. Four people standing around a hole in the ground. It was a gorgeous, sun-filled spring day, but she shivered as her mother's coffin was lowered into the ground. She glanced around the cemetery, hoping against hope that, maybe, Daniel would be there and they could go home together. But he wasn't. The priest's words of forgiveness were meaningless. Her mother had never done anything to hurt anyone, had never done anything but try to take care of Ellie and Daniel after she was left alone to raise them without a husband. How could she need forgiveness?

Ellie sat on the sofa in the pre-dawn twilight of her apartment and wiped her cheeks dry. KC lay curled up next to her in the dark. She'd sworn, after Mrs. Locke took her to see Father Patrick, that she would never set foot in a church again, but she was going to do just that in a couple of hours. She sniffed. There hadn't been a power on this earth that could have induced her to violate that oath—until Teresa.

It frightened Ellie a little that her love for Teresa could sway her that much. For years, she'd longed to love someone—and to be loved—to feel that kind of connection with another human being for the first time since losing her mother. *No, that's not true. For the first time since Katie lied.* But she was just beginning to see the risks of opening herself to that kind of love and the things it could make her do.

She knew Louise would say, "Darling, you deserve to be loved. You've got a good heart."

She hugged her knees to her chest. She was a survivor. She'd gotten along by herself for seven years—seven lonely years.

No, seven safe years, countered a stubborn voice in her head.

She was startled by the ringing of her telephone in the kitchen. She jumped up to answer it.

"Did I wake you?" From Teresa's whispered voice, Ellie knew she must be calling from inside the kitchen pantry again.

"No, you didn't wake me."

"Why were you up at this hour?"

Ellie didn't answer.

"It'll be okay," Teresa murmured.

Ellie swallowed. "How did you know?"

"I know. At least a little," Teresa said. "I know this will be hard, but it means a lot to me that you'll be there. And I really appreciate that you'll be there for Karen."

Ellie snorted. "I didn't think there was anything in this world that could ever get me in a church again."

She could hear a muffled chuckle as Teresa said, "You'd better stop before this power goes to my head."

"You have more power over me than you know," Ellie said softly.

For several seconds, there was only the sound of their breathing.

"I'll pick you up at nine," Teresa said at last.

A few hours later, Ellie sat sandwiched between Teresa and Rob. Sylvia and Lou and all of the aunts sat in the pew in front of them with Francesca and Chris and the kids, while Bernie and her mother sat in the pew behind. Even Gianni and Angelina were there. He, of course, had given Ellie a smug leer, and she had rolled her eyes. She glanced up now at Rob and saw the tightness of his jaw. If she had thought she would be the most uncomfortable one here, she was wrong. Sylvia and the aunts had given him tearful hugs while Karen tried to hang back, but Rob pulled her forward, forcing them to at least greet her, even if there were no hugs exchanged.

"Baby steps," Karen had whispered to Ellie after, and Ellie had to stifle a laugh.

It was weird, how automatic it was—the congregation's responses to the words the priest said, when to stand or sit or kneel. Little things had changed in the Mass, but mostly it was the same as Ellie remembered. *Maybe that's one of things people find comforting about it*, she realized. The sameness was something they could count on. She detected movement out of the corner of her eye and saw that Rob had reached over for Karen's hand. She felt like taking his other one. Teresa must have seen it, too, because she nudged her thigh over until it was firmly squeezed against Ellie's. Ellie glanced up to find Teresa watching her and it was all she could do not to press her face to Teresa's shoulder.

At the end of the Mass, most of the congregation left, which took a long time as everyone kept stopping to see the baby and congratulate Sylvia and Lou on another grandchild. At last, only a small group was left. The family all moved into the front two pews with a good bit of arguing over who should sit where while the parents and godparents were called up to the baptismal font.

"Rob looks very handsome," Ellie whispered to Karen.

"So does Teresa," Karen whispered back. Startled, Ellie looked up to find Karen smiling at her.

Teresa did look handsome, dressed in a navy pantsuit.

They watched as Teresa and Rob stepped forward, Teresa taking the baby and holding her while the priest intoned the baptismal blessing and poured water over her forehead. The water must have been cold, because little Annalisa let out a startled squawk. Everyone chuckled at such a big cry coming from such a little thing, and soon it was over.

There was more arguing and confusion as the family gathered for photos and the baby was passed around. At last, Teresa whispered something to Rob and came to Ellie.

"Come on," she said.

"Aren't we going to your house?" Ellie asked as Teresa led the way to the VW.

"We will, but we have a stop to make first," Teresa said.

Puzzled, Ellie got in. Teresa started the car and pulled out of the church parking lot. She drove a couple of blocks back toward Squirrel Hill before pulling over.

"Which cemetery are your parents buried in?" she asked.

"Why?" Ellie said, startled.

Teresa reached for her hand. "I know you were there at Christmas time, but we celebrated a new member of my family today. I have a couple of wreaths for your parents' graves. I thought we should celebrate your family, too."

Ellie looked at her and burst into tears. All the feelings she'd just relived from her mother's burial washed over her—the desolation, the utter aloneness. If Teresa wondered, she didn't ask. She reached over and wrapped her arms around Ellie, holding her tightly.

"You're not alone anymore," she whispered as Ellie sobbed.

CHAPTER 21

"HAPPY BIRTHDAY, BABY GIRL."

Louise beamed at Ellie as she set a wrapped package down on the table and slid into the booth next to Bernie.

"You didn't have to do that," Ellie said. "Can I open it now?"

Louise laughed. "Yes, you can open it now."

Ellie eagerly pulled the wrapping paper off to reveal a leather case. "It's beautiful," she said, lifting it to smell the leather. "What is it?"

"It's a passport case," Louise said. "For when you travel."

"You going somewhere?" Bernie asked.

Ellie nodded. "Everywhere. Some day." She reached across the table to hug Louise. "Thank you. It's perfect. By the time I'm ready to go, I'll have everything I need."

"So what are you girls doing to celebrate?" Louise asked.

"I'm not sure," Ellie said with a puzzled shrug. She eyed Bernie. "She won't tell me."

Bernie laughed. "It's a surprise. But first, we have to have burgers and shakes."

Louise jotted their orders. "You got it," she said, getting to her feet. "Coming right up."

"So, where are you taking us?" Teresa asked suspiciously when Louise had left them.

Bernie grinned wickedly. "You'll see."

— ⁓ —

"Where are you taking us?" Teresa asked again an hour later. She looked nervously right and left as she drove slowly down a street with run-down buildings on either side. Shadowy figures were visible on the corners and in the alleys.

Bernie checked the directions on the paper in her hand. "This is what she said. Keep going."

"What who said?" Ellie asked, leaning forward from the back seat.

"A place I thought y'uns might want to check out," Bernie said. "I been talking to one of the professors in the Women's Studies department and she told me about it."

"About what?" Teresa asked dubiously. "A place to go if you want to be robbed?"

"There." Bernie pointed.

"Where?"

"There, that sign on the left. Pull in there."

"Wild Sisters?" Ellie read.

"That's it," Bernie said, smiling.

"That's what?" Teresa's hands gripped the steering wheel tightly.

"Your kind of place," Bernie said, already opening her car door. "Come on."

Cautiously, Teresa got out. She locked the car, looking around at the surrounding buildings with distaste.

"I'll be right back." Ellie walked off into the darkness.

"Jesus Christ, where is she going?" Bernie muttered.

She and Teresa hurried after Ellie as she approached a group of people huddled around a fire burning in a trash barrel.

"Are you sure?" Ellie was saying when they caught up to her. The people gathered around the fire shook their head and turned their backs.

226

"What the fuck was that about?" Bernie hissed as they retraced their steps.

"They were different people than I usually see," Ellie said.

"No shit!"

"No," Teresa said in a low voice. "She's asking about her brother."

"Don't you know how dangerous that was?" Bernie demanded.

"Why? They wouldn't hurt me," Ellie said.

"Come on, you," Bernie urged. She took Teresa and Ellie by the arm and propelled them toward the entrance of Wild Sisters where a tall, burly woman stood guard. She was dressed in men's khakis and a button-down shirt with a necktie.

"Good evening, ladies," she said pleasantly. "IDs, please." She accepted their driver's licenses and scrutinized their birth dates. "Happy birthday," she said to Ellie. "Enjoy yourselves." She handed the licenses back and stepped aside to allow them in.

Bernie led the way to the cavernous interior of what looked like a converted warehouse with tables scattered about the floor, most of them already filled with groups of women. In fact, there wasn't a single man to be seen anywhere, including the waitstaff, all smartly dressed in shirts and ties, carrying dinner trays and drinks to the patrons at the tables. Bernie threaded her way to an empty table on the edge of the room, leaving Teresa and Ellie no choice but to follow.

"What kind of place is this?" Teresa asked over the loud hum of conversation.

Bernie picked up the drink menu. "I told you, your kind of place. Gay women, or I guess I should say Lesbians. With a capital L. That's what Judith said they like to be called."

"You mean everyone here is…?" Ellie looked around, her eyes wide.

"I assume so," Bernie said, looking around with open curiosity.

"Bernie," Teresa hissed, sinking low in her seat, trying to make herself invisible. "What are you doing? What if someone sees us?"

Bernie looked at her with a bemused smile as she lit a cigarette. "Well, then, I guess you'll have seen them, too, right? Jesus Christ, Bennie. It's just a club for women. It'll be like when we all used to dance together in school."

"Ladies, what can I get you to drink?" A server had just appeared at their table. When Teresa looked toward the exit, she said, "First time here?"

"Yes," Ellie said.

The server sat down at the fourth chair at their table. "I'm Jamie." She gestured around the room. "Everyone here knows the risks. No one would ever out anyone else. It's an unspoken rule." She smiled at Teresa. "You're among friends here."

Ellie placed a hand on Teresa's arm. "Please?"

Teresa looked back helplessly. "Budweiser?"

Jamie grinned and took Ellie and Bernie's orders. "Be right back." She returned in a couple of minutes with their drinks. "In about a half hour, the tables in the middle will all be moved to make room for dancing. Enjoy yourselves and just raise a hand if you need anything. I'll be watching." She laid a hand on Bernie's shoulder as she left them.

Ellie leaned toward Bernie and said, "I think you could have a new friend if you wanted one."

"Hmmph," Bernie grunted. "Who knows? Might be better than what I've had."

Teresa sipped her beer, trying to be nonchalant as she looked around, wondering if there was anyone here she knew. It wasn't long before people started getting up to move the tables in the middle of the floor as Jamie had said. Everyone shifted over to make room, and she watched women laughing and talking as they jostled. A haze of cigarette smoke hung over the room, swirling in the beams of light being cast by the large industrial fixtures hanging from the ceiling.

At the first notes of music, it seemed nearly the entire crowd of women moved as one to the cleared space to dance. Teresa watched, fascinated at the sight of women dancing openly with one another to a Donna Summers song.

"Want to dance?" Ellie asked.

"Um, not yet," Teresa said, taking a long pull from her bottle of beer.

An older woman with very short gray hair approached their table. "Care to dance, sweetheart?" she asked Bernie.

Teresa choked on her beer as Bernie shrugged and said, "Why not?" She laughed as she watched Bernie disappear into the crowd.

"They look like they're having fun," Ellie said, and Teresa caught the wistfulness in her voice.

With a resolute thunk, she set her beer down. "Okay." She stood and held a hand out.

They edged into the jostling crowd, dancing now to the Bee Gees.

"I haven't danced since Francesca's wedding," Teresa said, leaning to speak into Ellie's ear.

"I haven't since high school," Ellie said, laughing.

"I knew letting Bernie in on our secret would be dangerous," Teresa said.

Ellie twirled. "I love Bernie!"

The next song was a slow one, and Ellie moved into Teresa's arms before she could protest. At the feel of Ellie's body pressed close to hers, her arms wrapped around Teresa's neck as they swayed, just like all the other couples around them, Teresa let herself relax. She rested her cheek against Ellie's hair and closed her eyes. Just as the last notes of that song died away, the first drumbeats of Sister

Sledge's "We Are Family" thumped through the speakers, and the entire crowd was on its feet, arms swaying as everyone sang along.

Teresa had to shout to ask, "Why are they reacting like this?"

"Because that's what we are," said a woman next to them who had overheard. "Gays and Lesbians. That's what we call each other—family."

They caught sight of Bernie, now dancing with another woman. Teresa chuckled. "She looks like she's having a good time."

Ellie rose up on her toes and kissed Teresa on the cheek. "So am I."

Teresa stood at the stove, sprinkling a little more crushed oregano into the pot of sauce simmering there. From behind her, she heard Anita say, "Those should be a little smaller."

She turned around to see Anita showing Ellie what size to roll the meatballs. Ellie looked up and smiled. Karen and Rob came in carrying a bag of bread. Teresa turned back to the sauce, listening to the loud voices coming from throughout the house. She couldn't remember ever feeling this happy. Robbie and Karen were there most Sundays now, and Ellie was with them as well, though she hadn't returned to church again since the baptism.

"Sorry, but it's not going to happen," she said. "I did it that one time, for you."

Teresa herself hadn't been to Mass often lately, and when she did go, she didn't go to Communion. Her mother insisted it was a sin to go if she hadn't been to confession, and *I have no intention of confessing anything.* What was there to confess when she didn't feel she was doing anything wrong? But she knew her priest wouldn't agree. Neither would her mother. Sylvia was civil to Ellie, but Teresa could feel an undercurrent of disapproval when Ellie was around. Anita seemed to notice it as well, and stayed close to Ellie for which Teresa was grateful.

At least she was grateful until she heard, "let me show you some baby pictures of Teresa."

Teresa whipped around to find that they were done rolling meatballs, and Anita was leading Ellie from the kitchen. Ellie glanced back with an apologetic grin. Teresa groaned.

"What can I do to help?" Karen asked.

"Well, you can melt some garlic butter for the bread," Teresa said, getting a small saucepan out for her. "How are you and Rob?"

Karen peeled the wrapper off a stick of butter and dropped it into the pan. "We've waited a long time for this," she said. "I can't thank you enough."

"I didn't do anything," Teresa said.

"Yes, you did. You never cut him off. You made me feel welcome. Those things were huge by themselves," said Karen as she chopped a clove of garlic and scraped it into the pan. "But getting Francesca to ask him to be godfather... that meant a lot to him. To us."

Teresa looked at her. "I'm so glad you're both here."

Karen glanced out to the dining room where Anita and Ellie sat laughing over the photo album. "And Ellie?"

Teresa felt her face get hot. Karen laid a hand on her arm. "We're happy for you. You know that, right?"

Teresa met Karen's gaze for a long moment but simply nodded. "I know."

"You are so full of shit!"

"No, really." Sullivan skipped ahead so he could walk backward down the sidewalk and face them as he talked. "Just wait and see. In a few years, for just a couple hundred dollars, we'll all have personal computers on our desks and they'll be able to talk to one another."

"What could they possibly say that we can't just say like this?" Teresa asked.

"It's not this kind of talking," Sullivan said, and Ellie recognized the manic gleam in his eye, the one he got when he talked about his research. "We'll be able to talk to anyone, anywhere in the world. We'll have access to every library in the world. We'll be able to buy things over our computers and have them sent to our houses."

Bernie scoffed. "I can't wait to get out of my house. Why the hell would I want to sit on a computer in my house and have junk sent there?"

Ellie pushed open the door to the diner and led the way to a booth while Sullivan kept talking about how great this coming computer age was going to be. "It'd be good for him to have friends," she had pleaded with Teresa. "Friends other than me." But just now, she was regretting asking him to join them for an evening out.

"He doesn't get out much," Teresa had whispered to Bernie when they pulled up at the curb and Sullivan came bounding down the stairs behind Ellie.

"All right, Rod Serling," Bernie interrupted now as they slid into their booth. "Shut up and look the menu over. I'm starving."

Teresa grinned and picked up her menu. It had been weeks since Bernie had mentioned Tom. She had no idea if that meant they hadn't seen each other, or if Bernie just wasn't saying, but Teresa liked this happier Bernie much better than the brooding one who was always obsessing about her married lover. She loved that Bernie and Ellie got along, joking and laughing together. If Bernie ever resented it when Teresa dropped her off at home and then took Ellie home so they could have time alone together, she never gave any hint of it.

A different waitress came to take their order. Ellie looked around.

"Where's Louise tonight?"

The waitress glanced around the table. "You're Ellie, right?"

Ellie nodded.

"She just decided to take an evening off for a change," the waitress said.

Ellie frowned a bit. "Well, tell her I'm sorry I missed her."

"I will." The server took their orders and left to get their drinks.

"She deserves a night off every now and then," Teresa said, nudging Ellie with her shoulder.

"You're right," Ellie said, but she still looked worried.

They ate dinner as Bernie and Sullivan got into a debate over the relative merits of *Star Trek* versus *Star Wars*.

"This will go on all night," Teresa muttered in Ellie's ear.

"I wouldn't have picked you for a *Star Trek* fan," Ellie said to Bernie a while later as they walked back to the car.

"William Shatner," Bernie said with a sly smile.

"Let's leave the car here," Teresa said. "There's a bookstore nearby I've been wanting to get to."

Once in the bookstore, all four of them headed in different directions. Teresa was browsing the fiction aisle, a copy of Stephen King's *Firestarter* in her hand, when Bernie called from the end of the aisle.

"There you are."

She was carrying an upside-down book, a puzzled expression on her face.

"What are you reading?" Teresa asked.

"*The Joy of Lesbian Sex.*"

"What?" Teresa sputtered.

Bernie held the book out. "Look at this." But Teresa was already walking away from her. "Wait," Bernie called, hurrying after her.

"Bernie," Teresa hissed. "What are you doing?"

"What?" Bernie asked. "I'm looking at a goddamned book. I can look at a book for Christ's sake."

"Not that one," Teresa whispered. She looked around to see if anyone was within hearing.

"Why?" Bernie said in a normal tone.

"Lower your voice!"

"Why?" Bernie asked, even louder. "Have you looked at these drawings?" She held the book out again. Teresa looked helplessly for an escape route. "Have you and Ellie tried this one?"

Teresa covered her eyes with her hand.

"Hmmm, no. We haven't."

Teresa took her hand away to find Ellie standing there looking over Bernie's shoulder at the book. She tilted her head until she was almost upside-down.

Teresa could hear them laughing behind her as she took the opportunity to hurry up to the cash register to buy her book. She went outside where the cool April air felt good on her face.

She saw movement on the other side of the street in an alley between two buildings. There was a man with a dog. She hurried across, dodging cars, and ran to the entrance of the alley.

"Lucy!" she called. She took several steps into the alley.

The man turned, and the dog growled. Up close, Teresa could see that it wasn't Dogman and Lucy. Other shadows moved in the darkness, and Teresa saw that there were perhaps ten other people there.

"Sorry," she said. "I thought you were someone else."

Her heart leapt into her throat as the shadow people moved to flank her. She backed toward the entrance to the alley, but found her way blocked.

"Teresa!"

Bernie, Ellie and Sullivan trotted to the alley. The shadow people melted back into the darkness.

"What the hell are you doing?" Bernie demanded.

"I thought I saw someone I knew," Teresa said shakily, her heart still pounding.

"Come on," Bernie said. She grabbed Teresa by the arm and pulled her back out into the light.

Ellie, though, stepped into the alley and called out, "Daniel? Do any of you know a man named Daniel?"

"Go away," was the only reply.

Teresa took Ellie by the hand. "Come on. Let's go."

They walked back to where the car was parked. With some effort, Sullivan stuffed himself into the Volkswagen's back seat beside Ellie. Teresa drove Bernie home.

"You forgot your bag," Teresa called out when Bernie got out of the car. She held up a bag from the bookstore.

Bernie bent down to look into the car and grinned. "That's for you and Ellie."

CHAPTER 22

ELLIE QUIETLY SLIPPED OUT of bed and pulled on sweatpants and a sweatshirt. Creeping over to her dresser, she tugged out the bottom drawer where her drawing pad and pencils were kept. She sat in the chair near the window and looked back at the bed.

The light that came into this bedroom was one of the things she loved about this apartment, and right now, the early morning sunlight was spilling across Teresa's body as she lay sleeping. No longer shy about being naked with Ellie, Teresa was finally learning to relax and enjoy the pleasure she and Ellie shared when they made love. She lay now, one arm over her head, one breast exposed, the bedcovers making undulating shadows as they draped over her curves. KC was curled in a tight ball next to Teresa's leg. Outside, birds began to wake in the early morning, and Ellie's pencil flew in whispery scratches as she sketched.

She had a very good likeness laid out on the paper by the time Teresa stirred.

"What are you doing?" Teresa asked, rubbing her eyes.

"Drawing you."

Teresa sat up. "I didn't know you drew." She looked down and her eyes widened. "You're drawing me?" She pulled the sheet up to her neck.

Ellie smiled and got up. "Relax. See how beautiful you were?"

Teresa stared open-mouthed at the image on the paper. Ellie watched her, trying to tell what she thought, but all Teresa said was, "Could I see your others?"

Hesitantly, Ellie flipped to other pages in her drawing pad. Loose pages fell out upon the bed. Teresa picked them up. Something in her expression shifted.

"Katie?"

Ellie nodded. Teresa looked at them more intently, studying them.

"She was pretty. Nice hands."

Ellie sat on the bed. "She was. And she did have nice hands. It was one of the things I used to like watching." She reached out for Teresa's hand and raised it to her lips. "But now, it's your hands I like to watch."

Teresa pulled her hand away and rolled to the other side of the bed to get out. KC meowed at being disturbed.

"What's the matter?" Ellie asked.

"Nothing," Teresa said, looking around for her discarded clothing. "I just have to get going." She didn't look at Ellie as she quickly dressed. "I'll call you later."

Ellie, still sitting on the bed, said, "Sure." She heard the sounds of Teresa wrenching open the kitchen door and then pulling it shut. She closed her eyes for a few seconds, and then gathered up the scattered drawings and tucked them all back in their drawer.

———◆———

Not until she was at the bottom landing did Teresa pause. For a moment, she stood there with her hand on the doorknob, listening for Ellie, but there was only silence. At last, she yanked the door open and walked out to her car.

She felt almost nauseous as she drove. Her gut churned and she felt an acidic sourness in her throat. For a moment, she thought she might get sick, and she pulled over, willing herself not to throw up.

"What is the matter with me?" she muttered.

You're jealous, answered a voice that sounded suspiciously like Bernie's.

"What? No, I'm—" but she stopped mid-sentence.

This feeling was so totally foreign to her that she had to think about it for a moment. Maybe the Bernie voice was right. She'd never been jealous before—*because I've never had anyone to be jealous about.* It was a horrible emotion. *No wonder Bernie is like she is when Tom is with his wife.* The worst part was the way she'd stormed out, leaving Ellie sitting there, probably feeling just as awful as Teresa was feeling now.

Briefly, she considered going back to Ellie's apartment to apologize, but a glance at her watch stopped that thought. They both needed to get to work. *I'll apologize tonight.* She put the VW in gear and continued on to the store. She automatically scanned the alley for any sign of Dogman and Lucy, but saw nothing. She'd stopped putting any food out weeks ago.

She had the sidewalk swept and the front windows wiped down and Mrs. Schiavo's bread passed out before her parents got to the store.

"You stayed at Bernie's again last night?" Sylvia asked.

"Yes." Teresa busied herself restocking boxes of tampons and sanitary napkins.

"You been doing that a lot lately."

"I told you, Ma. Bernie's been having some trouble with this guy she's been seeing and she wants to talk. I'm there so late, it's just easier to stay."

Teresa could feel her mother's eyes on her, but she stayed squatted down straightening the shelves.

"Teresa! I need you to take the deposit to the bank," Lou called from the office.

Teresa closed her eyes. "Not today, Pop. I got a lot to do here."

"What do you have to do here?" Sylvia demanded. "I can take care of this while you go."

With a groan, Teresa got to her feet. She went to the office and pulled the money sling off the hook.

"You walking?" Lou asked as he entered the deposit in the ledger.

"Yeah. I feel like getting some exercise," Teresa said. She zipped the deposit bag into the sling and pulled on her sweater. "Be back in a little bit."

The beauty of the spring morning was completely lost on Teresa as she walked. She didn't see the sunlight bronzing the new leaves popping out on the trees; she didn't hear the birds singing as they hunted for nesting material or pecked in the flower beds for bugs and worms among the crocuses and daffodils that were popping up in some people's yards. All she saw was Ellie's drawings—the sketch of her looked as if it had been done by an Italian master—in a few strokes, Ellie had captured a fall of dark hair across the pillow, the sensuous curve of a breast, the soft mound of a hip. *I never thought I'd put 'me' and 'sensuous' in the same sentence,* Teresa had nearly said, but couldn't. Even to Ellie, she couldn't voice the thought that she was beautiful. But she also saw the innocence and beauty in the sketches of Katie—*Ellie's first love*—a place Teresa could never have.

When she got to the bank, her heart sank to the vicinity of her knees when she saw that Ellie's was the only open window.

"Miss Benedetto," Ellie said coolly as Teresa reached under her sweater and handed over the deposit bag. A faint patch of pink glowed in Ellie's cheeks.

Miserably, Teresa stood there, watching Ellie's face, hoping to catch her eye and convey to her how sorry she was, but Ellie wouldn't look up. In desperation, Teresa reached for a deposit slip and pen and scrawled, *Call me at lunch? Please.* She slid the note across the marble to Ellie, who gave a tiny nod. Teresa collected the empty deposit bag and tucked it back into her sling as she left to a chorus of good-byes from the other tellers.

The clock in the lobby ticked toward noon. Ellie saw Aaron Myers head toward the break room. She hid a smile as she reached under her teller window for her backpack and jacket. She'd been trapped by him one too many times and was doing everything she could to keep it from happening again. *Sooner or later, he'll get the hint.*

"Be back in thirty," she said to Bill White as he locked the front door behind her.

Ellie reached into her backpack and ate her sandwich as she walked. A couple of blocks from the bank was a payphone, the whole booth kind with a door. She wrinkled her nose as she stepped inside and slid the door shut behind her. Someone had obviously used it as a urinal. Probably several someones judging by the odor. She dropped a quarter into the slot and punched the number to the store. Teresa picked up on the first ring.

"Benedetto's—"

"It's me," Ellie cut in.

For a long moment, there was only the muffled sound of cars driving by outside the phone booth.

"Ellie, I'm so sorry," Teresa said in a low voice. "I don't know what came over me."

"Teresa, I can't change that Katie was in my life before you," Ellie said.

"I know. It was childish and stupid."

"Yes, it was," Ellie said. "Because *it* was childish. I was seventeen. It was child's play compared to what I feel for you. If you can't trust that—"

"I can. I do," Teresa said quickly. "I really do. I know better. I just... I don't know what it was. Like this monster reared up inside me."

Ellie smiled. "This was our first fight."

She could hear Teresa chuckle. "Not much of a fight," Teresa said.

"I hope all of our fights are settled this easily."

"I hope there aren't any more fights," Teresa said.

"That's not very realistic, is it?" Ellie asked, picturing the squabbles in the Benedetto house when they were all gathered together. She shook her head. "But we can fix anything if we just talk about it."

"You're right," Teresa said. "Can I see you tonight?"

"Can't. It's Thursday. *Magnum P.I.* with Sullivan, remember?"

"Oh."

"It's the only thing I do with him anymore. I can't break it. But you can take me out to dinner tomorrow night," Ellie said.

She heard Teresa laugh. "It's a date. Tomorrow."

———— ◦✐◦ ————

Teresa knocked and let herself into the D'Armelio house. "Hello?" she called.

"Oh, Teresa, it's you," said Mrs. D'Armelio, scuffing into the kitchen in her robe and slippers.

"Doughnuts," said Teresa, taking one for herself as she set the box on the table. She went to the bottom of the stairs and hollered for Bernie.

Mrs. D'Armelio shook her head as they heard feet stomping to the bathroom, accompanied by a lot of grumbling. She poured Teresa a cup of coffee and joined her at the table while they waited.

"How's the baby?"

"Oh, she's adorable," Teresa said, dunking her doughnut in her coffee. "My mother is in heaven." She saw sudden longing in Mrs. D'Armelio's eyes. "Hey, Francesca and the kids are coming over today. How about you and Bernie come, too? My folks would love to see you."

Mrs. D'Armelio's face brightened. "I haven't seen Sylvia and Lou except at church for ages."

Bernie made a grumpy entrance into the kitchen. "What the hell are you doing up at this hour?"

Teresa laughed. "It's eleven o'clock. You need to get showered and dressed. Y'uns are coming over for dinner."

Bernie dropped into a chair, a lit cigarette already in her lips as she took a deep drag and exhaled. "What?"

"I invited your mom and you over for Sunday dinner. She wants to see the baby."

Bernie rolled her eyes, but then saw the expression in her mother's eyes. "All right. What can we bring?"

"Just yourselves," Teresa said, finishing her doughnut. "You know how much food we'll have." She carried her coffee cup to the sink. "I'm going to go get Ellie and get started on the cooking. See y'uns about two?"

A couple of hours later, Teresa was up to her elbows in risotto with the aunts milling around, giving orders. Ellie and Karen were setting the table when Bernie came into the kitchen carrying a glass cake pan.

"Tiramisu. Needs a couple more hours in the fridge."

Teresa groaned. "No one makes tiramisu like your mom."

Bernie found space in the refrigerator for the pan. "She's already got the baby. She'll hold her until we leave. God, the comments I'm going to get now."

"I'm lucky," Teresa said with a sympathetic shake of her head. "No pressure. They're content to have one unmarried daughter at home to help out as long as at least one of us is reproducing."

Ellie came into the kitchen. "I just met your mom. She's so sweet."

"Yeah, that's my mother," Bernie said with a forced smile.

"What?"

"Italian mothers and daughters," Bernie said. "It's a love-hate relationship."

Ellie laughed. "I think that's all mothers and daughters."

Bernie snuck a meatball from the bowl waiting to be carried out to the table. "So Rob and Karen are coming every Sunday now?"

"Most," said Teresa, spooning the risotto into a bowl.

Anita came into the kitchen to check on the sauce. "Ellie," Anita called from the stove. "Come and taste the sauce. See if it needs more sugar."

Bernie sidled over to Teresa and said in a low voice, "And they're okay with Ellie?"

Teresa shrugged. "Seem to be."

"Unbelievable," said Bernie. "You are so lucky. Ellie here, and Robbie and Karen back, too. You are so goddamned lucky."

Teresa glanced over at Anita and Ellie. "I know. It's like some kind of dream."

<hr />

God, *how stupid could I be?* Teresa would ask herself not even an hour later.

Everyone had sat down at the table, which was a little different now, as Robbie refused to sit until Sylvia and the aunts did, which initially left everyone standing around in confusion.

"That training is paying off," Karen had whispered to Teresa when they first started coming back to the house for Sunday dinners, and Rob helped carry bowls of food out to the table, stunning Lou and Gianni into silence. He held the chair for Karen and for his mother, insisting the aunts sit and stop circling the table.

The noise dropped to a hum as everyone began eating—"the only time this house is quiet," Teresa often observed—when Sylvia said to Mrs. D'Armelio, "Well, Angela, are you getting tired of Teresa?"

"Why would I be tired of Teresa?" Mrs. D'Armelio asked innocently.

"All the time she's been spending over there," Sylvia said.

"Today's the first time I've seen Teresa in weeks."

Teresa froze. Around her, the rest of table conversation continued undisturbed, but she could feel the sudden chill emanating from her mother's direction.

Bernie, her instincts honed from years of lying to her mother, jumped in, saying, "Mom, don't be silly. I told you Teresa's been coming over late so we can shoot the shit."

"No," Mrs. D'Armelio said, shaking her head as she twirled spaghetti onto her fork. "I'm sure I'd have heard her. You two can never be quiet."

"That's very interesting," Sylvia said icily.

Teresa refused to look up, certain beyond a doubt that her mother was watching her and would instantly see the truth in Teresa's eyes.

"What the fuck?" Bernie hissed to Teresa a short while later when they escaped to the kitchen. "You told your mother you were staying with me? Why the hell did you invite us over today?"

"I didn't even think about this," Teresa moaned. "I'm not used to lying."

"Well, you'd better learn fast," Bernie said as Ellie came into the kitchen. "Tell her we went out for drinks to talk and didn't get in until late, and that's why my mother didn't hear us. You two are in for a shitload of grief from Sylvia. You," she pointed at Ellie, "you stick to me like glue until we get the hell out of here."

"Why?" Ellie asked in bewilderment.

Teresa nodded. "Just do it. We'll explain later."

Ellie was obviously confused at the immediate change in atmosphere. Teresa knew she had no idea what had happened, but the tension was palpable. Teresa wouldn't meet her questioning glances, and Bernie made sure Ellie stayed away from Sylvia and Teresa for the rest of the afternoon until it was time to leave, which Bernie arranged as soon she could.

"We'll give Ellie a ride home," Bernie said as her mother thanked Sylvia and Lou for having them over. "Come on, Mom." She gave Teresa a last glance as she herded them out the door.

"But I didn't get to say—" Ellie began, pointing toward Anita.

"Not today," Bernie said in a low voice. "We need to get you out of here."

Teresa saw Bernie push Ellie out the door. She wanted so badly to run after them, but all she could do was watch as Ellie turned for one last look before the door closed.

"Mom," Bernie said once they were safely in the car, "I'm going to drop you off and then take Ellie home."

Ellie sat silently in the back seat while Bernie drove to her house. She gave Mrs. D'Armelio a wave as Bernie got out to unlock the house for her mother. "I don't understand," she burst out when she got into the vacated passenger seat. "What's the problem?"

Bernie glanced at her. "My mother, God bless her, outed you two today."

Ellie heard the unaccustomed gravity of Bernie's voice. "You mean—?"

Bernie nodded. "Teresa's been telling her mother she's been staying with me when she's spent the night with you, and my mother blew that to hell. Sylvia will not let this drop." She shook her head. "Shit. This is not going to be good. I'm sorry for both of you."

Ellie sat silently beside her as she drove, feeling as if she were back in the car with Mrs. Locke after talking to Father Patrick.

"It would be a good idea for y'uns to plan to not see as much of each other for a while. Give this time to blow over."

Ellie felt a shiver run down her spine. "You don't think...?" She couldn't even voice the rest of that horrible question.

"I think," Bernie said quietly, "Teresa is going to be forced to make some hard choices."

She pulled up at the curb in front of Ellie's building. They sat there for a long moment.

"Thanks, Bernie."

"Jesus, I'm sorry, Ellie."

Ellie got out of the car and waved to Bernie as she drove off. Tears stung her eyes. She trudged up the stairs and let herself in. KC trotted out with little meows of welcome. Ellie scooped her up in her arms and heard a rap on the living room door. Ignoring Sullivan's knock, she buried her face in KC's fur, wondering when, or if, she'd see Teresa again.

"Do you want us to stay?" Rob asked in a low voice.

Teresa glanced in Sylvia's direction where she was wrapping some leftovers for Francesca to take home. She knew nothing would happen until everyone left, and she shook her head. "Gonna have to face it sooner or later."

"Call us if you need us," Karen said, squeezing Teresa's arm.

Anita, too, seemed to know something bad had happened. The other aunts were set to go, and still, Anita stalled, finding things to clean up in the kitchen.

"Anita, let's go," called Luisa. "My feet are killing me. I want to get home."

"Go," Teresa said from the sink where she was scrubbing a pan.

"What's wrong?" Anita asked worriedly.

Teresa couldn't meet her eye. She only shook her head. As much as her godmother loved her, she wasn't sure even Anita would forgive this if she knew. *Why should it need forgiveness?* But in their world, Teresa knew this was unforgiveable—more than Rob's divorce, more than his remarrying, more than anything else they'd never conceived of.

"You'd better go," she said to Anita.

Anita stood torn for a moment, wringing her hands, and then, reluctantly, went to get her coat. A moment later, Teresa heard all the aunts taking their leave. She continued to scrub the pots, and her heart pounded as she knew the inevitable was coming.

It was always inevitable, wasn't it?

Even Gianni seemed to sense some drama in the air. Normally the first to leave, he was hanging on, waiting to see what shit was about to hit the fan.

"You and Angelina need to go," Sylvia said from the living room and Teresa heard them leave a few minutes later.

At last, the house was empty, just Teresa and her parents. She placed the last pan in the dish drainer and dried her hands. No sense putting it off any longer.

She went out to the living room where Lou was pretending to read the paper. Teresa knew he didn't know what the problem was, but he was waiting for the explosion they all could feel building. Sylvia sat on the edge of her chair, her jaw set. Without a word, Teresa sat and waited for the storm to unleash itself.

"How could you?" Sylvia said at last.

Deciding to test just how far her mother's imagination had taken her, Teresa said, "How could I what?"

"Don't you dare!"

Sylvia jumped to her feet, her breast heaving. "How could you do this to us? After the way you were raised? After everything we gave up for you? To send you to school? Give you a future? This is how you repay us?"

Lou lowered his paper. "What are you—?"

"Her!" Sylvia shouted, pointing at Teresa. "Her and that whore! It's bad enough you're damning yourself to hell, but you'll drag all of us into your shame with you!"

Vaguely aware that her father had stood, Teresa got to her feet as well, stunned at the accuracy of her mother's instincts. Her brain froze—all thoughts of any kind of logical argument, any kind of appeal to her mother's love for her—all of it suddenly was distilled into just one thought, the only thing she could articulate.

"I love her."

So quickly Teresa didn't see it coming, Sylvia stepped forward and slapped her hard across the face. All three of them stood, paralyzed, as the sound of that slap seemed to reverberate through the room. Sylvia's face crumpled and she dropped into her chair, her hands covering her face as she cried.

"What did we do wrong?" she wailed, rocking and crossing herself. "Why is God punishing us like this?"

Lou bent over her, one arm wrapped protectively around her shoulders. Teresa raised a trembling hand to her cheek. Neither of her parents had ever struck her.

"Ma, please," Teresa pleaded, but her father stepped between them.

"I think you've done enough," Lou said.

Teresa backed away and then turned and ran upstairs to her room, slamming the door. She sat on her bed. Across the room, her face in the dresser mirror stared back at her, her left cheek glowing red. She was too shocked to cry. She'd known, if it ever came to light, her mother's reaction would not be good, but nothing could have prepared her for this.

"What now?" she whispered to her reflection, but there was no answer, only the sound of her mother's wails from downstairs.

CHAPTER 23

"Would you like some pie to go with that? You look like a coconut cream man to me."

Ellie couldn't help but smile as Louise hurried off to get the pie, bringing back a second plate for the man's wife. "Our apple pie is the best in town. If you don't agree, it's on the house."

Louise slid into Ellie's booth. "Now, tell me what's going on."

"Who said anything is going on?"

Louise cocked one eyebrow. "I know you better than that, missy. You never could hide it when something's wrong."

Ellie flushed. She couldn't tell Louise the truth—at least, not all of it. "It's Teresa."

"Did you have an argument?"

"Not us." She weighed her words. "Her family is kind of closed. Her mother didn't like her spending so much time with me, and they had words."

She guessed they'd had words. She hadn't heard anything since the day Bernie dropped her off at her apartment. No calls, no notes, no nothing. Two weeks of nothing. She didn't dare call the store or the Benedetto house. She kept hoping Teresa might bring a deposit to the bank, but none of the Benedettos had been by. She blinked hard as Louise studied her.

"Family can be hard sometimes," Louise said. "As much as we love them, they can drive us crazy." She nodded toward the cash register where her daughter, Patty, was ringing up a customer. "She decided I was working too hard, and won't leave me be."

As Ellie looked over, Patty glanced their way, frowning. She finished ringing up her customer and came to the booth. "Mama, are you okay? Do you need anything?"

"I don't need anything, except to be left alone to take care of my customers," Louise said.

Patty squeezed into the booth next to her mother. "Did you tell Ellie?"

"Tell me what?" Ellie asked.

"You didn't, did you?" Patty turned to Ellie. "She didn't tell you she had a heart attack."

"What?"

Louise waved a hand in irritation. "It was not a heart attack."

"The doctor said the chest pain and shortness of breath was probably a mild heart attack."

Ellie reached for Louise's hand. "Why didn't you tell me?"

"There was nothing to tell," Louise insisted. "He just said I need to take more time off."

"What he said," Patty interrupted, "is that she has to take at least two days off completely each week. But is she? No, she is not."

Patty pursed her lips, obviously curbing the other things she wanted to say.

"I need to be here to keep an eye on things," Louise said.

"But if he said you need to take it easy, you should be," Ellie said. "What would we do if anything happened to you?"

"That's what we said," Patty said. "Have you asked her?"

"Asked me what?" Ellie looked from Patty to Louise.

Patty glanced toward the register and saw that a customer was waiting. "You ask her or I will," she said as she scooted out of the booth.

"Ask me what?" Ellie repeated.

Louise looked down at Ellie's hand in hers. "Patty thought it might be time I need to hire someone to help me manage this place. Someone I trust. Someone like you."

"What? Don't you want Patty to take over?"

"She doesn't mind helping out," Louise said. "But she's busy with her children and doesn't want to be here all hours."

Ellie's mouth opened and closed a couple of times, but no sound came out.

"Before you give me an answer, I want you to think about it," Louise said. "You know sales and customer service. I could teach you to cook, but you don't even need to do much of that. Julius and the others have been with me for years. They're not going anywhere."

"I don't know what to say." Ellie stared down at their clasped hands.

"This could give you more freedom than you'll ever have at the bank," Louise said.

Or it could trap me in Pittsburgh forever. But Ellie didn't say it. She couldn't, not after everything Louise had done for her.

As if reading her mind, Louise said, "I don't want you to do this for me. Only if it's what you really want."

Ellie sat there, not knowing what to say.

"I know you weren't expecting this when you came in here," Louise said. "I'm going to tell you what my mama told me, Ellie Ryan. Life does not always give you what you want, but it usually gives you what you need."

***

Mrs. Schiavo had a cup of strong coffee and a doughnut waiting for Teresa when she came back inside with the empty bread tray.

"Sit down, Teresa."

Wearily, Teresa sat. Mrs. Schiavo waited a moment as Teresa took a sip of her coffee, leaving the doughnut untouched on the plate.

"You look... what's the word... terrible," Mrs. Schiavo said bluntly. "You're not sleeping, are you? What's wrong?"

Teresa looked at Mrs. Schiavo with eyes that stung and burned. "I'm fine, Mrs. Schiavo."

"Ha! I am an old woman, Teresita. I know unhappy when I see it and you are unhappy. Can you talk to your mama?"

Teresa scoffed.

"Ah," Mrs. Schiavo said, nodding. "Your mama, she is the trouble. Yes?"

Teresa nodded.

"My mama, too. When I want to marry my Eduardo. She say, 'NO!'"

Teresa looked up. "What did you do?"

Mrs. Schiavo reached over and took Teresa's hand in both of her gnarled ones. "I say to her, 'Mama, I love you, but I love Eduardo more. I am going to marry him.' And I did."

"What did your mother do?"

Mrs. Schiavo smiled, her eyes disappearing in the crinkles. "My mama, she try not to love Eduardo, but he was a good man. He bake for her every day, something different, something special. He say to her, 'You are the mama of my wife, and that makes you my mama, too.'" She cackled as she remembered. "He was so handsome, my mama, she come to love him like a son."

"I don't think that will happen for me," Teresa said wistfully.

Mrs. Schiavo peered at her. "Your mama, she love you. Love, she can make us do things we never thought we would."

Sudden tears stung Teresa's eyes. "I have to get back."

Mrs. Schiavo wrapped the doughnut in a napkin and patted Teresa's arm.

Back in the empty drugstore, Teresa angrily wiped away the wetness on her cheeks.

"She hasn't said a word?" Bernie had asked just the other day when she came by the store.

Since her outburst, Sylvia had adopted a policy of total silence on the topic of Ellie—a tactic that was the last one Teresa had expected. Her mother usually argued and nagged and hounded until she got what she wanted, but this strange avoidance of any arguments had Teresa knocked off-balance.

"She's just kind of pretending Ellie doesn't exist," Teresa said. She had told Bernie about the argument after everyone had left the house that awful Sunday. "She hasn't said one word to me about her." She busied herself with the espresso machine, hoping the noise would drown out any bits of their conversation her mother might overhear.

"Jesus, this is bad."

"She's also not leaving me alone for a minute," Teresa added, glancing back toward the office where her mother was fussing with the ledger. She lowered her voice to a whisper. "She's coming in early and staying late. I know it's to keep me from calling Ellie. I hear her get out of bed if I get up to pee during the night. I can't even sneak downstairs to call."

"So you haven't talked to her at all?"

Teresa shook her head. "I can't."

"Listen, Bennie. Sylvia's going to force you to be the one to bring it up, and she's betting you won't have the guts for a confrontation. She's hoping you'll just let it go, and everything will go back to being like it was. If you really love Ellie, you are going to have to stand up to your mother."

Teresa blanched. "You didn't hear her. The things she said."

"Seriously." Bernie leaned over the coffee counter. "What's the worst that could happen? She kicks you out? So, you come live

with me, or move in with Rob and Karen for a while. Or you and
Ellie actually live together like two grown-ups. Jesus Christ, it's
your life. You gotta stop letting your mother treat you like you're
sixteen."

Teresa thought about that conversation now as she counted the
store's cash drawer. She had been thinking about it every minute
of every day since she and Bernie had spoken. Bernie was right. It
was time.

"Hey."

Ellie blinked as Sullivan snapped his fingers in front of her
face.

"What?"

"You haven't heard a word I've said."

"Sorry." She shifted on the couch to face him. "What were you
saying?"

He shook his head. "It doesn't matter. I was boring myself. So,
where were you?"

Ellie shrugged. "Just trying to decide what to do about Louise's
offer."

"Free food. Sounds like a no-brainer to me."

Ellie laughed. "It would to you. I'm just afraid, if it wasn't
working out, I'd never be able to tell Louise I was quitting. And
what about travelling? How can I take two weeks or a month off
when Louise is supposed to be taking it easy?"

"Have you talked to her about it?"

"Not yet," Ellie said. "But I guess I should."

"Why don't you start spending some time there, learning more
about the diner? Kind of like an intern. Then you'll know whether
you'd like it." Sullivan's stomach growled. "How about we go down
there now?"

"You sure?"

"Yeah. Let me grab my wallet. I'll meet you downstairs."

A few minutes later, they were on a bus.

"Where's Teresa been?" Sullivan asked, giving her a sidelong glance. "I haven't seen her in weeks."

Ellie turned to look out the grimy window at the passing sidewalk below them. She hadn't confided in him, but Sullivan wasn't stupid. He knew Teresa had been spending several nights a week with Ellie, and, suddenly, she wasn't. Sullivan was a good guy, but he was a guy. "I guess she's been busy at their store." She closed her eyes, remembering how somber Bernie had been about the pressure Teresa was going to face from her mother. Ellie had hoped Teresa would find the courage to stand up to Sylvia, that this time, Ellie would be the prize worth choosing....

Ellie was up to her elbows in flour and piecrust when Louise came into the diner's kitchen, followed by Patty.

"Doesn't look like you need me at all," Louise said, taking in the piles of freshly cut apples waiting to fill the crust.

"I don't know," Ellie said. "I think I measured everything according to your recipe, but the proof will be when the customers eat it."

"Well, bake it up and we'll have a piece of pie to celebrate," Louise said.

"How was the doctor's visit?" Ellie asked as she spooned a sugar and cinnamon mixture over the apples.

She looked up when there was no answer. Patty crossed her arms over her chest.

"You gonna tell her? Or am I?"

Louise gave a wave of her hand. "He said there's a blockage."

"He said," Patty said, "that she has two blocked arteries and needs bypass surgery."

"What?" Ellie nearly dropped the measuring cup. "You have to have surgery?"

"Maybe," said Louise.

"Mama, there is no maybe about it," Patty said. "He said your arteries are over eighty percent blocked. If you don't have a bypass, you will have a full-blown heart attack."

"When? How long will you be out?"

Ellie looked around in a panic. She'd been coming down to the diner most evenings after she finished at the bank, trying to learn the ins and outs of running the place. There was so much to learn: ordering food and supplies, making a schedule, running payroll and taxes. And that was all in addition to actually working the diner—waiting on customers and ringing them up. It was overwhelming.

"The doctor said no work for at least six weeks," Patty said.

"Six weeks?" Ellie sat down hard on a stool.

Louise laid a hand on her shoulder. "Let's get that pie in the oven and then I'll show you how to do payroll."

Ellie finished scooping the pie filling into the waiting crust, then laid the upper crust out in a lattice pattern before sliding the pan into the oven. "Julius?" She set a timer. "Can you keep an eye on this for me?"

"Sure thing," he said from the grill as Ellie washed up the flour and sugar on the marble baking slab.

She knocked on Louise's office door—*the place my soul was laid bare*, she remembered with a droll smile. Her smile broadened as she saw a dill pickle lying on a plate on the desk. She tried to laugh, but it suddenly caught in her throat.

"What's the matter, baby girl?"

Ellie kept her eyes lowered. "Nothing important."

"You're a horrible liar." Louise leaned forward and took Ellie's hand. "Tell me."

Ellie looked up at her and tried to smile. She didn't want to tell Louise her worries—that the bank was becoming intolerable with Aaron Myers waiting to ambush her on an almost daily basis, or how lonely she was lately—not with Louise's health concerns.

"I just miss Teresa. She's been really busy and we haven't been able to see each other lately."

Louise squeezed Ellie's hand. "Some people are worth fighting for. I think Teresa is one of them. Don't you give up."

Ellie nodded. She took a breath and reached for the pickle. "All right. Show me how to do payroll."

Teresa sat on the porch step, watching the kids run around the aunts' front yard, hunting for the Easter eggs she had hidden earlier.

As far as she could tell, her mother hadn't said anything to anyone else. The aunts still treated her normally, though she kept catching Anita watching her with a worried expression on her face. Teresa knew she looked like crap. She still wasn't sleeping and she'd lost a lot more weight. *Any other time, I'd be happy to be this thin,* she thought sometimes, but she missed Ellie with a physical ache that never went away.

Just a few minutes ago, Karen had come to her. "We're concerned about you. Is there anything we can do?"

Blinking rapidly as sudden tears stung her eyes, Teresa had shaken her head. "No. There's nothing anyone can do."

Teresa sat now, thinking about that. There wasn't anything anyone else could do. Only she could do what needed to be done.

"What's the worst that could happen?"

Bernie's question rang in her mind, fighting to be heard over her mother's, *"How could you do this to us?"*

Bernie's voice spoke more loudly. *"Jesus Christ, it's your life. You gotta stop letting your mother treat you like you're sixteen."*

Francesca came outside, carrying the baby, while, down in the yard, Sylvia led Daniela and Rickie to a couple of the hidden eggs.

"Ma, they're supposed to find the eggs themselves," Francesca said. She looked at Teresa with a roll of her eyes. She sat beside Teresa, handing the baby over to her. "Where's Ellie? I haven't seen her in ages. I thought for sure she'd be here today."

Teresa lowered her head, smelling little Annalisa's soft hair. It was a moment before she could trust her voice to say, "She's been busy lately. I haven't seen much of her."

"Well, when you do, tell her I miss having her around." Francesca stood up to go to Rickie as he sat in the yard crying when Daniela took his egg.

What are you doing here? Teresa asked herself. *You know what you need to do.*

She started to stand, but then sat back down. Three times, she changed her mind, quailing from taking that step. Anita came out onto the porch.

"How's my goddaughter?"

Teresa got to her feet and handed the baby to her. "I'm not sure when I'll see you again," Teresa said breathlessly. She gave her aunt a quick hug and turned to descend the steps.

"Where are you going?" Sylvia demanded as Teresa went down the walk. "Teresa! Don't you walk away from me."

Teresa turned to look at her mother. "You know where I'm going."

"Don't you dare!" Sylvia said shrilly. "If you leave here now, don't you dare come back."

"What is this?" Anita asked, coming down off the porch. Annalisa started crying at the raised voices. "What's wrong?"

Teresa turned her back and walked to her car, ignoring her mother's threats and Anita's demands to know what was going on.

The yelling and commotion had brought the rest of the family out onto the porch. Teresa paused to look back. Robbie gave her a nod. Her heart was in her throat as she got in and turned the ignition. *If you drive away now, there's no going back.* She put the car in first gear and roared away from the curb.

She glanced at her watch and saw that it was nearly eleven. She drove straight to the cemetery. She parked and found her way to Ellie's mother's grave. No fresh flowers. She squatted down and plucked away some fallen leaves that had gathered against the headstone.

"I don't know if you would approve," she whispered. "I just hope I'm not too late."

She found a bench nearby and sat to wait. She wasn't sure how much time had passed when she saw Ellie coming from the direction of her father's grave. She didn't see Teresa sitting there. Teresa waited respectfully while Ellie visited with her mother, placing a fresh bouquet of flowers on her grave. Ellie stood and turned around. She stopped when she saw Teresa. Teresa got to her feet.

Ellie approached slowly. "What are you doing here?"

"Waiting for you." Teresa stood rooted to the spot. "I needed to see you."

"It's Easter," Ellie said.

Teresa nodded.

"What about your family?"

Teresa gave a funny shrug. "I'm not sure that will be an issue after today." Ellie frowned. "My mother pitched a fit when I left. She knew I was coming to find you."

Teresa suddenly felt light-headed and had to sit down again. Ellie sat beside her.

"Are you okay?"

Teresa looked at her and tried to smile. "That depends."

"On what?"

Teresa opened her mouth but no words would come out. She tried again. "On you. I just walked away from my mother. I'm not sure if there's any going back from that. What I don't know is if you can forgive me for these past few weeks."

Ellie took her hand. "There's nothing to forgive. I know this has been hard on you." Her voice had a catch.

"Hard on both of us, I think."

They looked into each other's eyes for a long moment before Teresa allowed herself to fall into Ellie's embrace.

"I've missed you so much," Ellie murmured when they parted.

"I have tried calling a few times," Teresa said, still holding Ellie's hand.

"Did you? I didn't dare call you. I was afraid your mother might answer, and I would just make things worse." Ellie searched Teresa's face. "I've been helping out down at the diner. Louise has had some health issues."

"Oh, Ellie. I am so sorry," Teresa said. "Is she okay?"

Ellie nodded. "She's all right. I'll tell you more about it later."

"You must be exhausted," Teresa said.

"I am," Ellie admitted with a wan smile. "But I'm learning a lot. I've learned how to run payroll and I'm a much better baker now."

"I can help," Teresa said.

"Really?"

Teresa's face fell. "I'm not sure I'll have a job tomorrow."

"You just walked away?"

"I had to," Teresa said. "I couldn't stand not being with you."

They sat side by side for a long time.

"What now?" Teresa forced herself to ask at last.

Ellie stood and tugged on Teresa's hand. "Let's go home."

CHAPTER 24

TERESA LAY WITH ELLIE'S back snugged up against her, soft and warm against Teresa's arm. She turned her head to the nightstand where the framed calligraphy stood—the only other one Ellie had ever made and the only one still in existence. Teresa knew now Ellie had made it for her mother.

Be still and know that I am God...

This psalm had become a touchstone these last three weeks. She hadn't seen or talked to her mother. Bernie had gone over to collect Teresa's clothes for her.

"Jesus Christ, Bennie," she'd said when she arrived at Ellie's. "I've seen your mother pissed over the years, but I've never seen her like this. It's like—"

Bernie stopped abruptly.

"Like I don't exist?" Teresa said with a tight-lipped smile. "I knew she would be like this."

"I got all your clothes, but...the framed thing you asked me to get? It was smashed and the paper inside was torn to bits. All over your bed."

Teresa nodded. She'd expected as much.

"I got this, though," Bernie said, holding up Teresa's rosary. "Was she this bad with Robbie?"

Teresa ran the familiar mother-of-pearl beads through her fingers. "It felt like it at the time, because Pop was angry, too. But that was different."

"Has your father said anything?"

"Not a word," Teresa said. "I called Pop and told him I could either work the Oakland store, or I'm leaving Benedetto's to work for someone else. His choice. In his world, if he doesn't have to talk about it or hear about it, it doesn't exist. So, I'm working at the Oakland store, Dom is at Morningside, and Gianni is in Bloomfield. He gets to deal with Ma. I can imagine the conversations they're having." She heard the bitterness in her own voice and saw the expression on Ellie's face. "I told you, this is not your fault."

"I know, but I feel awful," Ellie said.

Bernie gave a wave of her hand. "My mother tried to kick me out a hundred times when I was young. I'd go stay with Bennie for a couple of days and my mother would call and I'd go back. It's what we do."

Ellie didn't look reassured. Neither did Teresa.

"It'll be okay," Teresa forced herself to say. "I won't give in, but my mother can stay angry longer than Bernie's. Annalisa may be graduating from college before we're invited over again."

"Have you talked to anyone else?" Bernie asked.

"I gave Rob and Karen this phone number. We're going over there for dinner next Wednesday. Why don't you come along?"

"I will." Bernie got up. "I better get home." She paused at the door and looked back at Teresa and Ellie. "Who would've ever guessed that you'd be the real rebel?"

Teresa smiled now in the early morning twilight. Bernie was right. Part of what was making this so hard for her mother was that Teresa had never done anything wrong or rebellious—*Hell, I'd never done anything, period.*

Her smile faded. She would never say so to Ellie, but it was weird living with just one other person. Only Sullivan and Bernie had been by a few times. It was so quiet. As much as Teresa had longed for quiet when it was nowhere to be had, it felt strange now, and a niggling doubt had begun to make itself felt—a doubt that made her wonder if she could be happy with just Ellie forever. Forever. That was such a scary word. Could her mother stay angry forever? Would Teresa be forever cut off from everyone else she loved? Robbie and Karen would still see them, but she wasn't so sure about Francesca. She knew her sister liked Ellie, but she had become more like their mother as she had more kids. And then, there were the aunts. They were as conservative and close-minded as Sylvia about many things. But they were also naïve and innocent when it came to sex, and Teresa didn't know how explicit her mother might have been about Teresa's living arrangement with Ellie.

She felt positively sinful. She hadn't been to church. She had no desire to have another public confrontation with her mother. She could have gone to another mass or a different church, but she hadn't been to confession—"I have nothing to confess," she insisted to herself stubbornly—and so wouldn't have gone to Communion anyhow.

Ellie shrugged when Teresa mentioned this. "You know how I feel about church." She wrapped her arms around Teresa's neck. "I'm sure we can find better ways to spend Sunday mornings."

Teresa was more than willing to spend as much time in bed with Ellie as they could, but there hadn't been much of that, except for sleeping. She'd been joining Ellie at the diner most evenings after leaving the store, and by the time they got home, they were so exhausted, they'd been asleep almost before their heads hit their pillows.

Ellie stirred and rolled over.

"Hey there," Teresa whispered. She kissed Ellie on the cheek.

"Is it time to get up?" Ellie moaned, rubbing her eyes.

"It is if we intend to be at the diner before it opens."

Ellie's eyes snapped open. "It's Saturday."

"You know, if you do decide to manage the diner, you and Louise are going to have to work out who gets what days off. You can't keep working seven days a week." Teresa yawned. "And neither can I."

———— ✦ ————

"Mrs. Bland, your prescription is ready."

Teresa handed the bag to the cashier and went to fill the next prescription. The Oakland store was completely different from Bloomfield or Morningside. Here, there was no coffee bar, and people didn't come by to visit. The customers who came by this location were busy, on their way to or from work usually, and needed quick service. Lou had chosen this location, not because it was in an Italian neighborhood, but because it was in a busy section of medical office buildings between the University of Pittsburgh's Presbyterian Hospital, Magee-Womens Hospital and Children's Hospital.

"I really like being busier," Teresa had said to Ellie after her first week working there. It had taken her a while to become accustomed to the layout of the store, and the staff had been a little standoffish at first—"Staff! I've never had staff," Teresa had said with a laugh. "I was the staff." But when they saw Teresa unpacking boxes and restocking shelves, they seemed to have decided she was all right. Even though she was still working sixty to seventy hours a week, the hours flew by.

"Hi, Mr. Benedetto."

Teresa turned around so fast, she cricked her neck. Lou came by three or four times a week to check on things and take the deposits to the bank, but it still caught Teresa off-guard. There was no eye contact between them as he went back to the office. She continued filling prescriptions until she heard him holler for her.

"Yes?" she said as she went into the office. She couldn't bring herself to call him "Pop."

"Everything okay here?" he asked from where he was bent over the ledger.

"Everything's fine," she said.

"Anything you need?"

"How're Francesca and the baby? Is Ana Maria taking it easy? How's Anita's blood sugar?" All kinds of questions about the family nearly burst from her mouth, but she didn't dare. She had a feeling if she asked, she'd get some kind of response to the effect of "if you care that much, you can apologize and come home", and she wasn't going to do that.

"We're getting low on cash register tape."

Lou grunted, and Teresa went back to the pharmacy counter. All of her information about the family came from Rob now, and that was limited.

"They're okay," he said when she and Ellie were there for dinner.

She'd never realized how closely she kept tabs on everyone before, especially the aunts' health, but Robbie didn't know the answers to her questions.

"You could call them," Karen said, but Teresa shook her head.

She couldn't. Not yet. Not without knowing what her mother might or might not have said to them.

"They're fine, Bennie," Bernie had said to her. "You'd know if they weren't."

Teresa nodded, but she still worried. Sometimes she caught Ellie watching her with a guilty expression, and she tried then not to think about them so much.

Lou finished the deposit. Teresa looked up as he exited the office. "Well, I'll see y'uns in a couple days," he said to no one in particular.

Teresa watched through the store's front window as he got into his Cadillac and became aware of a hollow, empty feeling somewhere in the vicinity of her heart. *This was your choice,* she reminded herself as she returned to work.

She looked at her watch a while later. "Time to close up, Sandy," she called. She locked the pharmacy while the cashier reconciled the register.

"You going to the diner again tonight?" Sandy asked as she counted the drawer.

"Yes," said Teresa. "Louise's surgery is tomorrow. I thought I'd go over and help out."

"Go, then. I'm good here."

"You sure?"

Sandy glanced up. "I'm fine. I'll lock up when I'm done."

"Thanks. Have a good night." Teresa gathered her purse and drove over to the diner.

"Hi, Julius," she called to the grill cook as she came in. "Where's Ellie?"

He glanced up. "She took some sandwiches out. Been a while. Thought she'd be back by now."

Teresa deposited her purse in the office and went back outside, zipping her sweater against the cool May evening. She had no idea in which direction Ellie might have gone, and began searching the alleys and bus stops near the diner. The few street people she saw said that Ellie had been by offering sandwiches, but they couldn't say how long ago. There was no sign anywhere of Ellie, and no response when Teresa called. She circled back to the diner, hoping Ellie had returned, but Julius shook his head. Worried now, Teresa headed back out.

"Where are you?" she muttered as she tried to decide which direction to go. She walked several blocks, going toward some seedier sections of the city, afraid to venture too far into the dark alleys and spaces between buildings. She saw no sign of Ellie anywhere. Growing more desperate, she headed toward a small park where a lot of homeless people bedded down for the night. There, she saw a small figure seated on a bench, her knees hugged to her chest.

Teresa nearly ran to the bench. "Where have you been? I've been worried sick."

Ellie wiped tears from her cheeks.

"What's wrong? Did something happen?"

Ellie shook her head. "Nothing happened. Nothing ever happens. And everything is wrong."

"What do you mean? What is it?"

Fresh tears flowed from Ellie's eyes. "Louise is having open-heart surgery tomorrow. What if—?"

"She's stubborn and strong," Teresa said. "She'll be fine." But would she? Teresa knew how scared she'd be if it was one of the aunts facing such a serious surgery.

Ellie hiccupped. "And there's never any sign of Daniel. Nobody has ever heard of him. I have no idea if he's alive or dead. He's my only family and I have no idea where he is."

She leaned into Teresa, crying. Teresa held her, wishing there was something she could say to comfort her, but what could be said? How long could someone stay alive if they were on the streets? It had been years since he got out of the army. He could be anywhere. Privately, Teresa had doubted that he'd even come back to Pittsburgh, but she didn't say so to Ellie. That hope had seemed like a lifeline for Ellie, something she needed to cling to.

"Come on," Teresa said softly. "Let's go back."

Ellie nodded and got to her feet, allowing Teresa to steer her in the direction of the diner. When they got there, Teresa insisted they go home. "Enough for one night."

KC was waiting for them when they got to the apartment. Teresa fed her while Ellie got ready for bed. When Teresa got into bed, Ellie moved into her arms.

"Make love to me," she whispered. "I need to feel you."

Teresa kissed her as Ellie shifted to lie on top of her. Impatiently, Ellie stripped off her top, lifting herself up so that Teresa could get her mouth on Ellie's hardened nipples. As she sucked them, Ellie straddled her, begging for Teresa's touch, moving with her as Teresa's hand slid under her panties to find Ellie hot and wet, ready for her. Teresa nearly came herself as Ellie bucked against her hand. When her orgasm faded, Ellie collapsed against Teresa, crying again.

"Don't leave me," Ellie whispered into Teresa's neck.

Tenderly, Teresa held her. "I won't. I promise. I'll never leave."

CHAPTER 25

ELLIE GLANCED UP TO check which bus was approaching. It was hers. She stood, keeping her head bowed as she climbed the steps, handing her card to be punched.

"Hey, Ellie," said Larry. "How ya—" He stopped abruptly and shifted in his seat. "Look at me."

Reluctantly, Ellie lifted her face. Larry's nostrils flared.

"Who did that to you?"

She raised her hand to her bruised cheek. "I fell."

"Like hell you did. You tell me who did that, and I'll—"

"No!" She shook her head. "There's nothing you can do. I'll be fine."

He stared at her, his jaw working, but he said, "All right. You sit here behind me." He glared at the man sitting there, who immediately got up to move to another seat.

She could feel Larry watching her in his mirror, but she kept her eyes lowered. She was so angry, she was on the verge of tears, and she didn't want to cry on the bus, not in front of Larry. She'd fled from the bank before closing, before counting her drawer—*I don't even know if I'll have a job tomorrow.*

Had it all started only a half-hour ago, when she'd heard her name called from the second floor? She'd looked up to see Aaron Myers standing at the balcony.

"Could you bring me that file?"

He pointed to the counter where he'd set a file down while talking to Bill White a few minutes earlier. For weeks, she'd been avoiding going into the staff room by herself, knowing that he was watching for opportunities to corner her. He'd been getting more obvious in his attempts to get her alone. Grinding her teeth, she glanced over at Suzanne, who gave a tiny shrug. She came around the tellers' counter, picked up the folder, and carried it upstairs where she found Myers in his office.

"Here you—"

"Come on in," he said.

She hesitated, but he'd gone behind his desk. She entered the office and set the file on his desk. So quickly, she wasn't sure later how he'd done it, he had gotten around the desk and pushed the door shut, trapping her.

"It's about time we stopped this tease," he said. His gaze ran up and down her body, leaving her feeling dirty, as if he had touched her.

She took a step backwards.

"I think this has gone on long enough," he said, approaching her. "You've played very hard to get."

"I'm not playing anything," Ellie said. "I want you to open that door, please."

He laughed. For one fleeting moment, she considered running behind his desk, using it as a barrier between them, but it seemed so childish.

She pulled herself up to her full height and said, "I'm leaving." She began walking past him, but he grabbed her arm.

"Like hell you are." He grasped her other arm as well, pinning her and pulling her to him. He mashed his lips against hers as she squirmed, trying to get free. Desperately, she bit his lip. He jerked away from her and raised a hand to his bleeding mouth.

"You bitch!" He backhanded her across the face so hard that she was afraid he might have broken her cheekbone.

Ellie fought to clear her head and keep her wits as he yanked her to him again. She raised a knee and caught him in the groin. He grabbed his crotch and doubled over, gasping for breath. She ran for the door, wrenched it open, and rushed down the stairs to the lobby where Suzanne and Linda were talking to Bill White. She stood, breathing hard, her face throbbing where he'd hit her. Bill glanced up toward the balcony and cleared his throat.

"Well, I, uh..." He shuffled toward his office and closed the door.

Ellie stared at the closed door for a moment, and then ran to the staff room where she grabbed her backpack from her locker and rushed out the back door.

She raised her hand to her swollen cheek now, wincing. She felt Larry watching her in the bus mirror and, for a moment, she considered telling him who had hit her. *Why should that bastard keep getting away with this?* It was clear Bill White wasn't going to do anything about it. She had no idea what kind of recourse she might have for filing a complaint, but if the higher-ups' attitude was the same as White's, she couldn't count on any support from them.

But what if I don't have to go back?

"I'm going to get off here, Larry," she said, standing up.

"You sure you're okay?" He reached for her hand.

She nodded, giving his hand a squeeze. "I'm fine."

She descended the bus steps and began walking. She hadn't told anyone at the bank about Louise's offer. She felt she'd learned enough in these past few weeks that she could step in as manager. She'd been basically doing it all since Louise's surgery last week, going in every night after the bank to take care of the orders and paperwork. What if she just didn't go back? She didn't need the damned bank.

But every time she'd considered accepting Louise's offer and quitting the bank, there had been a moment of near-panic at the thought of being trapped in Pittsburgh forever. Ever since she was a little girl, she'd dreamed of leaving, of seeing other places, and now, it seemed life was conspiring to keep her here for the rest of her life.

"I can't leave Pittsburgh. I can't leave my family."

She and Teresa had never talked about moving away, and Teresa had never said those words, but Ellie could picture her saying it if she brought up the possibility of leaving.

Ellie looked around and realized she was only a block from her old house. She turned in that direction, slowing as she neared it. There, in the front yard was the elm tree she'd gotten stuck in when she was eight and Daniel's friend dared her to climb it. She could still feel the thrill of hearing Daniel say to his friend, "Don't ever dare Ellie to do anything, 'cause she'll do it." But she'd climbed so high, she became paralyzed at the thought of climbing back down again. Mortified at the thought of admitting she was afraid, she only replied, "I like it up here. I might stay up here forever," when they urged her to come down. She could see Daniel looking up at her, and he said to his friend, "She does crazy stuff like that, too. C'mon." They went away, leaving her up in the tree, but as soon as his friend had left, Daniel was back. "Hey, Jellybean. Don't cry. I'm coming. Don't be afraid." He climbed up to where she was and talked her back down, branch by branch. "No one else has to know," he said when they were safely back on the ground. "Just us."

Ellie stood looking up into the tree's branches now. "Just us."

———— ⋯⋯ ————

Teresa climbed quietly out of bed and went to get showered. When she came back into the bedroom to get dressed, Ellie hadn't moved.

In the half-light coming through the blinds, the ugly bruise on Ellie's cheek showed darkly, and her insides burned.

She leaned over and kissed Ellie lightly on the forehead.

Ellie stirred. "What time is it?"

"It's early," Teresa whispered. "It's Saturday. Stay in bed. I have to do a couple of things before I go to the store. I'll see you later."

"I love you," Ellie said sleepily, her eyes already closed.

Teresa smiled. "I love you, too."

Outside, it was a beautiful late May morning. Teresa got in the VW and headed, not to Oakland, but to Bloomfield. She had decided to come by early before either her mother or—God forbid—Gianni would be at the store.

"Good morning, Mrs. Schiavo."

Mrs. Schiavo's face lit up. "Teresita, it's so good to see you." She gave Teresa a tight hug. "Come sit down. Tell me how you are."

"Do you need help with the bread?"

"I already done it," Mrs. Schiavo said with a wave of her hand. "I want to know how you are. Sylvia, she won't tell me nothing."

She brought two cups of coffee and a doughnut to the table.

"I'm good," Teresa said. "I'm working down at our Oakland store now." She tilted her head in the direction of the drugstore. "How are things here?"

Mrs. Schiavo peered up at her. "I think not so good. She won't say so, but I think your mama misses having you around. Gianni, he's not a good worker, is he?"

Teresa laughed. "You always see everything, don't you? No, he is not a good worker. And now, maybe Ma and Pop see it, too." She took a bite of her doughnut and closed her eyes. "I've missed you. I kind of miss being here. Any news?"

Mrs. Schiavo filled her in on a few of the neighborhood births and hospitalizations and some gossip. "People ask about you, you know."

"Me?" Teresa said. "Who would ask about me?"

"Everyone!" Mrs. Schiavo tapped her arm. "Everyone knew you, and they like to see you and have you around." She looked at Teresa again. "They miss you. When are you coming back?"

Teresa blinked rapidly. She took a sip of her coffee. "I don't know. I'm really busy in Oakland. I might not be back."

Mrs. Schiavo studied her for a moment. "You and your mama, you're not talking, eh?"

Teresa shook her head. Surely, her mother was too proud to admit to anyone that her daughter was a lesbian, so she had no idea what Mrs. Schiavo might be thinking.

"You want to live your own life, eh? Not the life your mama she want for you."

Again, she sees straight through the bullshit. "That pretty much sums it up, Mrs. Schiavo."

"Well, that's a hard thing for your mama. I am sorry if you don't come back."

"I had to come by and see you, though." Teresa finished her coffee. "I need a dozen doughnuts."

A few minutes later, she sat in front of the aunts' house. It was still early, not yet seven, but she knew Anita, at least, would be up. It seemed a lifetime ago that she'd left here, knowing she might not be welcomed back. She could never have imagined going weeks without seeing her aunts. She reached over for the box of doughnuts and got out of the car.

Before she even climbed the last porch step, the front door opened, and Anita was standing there in her housedress. Teresa froze, waiting for a reaction.

"Come here," Anita said, hurrying to give her a hug, squeezing so hard, Teresa could barely breathe. "Oh, I missed you." Anita rocked her and patted her back.

"I've missed you, too."

Anita released her at last. "Come in."

Teresa hung back. "Who else is up?"

Anita glanced toward the house. "Let's sit out here." She guided Teresa toward the wicker chairs on the porch, freshly scrubbed for the spring. They sat, and Anita took Teresa's hand.

"I've been worried sick about you," Anita said. Her eyes scoured Teresa's face. "You've lost more weight. You sure you don't have cancer?"

Teresa smiled. "I don't have cancer. I'm good. Really." She looked down at their hands. "I'm sorry about the day I left."

"Your mother won't talk about it," Anita said. "She won't talk about you at all."

"I know," Teresa said quietly. "I don't want to put you in the middle. I just wanted to see you."

"You won't talk about it, either?"

Teresa shook her head.

"Okay. But you're all right?"

"I'm all right. I'm working down at the Oakland store."

"Where are you living?"

Teresa hesitated. "I'm living with Ellie."

Anita nodded. "I'm glad you have a friend, Teresa."

Sudden tears pricked Teresa's eyes. "She's been a good friend."

Anita looked out to the street, a far-away look in her eyes. "When I was young, there was a young man, a steelworker. He was Greek Orthodox. We met at a dance and dated for three years. We talked about getting married, but one of us would have had to convert. Neither of our families would accept that." Anita's fingers tightened around Teresa's. Teresa had never heard this story. She watched her godmother's face, seeing her as a beautiful young woman. "For a while, we talked about going away—away from Pittsburgh, away from family. It was the only way we could be together, but... We didn't do it." Anita dabbed at her eyes. "Not a day goes by that I don't think of him. Not a day."

"I didn't know that. Have you been unhappy?"

"Not completely unhappy." Anita looked at her. "I got to watch you grow up. But I can't help but wonder what my life could have been with a family of my own."

Teresa's brow furrowed. "How would you feel if I moved away from here? Not so far I couldn't visit, but... away."

Anita squeezed her hand. "I would understand. No one else can tell you how to make that decision. But you have to know, you'll have regrets no matter what you decide. Don't let anyone tell you you won't. You have to decide which regrets you can live with."

CHAPTER 26

ELLIE ENTERED THE BANK through the back door into the staff room. Bill White was there, pouring himself a cup of coffee. At the sight of her, he sloshed coffee all over the counter and placed the pot back on the burner, mumbling about something he needed to do in his office, and left as quickly as he could. It had been like that ever since the incident with Aaron Myers. The atmosphere at the bank was rife with tension.

"If they want to get rid of me for walking out, they'll have to fire me," Ellie had finally decided. "I'm not running away like I was the one in the wrong."

Teresa had been furious and had wanted to contact the police. "He attacked you!"

"It's my word against his," Ellie said. "Besides, I think I hurt him more than he hurt me."

Myers had looked startled to see Ellie at her window with Suzanne and Linda the next morning as he limped through the lobby. The bruise on her cheek had turned an ugly purple, and Ellie made no attempt to hide it. At the sight of him, the other two women had sidled closer to Ellie. *Like bison,* Ellie thought and she almost laughed at how he nearly tripped over himself as all three of them glared at him, watching him retreat upstairs. They had barely seen him since.

Linda had confided that Myers had tried cornering her a few times until she had her fiancé come by and stare him down. "He's a coward," she whispered. "He'll try anything he thinks he can get away with, but as soon as he's confronted, he looks for someone else."

Ellie looked balefully in the direction of Bill White's office. "And they let him keep getting away with it," she added, not bothering to lower her voice.

"Be careful," hissed Suzanne.

"Or what?"

A new kind of defiance had blossomed inside Ellie—*no, not new; it's old. As old as Katie's lies.* This job suddenly felt like another of the things keeping her chained to Pittsburgh, and she found herself fantasizing about what she would be free to do if they did fire her.

At noon, she left for her half-hour break. The park she'd found last fall had become her favorite lunch spot. The old men who played chess now recognized her and waved hello as she approached.

"Hey, Ernie, Sam," she called as she pulled her sandwich out of her backpack and sat on a bench. It was the same bench where the pie lady had sat down next to her, she realized. She watched a few other homeless people shuffling around, one woman carrying four shopping bags by their handles and another man pushing a shopping cart loaded with his belongings. She finished her sandwich and peeled a banana as she watched the bag lady approach a small group of mothers watching their kids play. She must have been asking for a handout because the other women were turning away or shaking their heads.

Could I have done that? Even when things were at their worst, could I have begged people for handouts?

You didn't have to beg. Louise saw and took care of you, a small voice reminded her.

The bag lady shuffled on, coming in Ellie's direction. The woman sat down on Ellie's bench, setting her bags down at her feet where she could keep an eye on them.

"Spare a quarter?" the woman asked.

Up close, Ellie could see that the woman was probably in her fifties, but it was hard to tell. Her gray hair was filthy as were her clothes, and a powerful odor of sweat and garlic settled around her as she sat.

"I can do better than that if you can do something for me." Ellie unzipped the pocket where she kept Daniel's photo. "Have you seen this man? He's older now, early thirties. His name is Daniel."

"May I?" the woman asked, looking at Ellie.

Startled at such a polite response, Ellie handed the photo over. The woman peered intently at the image and shook her head.

"Can't really tell anything from this picture, but there was a man, called himself Danny. Or was it Davy? He had a beard and a bum leg," she said.

Ellie stared at her for several seconds. "Where was this? When?"

The woman pursed her lips as she thought. "Wasn't near here. It was down at the Strip, or maybe the Point. So that would have been winter before this last one. I moved out this way. No idea where he'd be now."

"Oh, thank you," Ellie said, reaching into her backpack. She pulled out a five-dollar bill. "Thank you so much." She tucked Daniel's photo back into its pocket and stood. "I've got to go, but thank you."

"Thank you," said the woman, turning the five over and over in her hands.

"Jesus Christ, do you have any idea how long it's been since we did anything, just the two of us?"

Bernie grinned from the driver's seat.

"Since before Christmas," Teresa said.

"I mean, I like Ellie," Bernie added, "but this is going to be fun."

Teresa looked out the passenger window at the Monongahela River passing below them as they drove over the bridge.

"Go," Ellie had insisted when Bernie suggested going to Washington for some outlet shopping. "You two haven't done anything together in ages. I'll be fine. I'll probably be at the diner all day. Believe me, you'll get the better end of the deal."

She'd given Teresa a kiss that almost changed Teresa's mind and pushed her out the door when Bernie honked from the curb.

Teresa settled back in her seat. "So, why are we travelling an hour away when we have all the shopping in the world in Pittsburgh?"

"Because it's my fucking birthday and it's not Pittsburgh," Bernie said. She glanced in her rearview mirror at the city behind them. "We escaped."

She cranked up the music and talked about her latest issues with a student whose mother's boyfriend was arrested for beating them. Teresa half-listened, wondering where Ellie was. It felt weird to be separated from her, even though they rarely got to talk during the workday. *I wonder what she'll be doing at the diner today?* She was startled by a punch in the arm.

"What?"

"You haven't heard a goddamned word I've been saying, have you?"

"Sure I have," Teresa said. "You were talking about your student."

"That was five minutes ago," Bernie said, lighting a fresh cigarette. "Christ, you are pathetic. You can't even be gone from her for a day."

"Don't be stupid," Teresa said, but she could feel the heat rising in her cheeks. "I was thinking about the order I forgot to send in yesterday."

"Liar." Bernie exhaled, blowing the smoke out her window. "You are the worst liar in the world. No wonder your mother figured out the truth. Any contact from her?"

Teresa scoffed. "Are you kidding? I did go over to see Anita a couple of weeks ago."

"Really?" Bernie glanced over. "How was that?"

"It was good." Teresa shifted in her seat. "Ma hasn't talked about what happened, but I think Anita guessed. She told me she'd been in love. With a Greek boy, a steelworker, but neither family would let them be together."

"No way. Did you tell her about you and Ellie?"

"God, no." Teresa paused. "But I think she knows. She said she has always regretted not marrying him. Can you believe that?"

"Jesus. To live your whole life wishing you'd done it differently. That is fucking sad."

Teresa turned to the window again. "I know. She hasn't been completely unhappy, but she told me there would be regrets, no matter what choices you make. 'You have to pick the regrets you can live with,' she said."

"Shit. That's a cheerful thought. Do you think she was warning you you'd have to make a choice?"

"I already have, haven't I? I don't see Ma or Francesca or the kids, but I've got you and Robbie and Karen. And Anita, if I can see her away from the others.

Bernie flicked her ashes out the window. "Let's hope that's all the choices you'll have to make."

Ellie got off the bus on Liberty Avenue, near the Greyhound station. She'd slipped away as soon as Teresa and Bernie left, sneaking out of the apartment building so Sullivan wouldn't hear her. She hated lying to Teresa, but she had to have some time alone. Ever since her conversation with the bag lady in the park, she'd been obsessed with coming down to the Strip district to look for Daniel. It was the first clue she'd had in seven years as to where he might be, and she had to see for herself. She figured the bus station was a good place to start. The streets and alleys around the station had large numbers of street people hanging out, hoping for handouts from passersby. Ellie had to keep reminding herself that the woman said Daniel had a beard now. She'd been picturing him as she'd last seen him, clean-shaven, with his military buzz cut. The woman also said he had a bum leg. Ellie couldn't help worrying that he'd been injured somehow, or maybe he'd been wounded in Vietnam and came home with a bad leg.

He won't be the same, warned that careful voice in her head.

I don't care, Ellie answered. *I have to try and find him.*

Don't you think he'd have found you if he wanted to?

Ellie didn't like to think about that, about why Daniel hadn't come to find her. That question had plagued her for years, sometimes making her angry that he had simply abandoned her, and sometimes, she almost hated him for it—and then immediately felt guilty. But she knew, if she ever succeeded in finding him, one of the things she would have to ask him is why—*why did you just leave me there with them? Why didn't you come find me when you got back? Why have you let me search for you all these years?*

She paused at the entrance to a side street with sign after sign for strip clubs and bars. This was not like the alleyways she was used to searching near the diner or in Squirrel Hill. Driven by a recklessness triggered by all of her unanswered questions, she took a deep breath and began stopping people, showing them

Daniel's photo and asking if they'd seen him. Most of the men she encountered already smelled of alcohol, even though it wasn't yet ten o'clock. Judging by the sounds issuing from the bars when the doors opened, the strip shows took place all day long. A couple of men tried to talk her into going inside with them, but she kept moving. She knew she was taking a greater risk down here, but this was the last place someone had seen Daniel.

She wandered for hours, getting nowhere. No one else said they'd seen him. Glancing at her watch, she saw that it was three o'clock. She would have to hurry to get home before Teresa. She made her way back out to where she could catch a bus. She had to change buses three times, and was approaching the apartment when she stopped abruptly. Teresa was sitting on the front steps of the building.

"Hi," Ellie said, sauntering up the sidewalk.

Teresa didn't reply. She simply stared at Ellie.

Ellie forced a grin onto her face. "How was the shopping? We were crazy at the diner—"

"I just called the diner," Teresa said. "They said they haven't seen you today."

"Oh." Ellie sat beside Teresa, who immediately stood and stalked around the building to the side door. Ellie got up and followed her up the stairs to their apartment. Silently, she sat next to Teresa on the couch as KC jumped up into her lap.

"Where were you?"

The calmness of Teresa's voice worried Ellie more than if she'd yelled. "I was looking for Daniel."

Teresa turned to her. "Where?"

Ellie braced herself. "Down along the Strip district."

"What? Do you have any idea how dangerous that was?"

"That's why I didn't tell you," Ellie said, keeping her eyes on KC.

Teresa paused for a moment and Ellie could almost hear her trying to control her temper. "Why? Why did you go down there, and why did you lie to me?"

Ellie bit her lip, weighing how honest to be. At last, she sighed. "I ran into a woman, a street lady, a couple of weeks ago, near the bank, who said she might have recognized Daniel's name. She thought she'd seen him down there winter before this last one." She raised her gaze to meet Teresa's stony face. "I had to go. I'm sorry I lied, but you always worry so much, and you wouldn't have let me go if I'd told you." Ellie's eyes filled with tears. "It's the first clue I've had about him in seven years. I had to go."

She lowered her face to KC's head, sniffling. Teresa reached a hand out and laid it gently on her thigh.

"You should have told me," Teresa said quietly. "You should have trusted me to know how important this was to you."

Ellie raised her tear-stained face.

"From now on, you have to take someone else—Sullivan or me—if you're going to search in such dangerous places. Promise me."

"You... you would do that?"

Teresa laid a hand on Ellie's cheek. "You are everything to me. I know how much it means to you to find out what happened to your brother, but it would kill me if anything happened to you. Please don't do that to me."

Ellie closed her eyes, pressing her cheek into the warmth of Teresa's hand. "I won't. I promise."

"So, how is it, living with someone?" Karen glanced up as she twisted the corkscrew into a bottle of wine and extracted the cork. "An adjustment?"

"A little," Teresa admitted. She laid plates out on the table while Ellie and Bernie helped Robbie in the kitchen. "I mean, Ellie has been great about making room for my clothes and stuff, but..." She glanced toward the kitchen, but they were all busy, chatting. "I cannot stand going to a Laundromat. I never realized how spoiled I was, having access to a washer and dryer all these years. That is the first thing we're going to have to talk about, moving to an apartment or a house where we can have a washer and dryer."

Karen chuckled. "Your brother may be able to help. He gets rental listings all the time. Ask him."

Teresa lowered her voice. "I better talk to Ellie first. She likes the neighborhood she's in. It's... it's where she grew up." She looked around. "I'd love to have a place like this."

"Well, Shadyside isn't cheap, that's for sure. But we think it's worth it," Karen said. "We love this part of Pittsburgh. It has an old-fashioned neighborhood feel to it."

Teresa's expression became wistful. "I hate to admit it, but I kind of miss that part of Bloomfield. We knew everyone."

Karen looked at her. "And there's been no contact with your mother?"

Teresa shook her head. "There won't be. Not unless I come crawling back, alone, asking for forgiveness. I know now how Robbie felt."

Karen watched Rob for a moment as he had Ellie taste the glaze he had made for the ham. "I knew it hurt him, being cut off," she said. "But I didn't realize how much until these past few months since you fixed things. We never told you, but we were having some problems, Rob and I. He would get so moody and nasty, and I never really knew where it was coming from. He's so different now. I'm not close to my family. I can go to California to see them once every year or two and be perfectly fine with that, but I don't think you guys can. It's bred into you, that need to be around each other. How are you going to be if you and your mom can't patch things up?"

Teresa watched Ellie and Rob also. It hadn't been quite two months since she'd walked away from her family. What would birthdays and holidays be like? How would it be when Daniela made her First Communion and she wasn't there for it? What if one of the aunts ended up in the hospital? She turned back to the table.

"I don't know."

CHAPTER 27

"SHE'S HERE!"

The diner wasn't open yet, but the grill cooks were busy chopping potatoes and onions as they did their prep work in the kitchen, and the waitresses were wiping down all the booths and stools.

There was a lot of commotion as everyone crowded around to hug Louise and welcome her back.

Ellie came rushing into the kitchen from the office. "Did I hear—?"

She flew to Louise for a hug. Louise held her tightly.

"I've missed you so much," Ellie said happily. "How are you feeling?

"Like a bus ran me over," said Louise. She tugged at the upper part of her blouse to reveal an angry red scar over her breastbone. "My advice is to never have this done."

"It's better than the alternative," said Patty, coming in behind her mother.

Louise gave an impatient wave of her hand. "How are things here?"

"Everything is in good shape," Ellie said. "All the bills from last month are paid, all the orders are up to date, payroll taxes are done."

Louise shook her head. "I don't know what I would have done without you."

"How many times have I said that about you all these years? Want a pickle?"

Louise laughed. "Let me see the books." She and Ellie went into the office where Ellie had the diner's checkbook and ledger sitting out. Louise ran a finger down the columns. "I couldn't have done better myself. You didn't need me here at all."

"Don't be silly," Ellie said. "It's one thing to keep this up for a few weeks without you, but you are the heart and soul of this place. It would never be the same if you weren't here."

Louise sat back in her chair, searching Ellie's face. "And how are you?"

"I'm okay," Ellie said.

"That's not really an answer."

Ellie shrugged. "I'm busy. Between the bank and the diner and... I'm fine."

Louise watched her for long seconds. "How's Teresa?"

"She's good. She's busy at her store, and she's been helping out here." Ellie stood. "We should get back out there. I know everyone wants to visit with you before Patty makes you go home and rest."

Louise chuckled. "You are very good at changing the subject, Ellie Ryan. We'll talk more later."

"Sandy, I'm taking a couple of hours off." Teresa locked the pharmacy. "I'll be back by two to take care of any prescriptions."

"Okay, Boss."

Teresa stopped short and grinned. "Boss," she muttered, going to the office to get her purse. "I like that."

The air was hot and humid as she left the store's air conditioning, and it made her miss Bloomfield with its trees and shady sidewalks. This part of the city was ugly–good for business, but ugly. She felt a pang of nostalgia for the walks she used to take to deliver prescriptions for their older customers, the way they used to invite her in for a bite of whatever they had cooking, the way they told her what was happening in their families. She rolled down the VW's windows and drove to Francesca's house.

She parked in their driveway behind Francesca's Mercedes station wagon. Climbing the porch steps, she paused and took a deep breath.

When she rang the bell, she heard the kids running to the door. Rickie yanked it open.

"Aunt Resa! Where have you been?" He hugged her around the waist.

Daniela ran up behind him. "Did you bring us anything?"

"Daniela!" Francesca hurried after them, holding the baby. "That is not polite."

"But I do have something for you," Teresa said. She held up two bags. "One for each of you."

The kids grabbed their bags and dumped them on the living room floor, squealing over new coloring books and crayons and bottles of bubbles.

"I have something for you, too," she crooned to Annalisa, offering a plush teddy bear.

She looked at her sister who stood looking back. "Hi."

Francesca stood there for several seconds. "You haven't talked to me for three months, and all you can say is 'hi'?"

She turned toward the kitchen. Teresa followed.

Francesca put Annalisa in her high chair and scattered some Cheerios on the tray. She turned to Teresa with her arms folded. "Well?"

Teresa suddenly felt as if her legs might not hold her up. She sat at the kitchen table. "I've wanted to call you so many times."

"Then why didn't you?" Francesca got two glasses down and filled them with iced tea. She set one glass in front of Teresa and joined her at the table.

Teresa opened and closed her mouth a couple of times. All of her reasons and excuses for not calling suddenly seemed very feeble. "I didn't know what to say."

She glanced up to gauge the expression on Francesca's face and was startled at how much her sister looked like Sylvia. "Has Ma talked to you at all?"

"Not really," Francesca said. "For the first few weeks, she muttered a lot about how ungrateful you were, and how you were no daughter of hers, but she never really said what happened. What did happen?"

Teresa gulped her tea. "I... it was about Ellie," she managed to say. She reached over and rearranged the Cheerios on Annalisa's tray while she waited for Francesca's response.

"Is she your lover?"

That should be such a simple question to answer, Teresa would think later. She forced herself to meet her sister's gaze. "Yes."

"Wow." Francesca sat back. "That explains a lot. You should have heard Ma go off about the whole Billie Jean King thing."

Teresa laughed at the absurdity of that scenario. "Yeah, the timing of that could have been better."

They both sipped their tea while Annalisa gurgled happily.

Francesca gave Teresa a sidelong glance. "So, you're really...?"

Teresa took a deep breath. "I love her."

"Wow," Francesca said again. She shook her head. "No wonder Ma won't talk about it."

"It was awful. She said—" Teresa shook her head. "It doesn't matter what she said. I had to leave. I haven't meant to stay away, I just didn't know how you would feel about everything."

Francesca leaned forward. "I miss you. We all do. The kids, the aunts. It's worse than when Rob wasn't coming over. You were always in the middle of everything. It's weird without you there."

"Really?"

"Yes, really. Why would you even question that?"

Teresa blinked at the sudden tears stinging her eyes. "I've missed everyone so much."

"Can't you... can't you come without Ellie?"

Teresa shook her head. "It's not just coming over without Ellie. You know Ma. I'd have to crawl back, say I was wrong about everything. Never see her again." She met her sister's gaze. "I just can't."

Annalisa threw a handful of Cheerios at them and giggled. Teresa smiled. "I've missed this. But I have to live my life. I wasn't sure how you'd feel about this."

Francesca reached for Teresa's hand. "You're my sister. I love you. I want you to be happy." Her expression sobered. "I just don't know how you're going to be happy being torn in two."

———◦✦◦———

"What do you think is going on in there?"

Linda tilted her head toward Bill White's office where White, two other men they didn't know, and Aaron Myers had been sequestered for the past hour. It was late afternoon, nearly time to start counting their drawers. The door opened, and Myers walked out, not looking in their direction as he went back upstairs to the loan department.

"Miss Ryan?"

Ellie's head snapped up. Bill White was standing in his doorway. He gestured toward the office where the other two men sat with somber expressions. Ellie glanced toward Suzanne and Linda, and then walked to his office.

"Please, have a seat." Bill White indicated the chair Aaron Myers must have just vacated.

Ellie sat on the edge of the seat, looking from Bill to the other men.

One of them cleared his throat and said, "Miss Ryan, we're here about the alleged incident of last month."

"Alleged?" Ellie interrupted. "There is nothing alleged about it. He attacked me. I defended myself."

The other man shifted in his seat and cleared his throat. "That's not how Mr. Myers tells the story."

Ellie's mouth fell open. "And you're going to believe him? I suppose I hit myself across the cheek?"

The first man said, "He said you fell and struck your cheek against the desk."

"That's a lie!" Ellie stood. "He grabbed me, and when I kneed him in the balls, he hit me."

"Well," said the second man with a hint of a smile. "He said you would say something like that."

"He's a pervert! Just ask the other girls how many times he tried to grope them," Ellie said furiously. She turned on Bill White. "You know what he's like. Why are you just sitting there?"

Bill's jaw worked from side to side. "Aaron means no harm, he just—"

"I don't believe this!" Ellie looked from one of them to another.

"Look," said the second man. "The bottom line is, you've become a distraction at this branch. We're offering you a transfer to one of our branches down—"

"A transfer?" Ellie's eyes blazed. "Instead of doing something about him, you're going to get rid of me?"

"Now see here," said the first man. "We're offering you a diplomatic solution to your problem."

"My problem?" Ellie laughed. "I'll give you a diplomatic solution. Go to hell."

She yanked the door open and stormed through the lobby into the staff room where she pulled her backpack from her locker. She came back into the lobby, unpinned her name badge, and slammed it on the teller counter. "Good-bye," she said to Linda and Suzanne, who were watching with wide eyes. With one last disdainful glance toward the men peering around the door of Bill White's office, she turned on her heel and walked out the front door.

Teresa unlocked the apartment door to find KC sitting there scolding her for leaving her alone so long. "Where's your mother?" Teresa picked her up. "Ellie?" There was no answer. Teresa got a can of cat food from the refrigerator and fed KC. She glanced over and saw that the light was blinking on their new answering machine.

"Teresa," came Ellie's voice. There was so much background traffic noise that Teresa had a hard time hearing her. She leaned closer to the machine as Ellie's message continued, "I may not have a choice any more about taking Louise's job offer. I walked out at the bank. Those bastards were—"

There was a long pause on the machine, and Teresa could hear that Ellie was crying. "Anyway, I'll be home later. I just need some time." There was another pause, and then, "I love you."

Teresa looked around in dismay. How long ago had Ellie called? And where from? She played the message again and again, listening to the background noise. She thought she heard an amplified voice in the background saying something that sounded like "Philadelphia", but she couldn't be sure.

"Shit."

She was down at the Greyhound station. She was searching for Daniel down there again. She raced across the hall and pounded on Sullivan's door.

"What's up?"

"It's Ellie. I need your help," Teresa said.

Sullivan pulled his door shut and followed Teresa down to the VW. She explained as she drove.

"But why's she looking down there?"

"Because some bag lady thought she recognized Daniel's name, and thought that's where she'd seen him," Teresa said.

"That's a rough part of town," Sullivan muttered.

"Tell me about it," Teresa said, her voice tight. "I've asked her before not to go down there alone, but she sounded so upset about whatever happened at the bank."

They sat in a tense silence as Teresa wove through traffic. She found a parking space not too far from the bus station.

"What now?" Sullivan asked.

Teresa looked around. "I hate to say it, but we should probably split up." She glanced at her watch. "Let's meet back here in an hour, okay?"

He nodded and went in one direction while she headed in the other. She glanced through the doors of the topless bars, open to the warm summer night. Music thumped with amplified basses that she felt in her abdomen, and she saw women gyrating on the bars while men sat on the barstools, ogling them. Surely, Ellie wouldn't have been stupid enough to go inside any of those places. She turned to the alleys between buildings, calling for Ellie. The stench of rotting garbage and excrement was suffocating in the still, humid air. Where there were street people, she stopped to ask if they'd seen Ellie. A group of them had.

"She went that way," one toothless man said, pointing.

"Thank you." Teresa hurried in the direction he had indicated.

She was in a dank tangle of dark streets. The buildings had their windows thrown open to the night, and the sounds of televisions, people shouting, music—it all tumbled to the curb below in a cacophony of noise.

"Ellie?" she called hesitantly.

"What you doin' down here, Snow White?"

She turned to find three men approaching. They spread out to cut off any avenue of retreat. They were all dressed similarly in jeans and dingy T-shirts that used to be white, but now were stained under the armpits and yellowed under the dim light falling to the sidewalk in patches from the open windows above them. Two of them held open cans of beer, and the third had a lit cigarette hanging from the corner of his mouth.

She tried to push between two of them, but one sidestepped, blocking her.

"Let me pass," she said, and she could hear the tremor in her voice.

"Don't be so unfriendly," said the one with the cigarette. "We just wanna talk."

"I have to—" She tried again to shoulder her way through, but one of the guys with beer grabbed her arm while the third moved in behind her.

"Leave me alone!" She twisted out of his grasp, looking around in a panic for an escape route, but the one with the cigarette stepped in front of her.

"You shouldna come down here if you wasn't lookin' for company." Grinding the cigarette under his heel, he moved closer. She could smell the beer and tobacco on his foul breath.

"I was just looking for someone," Teresa said.

They closed in, their sweat and body odor almost gagging her.

"Well, you found three someones," said one of them.

"Please..." Teresa looked around desperately. The street they were in was dark and deserted.

One of the men reached for her hair. She jerked away.

"Don't touch me!"

They laughed. "You know you want it. That's why you came down here."

The two with beer in their hands threw the cans down and reached for her arms, dragging her deeper into the shadows. Teresa screamed for help. One of the men slapped her hard across the face and clamped a filthy hand over her mouth. She kicked and struggled, but they laughed harder and pinned her against the building. The roughness of the bricks and mortar ground against her shoulders and back as she fought. Two of them held her tightly while the third ripped open her blouse and shoved his hand under her bra. His other hand tugged on his belt. She bit at the fingers of the hand over her mouth and yelled for help again when the hand was yanked away. The man she'd bitten cursed and then punched her. Her head slammed against the brick wall behind her. Lights popped in front of her eyes and she fought to stay conscious. It seemed everything was happening from a long way away. There were other noises—yells and something that sounded like growling. She couldn't tell what was happening, but she realized the men weren't holding her anymore as she slid to the ground. Her legs refused to support her. As she slumped sideways, she had foggy images of a scuffle and a dog leaping before everything went black.

CHAPTER 28

TERESA LAY ON HER side with her eyes scrunched tightly shut, the covers pulled up over her head to shut out even the little bit of sunlight coming through the closed blinds of her hospital room. She stuffed a corner of the sheet into her mouth to keep from shouting at everyone to leave.

"Is the doctor sure there's no brain damage? Three days is a long time to be unconscious."

"They say she should be fine, but she'll have headaches for a long time from the concussion."

"How could this happen? Why was she even down there?"

"That's what the police want to know. Thank goodness they got the man."

Teresa's eyes snapped open. *The man? Why only one?*

"Is she awake?"

"I don't think so."

A shadow loomed over the bed, but she remained still.

"Let's go get something to eat, and then we can come back and see if she's awake."

Footsteps shuffled from the room, and all was blessedly quiet for a moment. Her parents and all of the aunts had been there nearly constantly since she'd awakened—was it only yesterday? She was losing track of days. She rolled onto her back and stared up at the ceiling. Every pulse of blood through the arteries in her brain felt as if her head was going to split apart. She tried to sit up and immediately began to retch. She grabbed for the emesis basin on her bedside table and vomited into it. A nurse heard the sounds and came in.

"Still nauseous?"

Teresa moaned and lay back again. "When is this going to stop?"

"You had a nasty concussion. Hard enough to crack your skull."

There was a knock on the door.

"Excuse us. Is Miss Benedetto awake?"

Two uniformed police officers stepped into the room.

"She is," said the nurse.

"Is she up to answering some questions?"

The nurse looked questioningly at Teresa, who nodded.

"Sorry, I can't sit up," Teresa said.

"That's okay, miss," said one of the policemen. "I'm Officer Pulaski, and this is Officer Benson. We just have a few questions about your attack. Do you remember what happened?"

"Yes. I was looking for a friend, and these three guys surrounded me—"

The two officers exchanged puzzled glances. "Three guys?"

"Yes. They cornered me, and two pinned me against a wall while the third started to... He started to..." She closed her eyes.

"Miss, there was only one man when we arrived on the scene."

"No," Teresa said. "There were three. They all wore jeans and T-shirts. They'd been drinking. They were white, in their thirties, about my height, dark hair, a few days' worth of beard."

Officer Benson pulled a notebook and pencil from a pocket and jotted notes while Teresa spoke.

"You're sure?" Pulaski hooked his thumbs in his belt. "You don't think you could be confused, you know, with the blow to your head?"

"No," Teresa said firmly. "One of the ones pinning me had his hand over my mouth. I bit him and he punched me. That's when my head hit the wall. After that, I don't remember much. I did hear a dog. That's when I blacked out."

Benson looked up from his notes and nodded. "That's right. Your attacker had a dog with him. We found a winter coat in his backpack that belonged to your father. We think he was stalking you, waiting for a chance to get you off by yourself."

"Wait, what?" Teresa pressed her fingers to her head, willing it to stop pounding so she could make sense of what they were saying. "No. That's not right."

"We have a photo of him." Pulaski reached into his chest pocket and pulled out a mug shot.

Teresa sat up, forcing the nausea back down, and took the picture. She blinked and tried to make her eyes focus.

"Do you recognize him?"

"Yes, but—"

"This is the man who attacked you."

"No. It isn't." Teresa looked up at the officer. "I know this man and his dog. They're homeless. They slept in the alley behind our store in Bloomfield last winter, but I haven't seen him since..." She tried to remember. "Like, last January." She looked at the photo again. She'd know Dogman's eyes anywhere. "This is not the man who attacked me."

"But your parents identified a coat he had as belonging to your father."

"No. You have it all wrong." Teresa closed her eyes, her palm pressed to her forehead. "That coat was in a bag for the Salvation Army. I gave it to him. He didn't steal anything." She looked at them. "I don't understand. Why would you think he attacked me?"

"When we got the call that there was an altercation in that alley, the first officers on the scene found this man kneeling over you. There was no one else in the alley, Miss Benedetto."

The expression in their eyes told her they did not believe her.

"Look, I don't know what happened after I blacked out, but I'm telling you, this is not the man who attacked me. There were three of them. I would know them if I saw them again, but it was not Dogman."

"Dogman?"

Teresa shook her head, but that only made it pound more. "It's what I called him. I never knew his name. Where is he now?"

The officers glanced at each other. "He won't give a name and we haven't gotten any word back on his fingerprints. A couple of army tattoos, but no other identification. He's a John Doe to us. We've got him in the city jail."

"What? No." She looked from one to the other. "You can't jail him. He didn't do anything."

"He won't give us a name," Benson repeated, his pencil poised over his notebook. "He hasn't acted innocent."

"Well, now that I've told you what happened, can't you let him go?"

Pulaski shook his head. "We'll have to let the city attorney know what you've told us, but he can't post bond, and they won't let him go just like that. When you get out of the hospital, they'll probably need you to come downtown and make a formal statement. Until then, he's staying put."

"Thank you, Miss Benedetto." The officers tipped their caps and left.

Teresa lay staring up at the ceiling. How did everything go so very wrong? Her head was splitting again, Dogman was in jail, and Ellie was gone forever.

Ellie sat on her bed, her drawing pad on her lap, sketches scattered around her on the comforter. KC lay curled up on Teresa's pillow.

The pillow that used to be Teresa's. Her pencil flew, feathery lines appearing like magic on the white paper—lines gradually growing darker and thicker, more jumbled, more confusing—like her memory of that night in the alley. She'd heard the sirens. There was a large crowd gathered by the time she got there. Police lights strobed from four or five cruisers. An ambulance rolled up, lights flashing and siren blaring to part the crowd. She'd caught only a glimpse of what looked like Teresa being wheeled into the back of the ambulance and whisked away. The police were asking for witnesses, but Ellie hadn't seen anything, and they wouldn't tell her what had happened. She'd seen a scruffy-looking man being taken away in handcuffs and a dog yowling pitifully as it was hauled away on the end of a leash. That's when Sullivan had found her.

By the time she'd gotten to Mercy Hospital, Teresa's parents and aunts were already there. No one knew anything except that Teresa had been attacked and was unconscious. When Ellie and Sullivan had entered the emergency room waiting area, Sylvia Benedetto had flown at her, yelling that this was all her fault, that Teresa had never gone anywhere like that part of town before. Ellie couldn't argue. It was true. Every bit of it. Sullivan and Teresa had both come, looking for her. Teresa, who had always been afraid, had gone anyway. *If only I hadn't done it...* How many times had Ellie wished that these past days?

The other aunts steered Sylvia to another part of the waiting room, but Anita had come to sit with Ellie, patting her hand as they waited for what seemed like hours for news. The doctors had finally told them that Teresa had suffered a fractured skull and concussion, and that they were transferring her to the neuro intensive care unit. When Ellie got upstairs, Sylvia had forbidden the hospital staff to let her see Teresa. It had been the most helpless feeling. Right there, through those ICU doors, was the woman she loved, only Ellie couldn't get to her. Rob and Karen and Bernie were there by then. Bernie said it didn't matter. Teresa was still unconscious. If she'd thought that would comfort Ellie, she was wrong. Teresa was hurt, and it was all her fault.

Ellie sat back, looking at the jumbled lines on the paper. The sketch captured all the chaos of the scene at the alley—all sharp angles and heavy lines and angry shadows.

There was a soft knock at the living room door. "Ellie?" She knew Sullivan was listening, waiting for her. "Ellie, I know you're in there." When she didn't respond, he went back to his apartment.

She set the pad aside and pulled other sketches to her. There, so beautiful, was Teresa the morning Ellie had drawn her as she slept. Ellie traced a fingertip over the curve of the breast and the swell of the hip. She turned to another sketch, one that was just lots of disjointed images —a sensuous mouth, soft eyes framed by long lashes, the sweep of a jaw and lustrous, dark hair....

When Teresa finally regained consciousness, Rob and Karen had arranged for everyone to be away from the room while Bernie sneaked Ellie in. Teresa had turned to see who had come in, and—*if I live to be a hundred, I'll never forget*—the hardening of her expression, the anger, the accusation. It was as powerful to Ellie as if Teresa had shouted it. And then, Teresa had simply turned away, rolled onto her side, her back to Ellie, without saying a word.

Her eyes filled with tears now as she stared at the eyes on the page. *She'll never look at me like that again.* She set the drawings aside and curled up on her side, sobbing.

The pronouncement by the doctors that Teresa was ready to be discharged from the hospital prompted a loud discussion as to where she would go.

"Of course she's coming home," said Sylvia, her hands on her hips. "Why on earth would she not come home?"

"And what's she going to do all day while y'uns are at the store?" asked Ana Maria. "She should come home with us. We can take care of her."

Teresa let them argue for a while, until she stunned them all into silence by saying quietly, "I'm not going with any of you."

The new reality of her situation hadn't hit for a few days, but, when it had, she'd had hours lying in a hospital bed to think about it. She didn't have a home. She didn't have a relationship. All of her clothes were at Ellie's. Other than retrieving them, she was free to go anywhere she wished. The irony of the situation didn't escape her, either. *Because of Ellie's relentless search for a homeless man who doesn't want to be found, I'm now homeless.* She lay there, trying to remember what it felt like to love Ellie, but it was as if those feelings had evaporated or belonged to some other person's life. Whenever she thought of Ellie, what she saw instead were the leering faces of the men who had attacked her; she felt again the paralyzing terror that they were going to rape her, that horrible feeling of helplessness as they had her pinned against the wall. She couldn't sleep for more than an hour or two before waking, soaked in sweat, her heart pounding, as she looked around to make sure there were no shadows lurking in the room. Somehow, all of these things had destroyed any feelings for Ellie other than anger, and Teresa found herself wondering how real her love had been, if it could be killed by something like this. *Am I even capable of real love?*

"Aren't you even going to talk to her?" Bernie had asked when they had a few minutes alone the day Teresa was discharged.

"There's nothing to say." Teresa avoided Bernie's gaze. "Rob and Karen have plenty of room. They said I'm welcome to stay with them as long as I want."

"You sure you don't want to come stay with us? You know my mother would love to have you. You're the daughter she really wanted."

Teresa laughed a little, but her head still hurt so she stopped. "No, thanks. I do have another favor to ask, though."

"You sure about this?" Bernie asked a couple of days later as she drove downtown. She'd been driving Teresa all over town since she got out of the hospital—the police station, the city attorney's office, and now, the city animal control office.

"I'm sure." Teresa walked up to the reception desk where a large black man was listening to a Pirates game on a radio.

"Excuse me?" Teresa smiled at him. "I was told by the police that my stolen dog had been found and brought here."

"What's the name?" the man asked, pulling a clipboard off a hook.

"The dog's name? Or mine?"

The man tilted his head and looked at her. "The dog's."

"Lucy."

"I don't see no Lucy."

"Well, she was stolen," Teresa said. "They didn't know her name. That's why I'm here. May we go back and look at the dogs?"

He glanced at the radio where the announcer was shouting about a double play. With an irritated shake of his head, he pushed heavily to his feet. "This way."

"What are you doing?" Bernie asked in an undertone.

Teresa shushed her and followed the attendant through a metal door, where their sudden entrance prompted nearly all of the dogs there to start barking. Teresa scanned the cages as they walked down the central aisle until she saw a brown dog cowering in the back of her cage.

"This one."

He stopped. "You sure?"

"I know my own dog," Teresa said. She could see Bernie's mouth drop at the lies she was telling and hoped the man wouldn't notice how obvious she was being.

He unlocked the door of the cage and Teresa squatted down, holding out some dog treats she'd thought to put in her pocket. "Lucy. Lucy, it's me. Come on, girl."

She held her breath for several seconds as Lucy simply stared at her, and then she crab-walked toward Teresa, wagging her whole back end, crouching and whining as she licked Teresa's face.

"Guess it's your dog, all right," the attendant said. "I got to have you sign for her."

Teresa stood and patted her leg. "Come on, Lucy."

"You can't take her out of here like that," he said. "She got no collar, and you got no dog license or leash."

Teresa thought quickly. "I guess the guy who stole her got rid of her collar with her tags. I'll pay for her license again if you have a bit of rope I could use." She gave him another smile, and he sighed.

"Follow me." He led the way back to the reception desk where he slapped a form on the counter. "Fill that out."

Fifteen minutes later, Lucy was in the back seat of the car, and Bernie was staring at Teresa. "Did that concussion do something to you? Where the hell did you learn to lie like that?"

Teresa gave her a sardonic look. "I grew up with you. And I'm finally learning it doesn't always pay to be honest. I knew they'd never let me have her to take care of her for Dogman, and I couldn't stand the thought of leaving her in that place."

"Shit." Bernie started the ignition. "I am impressed. So, where to now?"

"The city jail."

⚬

"I think this is everything."

Ellie had Teresa's clothes packed up in boxes and shopping bags. Bernie stood there, looking hesitant to grab them and go.

"Do you want to sit down?" Ellie asked, pointing toward the kitchen table.

"Yeah, I do." Bernie pulled out a chair and dropped into it.

"Coke?"

"Thanks."

Ellie got out two cans of Coke and joined her.

Bernie popped the top of her can. "I miss the tabs. Remember pulling them off and wearing them like rings?"

Ellie smiled a little. "Where is she?"

"At Rob's. Her mother's pissed, but she didn't want to go home."

Ellie glanced up at Bernie. "How is she?"

Bernie didn't answer right away. She reached for her cigarettes, then seemed to remember where she was and put them back in her purse. "Different. She changed when she met you, but this is different. She doesn't laugh. She doesn't really talk much. I think whatever those bastards did to her in that alley really messed her up."

Ellie nodded, but her eyes were dry. She seemed to have cried herself out. "And she blames me."

Bernie sighed. "I'm afraid she does." She leaned her elbows on the table. "I wish you'd go talk to her. It's stupid for y'uns to let this end without even talking. If it still ends after you talk, then okay. You'll deal with it. But this is bullshit."

Ellie shook her head, her fingertip drawing patterns in the frost on her can. "I can't. You saw what she was like in the hospital."

"Do you love her?"

"What?" Ellie looked up.

Bernie set her can down hard. "I said, do you fucking love her?"

"Yes. Of course I do."

"Then fight for her, goddammit." Bernie glared at her. "I have waited my entire life for what you two have. I would kill for someone to want me that bad. Yes, she's scared and angry and traumatized by what happened. Fight for her! Help her through this. Isn't she worth it?"

Ellie stared into Bernie's eyes. Her mouth opened and closed. "I'll... I'll think about it."

CHAPTER 29

TERESA AND LUCY WALKED the sidewalks of Rob and Karen's neighborhood, appreciating the thick shade of the sheltering trees warding off the hot June sun. Even in the shade, Teresa wore dark sunglasses, as her eyes were still sensitive to bright light. Lucy was on a leash, but there was no need. She never strayed far from Teresa's side. She was friendly with Rob and Karen, but it was clearly Teresa she had bonded to in Dogman's absence.

"I'm so sorry this happened," she'd said to him when they let her see him in jail. She frowned at her clasped hands on the counter that separated them. "I don't know how to thank you for what you did, getting them off me. I've talked to everyone I can and explained that it wasn't you. I think they believe me, but it's going to take a while before they let you go."

She didn't repeat what the assistant city attorney had said about having one John Doe in jail, even if it was the wrong man, being better than having three unknown suspects at large. She couldn't tell if he was really that arrogant, or if he still didn't believe her that Dogman wasn't her attacker.

Dogman had looked at her through the glass panel. "Do you know if Lucy is okay?"

Teresa nodded. "She is. I have her." She squirmed. "I had to tell them she was mine so they would let me have her, but I'll take care of her for you until you're released."

He'd nodded, staring at her with those eyes that seemed to burn through her.

She slid a piece of paper through the slot in the glass. The attending police officer checked it and handed it to Dogman. "Call me when they let you out, and I'll bring Lucy to you. Is there... is there anything you need? Anything I can get you?"

He shook his head. "They'll give me my stuff back when they let me out. All I need is Lucy." He stood.

"Okay." Teresa stood also. "Call me."

He nodded. "Thanks."

She knew he was only thanking her for Lucy's sake. She reached down now and patted Lucy's head as they walked. The dog had actually been good company. She'd been perfectly well behaved in the house, not messing or begging. Teresa had given her a bath and taken her to a veterinarian for her shots. She lay beside Teresa's bed at night and was always there when Teresa woke from her nightmares—the nightmares that weren't going away. Sometimes, Teresa would sit on the floor after one of her bad dreams, Lucy curled up against her thigh, warm and comforting. She'd been thinking lately that after Lucy went back to Dogman, maybe she'd get a dog of her own, but every time she thought it, she drew a blank on where that might be. She couldn't stay with Rob and Karen forever, and she could never move back home.

They approached the house, and Teresa stopped short. Ellie was sitting on the front porch. Bracing herself, Teresa walked up to her.

"Hi."

Ellie stood, brushing her backside off. Teresa had never seen Ellie in shorts and diverted her eyes from her bare legs.

"Hi," Ellie said. She glanced down at Lucy who wagged her tail. "Who's this?"

"Lucy."

Ellie glanced up sharply. "Lucy. As in Dogman's Lucy? The one who was behind your store?"

"Yes," Teresa said. "He was the one who saved me."

There it was again—that note of accusation. It hung like a palpable thing between them.

"Teresa, there's a lot we need to talk about." Ellie waited, her hands shoved into her shorts pockets as Teresa stared at the sidewalk for several seconds.

"Come in," Teresa said at last. "Rob and Karen are at work. I was just going to get dinner started."

Ellie followed Teresa inside. Lucy got a drink from a bowl on the kitchen floor and lay down where she could keep an eye on Teresa as she got a pasta pot out and started to fill it with water.

"Can we talk? Please?" Ellie said. "Without interruption?"

Teresa turned the faucet off and joined her at the kitchen table.

"Why aren't you at work?" Teresa asked.

Ellie sat back and exhaled. "There is so much... I don't have a job at the bank anymore."

"What? You said something in your message..." Teresa tried to remember.

"The day everything happened, I was pulled into the manager's office and—"

"They didn't fire you!"

Ellie shook her head. "No. They didn't fire me. They offered me a transfer to get me out of the way. Instead of dealing with the pervert who hit me, they figured it was easier to move me to another branch."

"What did you say?"

Ellie shrugged. "I told them to go to hell and walked out. That's when everything went haywire. I left you that message. I went downtown. I was just feeling angry and reckless and... I honestly didn't care if something happened to me that night." Ellie's eyes shone with tears. "But I never meant for it to happen to you."

Teresa watched Ellie, trying to feel something, anything other than anger. "And what if it had been you? Do you think that would have been any easier for me? What were you thinking?"

"I guess I wasn't." Ellie shook her head. "I was just so angry—"

"And reckless," Teresa cut in. "Got that."

Ellie opened her mouth to respond but closed it again. "What now?"

"Are you working for Louise?"

"Kind of," Ellie said. "I'm working there about forty hours a week, but we don't have a formal agreement. What about you? Are you back to work?"

Teresa looked down at her folded hands. "Not yet. I haven't decided what I'm doing."

Ellie leaned forward, placing her hands over top of Teresa's. "Please, can we fix this? Can't we go away together? Leave Pittsburgh, go somewhere new, somewhere where nothing else pulls us apart."

For long seconds, Teresa stared at their hands. "I don't know."

"Do you still love me?"

Teresa looked up. "What?"

"Do you still love me? Isn't that worth hanging on to?"

Teresa sat back, sliding her hands out from under Ellie's. "I don't know," she repeated. "I don't know what I feel." She stood and went back to the sink, not wanting to see the hurt and confusion in Ellie's eyes.

A moment later, she heard the front door open and close. When she turned around, Ellie was gone.

❧

"What are you doing? You shouldn't be here."

Louise gently pulled the spatula from Ellie's hand. Ellie wiped the back of her hand across her eyes.

"I need to keep busy." Ellie gave Louise a watery smile. "Who would've believed that making pies would be my way of keeping my mind off—"

Louise handed the spatula back. "Need some help with the dough?"

Ellie shrugged. "Sure. My dough's still not as good as yours."

Ellie measured sugar for the cherries while Louise added a little flour to the dough and kneaded it in.

"So, what's going on?"

Ellie blinked and kept her eyes on what she was doing. "Everything."

Louise raised her eyebrows in question as she pounded the dough.

"I lost my job. I lost my best friend." Ellie sniffed. "I feel like I can't do anything right."

"You miss the bank that much?"

Ellie snorted and clamped her forearm over her nose and mouth to avoid spraying snot into the cherries. "No. But it's not how I pictured myself leaving."

Louise chuckled. "Bet they'll remember it, though."

Ellie started laughing. Louise laughed along with her. A couple of the cooks and waitresses peeked back at them to see what was so funny.

Louise rolled the dough out to the perfect thickness and slapped it into a pie pan. Ellie spooned the cherry mix into the dough and turned to the sink to wash the bowl, while Louise laid out strips of dough in a basket weave pattern over top of the cherries. She slid the pan into the waiting oven.

"Come with me."

Ellie dried her hands and followed Louise to her office. Louise sat in her chair, and Ellie took the other seat.

"What are you going to do?"

Ellie sat there a moment. "About what?"

"About your life."

"What do you mean?"

Louise leaned forward. "I mean, you need some momentum. You aren't happy here. You need to move on. You need to let Daniel go, Ellie. You need to let Teresa go, too, if she won't go with you. And you need to let me go."

Sudden tears sprang to Ellie's eyes again. Exasperated, she wiped them away. "I'm so sick of crying. I feel like it's all I've been doing for weeks. And where do you get off, telling me all those things?"

Louise tilted her head and gave Ellie a knowing smile. "Ellie Ryan, I've known you for how many years now? I'm saying this because I love you. You have lived your life for your dead mother and your lost brother. You don't even know for sure he's here. You are suffocating here in this city. You've done the hard part. You walked away from your job. The next step should be easy. Pick a place and go."

Ellie shook her head. "I can't leave you. What about the diner? You can't work like you used to."

"Baby girl, you're never going to leave me. That's never going to happen. Patty's been reconsidering helping me out here. I think she got a little taste of it and liked it." Louise opened her desk drawer and pulled out a slip of paper. "This is the name, address and phone number of my cousin in Baltimore. She owns a seafood restaurant and just opened a second one. She needs a manager to help her out. It may not be what you want to do forever, but you learned enough here to step in, no problem. I told her all about you, and she'd love to have you call her for a telephone interview. No guarantees, but I did tell her I'd never make her favorite sweet potato pie again if she didn't hire you."

"Baltimore?"

"Not too far away," Louise said, reading Ellie's mind. "You'd be close enough to get back here for visits. You could explore a new city, see the Chesapeake Bay, and start your traveling the way you always planned."

Ellie considered. "Maybe Baltimore wouldn't be so bad."

"Thanks for driving us again."

Bernie glanced in the side view mirror at Lucy, who had her head out the backseat window. "I don't mind. You're still dizzy?"

"Yeah." Teresa rubbed her forehead. "It's irritating. It's like being a little drunk all the time."

"Shit. I wish I could feel that way without having to drink. It would make going back to school in the fall much easier."

Teresa smiled and looked back at Lucy. "I'm really going to miss her. She's been good company."

Bernie gave her a sidelong glance. "Missing anyone else?"

Teresa was glad for the concealing sunglasses she was wearing, but she knew Bernie could see the flush creeping into her cheeks. "I'm dealing with it."

"She really asked you to leave Pittsburgh and go away with her?"

"Yes. I told you." Teresa shook her head. "I just can't let go of what she did."

Bernie lit a fresh cigarette and took a deep drag. "What are you going to do about work?"

Teresa didn't answer immediately. "I don't know yet. Pop hasn't pushed me. And he's been paying me. Can you believe it?" She sighed. "I'll have to make a decision soon. I'll probably go back."

"To which store?" Bernie flicked her ashes out the window, and Lucy sneezed. "Sorry, dog." She pulled open her ashtray and turned back to Teresa. "You could go back to Bloomfield now, if Ellie's not in the picture."

"I know. I've been thinking about that." Teresa bit her lip as she thought. "It still feels like I'd be crawling back to Ma, though. Don't know if I can do it, but I do miss that neighborhood. It's so much nicer than Oakland."

"Where should I park?" Bernie asked as they neared the jail. "I've never done this."

"Me, either." Teresa pointed. "Park here. I'm not sure how long this will take."

"Do you want me to wait here?"

"Yeah, maybe. You mind?"

"Shit, no." Bernie ground out her cigarette and lit another. "The city jail is one place I can honestly say I've never had any desire to visit."

Teresa got out and opened the back door of the car. Lucy stood quietly while Teresa clipped her leash onto her new collar. Teresa reached back into the car and gathered up another large shopping bag before bumping the door shut with her hip. "I shouldn't be long."

She and Lucy walked through the jail's front entrance. The police officer behind the desk frowned at Lucy.

"I'm here for someone who's being released today," Teresa said quickly, before he could say dogs weren't allowed. She took her sunglasses off. "This is his dog."

"Who is it?" The officer consulted a clipboard.

"Dog—uh, John Doe," she corrected herself.

He looked up and peered at her more closely. "You the one he saved?"

Teresa nodded in relief. "Yes." It had taken forever to get the people in authority to believe that he had been her rescuer, not her attacker.

"Wait here." He gave Lucy one last curious glance and disappeared through a door.

A few minutes later, Dogman emerged through another heavy steel door, his backpack slung over one shoulder. Lucy immediately began whining and dancing in an effort to get to him. Teresa let go of the leash. He dropped the backpack, knelt down, and buried his face in her neck as she licked every bit of him she could reach. After a few minutes, he stood, wiping his hand roughly across his eyes.

"Thanks for taking care of her."

Teresa smiled. "I couldn't leave her in the pound. She's been no trouble at all." She hefted the shopping bag. "I have what's left of her food in here. And," she pulled out a dark-gray bundle. "I thought you might not want to have my father's old winter coat anymore after the trouble it caused. Here's another."

He looked from the coat to her as he picked up his backpack. "You didn't have to do that. You don't owe me anything."

"But I do," Teresa said. She pushed the coat back into the bag. "I will never know how you happened to be there that night, but I can never repay you for what you did."

He nodded and accepted the bag. They turned toward the front door and descended the steps to the sidewalk below. Dogman stopped and looked up at the summer sky.

"It's been a while," he said.

He knelt down and stuffed the dog food and coat into his backpack and refastened the flap. Slipping the straps over his shoulders, he picked up Lucy's leash and stood. He gave Teresa one last nod.

"Are you Daniel?" she blurted. She knew it was impossible, but she had to ask.

He turned and looked at her. "I don't know who that is."

CHAPTER 30

ELLIE MADE HER WAY through the cemetery to her mother's grave. There, she laid a sealed plastic baggie at the foot of the tombstone. Inside the bag was Daniel's Bronze Star. She'd included a note with the address of Louise's diner if he wanted to know where to find her.

"I don't know when I'll be back, Mom. It might be a while." She sat back on her heels and looked around at the squirrels running around like mad, gathering nuts as summer drew to a close. "I might finally get to travel and see some places. I'll tell you about it when I come back."

Are you doing the right thing?

She closed her eyes. She'd asked herself that question a million times. She still didn't know if it was the right thing to do, but Louise was right. She had to start living her life instead of spending it in one place waiting for people who weren't coming back. Including Teresa.

Ellie had hoped, after her talk with Teresa at Rob and Karen's house, that she'd come around, and they could leave together. All through her conversations with Marion, Louise's cousin, during all the hours of her bus trip to Baltimore to meet her and look for an apartment, the days spent packing up her things. Through all of those preparations, she kept hoping for Teresa's knock on the door, for a phone call saying she'd changed her mind, but there had been nothing.

"Bye, Mom."

She got to her feet and walked back to her apartment. Sullivan had borrowed a pickup truck from a friend, and they had loaded her bed, sofa and television into the back of it. She had sold or given away all of the rest of her furniture. Her clothes fit into two new suitcases—a bon voyage gift from Louise.

"I'm going to miss you so much," Ellie had whispered last night, holding Louise tightly.

"I'll miss you, too, Ellie." Louise rocked her. "But you'll be back to visit, and now I'll have another reason to come see my cousin."

Upstairs, Ellie took one more trip around her empty apartment, stripped now of all the travel posters. It felt sad and lonely. *Any lonelier than it has been since she left?* KC meowed pitifully from inside her carrier. Sullivan knocked on the open door into the living room.

"All set?"

Ellie sighed. "I guess." She picked up a paper-wrapped parcel. "You sure you don't mind delivering this?"

"I don't mind. I'll get it to her."

She picked up the cat carrier. "Let's go."

Teresa sat in a pew in St. Rafael's, breathing in the familiar scent of incense and automatically responding to the priest along with everyone else.

"Remember when it was our First Communion?" Bernie whispered. "God, that seems like someone else's life, doesn't it?"

Teresa nodded. Everything she did lately felt like it belonged to someone else's life. She was back at the Bloomfield store, but not back home. Rob had helped her find a small house to rent—"with a washer and dryer," she'd noted with a wry smile.

"Are you going to bring your bedroom furniture from home?" Bernie had asked.

Teresa had scoffed. "I've had that bedroom furniture almost since I got out of a crib. I think I'm ready to buy my own stuff."

The house still looked pretty empty—only a bed and dresser, a chair with an ottoman and a good reading lamp, and a small kitchen table with two chairs.

"You sure you don't want a television at least?" Karen had asked when she and Rob came over to see how she was doing.

Teresa shook her head. "I'm enjoying the quiet. I'm getting tons of reading done." *And the more furniture I buy, the more permanent this feels,* only she didn't say that part out loud.

She couldn't explain, even to herself, why she wasn't ready to make it feel more permanent, but ever since Sullivan had come by the store with Ellie's package...

"Baltimore? She really moved to Baltimore?" she'd asked.

"Yeah. I helped her move," he said. "She's working for Louise's cousin. Got a nice apartment. Starting over."

Starting over.

She closed her eyes now as Father Luigi droned on with his homily on original sin and how sacraments like First Communion bring sinners back to that state of innocence abandoned after childhood. She hadn't really believed Ellie could do it—leave Pittsburgh, leave her parents' graves, leave Daniel and her never-ending search for him—but she had.

Could you?

That question had been nagging at her more and more.

It's not that simple.

Sitting on her dresser—the only ornamental thing in her entire apartment—was the calligraphy Ellie had made for her mother and asked Sullivan to deliver to her. Sitting beside it was Ellie's note. *I hope one day you'll come to me with this, but if you don't, keep it to remember me.*

Lately, Teresa had felt stirrings of something she couldn't at first identify. She found herself daydreaming about what Ellie might be doing now, or she would read something and her first thought was, *I have to remember to tell Ellie about that.* Her nightmares were becoming less frequent and less vivid. There had been a few good dreams, too, even some erotic ones in which Ellie was making love to her, and she woke throbbing with an orgasm.

Teresa snapped to as the homily ended, and everyone shifted.

Father Luigi began blessing the bread and wine for Communion, and there was a stir of excitement. Daniela's second grade class filled the first two rows so they could watch the momentous preparations for this milestone in their lives. When it was time, the nuns whispered to the children, herding them to the back of the nave so they could line up two by two, girls on the right, boys on the left. In their columns, they marched solemnly down the center aisle, the boys wearing their first suits, hair slicked back, cheeks soft and rosy, while the girls patted the full skirts of their white dresses, some still wearing lace pinned to their hair, a few with white gloves. Daniela gave a nervous wave as she marched by, almost walking up the heels of the girl in front of her. Francesca put a hand over her eyes and shook her head.

Can you even remember what it felt like to be that excited by something? Teresa frowned, trying to recall. She'd certainly been excited, giddy even, about things as a girl—First Communion, first bicycle, starting high school, going to college—but then, her life had settled into a... a flatness, where nothing seemed extraordinary, nothing stood out. Until Ellie. Ellie had brought color and joy and excitement back into a life that had become merely existence. Teresa shook her head. *I'm reading too much,* she thought with a droll smile. But she couldn't shake the feeling that her life had become flat again, monochromatic, like a black and white photo.

After the Mass was over, every family jostled for photos of their child standing on the steps in front of the altar.

"This is going to take forever," Bernie whispered. "Come on."

"I'm going to stay," Mrs. D'Armelio said. "I'll see you at the Martellis."

Together, Teresa and Bernie escaped into the bright September sunshine. "Shit. This is going to be a big deal, isn't it?"

"Yup. As big as Christmas," Teresa said. She retrieved her sunglasses from her purse. "My family hasn't had an occasion like this for ages. My mother and the aunts are going to make the most of it." She grabbed Bernie's elbow. "Let's walk. Leave the car here."

Bernie looked at her as if she were crazy, but shrugged and reached for a cigarette. "So, how's the new place?"

"Different." Teresa squinted up at the brilliantly blue sky. "I have never lived alone. You have any idea how weird that feels?"

Bernie thought about it. "I haven't, either. Jesus, I won't live alone until Mom dies. That might not be until I'm retired. She'll live forever."

Teresa chuckled. For all of Bernie's complaining about her mother, Teresa could not see her living alone, cooking or cleaning for herself. She didn't want to think about what that house would look like if Bernie lived there by herself.

"What are you going to do for your birthday?"

Teresa looked at her in shock. "I forgot. Thirty-five next month. Damn. Can you believe we're this old?"

Bernie snorted. "You mean, this old and exactly where we were when we got out of college. Are we still going to be here in another thirty-five years?"

"Good night, you guys. See you tomorrow."

Ellie waved to the cooks and waitstaff as she locked up the restaurant. Marion's original restaurant was in Riverside, on the west side of the Inner Harbor, but she had reasoned that having another location on the east side would be a smart move for those customers who didn't want to navigate Baltimore's downtown traffic. The new location in Fell's Point was doing well. Ellie liked the artsy feel of this section of the city. The only downside was the smell. She sniffed her sleeve as she walked under the streetlights. It was hard to get the fishy smell out of her clothes and hair. She'd been lucky enough to find a small apartment on the second floor over an art gallery. It had been the artist's living quarters and studio before he started becoming successful. It had large windows that gave her a wonderful view of the city's skyline. She carried a stout walking stick. She hadn't had any trouble, but most nights, she got out of the restaurant after the buses stopped running, and walking was her only option. She only had to go eight blocks to get home, but she kept scanning her surroundings as she walked.

Funny, she thought, *I used to walk around Pittsburgh at all hours and never worried at all.*

Maybe you should have worried more, replied a small voice in her head. *If you had, she'd still be with you.*

She walked faster, trying to outpace those unwelcome thoughts, but she knew better. They'd been her constant companions since that night. For Ellie, life would never be the same. One stupid decision had changed things forever. Teresa could not forgive her, and now she was alone —again—but more alone than she'd ever been in her life. Marion was nice, but she wasn't Louise. She was Ellie's boss, not her friend, and though she had helped get Ellie set up in the new restaurant, she only came by three or four times a week to check on things.

Approaching her building, she looked around to make sure no one was nearby, waiting to pounce as she unlocked the door. The area looked deserted. She unlocked the door and quickly flipped the lock again as soon as she was inside. There, pushed through the mail slot, was the day's mail. She gathered it up and climbed the stairs to her apartment. She could hear KC meowing as she unlocked the door at the top of the stairs.

"Hi, little one." She picked KC up and felt the vibration of her purr against her chest. She carried the cat into the kitchen and spooned a little canned food for her. She set cat and food on the table and sat to leaf through her mail, smiling when she saw a letter from Louise. She'd never been much of a letter writer—*who did I ever have to write before?*—but she had written Louise and Sullivan regularly since moving. Sullivan didn't write back very often, but Ellie didn't expect much from him. She wrote because it gave her something to do. Her schedule was much different now. She was working a lot of hours, often not getting home until after midnight and then back at work by ten the next morning, but the pay was good. She was saving money, *and what else would you do with your time anyhow?* She wondered sometimes how Suzanne and Linda were doing, but she found she didn't miss the bank at all. She did miss other things, though. She'd said good-bye to Larry, riding his bus one last time before she left, and she'd gone to the little park near the bank to sit one last time, watching the old men play chess, and the mothers with their babies, and the street people wandering around.

She read Louise's letter, full of bits of this and that, nothing special, but it warmed her heart to read it. She placed it with all the others in a stack on the table. She turned out all the lights and went to shower. A few minutes later, she was sitting on the couch, a towel draped over her shoulders as she continued rubbing her hair dry, looking out the windows at the lit silhouettes of the skyscrapers in the distance. KC jumped into her lap and settled contentedly. Ellie reached over to the side table where stood a vase with a dried white rose—the one Teresa had left at her door—and she felt again that ache where her heart used to be. *It's still there,* she reminded herself, touching a finger to the gold heart hanging around her neck—*crooked and bent, but whole.*

"Teresa, you don't have to do that," Mrs. Schiavo said as Teresa paused her sweeping of the sidewalk in front of the store to help distribute the bread.

"I don't mind." Teresa took the leftover loaves and broke them in half. She kept glancing over the heads of the people gathered there, hoping to catch a glimpse of Dogman and Lucy, but she suspected she would never see them again. She gave out the last of the bread and returned the tray to Mrs. Schiavo.

"Come inside." Mrs. Schiavo led the way into the bakery and poured two cups of strong coffee. She joined Teresa at a table, setting a doughnut down in front of her. "How are you doing?"

Teresa tore off a bite of doughnut and dunked it in her coffee before eating it. "I'm doing okay."

Mrs. Schiavo peered into her face. "Just okay?"

Teresa nodded. "Just okay. But okay is better than it has been."

Mrs. Schiavo thought about this as she sipped her coffee. "What would make it better than okay? Is it your mama?"

"No, surprisingly." Teresa gave a tight-lipped smile. "It isn't my mother."

"Then it's love," Mrs. Schiavo said. "Love, she doesn't always go smooth, does she?"

Teresa opened her mouth and closed it. "No. She doesn't always go smooth."

"How old are you?"

Teresa blinked. "Thirty-five next week."

"So young." Mrs. Schiavo clucked her tongue. "So much life ahead of you. Are you better? From the hospital?"

"Yes." Teresa kept her gaze on her doughnut. "I'm better."

"But still afraid?"

Teresa looked up sharply. "Yes, sometimes."

"And angry." Mrs. Schiavo nodded. "Fear and anger, they go like this." She clasped her gnarled hands together. "When the fear, she goes away, the anger, she will go, also."

"I'd better get back to the store," Teresa said. "Thanks, Mrs. Schiavo."

The drugstore was still empty when she got back inside. Her mother had been coming in a bit later than she used to. It wasn't exactly angry between them anymore. It was just strained. They talked about the store and inventory; they talked about Francesca and the kids; they talked about the aunts, but Sylvia never mentioned Ellie or asked how Teresa was doing in her house. Teresa brought her own dinner; Sylvia didn't come back with a plate in the evenings.

"I always wished she would stop being so nosy, butting into my life all the time," Teresa had confided to Bernie a couple of days ago. "But now that she has, it's really weird."

"Good weird or bad weird?"

"More good than bad," Teresa said. "Makes it hard to think of things to say sometimes, so we just don't talk for long periods of time."

"Jesus, that would be weird," Bernie said. "I can't picture your mother keeping her mouth shut. What do you want to do for your birthday?"

"That was an abrupt change of topic," Teresa said, narrowing her eyes. "Why? What do you have in mind?"

Bernie grinned with a wicked gleam in her eyes. "Want to go dancing? I kind of miss going out to Wild Sisters. It was fun. And it's not like the asshole will ever take me dancing. Too afraid someone will see us and tell his fucking wife."

"I'll think about it," Teresa said, but privately, she knew she had no intention of going near that place again. To be there without Ellie would feel as if she were cheating. That made no sense, but she couldn't imagine being with another woman, even if it was just dancing. "In the meantime, I need you and your mom to come to dinner on Sunday. I don't know if I can stand them celebrating my birthday without some backup."

CHAPTER 31

TERESA KNOCKED ON THE door and opened it. "Anyone home?"

"Come on in," Karen called from the kitchen. "Rob should be home any minute."

Teresa took off her jacket and hung it in the foyer closet. "What can I help with?"

"Pour us some wine, and then you can take over with the fettuccini." Karen moved over to chop up some carrots for a salad.

"Fettuccini?" Teresa went to the pot where the water was boiling. "Y'uns don't usually eat this heavy."

Karen shrugged. "We are tonight."

Teresa's eyes narrowed. "What's up?"

Her question was answered immediately by Rob's entrance, accompanied by Anita. Teresa gave Karen an "I should have known" kind of look. Robbie, taking Anita's coat for her, looked a little embarrassed.

"What can I do?" Anita asked. She hurried into the kitchen where Karen set her to work on the salad while she went to finish setting the table.

"So how are you, Nita?" Teresa asked, stirring the fettuccini noodles.

"Same old things," Anita said. She waved her knife, sending a bit of celery flying through the air. "Everything hurts. I don't know how long I'm going to last."

Teresa smiled and picked up the celery. She lifted the cover on the alfredo sauce, giving it a stir and then raised the spoon to her lips. She sprinkled a little more salt into the sauce. "You'd better be here a good, long time. I don't know what I'd do without you."

Anita scoffed. "You never come to see us. When you come to Sunday dinner, you don't say two words. You're like a ghost of the old Teresa."

Teresa didn't respond. She could feel Anita's eyes boring into her back, but she busied herself stirring the sauce again.

"Smells great," Robbie said. He rolled his shirtsleeves and washed up.

They finished dinner preparations and sat, where Anita insisted on saying grace before they ate. Rob passed the bread while Teresa looked suspiciously from one of them to another. They ate for several minutes, but no one said anything and no one made eye contact.

"All right." Teresa set her fork down. "What's up? Nita isn't here by chance. Y'uns are up to something, so out with it."

Anita suddenly found her salad very interesting while Rob shoveled another forkful of fettuccini into his mouth. Karen gave them a disapproving glance.

"Since these two are turning chicken," Karen said, "I'll tell you what's going on." She set her fork down as well and placed her elbows on the table. "We're worried about you."

Teresa sat back. Conversations like this never happened in this family. It was one thing to yell or squabble, but no one talked about feelings. She waited nervously.

"Let her eat first," Rob said, but at Karen's glower, he lowered his fork as well. "She's right. We are worried about you."

"You're not happy," Anita said.

"I'm fine," Teresa said. "I've just been through a lot."

"Yes, you have," Karen said. "I can't imagine what you went through that night, but this is more than that, and you know it."

Teresa's heart hammered in her chest. Except for blurting out to her mother that she loved Ellie, she'd never talked about this to anyone. She didn't know exactly how much they knew or guessed.

"Resa," Rob said. "Look, we know this is hard. And it's not something you can just talk about. But we want to tell you, all of us, that we support you. We'll be here for you, no matter what."

Teresa stared at her plate. They still weren't saying precisely what it was they supported—*do they really know?* She couldn't speak, couldn't take the chance that they weren't talking about the same thing.

"Teresa." Anita reached over and placed her hand on Teresa's arm. "I told you about Nikolas. How we let our families keep us apart. How I've regretted that decision my whole life. I may not understand loving another girl, but I understand love. If you love Ellie, you need to go to her."

Teresa couldn't have been more shocked if Anita had slapped her. She looked up warily, meeting their eyes one at a time, watching for signs of judgment or disgust—the things she'd seen in her mother's eyes—but there was none of that.

Karen spoke first. "We've never seen you as alive as you were with Ellie."

"And this," Rob said, waving his hand in her direction, "is bullshit."

Teresa snorted with laughter, her eyes filling with tears.

Rob pressed his advantage. "We'll deal with Ma and Pop. Go to her."

Teresa blinked rapidly. "It's not that simple. We didn't—things weren't good between us when she left."

Karen reached for Rob's hand. "Love isn't always easy. We've had our rough patches. But it's always worth it. Do you love her?"

Do you still love me?

Teresa hadn't been able to answer that question when Ellie asked it. She hadn't felt anything except fear and anger then, but, as Mrs. Schiavo had said, when she'd finally been able to let go of the fear, the anger had gone as well. What was left now, was an ache—a terrible, empty ache.

"I... I have to think about it," was all Teresa could say.

"But—"

Karen started to argue, but Anita cut in.

"That's enough for now. The food's getting cold. Let's eat."

Teresa shot her godmother a look of gratitude. She knew Teresa well enough to know that more talking was not productive. All her life, the best way to talk Teresa into anything was to plant the seed and leave her alone to think it over.

When dinner was over, Teresa and Anita insisted on helping to clean up.

"Thanks," Teresa mumbled to Rob and Karen as she said good night. "I'll take Nita home."

In the car, Anita talked about nothing important—Luisa's gout in her big toe, was Gianni ever going to get engaged to Angelina, what a stinker little Rickie was—and Teresa was again grateful to her aunt for not expecting her to talk. She couldn't have talked right now, not without bursting into tears.

She pulled up at the curb. "I'll walk you up." She accompanied Anita up to the front door where Anita turned to her.

"Good night, my angel."

"You haven't said that since I was little," Teresa said, her voice cracking.

Anita laid a loving hand on Teresa's cheek. "I know."

She went inside, and Teresa walked slowly back to her VW. As she drove, Teresa felt a slow upwelling of emotion, a tidal wave of things she'd kept in, walled up, ever since the terror of that night in the alley. She stumbled through her front door, dropped into her chair, and wrapped her arms around herself as she sobbed.

It was still dark when Ellie woke. For a moment, she lay there, trying to hold on to her dream… It had been a good one, about the Christmas when she'd been five. She'd crept downstairs first to check out what Santa left and then had run back upstairs to get Daniel, who groggily followed her downstairs.

"This pile is yours," she said excitedly.

Daniel was fully awake by then and turned on the kitchen light so the illumination wouldn't reach upstairs and wake their parents. "Hey, I got a new guitar!"

"And I got drawing pencils and new books," Ellie whispered.

They froze as they heard footsteps upstairs, and, a moment later, their parents came down.

"Merry Christmas," Michael said.

"Merry Christmas, Daddy," said Ellie, running to give him a hug.

"Play us some music," Ellen said.

Daniel lifted the guitar out of its case, adjusted the tuning, and played "Silent Night".

Ellie smiled now, remembering how he had loved that guitar. It had broken her heart to have to let it be sold when her mom died, but she could only take a few things with her to foster care. She rolled over and hugged KC. The holidays were edging closer. This had been one thing she hadn't been looking forward to. She still hadn't made any friends here in Baltimore. *Hard to meet people when you're always working.*

Last year at this time, she and Teresa had been dancing around their attraction to each other, neither confident enough to say or do anything... until that magical New Year's Eve.

Has it really been a year since I met her? She tried to think back. It had been fall, just before the holidays because she helped decorate the store window. *How could so much good and bad happen in one year?*

She felt homesick for Pittsburgh, for Louise, for Teresa. Getting to spend Christmas with Teresa last year had felt so special. For a little while, she had thought she might never have to spend another holiday alone. *Stupid you.*

She got out of bed and padded into the bathroom. She had a rare day off and had booked a spot on a lunch cruise of the harbor. She glanced out the window. The sky was cloudless. It looked as if it was going to be a gorgeous day.

She showered, and then she and KC had breakfast. "What do you think about this cruise, little one?" Ellie asked as she ate her Shredded Wheat. "On a boat for three hours with a bunch of strangers." KC looked up and gave a tiny meow. "But if I don't do things like this, I'll never meet people, will I?" KC meowed again. Ellie nodded. "That's exactly what I thought. Thanks."

She gave KC's head a pat and carried her bowl to the sink.

An hour later, she was on a dock at the Inner Harbor, lining up with about twenty other people to board a boat. A group of three women a few places in front of her in line caught her attention, all of them stocky with short hair and baseball caps. They had to be family. She smiled to herself as the crewmembers started letting people board. Ellie found a place on the upper deck that gave her an unobstructed view. The sun was warm, but the air was still chilly, and she zipped her jacket as she stood at the rail. She heard voices and turned to see the three women climbing the metal steps to the upper deck. They said hello, and Ellie nodded in return before turning her attention to the crew making preparations to begin the cruise. Someone's amplified voice came over a loudspeaker, explaining their route and inviting them to wander the boat freely.

Ellie put on her sunglasses and settled in a chair, her face lifted to the sun, enjoying the rolling motion of the boat as it moved away from the dock. She could feel the vibration of the boat's engines as they rumbled. Over the rumble, she became aware of the women's voices off to her side. Two of them were telling the third she was better off without her cheating girlfriend, but the third woman, Darlene, was apparently still lamenting the breakup. Ellie rolled her eyes behind her sunglasses. It had never occurred to her that she'd had no one to confide in when she and Teresa broke up. Louise seemed to know, but they'd never talked about it. She probably could have talked to Bernie, but she was Teresa's friend. And Sullivan was just...Sullivan. *I never even thought of it as a breakup*, she realized. *It was just another thing ending. Like everything else in my life.*

The amplified voice returned, pointing out landmarks as they traveled south through the harbor. Ellie sat up, ignoring the continued conversation near her, taking in the views as the boat churned along at a leisurely pace. Before long, the crew was inviting people to head toward the dining room.

Now, for the awkward part. Ellie took a deep breath, reminding herself that she'd chosen this cruise to meet people. She followed the other women down the stairs to the main deck and inside to the dining room, where most of the passengers were already seated at tables. She stood there for a moment, looking around.

"Won't you join us?"

She turned to find one of the three women from the upper deck standing near her, indicating their table. "Thank you."

"I'm Olivia," said the woman who had invited her. "This is Sue, and this is Darlene."

Ellie nodded to each of them, introducing herself. "Are y'uns from Baltimore?" she asked as she placed her napkin in her lap.

They glanced at each other. "Sorry, what?" said Sue.

Ellie smiled. "I forgot. That's Pittsburgh. Are you guys all from Baltimore?"

"We are," Olivia said, indicating herself and Darlene. "Sue is from Frederick."

Ellie had no idea where that was, but she nodded politely.

The crew began serving lunches. The four women chatted through lunch, and Ellie told them about the job that had brought her to Baltimore. She learned that Sue and Darlene were guidance counselors for Baltimore schools, and Olivia was a legal assistant.

The boat made a wide, sweeping turn and began the return trip to the dock. They finished lunch and went back to the upper deck, where the day had warmed enough to take their jackets off.

"Would you mind giving us your phone number?" Olivia asked, pulling a business card from her wallet. She asked a crewmember for a pen and jotted a couple of numbers down. "This is us, and that's Darlene," she said. "We've never been to your restaurant. Maybe we can come by some night. Are you allowed to join us?"

"Probably not," Ellie said. "But I'll make sure you have a great dinner."

The boat docked and all the passengers got off. Ellie stood there for a moment.

"It was nice to meet all of you," she said.

"You, too," said Darlene, looking at Ellie as if she wanted to say something more.

"Well, I have to get going," Ellie said before Darlene could say anything else. "Bye."

She turned and walked away with a wave. "You wanted to meet people," she said with a wry smile as she turned a corner.

A hard frost had descended overnight, covering Teresa's car windows, and making the bushes and trees glitter in the early morning light. She scraped her windshield clean and gave the side windows a cursory scrape, and then got in and headed toward the store. As she turned into the alley, her eyes automatically scanned for Dogman and Lucy. Even after all these months, she still hoped she might see them.

Inside the store, she busied herself putting out the boxes of Halloween candy that had been delivered yesterday. *Ellie's idea*, she recalled. And right after Halloween, it would be time to decorate the window for Thanksgiving. She went to the storeroom and found the box labeled "Macy's Parade". Inside were all of the miniatures Ellie had made for the display last year, with the toy soldiers holding the strings attached to their Popeye and Superman balloons. She fingered one of the figures, biting her lip for a moment before setting the box down and going to the telephone.

She dialed and waited impatiently for someone to answer. "Hi, Mrs. D'Armelio? Has Bernie left for school yet?" She waited, listening to the voices coming over the phone. "Hey," she said when Bernie picked up. "You doing anything tonight?"

"No," said Bernie. "Why?"

"Want to go to the diner?"

There was a long pause. "Sure. We can do that. Want me to pick you up?"

"No," said Teresa. "I'll come get you. Five o'clock?"

"Sounds good. See you then."

Teresa hung up and went outside to sweep and pass out bread for Mrs. Schiavo. She'd have to figure out how to get her mother to close the store for her.

"Just tell her you have something to do," she muttered. "It's not like you do this every night. You're allowed to have an evening off."

If Sylvia wondered what Teresa wanted with her evening off, she didn't ask. Teresa kept an eye on the clock, wondering a few times if it was broken, as it seemed to have stopped. At last, four-thirty rolled by, and she went to get her jacket and purse from the office.

"Bye, Ma," she said as she hurried out the back door.

She drove to Bernie's house and beeped. Bernie appeared immediately and got in.

"So, what's up?" Bernie asked.

"Nothing," said Teresa. "I just got hungry for one of Louise's burgers."

"Jesus, Bennie, it's me. Stop with the bullshit."

Teresa sighed. "All right. I want to get her address. I figure Louise will have it."

Bernie grinned. "It's about fucking time." She chatted about school and the nun who was their new principal as Teresa drove through downtown traffic.

When they got to the diner, Teresa's heart fell as she saw Patty at the register. "Damn. She's not here."

They slid into a booth and picked up menus. A waitress Teresa didn't recognize came to take their drink orders.

"Is Louise here tonight?" Bernie asked.

The waitress glanced up at them. "Yes. She's in the office. May I tell her who's asking?"

"Friends of Ellie's."

"I'll tell her right away."

Louise appeared a couple of minutes later and sat beside Teresa, giving her a hug. "How are you two?"

"We're good," Teresa said. "How are you feeling?"

Louise laughed. "I couldn't be better. Patty is here at least half-time now, so I can take some time off. Something I never thought I'd say." She eyed both of them. "So what brings you down here?"

"Your burgers and shakes," Teresa said quickly. "What else?"

Louise nodded. "What else, indeed." She slid out of the booth. "I'll let you enjoy your meal. Good to see you."

Bernie leaned across the table. "Why didn't you ask?"

"I just couldn't," Teresa said miserably. "Then she'd know Ellie and I haven't talked or written."

Bernie shook her head. "You are so fucked. Do you think she doesn't know that already?"

Teresa sat there, her appetite gone, when Louise reappeared.

"I don't know if you need this," she said, laying a slip of paper on the table. "Oh, and I'm driving down there in a couple of weeks, if you'd like to go with me."

She left, and Teresa stared after her.

"Close your mouth," Bernie said reaching for the paper. "You look like an imbecile." Her face broke into a big grin, and she held the paper up. "Ellie's address."

"Why are you doing that?"

Marion had entered the restaurant on a busy Friday night, unannounced as she often did, to find Ellie hurrying through the dining room, carrying a tub of dirty dishes.

"One of the bus boys didn't show tonight," Ellie said in a harassed voice. It wasn't just the missing bus boy—it was the bus boy, a squabble between two of the waitresses over a bartender, and Darlene. She could feel Darlene's gaze following her from the bar, though she refused to look over. Ever since the cruise, Darlene had been coming to the restaurant two or three nights a week. She sat at the bar, ate a little, drank quite a bit, but mostly tried to engage Ellie in conversation. Ellie had quickly figured out that maybe Darlene's girlfriend had her reasons for leaving. Ellie made her apologies, but kept moving, grateful on the nights the restaurant was busy.

"I want to check on the new guy," Marion said, heading to the kitchen where they had a new cook, whose only experience was cooking in his family's Chinese restaurant. Marion hadn't been so sure about hiring him, but Ellie had talked her into giving him a chance.

"I'm surprised this joint isn't serving fried chicken and chitt'lins," Ming, the new guy, was saying to the other cooks as they entered.

The other cooks stopped laughing when they saw Marion and Ellie, and there was dead silence, except for the sizzle of cooking food.

Marion put her hands on her hips, reminding Ellie forcefully of Louise, and said, "I suppose if you had your way, we'd be serving chow mein and egg rolls." Ming whipped around to face her as a few of the other cooks smirked. "If you have a problem working for a black woman," Marion continued, "you'd better speak up now."

"No, ma'am," he said.

"Glad to hear it. Now get back to work, all of you."

Marion went down the line, tasting and inspecting. "Good work, everyone." She made for the kitchen doors, adding in a fake Southern accent, "Even if we ain't serving fried chicken and chitt'lins."

They heard loud laughter follow them as the doors swung closed. Marion pulled Ellie aside. "What's with the woman at the bar? A friend of yours?"

Ellie felt her face get hot. "No. I mean, I know her, but I don't know how to get rid of her."

"Leave that to me." Marion went behind the bar and stood in front of Darlene. "How many have you had tonight, sweetheart?"

"Just a couple," Darlene said, holding her beer.

"Well, I never let anyone leave my place three sheets to the wind," Marion said. "And I don't let customers interfere with my staff when they're on the clock. So, this is your last one for tonight, all right?"

How does she do that and not piss people off? Ellie thought, watching from a distance.

"Sure," Darlene said, draining her glass. She slid down from her bar stool and left with one last glance in Ellie's direction.

"If that happens again, you let me know," Marion said.

"Thanks."

Marion glanced at her watch. "Louise should be here soon. Let's go to the office."

Ellie told the hostess where they'd be and followed Marion.

"Close the door," Marion said.

Ellie closed the door and sat.

"Are you happy here?"

Ellie's mouth opened and closed a couple of times. "I don't know what you mean."

Marion sat back, one perfectly plucked eyebrow arched as she looked at Ellie. "I mean, are you happy here? Happy at work? Happy in Baltimore? It's not a hard question."

"Well," Ellie stalled. "I guess I've been a little homesick for Pittsburgh, but I've been exploring more of Baltimore. It's a nice city."

"Yes, it is," Marion agreed with a hint of a smile, but only a hint. "And you still didn't answer my question."

Ellie's shoulders slumped a little. "I'm tired, I guess. Working a lot of hours."

At this admission, Marion leaned forward, her elbows on the desk. "Yes, it has been a lot of hours. And you've done a fantastic job. I would have had a hard time getting this second location up and running without you. Louise wasn't lying when she said you were the hardest working person she knew. That's quite a compliment coming from her."

Ellie felt her cheeks glow at the praise.

"But is this what you want to do as your career?"

Ellie thought for a moment. "I've worked since I was eighteen, two and three jobs. I've never really given any thought to a career. I guess I could go back to banking."

Marion sat back with a scowl. "Banking. You're better than that. But you need more education if you're going to have a real future." She opened her enormous purse and pulled out a thick catalog. "From the University of Baltimore. You look through this, give some thought to what it is you really want to do, and I'll help you get there. We can cut your hours back, let you attend classes, and I'll help with tuition."

Ellie stared at her. "Why would you do that?"

Marion threw her head back and laughed. "Louise told me that would be your reaction. I'll tell you why, Ellie Ryan. Because the first woman I worked for did the same for me. Not a college degree, but business school, so I didn't have to be a cook all my life. She gave me a leg up and told me to pass it on to someone else when I could. So I'm offering this to you. And when you can, you pass it on."

Sudden tears stung Ellie's eyes as she accepted the course catalog. "I don't know what to say."

"Say yes."

There, in the doorway, unheard by either of them, stood Louise. Ellie flew into her arms, hugging her tightly.

"Oh, I have missed you so much," Ellie said, her voice muffled from somewhere in Louise's soft bosom.

"And I've missed you, baby girl," Louise said. "I've brought you a surprise."

She released Ellie and stepped aside.

Ellie's mouth fell open.

"Hi," said Teresa.

CHAPTER 32

TERESA TURNED OVER, LOOKING out the windows at the nighttime Baltimore skyline from Ellie's couch. Impatiently, she tugged at the sheet and punched the pillow.

"I told you surprising her might not be a good idea," she could hear Bernie saying.

She closed her eyes, trying to shut out the expression on Ellie's face once the initial shock of her unexpected appearance had faded.

Louise, apparently reading the situation, had said to Marion, "Come buy me a drink. We'll leave these two here to catch up."

She and Marion had left the office, pulling the door shut. Teresa had stood there awkwardly, waiting for Ellie to say something.

Ellie's affect was completely flat as she said, "Can I get you anything? Are you hungry or thirsty?"

What did you expect, that she'd collapse into your arms?

Grudgingly, Teresa had to admit she had pictured something like that. Ellie, though, had not seemed to want to be alone with her. Rather than staying in the office to talk, she'd taken Teresa out to the bar and served her a glass of wine, handing her a menu.

"I won't be off for a couple of hours," Ellie said, not meeting Teresa's eyes.

"That's okay," Teresa said. "I know this was unexpected. I'll wait."

Ellie nodded. "I have to go check on the kitchen."

Teresa had nibbled on some steamed shrimp, trying to ignore the uneasiness in her stomach. *She doesn't want to see you. She may not even want you to stay with her.* Teresa hadn't considered any of those possibilities before saying she'd come with Louise.

When Louise left with Marion, Ellie had said, "My place isn't far from here. I'll just be a few more minutes."

She'd seen to the closing of the restaurant, and left the kitchen crew to clean up. "Ready?"

They'd gone out to Teresa's VW. Apart from Ellie's directions, it was a silent ride to her apartment. She went to shower while Teresa sat on the couch with KC.

"At least you're happy to see me," Teresa had whispered as KC rubbed all over her, purring loudly.

When Ellie came out, smelling clean, her hair still damp, she'd sat on the far end of the couch from Teresa, her legs drawn to her chest. "How are you? I mean, the last time I saw you, you were..."

"I was still kind of a mess." Teresa nodded. "I'm better now. It took a while."

"Are you still living with Rob and Karen?"

"No," Teresa said. "Rob helped me find a house to rent. I'm back working at the Bloomfield store."

Ellie seemed surprised as she took that information in. "Working with your mother?"

"Yes, but it's different now. I have more of a life of my own. It's different."

Ellie searched Teresa's face, her eyes wary. Suddenly, she asked, "Why are you here?"

It was Teresa's turn to gape. She'd not expected any of this. In her imaginings, everything would be forgiven as soon as she showed up. *You are such an idiot.* "I miss you," she said at last.

Ellie's eyes were hard. "It's been almost four months. Almost four months since I stood in front of you, telling you I loved you and practically begging you to go away with me. You turned away. Do you remember that?"

Miserably, Teresa nodded. "I know. I was still so angry—at you, at the bastards who attacked me, at the world basically. I wasn't ready to let anyone close again."

Ellie watched her, but said nothing for long seconds. "And now you are?" Without waiting for an answer, she continued, "But now, I've moved on. I'm making a new life for myself. I... I've met someone."

Teresa stared at this admission. This was one thing she had absolutely not been prepared to hear. Not for one second over these past months had she thought of being with someone else. She wasn't with Ellie, but she'd not had any desire to find someone new. *But Ellie has.*

"Oh."

She turned away from Ellie, facing the windows. "I didn't know. I'm sorry to have barged in on you like this. It's kind of awkward now. Louise wants to visit with Marion all weekend. And you. I can go to a hotel if you'd rather."

"You don't have to do that," Ellie said, looking anywhere but at Teresa. "I'll get some sheets and a blanket. You can sleep out here."

Teresa pressed the sheet to her eyes now, willing herself not to cry. *You've got two days to get through, and then you can leave and never have to see her again. Just two days.*

Ellie woke from a bit of fitful sleep just as dawn began to chase the shadows from her room. She'd lain awake most of the night, listening to the creaking of the sofa springs as Teresa tossed and turned. She was sure Teresa wasn't sleeping, either. All night long, a circular argument had run through Ellie's head.

She came back to you.

She came back when she was damn good and ready to come back. With no warning. Just assuming I'd be alone, waiting for her.

Well, you are alone. And what was with the "I met someone" comment?

Ellie threw her arms over her face. *It just came out. I didn't want her to think I've just been sitting around wishing she'd come back to me.*

But that's exactly what you've been doing. Why can't you just say so?

She couldn't answer that. There was nothing to keep her from just going to Teresa, just going out there and kissing her and telling her how much she'd been missed. Ellie actually sat up on the side of the bed. KC sleepily raised her head to look at her. For a long moment, Ellie wavered—*just go*, said that voice—but, with an exasperated sigh, she flung herself back down on the bed and yanked the covers up to her chin.

Ellie lay there now, wondering if Teresa was awake. Giving up at last on getting any more sleep herself, she went to the bathroom and then pulled on a sweatshirt and slippers and quietly opened the bedroom door. She immediately smelled coffee. Stepping out into the living room, she saw Teresa sitting cross-legged on the sofa, her blanket over her legs, holding a cup of coffee.

"Morning," Teresa said.

"Morning." Ellie pointed toward the kitchen. "Be right back." She poured herself a cup of coffee. KC trotted into the kitchen meowing for some breakfast. Ellie fed her and carried her coffee back to the living room. She curled up on the opposite end of the couch again. It seemed this distance between them—two cushions' worth—was as impenetrable as a stone wall.

"So did you ever... I mean," Teresa hemmed. "I just thought you would never be able to leave Pittsburgh unless you found out something definitive about Daniel."

Ellie took a sip of her coffee before saying, "I never did. I might still have been there if not for Louise. She told me I had to stop living my life waiting for people who weren't coming back."

"Like me."

Ellie didn't respond.

Teresa shifted on the sofa. "I am so sorry..." she said. "About everything that happened."

"So am I." Ellie shook her head. "I never meant for you to get hurt. It was so horrible, not being able to come to you, and then, when I did..."

"I know." Teresa frowned at her coffee cup. "I wanted you to hurt. I couldn't admit that to myself for a long time. All those times you went out, wandering around, never worrying, never afraid. It felt like—" She stopped.

"What? It felt like what?" Ellie leaned forward.

Teresa met her gaze. "It felt like you never had to face any consequences for your actions. It felt like I paid instead."

Ellie watched her. "I think, in some ways, I paid through you. I can't imagine how terrifying that must have been for you, but the guilt of knowing you were lying there because of me was terrible."

Teresa closed her eyes. "I hated those men. I've never felt anything so... so toxic. It poisoned me. For a long time."

Her eyes opened, and, just for a moment, Ellie could see a hardness in Teresa's gaze. It only lasted an instant, and then Teresa's eyes were soft again—the way she'd drawn them.

"You blamed me," Ellie said. "You wanted me to feel what you felt."

Teresa nodded.

They sat in silence for a long time, each lost in her thoughts.

"Are you really seeing someone else?" Teresa asked as if the words were being dragged out of her.

"Well, I did meet someone." Ellie gave a little shrug. "A creepy someone."

They both laughed a little and then lapsed into silence again.

"What now?" Teresa asked at last.

Ellie didn't answer immediately. "I don't know." She glanced at the clock. "We'd better shower and eat breakfast. Marion and Louise are expecting us."

It seemed to Teresa later that every minute of that day was burned into her memory with a kind of super clarity. Knowing it would probably be the last day she would ever spend with Ellie, she found herself paying special attention to every detail—the gleam of sunlight on Ellie's hair as they walked the streets of Fell's Point with Marion and Louise, the music of Ellie's laughter at something Louise said, the way Ellie spontaneously slipped her arm through Louise's as she pointed out some gulls squawking and squabbling over a piece of bread. Teresa followed behind, wishing it were her arm that Ellie had taken.

She tried to put aside the gut-wrenching thoughts of what it would feel like to say good-bye to her tomorrow. *Just be here with her now, today,* she kept telling herself. Her life, she knew, would never again feel complete. Perhaps it had never been complete; she simply hadn't known what was missing until she had Ellie to love.

They toured the campus of Johns Hopkins University, and then went to the Baltimore Museum of Art, where they had lunch at the museum's café. Local artists' paintings hung on the walls.

Ellie asked Louise for updates on everyone at the diner. Louise filled her in.

"Patty's still working at the diner?" Ellie asked.

"Yes," Louise said. "And I'm taking it easier. I know that's your next question."

Ellie smiled. "I just want to make sure you'll be around a good, long time."

After lunch, Marion drove them back to the Inner Harbor, where she and Louise decided to settle on a bench and catch up on family news while Teresa and Ellie wandered around.

"Any news with your family?" Ellie asked.

"Well, there's going to be a new addition to Robbie and Karen's family," Teresa said with a smile.

"Really?" Ellie reached out and grasped Teresa's arm.

Startled, Teresa looked down, and Ellie withdrew as if she'd been stung, her cheeks burning furiously. "It's a golden retriever puppy." Teresa still felt the warmth where Ellie had touched her. "They enjoyed having Lucy there so much, they decided to get a puppy. They're four weeks old now, so they have wait a month before she'll be ready to take home."

"You're kidding," Ellie said. "No one in your family has a dog."

"I know." Teresa wished with all her heart she were brave enough to take Ellie's hand. She twitched in her direction, but pulled back, slipping her hand into her jacket pocket. "My mother had plenty to say about it, but you know Rob. He got over that a long time ago."

"Too bad you couldn't."

Ellie didn't say it, but Teresa could hear the words as clearly as if Ellie had shouted them.

She walked on. Ellie followed. "Bernie asked me to say hello," Teresa said.

Ellie smiled. "More likely she told you to ask me what the hell I'm doing in Baltimore."

Teresa chuckled. "Well, that kind of was her reaction when I told her where you were."

"You ever see Sullivan?"

"Not since..." She paused. "Thank you for the calligraphy."

Ellie stood watching the historic boats bobbing at the dock. Teresa stood beside her, wondering what she could say or do to fix things between them. Searching for something, anything, to fill the void, Teresa said, "I heard Marion saying something last night about you attending classes. Are you going to?"

Ellie shrugged, walking along the dock. "I had never thought of myself as being able to go to college. Not since before Mom died."

"What did you want to be when you were little?"

Ellie smiled. "You mean, after I decided I couldn't be Jo March? I thought I'd probably end up being a teacher, like Mom."

"You'd be a wonderful teacher," Teresa said. "You should take Marion up on her offer."

"It's kind of scary, thinking about going back to school now," Ellie admitted. "I mean, I'm so much older than everyone else, and my last year of high school wasn't so great."

"Only because you were working to support yourself," Teresa said. "You are the kind of student they would kill for. Motivated, hard-working, old enough to want to be there."

Ellie looked at her. "You think so?"

Teresa stared into Ellie's eyes, those eyes that used to look at her with so much love in them. For a long moment, they stood like that. For the first time since Teresa's arrival, Ellie's eyes were soft and unguarded—until a group of elementary students swarmed around them to see the ships. Just like that, Ellie shut down and she broke eye contact.

"We should probably get back to Marion and Louise," she said. "They might be ready to leave."

Reluctantly, Teresa accompanied Ellie back to where the older women were just getting to their feet.

"I need sweet potato pie," Marion declared. "Come on home and we'll cook up a storm."

Marion led them to her apartment on the fourth floor of an upscale building nearby.

Ellie gasped when they stepped inside. "Look at that view!"

"That's what I wanted," Marion said proudly. "This is what I've worked so hard for. I don't want a husband and children, expecting me to wait on them after I get home from a long day. I don't want to have to worry about a yard and flowers when I've already got no time."

She uncorked a bottle of wine and poured four glasses. "You two sit and visit," she said to Louise and Ellie. To Teresa, she said, "I hear you're quite a cook. Come on, and we'll see what we can fry up together."

"That was nice," Teresa said a few hours later as she drove them back to Ellie's apartment. "I like Marion."

"Mmm," Ellie said, watching the passing scenery. "She's no Louise, but I'm learning a lot. She doesn't take any nonsense from anyone."

Teresa was tempted to keep driving, just to delay the inevitable separation of Ellie's going to her room, leaving Teresa on the living room sofa, but Ellie said, "Turn right here."

Upstairs, KC greeted them. Ellie fed her. Putting the cat food back in the refrigerator, she asked, "You want some more wine? You only had one glass because you were driving."

"I'll have one if you do," Teresa said.

"Sure."

They carried their wine out to the living room, leaving the lights off, and taking their accustomed places on the couch.

"You have a nice view, too," Teresa said.

Ellie nodded. "I know. I was lucky to find this place. There are still paint splatters on the floor from when this was the studio of the guy downstairs."

They settled into a silence that didn't have the prickliness that had been there the night before. *Do something.* Teresa got up and went to where her suitcase sat in a corner. Reaching between folded clothing, she pulled out a frame.

She laid the calligraphy on Ellie's lap and sat again. "Your note said I could bring this back to you someday," she said softly. "This isn't exactly how I pictured it, but you should have this back."

Ellie looked up at her, her face half-lit by the illumination of the picture window. Teresa impulsively reached out for Ellie's hand. "I know we've been through a bad time. I know I hurt you, but I love you. I will never love anyone the way I love you. Can't we find a way to move past this?"

She held her breath for long seconds as Ellie stared into her eyes, and then her heart fell as Ellie pulled her hand away.

"We probably could," said Ellie. "If it was just us. But it isn't, is it? What happens the next time your mother gives you a demand or ultimatum? What happens when your family needs you to be there? What happens to me the next time you feel pulled back to a family that won't accept me?" Tears filled her eyes and spilled over, leaving tracks that glittered on her cheeks. "I don't think my heart could take that again."

Teresa shifted closer and reached out, gently wiping the tears away with her thumb as she cradled Ellie's cheek. "When you came to see me at Rob's, you asked me if I still loved you. I just told you I do. Now, I'm the one asking. Do you still love me? Never mind those other things. Do you still love me?"

Ellie pushed to her feet and went to the window, her arms wrapped tightly around herself as she stared out at the city. Teresa followed, standing near, but not touching her again.

"I'm not sure I would have found the courage to come to you by myself," Teresa said softly.

Ellie wiped a hand across her cheek. "I don't understand."

"A few weeks ago, Robbie and Karen and Anita ambushed me," Teresa said. "They sat me down and told me they supported us. Anita has a story she'll have to tell you herself, a heartbreaking story. She doesn't want me to end up like she did. She told me..." She had to pause; her heart was pounding so fast, she thought she might not be able to take another breath. "She told me if I loved you, I had to come to you."

Ellie half-turned toward her. "Anita said that?"

"Yes." Teresa's voice was barely more than a whisper.

Ellie placed her hand over her mouth, and Teresa could feel her fighting to hold in her emotions. Teresa stepped closer, taking Ellie's face in her hands. Ellie lifted her face as Teresa bent to her. She'd nearly forgotten the exquisite softness of Ellie's lips as their mouths met and they melted into each other. Time stopped as they stood there—*please don't let it start up again*, Teresa thought vaguely—but eventually, they parted, but only far enough for Ellie to unbutton Teresa's blouse and push it from her shoulders. Teresa gasped at the feel of Ellie's fingers on her bare skin. Goose bumps erupted in the wake of her touch.

She tugged Ellie's shirt and bra off, wrapping her arms around her and lifting her off her feet. She carried Ellie into the bedroom, where she gently laid her on the mattress. Impatiently, they pulled the remainder of their clothing off. Teresa lay down, and Ellie lowered herself onto Teresa, their full nakedness almost more than Teresa could take.

"I need you," Teresa whispered.

They made love—mouths and hands touching and teasing, arms and legs tangled as they moved together, sinuously, seamlessly, blending until it was nearly impossible to tell where one ended and the other began. Together, they gasped and shuddered and collapsed, no matter who was having an orgasm, only to begin again.

At last, they lay, exhausted, Ellie's head resting on Teresa's shoulder. Teresa pressed her cheek to Ellie's head.

"We may not have the support of my entire family," Teresa murmured. "That's something I'll have to learn to live with. But we have Anita, Robbie, and Karen. I think Francesca's on our side. And we have Bernie and Louise. It's small for me, but can you live with a family that size?"

Ellie lifted her head, and Teresa thought she might die at the love shining through her eyes.

"I haven't been part of an 'us' for so long," Ellie said.

"Will you?" Teresa murmured. "Will you be part of us, forever, with me?"

Ellie looked at her for a long moment. "Are you sure?"

Teresa's voice was strong now as she said, "I've never been so sure of anything in my life."

Ellie lowered her head to Teresa's shoulder again. "Where?"

Teresa was quiet for a moment. "It might be easier for us to start somewhere else. Here? I don't care as long as we're together."

Ellie played with Teresa's hair as she thought. "We could always go back home someday, when we're ready."

Teresa's arms tightened around Ellie. "I'm already home."

###

About Caren J. Werlinger

Caren was raised in Ohio, the oldest of four children. Much of her childhood was spent reading every book she could get her hands on and crafting her own stories. She completed a degree in foreign languages and later another degree in physical therapy. For many years, her only writing was research-based, including a therapeutic exercise textbook. She has lived in Virginia for over twenty years, where she practices physical therapy, teaches anatomy, and lives with her partner and their canine fur-children. She began writing creatively again several years ago. Her first novel, *Looking Through Windows*, won a Debut Author award from the Golden Crown Literary Society in 2009. In 2013, *Miserere, In This Small Spot*, and *Neither Present Time* all won or placed in the 2013 Rainbow Awards. *In This Small Spot* won Best Dramatic Fiction in the 2014 Golden Crown Literary Awards.

Connect with Caren online

E-mail her at: cjwerlingerbooks@yahoo.com

Visit her website: http://www.cjwerlinger.wordpress.com

Other Books from Ylva Publishing

www.ylva-publishing.com

Turning for Home

Caren J. Werlinger

ISBN: 978-3-95533-323-2
Length: 345 pages (approx. 85,000 words)

When Jules goes home for her grandfather's funeral, the visit unleashes a flood of memories and sends her on a lonely—and familiar—path. Her partner, Kelli, feels Jules slipping away but can't figure out how to pull her back. In desperation, she turns to Jules's oldest friend—and her ex—Donna. When a lonely girl reaches out to Jules for help, the past and present are set on a collision course.

Barring Complications

Blythe Rippon

ISBN: 978-3-95533-191-7
Length: 374 pages (approx. 77,000 words)

When a gay marriage case arrives at the US Supreme Court, two women find themselves at the center of the fight for marriage equality. Closeted Justice Victoria Willoughby must sway a conservative colleague and attorney Genevieve Fornier must craft compelling arguments to win five votes. Complicating matters, despite their shared history, the law forbids the two from talking to each other.

Coming Home
(revised edition)

Lois Cloarec Hart

ISBN: 978-3-95533-064-4
Length: 371 pages (approx. 104,000 words)

Rob, a charismatic ex-fighter pilot severely disabled with MS, has been steadfastly cared for by his wife, Jan, for many years. Quite by accident one day, Terry, a young writer/postal carrier, enters their lives and turns it upside down.

All the Little Moments

G Benson

ISBN: 978-3-95533-341-6
Length: approx. 139,000 words

Anna is focused on her career as an anaesthetist. When a tragic accident leaves her responsible for her young niece and nephew, her life changes abruptly. Completely overwhelmed, Anna barely has time to brush her teeth in the morning let alone date a woman. But then she collides with a long-legged stranger...

Coming from Ylva Publishing in 2015

www.ylva-publishing.com

Times of Our Lives

Jane Waterton

For the residents of OWL's Haven, Australia's first exclusively lesbian retirement community, life is about not being afraid to take chances. Together, Meg, Allie and their spirited group of friends share their lives, hopes and dreams, proving that whatever the setbacks, hearts that love are always young.

Across the Pond

Cheri Crystal

After having been betrayed by her partner of thirteen years, Janalyn isn't looking for another relationship, especially not one separated by miles of ocean.

But when she travels to Devon, England, for a conference and meets a sporty Brit named Robyn, desires Janalyn thought were permanently lost are suddenly back and stronger than ever.

Despite cultural differences, poking fun at each other's use of the English language, and Robyn coming off as a player, Janalyn can't help the attraction she feels, no matter how hard she tries.

Can she and Robyn find a common ground upon which to make a life together? Will Janalyn throw caution to the wind and risk her heart again? If Janalyn does indeed venture across the pond, will love be her life preserver?

Cast Me Gently
© by Caren J. Werlinger

ISBN 978-3-95533-391-1

Also available as e-book.

Published by Ylva Publishing, legal entity of Ylva Verlag, e.Kfr.

Ylva Verlag, e.Kfr.
Owner: Astrid Ohletz
Am Kirschgarten 2
65830 Kriftel
Germany

www.ylva-publishing.com

First edition: October 2015

No part of this book may be reproduced, scanned, or distributed in any printed or electronic form without permission. Please do not participate in or encourage piracy of copyrighted materials in violation of the author's rights. Thank you for respecting the hard work of this author.

This is a work of fiction. Names, characters, places, and incidents either are a product of the author's imagination or are used fictitiously, and any resemblance to locales, events, business establishments, or actual persons—living or dead—is entirely coincidental.

Credits
Edited by Sandra Gerth & Michelle Aguilar
Proofread by May Dawney
Cover Design and Print Layout by Streetlight Graphics

CPSIA information can be obtained at www.ICGtesting.com
Printed in the USA
LVOW11s1918130116

470476LV00003B/90/P